FRESH TRACKS

ON THE SLOPES
BOOK 3

DAKOTA FOREST

To the readers and dreamers looking for their person, the one that makes any place feel like home, this one is for you.

PROLOGUE

TJ
7 Months Earlier

I CAST my line out into the rippling current of the river, breathing in the fresh air of the Cascade Mountains in Central Oregon. At the crack of dawn, I'm the only one out here, wading in the shallow waters to fly fish behind my house. It's practically perfect. With a gentle breeze, birds chirping, the sound of the water, and the sun rising in the distance, I couldn't think of another place I'd rather be right now.

That's why I had Clay design this house and why I built it right here on the banks of the river. The city of Bend is the best place to be in May. The mountain nearby is still open for spring skiing, the hiking trails below the mountain are starting to open, and the warm spring air is helping to feed the Deschutes River with fresh snow melt. Out of all my homes, only the one in Wyoming competes with this place as my favorite.

I like to spend as much time here and in Wyoming as possible. I love being by the mountains and river, especially this time of year. Everything should be great right now, except there's just something missing.

I shake my head. "What am I doing with my life?" I mutter to myself for no one to hear.

I give my fishing rod a quick flip of my wrist and give the line some action.

After leaving my band, Teal Tigers, almost ten years ago at the peak of our fame, the past decade has flown by in a blur and this is where I've ended up.

Alone. Ticking away my time fishing, running a real estate empire that I never wanted in the first place, and getting overly involved in the restaurants I backed with my friends.

Even this weekend, I was supposed to be in Seattle to meet with my former band manager, but I cancelled at the last minute. I guess there are some perks to being known as the flakey rock-star, even all these years later. I don't know what I want to do anymore and don't feel like rehashing those details or opening up that part of my life again — at least not yet.

So that's how I ended up here, sharing my house with the Chapman family and their friends this weekend. When I origi-nally offered to let them stay, I was planning to be in Seattle and they'd have the place to themselves. Instead, I'm out here because my giant house suddenly feels too crowded.

Getting out here is my normal morning routine, but it feels like even more of an escape this morning while my house is crawling with people.

My eyes drift over the river, trying to enjoy the calm, peaceful setting when a snapping sound grabs my attention. I look over my shoulder along the banks of the river but see noth-ing. It's probably just an animal rustling around in the brush, snapping a twig.

I focus again on the water in front of me, with the sunrise

warming my back. There's a light mist from the rapids at the bend in the river and a small, beautiful rainbow forms, arching just over the water.

CHAPTER 1
GRACE
THANK YOU

"I CAN'T THANK YOU ENOUGH," I say to my friend, Kayleigh, when she sits down on the bench next to me. She pats me on the thigh and we both look out over the bunny slopes of the Park City resort. Sitting here, we have a perfect view of Clay, my brother and her best friend, trying to wrangle a group of kids on skis.

"This was fun. Seeing things through the eyes of these kids reminds me why I love this. I mean really, what are friends for?" she says. I take my earbuds out and put them back in my pocket.

"Still, you took time out of your hectic December training schedule to help teach these kids. I'm pretty sure they'll never forget getting lessons from *The* Kayleigh Jensen, local legend and Utah's homegrown Olympian." She shrugs, but I still notice the way her cheeks turn a gentle shade of pink, contrasting her black hair.

"Well, I need a backup plan. I can't be a professional skier forever. I could see myself doing this someday though."

Pride wells in me as I remember why she has been such a good friend for so long.

I beam back at her. "If you're serious, Wasatch Wishes would love to have you. We can never get enough volunteers, especially ones that the kids flock to like they do with you. You just have to say the word."

"Definitely." She smiles softly back at me and I know she genuinely means it.

I started with Wasatch Wishes in my late teens after my accident. There's just something about it that's always called to me. I love teaching these at-risk kids to ski, snowboard, and enjoy the winter outdoors like I did growing up. Being raised in a ski town like Jackson, Wyoming, my parents and brothers taught me to ski when I could barely walk. But until I moved to Utah, I took it for granted that skiing was so accessible.

After moving to Utah to finish high school and attend college here too, volunteering made me realize just how fortunate I was. I still remember the joy it brought me when I started volunteering here. After graduating, it was a dream come true to get a full time job with the organization I had spent so many hours volunteering with.

Nothing makes me happier than spending time outdoors and getting to share it with these kids. So here I am, always trying to rope my brother and friends into volunteering with me.

"Seriously, you're a natural with them. But him?" I gesture out toward my brother. "Not so much."

We both look out to Clay, who's palming his face, looking down at one of the kids sitting on the ground making snowballs, taking bites out of them. Kayleigh watches him for a moment before letting out an amused laugh.

"What's so funny?" I grin back at her curiously, spinning the lid off my emotional support water bottle.

"That." She tilts her head toward my brother on the beginner ski run. "I never thought I'd see *that* again." I still can't believe he finally agreed to help with the class I teach when I'm not back at the office hounding donors.

A warm smile spreads across my face. She's right. My

brother didn't ski for years after injuries derailed his skiing career, but his girlfriend, Lizzy, gave him the courage to try again last winter. Even though he's not competing anymore, it's good to see him enjoying something that used to mean so much to him.

"Yeah, but he's a pretty terrible teacher," I tease Kayleigh, loud enough for him to hear.

"Very funny!" he calls out before sending the kids to the racks to put their gear away.

He skis over, stopping in front of us.

"These kids are a lot of work. I don't know how you do this." He takes his goggles off, propping them on top of his helmet.

"Oh, come on. They aren't that bad." I flick some snow up with my boot, hitting him right in his now uncovered face.

He glares down at me, wiping the snow off. "Yeah, you're worse. No wonder they're a handful if they're always with you."

I shrug my shoulders, smiling innocently.

"So pizza at your place tonight, right?" he asks. And I know he's asking Kayleigh and not me.

I love my studio apartment and my Sprinter van that I split my time between, but neither are exactly great options for hosting dinners. My small apartment gives me the freedom to hop in my camper van at the drop of a hat for a last minute adventure. It's perfect because I have a serious case of squirrel brain and don't do well with maintenance.

Oh, I want to go rock climbing in Moab? I can be there in six hours.

My best friend Josie's going to a music festival in the desert this weekend? Heck yes, I'll be there.

Kayleigh nods back to Clay. "Yep. That's still the plan."

"Good. We still need to talk about Tanner and V's wedding. It's only a week away," says Clay.

"Perfect." I stand up, clapping my hands together once.

"Thank you both again for helping today, but I need to get these kids back to the office for pick up. I'll see you tonight!"

AFTER SEEING the last of my class head home, I make my way inside. Calling this place an *office* might be generous. Wasatch Wishes is based out of an old auto body garage in a shopping center just outside of Park City. It was donated before I started here and the early volunteers helped spruce the place up, convert part of the space into storage for all of the ski equipment, an entertainment space to host events, and a small office area. It's still a little rough around the edges and we could use a proper space, but that costs money. This place is practically my second home since I've come here almost every day since high school.

Originally, I was just a volunteer working with the youth ski classes. After graduating college, I started working with activity programming. Being a small non-profit though, I've worn a lot of hats over the years, including finding and recruiting donors when I'm not helping with the kids' activities.

I make my way into the shared open office area and find my desk along the back wall. I open my laptop to check my email, looking down at my nails. The glittery, rainbow flecked gel is wearing off.

Scrolling through my inbox, nothing jumps out as too pressing. I just might make it out of here in time for happy hour at Roxy's before dinner with Clay, Lizzy, and Kayleigh.

I look up when I hear the front door shut and spot my boss walking in. Kathy is great, but she always finds a way to corner me at the end of the day with something that needs to be done right away.

I smile and I give her a two finger salute. She looks back at me with a forced smile.

"How was today's class?" she asks, walking toward my desk, still wearing that forced smile. That's the face she makes when she needs me to stay late, or cancel my plans to meet with a possible donor. Maybe I won't be making it to happy hour after all.

"The kids loved Kayleigh. I mean, how could they not?" I snort a quick laugh. "I think they even liked my brother."

"That's great. I can't thank you enough for organizing that. We need all the volunteers we can get."

I don't know why, but I'm not thrilled about the way she emphasized 'volunteers'. I wonder if funding is short again. It's the constant struggle of a non-profit, but the small donors I've been working with have been reliable. And for as long as I can remember, the bigger private and corporate donors have always come through with their end of year donations.

"So, what's up? Need help with something before we close up for the night?"

Her smile falters and she nods before grabbing the chair from the desk next to mine and sitting down in front of me.

"There's no easy way to say this."

I shift in my seat, fidgeting with the lid of my water bottle. This sounds worse than missing happy hour.

"One of our bigger donors isn't making a contribution this year. I just found out earlier this week."

Yeah, this is definitely worse than missing happy hour.

"I've had to make some hard decisions with the impact to our budget." Her already weak smile wavers into something closer to a pitying grimace.

"So, are we looking at cutting hours or programs again?" I ask. This has happened before when we've lost a grant or donations got tight. That's just part of working for smaller, local organizations like this.

"Grace," Kathy says, but I already know what's coming. "I'm

so sorry to do this, especially right before the holidays. But we're not going to be able to keep you on next year. We just can't fit your position in the budget right now."

My throat tightens and water pricks the corner of my eyes. This is not how I saw today going.

A million things are racing through my mind when I feel Kathy pat me on the shoulder. "We can't thank you enough for everything you've done, Grace. I know it's not much, but you'll still get paid through the end of the month. And if something changes and we can afford the position again, you're always welcome back."

I look up at her, seeing her look of genuine remorse. I've always known this was a possibility working here with a razor thin budget each year, but that doesn't change the fact that it still stings.

I hang my head for a moment, take a deep breath, and put on a brave face. There's no point in sulking. I might as well make the most of it. My mom always said when one door closes, another blows open.

"I STILL CAN'T BELIEVE TJ is letting them use his house for the wedding," Clay says, reaching for another slice of pizza, before Lizzy bats his hand away.

"I wanted that one. You take the other," she says, playfully glaring at my brother before she grabs the slice with more toppings.

He throws his head back, groaning. "Always such a brat."

She cocks her head and smirks. "Yeah, but you love me."

He leans over and drops a kiss to the top of her head.

Kayleigh and I share a glance, understanding just how unlikely this scene would have been ten months ago. Clay was practically a recluse, grumpy and self-loathing, for nearly the entire decade since my accident when we also lost Mom. That was until our older brother Tanner's fiancée, Veronica, brought her best friend, Lizzy, into our lives earlier this year. But that's a whole other story.

Watching them is almost enough to distract me from losing my job earlier today. I was always supposed to be the sibling that had their shit together, even if I'm the free spirit. While I may not have had a plan for my life, I always seemed to end up in the right place at the right time. I was the first one in my family to graduate college. I got my dream job here in Park City working for a non-profit I was passionate about. Even being set back for nearly six months recovering from the car accident in my teens, I was exactly where I wanted to be up until a few hours ago.

I get up and head to the kitchen island. "Anybody need a refill? It's Friday night after all."

I pour myself a glass of red wine, leaning against the counter, watching them in the dining room. Seeing my brother with Lizzy, I'm beyond happy for them. Having someone in my corner like that would be great right now, even if I don't need them, but here I am still very single.

I know what I want from my life. That will never change. I want to see the world and keep traveling. Aside from losing my job today, I still want to work with non-profits and make a difference. And I can do that alone or with someone that will enjoy it with me. If I did have someone with me, I'd want someone who's comfortable in their own skin and knows what they want. It shouldn't be this hard to find a confident man that makes me feel valued, the way I value myself.

"You alright?" Kayleigh's voice catches me off guard when she joins me in the kitchen. "I've never known you to be all doom and gloom when there's pizza around."

She's got me there. I love pizza. Pizza party at school or

work? I know everyone thinks they're cliché, but I have always thought they were fun. Growing up in Jackson, Big Red's pizza was a staple in our house on Friday nights. I loved standing around, sharing food, and pouring soda out of the big bottles. That's why I always love it when we do pizza here on Friday nights.

I smile half-heartedly back at Kayleigh, taking a sip of my wine. "Yeah, I'm fine. Just a long day."

She eyes me skeptically. "You sure?" She points to my wine glass. "That's the second glass you've poured in the last ten minutes. Starting to worry there won't be any left for the rest of us."

Clay is easy to hide my feelings from when he's distracted by Lizzy, but I'm clearly not fooling Kayleigh tonight.

"Look, I don't want to make a big deal about this, especially with my family and the wedding next week. So can we keep this just between us?"

She grabs the bottle of wine to top off her glass and nods. "Your secret is safe with me. Promise."

I let out a long sigh. "I got laid off today."

She jerks her head back. "Are you serious? We were just volunteering with you this morning."

I hold my finger to my lips in a shushing gesture. "Don't let them hear you, but yeah." I take a drink and shrug. "It is what it is."

"Is there anything I can do?" She rests her hand on my shoulder. This is why Kayleigh and Clay have been best friends for years. It's why the two of us became such good friends too. She will always ask how she can help those close to her.

"No, I'll be fine. Just a bit of a shock, that's all." That's an understatement. It's still just settling in that come Monday morning, I won't have to go into the office I've been going to for basically my entire adult life.

She reaches down, opening the wine fridge and emerges with another bottle.

"I feel like we might need this tonight."

I let out a short laugh. "You don't have to twist my arm."

"Timing is good for you though."

I arch a brow at her. "Is there ever a good time to get laid off?"

"Oh, come on. You just turned twenty-seven. You have some time off for the holidays anyway. Take your van up to Jackson early, before the wedding. Ski bum around for a bit. It's not like you have anything or *anyone* tying you down here." She looks at her wine for a second before bringing her eyes back to mine.

Sure, I have the occasional hook up partner from time to time, but I haven't found someone worth dating yet and she knows that. I don't even feel like my standards are unreasonable. I shouldn't have to apologize for being tall and quirky or worry about intimidating guys with a Napoleon complex.

I give her a light slap on the wrist that's not holding her wine. "OK. Ouch. Way to throw salt in the wound. No need to remind me of my lack of a love life."

"What's your line again, 'too many boys, not enough men'? Thankfully, I'm not interested in either." She smirks at me playfully. She's throwing my trademark line of why I've never had a serious boyfriend right back in my face. It might be self-inflicted, but if there's one thing I learned from my family growing up, it's knowing your own worth and having standards. Both of my brothers held out and landed their perfect matches.

"Really though. If I didn't have my insane training schedule, I would do that in a heartbeat. Come on, let me live vicariously through you," she says, her hands raised in a pleading gesture.

"That's," I pause for a second, "not the worst idea."

This time, she quirks a brow at me. "Think about it. Try to make the best of the situation."

"If you come visit me to do some backcountry skiing finally,

I'll do it." I say, glaring at her in challenge. I've always tried to get her to go backcountry skiing with me and she always turns me down. This time, I see the sparkle in her eyes, the one that tells me I pushed the right button to stoke the competitive side of an Olympic skier.

"Deal," she says, grinning wide before patting me on the shoulder again and heading back to the table.

I hear Clay burst out laughing from the dining table, dragging my attention away from the kitchen. I take a second to look around Kayleigh's sprawling slopeside home before heading back to the dining room to join them.

Her place is massive compared to mine. Fortunately, that's a positive right now. My place is easy to afford and maintain if I'm gone for a few weeks, or even a couple months.

Maybe Kayleigh's right. Maybe I should just make the best of it. Maybe being jobless going into ski season isn't so bad. I've been so caught up about losing my dream job that I haven't thought of the upside.

The universe takes, but the universe gives back too. Sometimes we just have to be willing to see it. It's the start of winter, my favorite season. I have savings, I have my camper van, and now I have some time for myself.

I'm sure I can convince my van buddy, Josie, to meet up. She's bouncing around ski resorts in her van this winter. And we always like to hang out and explore a new small town or spend time outdoors.

Yeah, maybe this isn't the worst idea I've ever had.

CHAPTER 2
TJ
REMIND ME

One Week Later

"IS it a good deal or not, Slade?" I stand in my recording studio, looking out toward the backyard of my house in Jackson, Wyoming. I have a clear view of my guesthouse where Veronica and her friends are getting ready for the wedding. Everywhere around me is chaos right now and this is the only room where I can get away from it. I might not have used it much since I built this house a few years ago, but I'm appreciating the soundproof studio today. For a small wedding, there's still a lot going on to get set up. But I'm still more than happy to let Chapman and V get married here.

Tanner Chapman has become a good friend over the years. He's gone from someone I hired to take care of this house when I'm not in town, to one of the few people I trust to be straight with me. I practically had to beg him to use my house for this wedding. And V, she's as sweet as they come. That still doesn't mean I'm exactly enjoying this many people in my space today though.

"I mean, I think so. Good bones. Great location with a view

of the Space Needle and Mount Rainier. The first floor will be perfect for opening my next restaurant and you've got great potential for condos or office space on the top three floors." Slade's gruff voice on the other end of the call is confident as always.

"Fine. Call Jake. He'll take care of the offer and the financing."

"Alright, I'll call your brother as soon as I'm off the phone with you." He pauses for a moment and I hear a questioning hum. "So are you good? You seem a little less chill than usual, TJ."

I groan and scrub my palm over my face. "Yeah. Just chaos here. Chapman and his girl are getting married today. We're doing it at my place. Actually your dumbass little brother is catering it too."

"Oh shit, dude." He lets out a laugh and his usual serious demeanor disappears. "You must really like them if you're letting that many people up in your space. Don't let me keep you. I'll talk to Jake. Give Sutton some shit for me."

"Will do. Let me know if Jake doesn't get you what you need to make it happen."

I hang up the phone and drop my head against the window, keeping my eyes focused outside. For someone that was so used to loud music and huge crowds, Slade's right, I don't like commotion around me if I can avoid it. I grew up with that in all the homes I lived in and it's something I don't need or like anymore.

Looking past the guesthouse, I glance up at the slopes of Jackson Hole. For late December, the snow coverage is already great. Sure, the Snake River might be too frozen for me to go fishing — my favorite quiet escape whether I'm here or in Bend most of the year — but this cold does mean prime skiing. I may not be a diehard skier like Chapman, but I do like to get out at least once a week when I'm in town.

I take another glance further up the mountains, soaking up the view of the jagged granite mountain peaks of the Tetons and enjoy this moment of peace and quiet. *This* is why I have houses in places like this, to get away from all the noise of the world. I need to be able to disconnect from everything else.

A flash of pink, orange, and purple from the corner of my vision snags my attention. I jerk my head and my whole body tenses when I see *her*.

Fuck.

I lean against the window and I can see my breath fog the cold glass. She walks down the path from the driveway to the guesthouse. I haven't seen her in seven months, but everything about her is ingrained in my mind like the lyrics to my old songs. Something I could truly never forget.

Her flowing rainbow hair. Her tall, fit frame. Those impossibly long legs that let her stride gracefully away from me. Something stirs in my chest, the same feeling I had that day on the river in Oregon. I know I shouldn't be transfixed by her, but my body won't listen to my mind telling me to look away.

Just before she reaches the door to the guesthouse, V swings it open, practically bursting out toward Grace. She flashes V a smile — the mischievous, infectious one that I haven't been able to get out of my head since that morning in May.

My phone buzzes in my hand, pulling me back to the present. Is Slade already calling me back? Jake better not be giving him a hard time.

I look at the screen and feel my brow furrow when I see the message.

Miles: Got time to talk? The guys still want you back for a reunion tour this spring.

I should have just said 'no' seven months ago. That's what

every bone in my body told me to do and that's how I like to make decisions. It's rarely failed me in life. But for some reason that day, I was in my head too much and said I'd think about it. Now, I've had to avoid the weekly calls and messages because I honestly don't think I want to get back with the band. Even if it was a one time deal, I don't know if that's a chapter in my life I want to revisit. There's still a nagging voice in the back of my head though that says I owe it to them. I don't want to think about where I'd be if I hadn't been in the band.

"Hey, TJ." I practically jump out of my skin and my head whips around to see Sutton, leaning in the doorway to my studio.

"Shit. Are you trying to give an old man a heart attack?"

He chuckles and walks into the room. I take one last glance out toward the guesthouse hoping to see her, but she's already inside.

"You're forty-two. I'd hardly call you an old man."

I lean against the black foam padded wall and fold my arms over my chest, feeling my heart that was pounding for an entirely different reason settle back into its proper place. "Yeah. We'll see what you're saying when you're a decade older."

"What are you doing in here anyway? Hiding as usual?" He steps toward a stack of speakers and amplifiers and grabs one of my guitar picks.

"Actually, I was just on the phone with your brother. He wants me to buy another building in Seattle. He already has his mind made up on a new restaurant."

Sutton palms his face in both of his hands with an exasperated sigh. He takes another step toward me and looking at his fingers, he spins my guitar pick between the tips. I can see why his knife work in the kitchen is always so precise.

"Fuck. He's really going to burn himself out and probably drag me down with him if he keeps trying to expand like this." He's right. I met them and Tanner because of Gloria's, their restaurant here in town. I've watched how Sutton busts his ass running it while Slade runs his other spots in Denver and Park City.

"So, everything going alright with the food prep?" I change the topic because I know all too well what it feels like to get burned out. That's something I'd rather not relive.

He shrugs. "So far, so good. Besides..." He walks along the wall where my guitars are hanging and eyes my favorite acoustic one. "I'm enjoying the added bonus of trashing your kitchen today." He mindlessly drags the pick across the strings, sending a stray note echoing across the room.

"Hey! Not that one." I level a glare at him, watching him pull his hand away from my first guitar, the one that went from foster home to foster home with me. "You should know better than that. You get all protective when I mess with your knives at your place."

He smirks at me, flaring an eyebrow up. "Yeah, but I'm a chef that cooks and uses my knives. You're a rockstar that hasn't performed in years." He swipes his finger across the guitar again and flicks the dust from his fingertip. "Seriously, when was the last time you picked up a guitar? This place feels like a morgue."

I grasp my chest and feign agony. "You wound me, Sutton." I play it off well enough because he rolls his eyes. Deep down, I know he's not wrong, he's entirely right.

I'm a musician who spends more time fishing and managing my real estate holdings than I do making or playing music.

"Remind me why we're friends again?"

He shakes his head, still smirking at me. "I'm pretty sure it's because you have a thing for the pasta at Gloria's and you spend an unhealthy amount of time at the chef's tasting counter. You know, *my* counter? Speaking of..." He checks the time on his phone and slaps his thigh. "I have food to prep."

"Ass." I call after him when he turns to leave. He flips me the bird over his shoulder before shutting the door behind him.

This is why I like him and his brothers. Yeah, we do business together. But that started after I was friends with Sutton. They don't give a damn that I'm famous, and they will never stop giving me shit.

Looking at my phone, I realize what time it is.

Three hours until the wedding.

It's only going to get more hectic as the day goes on. I turn back toward the window, looking out at the guesthouse with the mountains towering in the background. Like a reflex, my eyes drift back to the door, hoping to catch another glimpse or flash of that colorful hair.

I shake my head and peel my gaze away from the window, trying to clear those memories out of my head.

Those eyes. That voice. That smile.

What is wrong with me?

I let out a long, ragged sigh before looking around my studio. I key in on the guitar that Sutton was messing with. A decade ago, that's what I'd do right now to distract myself.

But now? I just want to crawl away and enjoy my peace and quiet.

Yeah. Maybe that's what I'll do. I can just lock the door to the studio and come out when everyone has left and I have my house back to myself again.

But no, I can't do that. My friends are here. My *real* friends. Not like the ones from years ago that just clung on to me because of Teal Tigers, my fame, and my money.

No, the Chapmans are genuine friends. Now V, her brother, Collin, and Lizzy are too. They are real friends and couldn't care less about any of that stuff. And even Sutton too, I'm glad he's here. I'd even list Grace as a friend, but I don't think that's quite the right word.

No. I think she's something else entirely.

And that's why I'm going to power through and be here for their wedding today. Even if there's a certain distraction looming around here that I clearly haven't been able to get out of my head over the last seven months.

It's just a few hours and then I can go back to my nice, quiet, calm life.

I HAVE to give Tanner and V credit. When he said she's a fanatical planner and detail oriented, he meant it. She spent the last two days with her best friend, Lizzy, transforming the open living space of my house into an intimate wedding venue. My large living room, entryway, and dining room with the floor to ceiling windows looking out over the mountains now has seating for forty. I told them they could probably invite more, but she said she was keeping it small and with the way she laid it out, the house looks like it was designed as a damned wedding venue.

Standing in the kitchen, I keep my distance, quietly nursing a beer and watching the last guests trickle in.

"Shouldn't we get seated? It looks like everyone is here," Sutton whispers.

I look over to shoot him a glare, but he's still focused on putting the finishing touches on the hors d'oeuvres for the casual cocktail hour they wanted instead of a formal dinner.

"Yeah. You're probably right." I take the last sip of my beer and toss it in the recycling. "You sitting on the groom's side?"

Sutton nods, but keeps his attention on perfectly placing the last garnish on the tower of bite sized snacks. I groan, clearly impatient waiting on my friend.

He chuckles to himself. "Hold your horses. You're awfully antsy for someone that doesn't even like going to these kinds of things." He finishes and wipes his hands off on his apron before taking it off and setting it aside. "There. All done."

I shake my head and start to make our way to our seats. Sutton is right behind me when we take two spots in the back row. From here, I have an even better view of how V and Lizzy decorated my place.

The seats are laid out to capitalize on the angular shape of the room, almost making it look like a cathedral to the mountains outside, with the small, white altar right in front of the windows. Sprigs of evergreens are placed throughout the space and with it being late in the afternoon, facing the Northwest like this, the mountains are framed by the glowing sunset.

I always joked with the architect about the million dollar views from every room, but shit, this is a billion dollar view. And it should be, as much as I spent on building this place.

"Do you think our boy, Chap, cries?" Sutton whispers playfully into my ear, grabbing my attention away from admiring the view that never gets old.

The corner of my lips tug up into a wry smile and I elbow him in the ribs. "My money's actually on Clay. I think he's the closet softy after seeing him with Lizzy when they stayed with me in Bend."

Sutton starts to say something, but I ignore him when the guests quiet down. I turn around to see Collin make his way from the back of the house and lead the way down the aisle to start the ceremony. He takes his place at the altar as the officiant, fitting since he's also Tanner's best friend.

I turn back toward the hall just in time to see Grace walk in next, arm in arm with Collin's boyfriend, Walker.

I feel my heart stop and my mind blocks out every sound around me, just like the moment before I would go on stage for a concert. Her long, bright colored hair is up in a crown of braids. Her dark purple bridesmaid dress accentuates her tall, toned body. Some of her tattoos that are still etched into my psyche are peeking out of the low cut back and slit on the side.

She practically glides across the room, smiling at everyone her eyes meet, looking around the room at her friends and family on Tanner's side of the aisle. Her eyes meet mine for just a second and she drops them to the flowers in her hands. Even with her makeup, I swear I see a hint of adorable pink stain her freckled cheeks. When she looks back up, her eyes are focused forward toward Collin, like I don't even exist.

I don't even notice when Lizzy and Clay or V come into the room. My eyes never leave *her*.

I'm transfixed by her.

The smile she's wearing is the same bright, playful one that she flashed at me like a siren song to get me on stage to do karaoke at a shitty dive bar with her.

She looked like a dream earlier today when she showed up to the guesthouse. Christ. I doubt she could ever look anything but stunning. But as she stands there next to the altar, I can't help but notice what looks like the slightest glimmer of worry in her eyes.

Whatever it was, it's gone before I can blink and that wide, bright smile is back and I just can't look away from her. The way she's silhouetted with the sunset behind her, the vivid hues matching the streaks of color in her hair. She's perfection.

"Hey there, buddy." Sutton whispers into my ear after he elbows me in the ribs, snapping me out of my trance. "Are you really that cliché, man? I know she's a bridesmaid, but she's the Chapman brothers' baby sister. You know, the two giant six-foot-god-knows-what mountain men we're *friends* with? They won't give a shit that you're a rockstar. They'd still murder you and I have a feeling Chap knows where to hide bodies around here."

Fuck my life. I need to get my shit together.

I should be thinking about the eight figure real estate deal in Seattle that I know Jake is busy working on right now. I should be celebrating with my friends at their wedding. Or maybe I should be thinking about reviving my dormant music career.

But I should definitely not be fawning over Grace like a lovesick puppy.

I take a deep breath and lean toward Sutton, still keeping my eyes forward. "I don't know what you're talking about," I mutter, taking one final glance at her. "And again, retired rockstar."

"Yeah, keep telling yourself that." He chuckles to himself and I focus back on the ceremony.

If Sutton can notice her throwing me off my game like this, I'm clearly being too obvious.

Does she even have a clue what she does to me?

CHAPTER 3
GRACE
CRYSTALLINE

I STILL CAN'T BELIEVE this is finally happening. I'm back in Jackson, watching my oldest brother get married to the woman of his dreams. The one he's been in love with basically my whole life. Everything about it feels surreal, yet perfect at the same time.

Well, nearly perfect.

I look to our family's side of the aisle, seeing the empty seat next to Dad, the one left in memory of our mom. It's been a decade since the car accident that took her from us and nearly took my life too. A shiver racks through me, pricking my skin along the scars I still carry from that day. I remember the times during my recovery that I would have never imagined being here with them. Not a day goes by that I don't think about her and the hole left in my life.

I would give anything for her to be here today. To see the man my brother became. She always knew Tanner loved V growing up, even if he was too afraid to ever do anything about it.

I wipe a stray tear away at the thought of how happy she would be to finally witness this.

But selfishly, I wish I could talk to her.

Everyone thinks I'm just here for the wedding this weekend

and then it'll be back to my life in Salt Lake City. Except that's not the case. I'm planning to stay here for a while until I figure out what's next on my journey in life. Mom was my guiding influence, subtly giving me the strength to find my own path in life. Sure, Kayleigh is right and Mom would have said the same thing.

Make the best out of it. It'll all work out in the end.

Looking at Tanner and V, I smile at that little bit of wisdom Mom always liked to drop on us because that's exactly what happened with these two, finally ending up together. It still doesn't change how I feel though. Wasatch Wishes was my dream job and now I need to find something else to do. I don't even know where to start.

The rustling of paper gets my attention back on the ceremony as Tanner unfolds his handwritten vows. It's times like these when I'm glad I'm five-ten and even in heels, I can easily peer over Lizzy to watch.

In typical Tanner fashion, he works in a couple of sappy jokes that has everyone laughing. I scan the crowd, seeing all of our friends and family. I look through the rows, noting that everyone they wanted here made it.

My gaze finally lands on the back row. My skin heats and my brows knit together. Everyone in the room right now is focused on my brother and V, except for TJ, whose eyes are locked on me.

What is his deal? He always seems to be glaring at me. Ever since the first morning of our spring trip to Bend, when my brothers, their partners, and me as the fifth wheel stayed at his house, it's been this way.

Yeah, I know I interrupted his quiet mornings of fly fishing with my cold plunges in the river. But I wanted to try it, the cold river was right there, and my apartment in Utah definitely doesn't have space for a cold tub.

Did I get a little carried away after that first morning where I accidentally scared him? Maybe, but how was I supposed to know he was on the other side of that boulder at the crack of dawn? I figured no one else would be up as early as I was.

I did enjoy trying to sneak up and scare him over the next couple days. And OK, I definitely dragged him up on stage at a shitty dive bar for karaoke and made him sing ridiculous pop songs.

He can't really still be annoyed with me, can he? And it's his friend's wedding day. He should be focused on the ceremony, like everyone else.

Except I don't really have room to talk because I'm still staring right back at him. I meet his gaze, smirk, and flare my eyebrows in question. But his crystalline blue eyes never leave mine, only making the temperature of my skin creep even higher.

I overexaggerate rolling my eyes before matching his glare and tilting my head toward the altar. He finally snaps out of whatever that was, nods, and looks toward the altar.

IT'S BEEN years since I've been in The Chairlift, the old bar down the street from Tanner's cabin. It's got that perfect homey mix of old school locals like our family, recent transplants, and out-of-towners coming in after skiing. Nothing about it screams wedding reception venue, but it's perfect for the newlyweds. It's been here since the days our grandparents owned the land surrounding it along Moose Wilson Road, back when they still had a small ranch. These days, my brother's cabin and the bar are all that's left from that time so it's fitting that my brother and V would want to have their reception here.

Everyone is ecstatic and rightfully so. I have never seen either of my brothers this happy. Veronica has been grinning ear to ear all night and Lizzy is in full Maid of Honor mode, working with Collin to keep the party rolling according to V's strict itinerary.

Even my grandparents are here and enjoying the lively scene in the dingy old bar.

I'm genuinely thrilled for my brother, but seeing all of my family like this, like everything is all coming together for everyone else, just reminds me that I don't know what's next for me. I'm going to take some time for me, but I still want to find a way to make an impact with others. And I feel like shit for even thinking about myself on a day like this.

I had my dream job. I was having fun, I was helping people, I was making a difference. It never even felt like work.

And now? Now, I don't know what's next .

Which, of course, is exactly what my grandparents want to ask me about. I did my best to hide away in the back of the bar at a high-top by myself, but they're like bloodhounds. Somehow they're always honed in on 'Where is Grace?' They're always well-meaning and normally I would love to talk to them about my work.

But today? I just want to enjoy my drink and wind down the night on my own. Trying to convince everyone you're perfectly fine is exhausting and I'm reaching my limit for socializing tonight. That's why I changed as soon as the ceremony was over into my comfortable overalls and flannel and found a high-top table away from the crowd.

"Oh sweetie, what are you doing hiding over here?" Grandma asks, clutching her champagne flute to her chest. "I'm glad you could get some time away from working with those kids to come see us." I'm positive this grungy bar has never seen a champagne flute come through its doors until today. And judging by her smile and giddiness, Lizzy, must have clearly gotten to her with more than one glass of celebratory bubbles tonight.

My grandpa rolls his eyes. "Nancy, you know that hasn't been her job for years. She's in charge of getting the money to pay for those classes and lessons now."

My heart sinks and warms simultaneously, seeing just how invested and proud they are with my life.

I huff a laugh, trying to mask my emotions, but I can feel my shoulders sag. I don't want to lie to them, but I'm not ready to tell the full story to anyone else yet. I don't want to take away from their day and bring down the vibe with my own pity party.

My grandma doesn't catch the subtle hint that for once, this is a subject I'd prefer to move on from. Literally, we could talk about anything else right now and I'd be thrilled. We could even talk about my continual lack of a boyfriend, her normal favorite topic to gossip about with me. I'd be fine with that for a change, considering it's something I assume will only continue now that Tanner is married and Clay has a girlfriend.

"So, when are you driving back to Utah? I imagine they can't let you out of their hands very long knowing how much you do for them." She smiles at me so warmly, but that doesn't dull the still fresh wound. I know she's trying to compliment me, but that one hurts.

I take a sip of my own Champagne, which hardly feels appropriate for my current feelings, and plaster on a smile as I try to come up with some kind of noncommittal answer. I start to open my mouth, but I realize neither of them are looking at me now. Their collective gaze is locked on something behind me.

I start to shift in my seat to see what has my grandparents' attention, but before I can even move, a hand gently grazes the back of my shoulder. The warmth, the pressure, it instantly electrifies my skin, waking up every nerve in my body.

OK, maybe it was more of a *who* has their attention, not a *what*.

Before I can turn around, a voice I could never forget stops me midturn. "Hey there, Rainbow," that deep, well-worn voice rasps. I would know it anywhere.

So would a lot of people actually, considering it's a famous one, played on radio stations across the planet for more than two decades.

But that nickname. That isn't so well known. That was just for me.

Freaking TJ.

"I was wondering where you were hiding," he says, his thumb rubbing a circle on the back of my shoulder. I know it's just a casual, friendly touch, but something about it and his presence sends a shiver down my spine.

I remember him being that way in Bend, always greeting you with a hug, resting a hand on someone's shoulders, the way he'd look you in the eye to talk to you, or clasping both of your hands to shake. Maybe it's a musician thing, needing physical contact to connect.

Either way, I don't know if he senses my reaction, but he quickly removes his hand and extends it across the table, reaching to greet my grandparents.

I palm my face, groaning in frustration before looking up to catch the look of pure excitement on my grandma's shocked face.

"Oh my goodness, Mr. Jacob." Her voice is flustered as he clasps both of her hands. "It was so sweet of you to let them use your house for their wedding."

I let out an exasperated sigh.

He chuckles to himself and to my chagrin, he pulls up a stool and sits down right between the three of us. I guess he didn't get my memo about wanting to enjoy my drink alone tonight either.

"There's no way you can be the infamous Grandma Chapman they all talk about." He flashes a wide smile at my grandma and she flushes like a swooning fangirl. "You hardly look old enough."

Really, Grandma? Falling for his charisma that easy? If you haven't spent time with him, it'd be easy to call this an act. But I've spent almost a week with him, with my brothers and their girlfriends, seeing how he is in private. So I know this isn't an act, this is him — genuinely kind and polite to total strangers or friends of friends. There's something heartwarming about it, someone in his position that can talk with a couple of old ranchers like they're lifelong friends.

"How do you know our little Gracie?" Grandma asks, still blushing.

I drop my head and groan. Really Grandma, you're really so easily charmed? I mean, I guess I get it. He's famous, he's got the whole musician vibe going on, and he is definitely easy on the eyes. As tall as I am, I'm used to being eye to eye with most men, but even I have to look up to meet his eyes. He must be at least six-two or something.

And he clearly takes care of himself. I'll begrudgingly admit, I watched his old music videos when I was younger. In those days, he always looked lean and slender. After getting to meet him in person when we were in Bend, it's impossible to not see that he's built, with subtly toned muscles hiding under his well-tanned skin.

But I'm not falling for that today. I lower my eyes at him, showing that I'm not in the mood for his charm and games.

He just tosses me a playful wink and carries on. "We're old friends. She stayed with me and your grandsons in Bend back in May for some spring skiing with their girlfriends. It was a wonderful time."

I turn in my seat to face him, tip my chin, and shoot him a conspiratorial grin. "Oh. It was a wonderful time, if by wonderful you mean hearing you complain about me swimming and scaring away your precious fish on the river every morning."

His blue eyes sparkle with mischief when he grins back at me. "I think swimming would be generous. It was more like..." He brings a knuckle to his lips as he looks up in thought. For some reason, my eyes are drawn to the ticking of the muscles in his defined forearms revealed by the rolled up sleeves of his plaid flannel.

OK. I guess I'm not immune to his looks either.

He brings his eyes back to mine and I note the small scar splitting his eyebrow next to a piercing. I wonder how many times that's been ripped out to scar like that. He was known for being a bad boy rocker after all.

"... Floundering? Yeah, I think I'd call it floundering. I was more scared that I might have to dive in and rescue you than I was from you sneaking up on me."

Alright. This was not the exchange I was expecting tonight. I roll my eyes at him. "Whatever, *Mr. Jacob*."

A low laugh rumbles from his chest and he leans against the table, swirling his beer bottle. I watch the motion, seeing that little tattoo around his ring finger that none of us had the nerve to ask him about.

I turn to look at my grandma and her eyes show nothing but fascination with this exchange. Great. I can add this to the list of things she'll want to discuss later. Thankfully, my misery is interrupted by my grandpa clearing his throat.

"Come on, Nancy. I want to go see Clay and Lizzy. You know she was asking about your meatloaf earlier." He wraps his arm around her waist and gives us a little wave goodbye. Clearly he gets social cues more than Grandma.

After they leave, I turn in my seat to face TJ. "What the hell was that about?"

He shrugs, the gesture making a lock of his shaggy, dark blond hair drift across his forehead. He tucks it out of the way, takes a sip of his beer, and smirks. "I have absolutely no idea what you're talking about, Rainbow."

CHAPTER 4
TJ
RAINBOW

JUDGING by the look on her face, Grace is clearly not amused by me interrupting her conversation with her grandparents. I can see her chest rise and fall with irritated breaths, her nostrils flaring each time. Her normally soft evergreen eyes are narrowed on me with annoyance. No one looks at me with this much open hostility, except maybe Sutton because he's always a shit-starter.

But I like seeing her like this.

I've spent most of my adult life having people not act like themselves around me. Some fawn over me, some ask the same dumb questions about being the famous frontman for Teal Tigers, while others just freeze, not knowing what to do in my presence. But I couldn't care less, I'm just a guy from Seattle that grew up in foster care.

I've never wanted the attention of being a celebrity and that's what makes Grace special. Ever since that day we met, she's treated me like just another guy, the same way her brothers did when I hired Tanner as my property manager and then Clay to design one of my houses.

She dragged me on stage to sing karaoke at a shitty dive bar all night. It wasn't because she wanted to see Tommy Jacob from Teal

Tigers perform. She was just having fun and wanted others to enjoy themselves too. She wouldn't even let me sing anything rock, it was girl anthem after girl anthem. She toyed with me every morning on that trip while I was trying to fish, doing her morning cold plunges, making me watch the cold water glisten on her body in the sunrise. She joked and laughed, both with me and at me, flashing that glowing, kind smile that still haunts my dreams. Nothing about the way she treated me said awestruck or fangirl. People like that are... rare —the kind I want to surround myself with.

Looking across the small table at her, I would do anything to make that smile appear again. I start to work through every idea in my head to lighten the mood when her eyes meet mine again. She glares for just a moment before dropping her head into her hands with a long sigh.

Yep. She's annoyed with me.

Maybe it's for the best, like Sutton said. She should be off limits and if she's pissed at me, maybe that'll make it easier to stay away.

But I saw her body language. She was floundering in that conversation with her grandparents. I don't know what they were talking about, but I could tell from across the bar she wanted to be anywhere else than answering whatever they were asking her. At least now she's just annoyed, with fire in her eyes, instead of looking miserable on a day she should be anything but.

Unaware of my intentions, her unrelenting glare returns. I take the opportunity to look at those freckles, highlighted by her tanned cheeks. If I had the time, I would count each and every one of those little dots.

"Seriously, what do you want? I'm not exactly in the mood for karaoke tonight."

I snort a laugh and take another sip of my beer, feeling the corner of my mouth pull up into a smirk. "You looked miserable. I figured I'd come over and lighten the mood." Honestly, that's all I want. I want her to feel half as good as she makes me feel just by being near her. Anytime I've ever been near her, it feels like nothing else in the world matters.

She rolls her eyes, throwing her head back with an exaggerated groan. The move exposes the column of her neck and for a moment, my mind drifts to what it would feel like to run my fingertips along it. Or what it would be like to leave a trail of kisses along it, dragging my lips along her neck, working my way down to...

Holy shit, I need to get myself in check.

She drops her head forward, finally looking back at me. Thankfully, I don't think she caught me staring at her, again.

"Lighten the mood?" she finally responds, setting her drink down. "You definitely did something to my grandma's mood." She shakes her head and huffs a laugh. "I think you've got yourself a new admirer."

She raises her eyes to mine and some of that annoyance has worn off, but now I see something else... what I saw at the ceremony. Her smile is there, but there's something else lurking just under the surface. I'm determined to know what could make someone so bright and vibrant feel that way on a day like this.

"Now, do you want to tell me why you were dying for that conversation to end?" I raise my pierced eyebrow in question.

She sighs and rolls her head back and forth like she's internally debating if she should humor me or rightfully tell me to fuck off. Finally, she turns to face me straight on, looking down her thin straight nose. Even with her brow furrowed and the obvious tension on her face, she's still striking. Her green, feline eyes peeking out from under her bangs are breathtaking and right now, they're burning a hole into me.

"No, not particularly."

I shake my head, laughing. That's better than fuck off, so I'll take it.

"You're going to make this hard on me, aren't you?" I tease.

She lifts her champagne flute, tilting it back and finishing it in one, long swig. Suddenly, I'm jealous of a stupid glass with the way her full lips wrap around it.

Damn. I definitely don't have my shit in check.

"I'm not really in the mood to talk to anyone tonight, TJ. Not you, not my grandparents, not anyone."

I lean forward, humming to myself. I'm not ready to give up just yet.

"How about we make it a game?"

"Aren't you a little old for games?" she scoffs.

My shoulders rise with a hushed laugh. "Ouch. Is that a no then?"

She tilts her head, eyeing me curiously. This time, I can tell she's taking my offer a bit more seriously. I find myself craving the feeling of her eyes on me, but equally afraid she might see how I really feel about her if she keeps looking.

She finally shrugs. "Whatever, OK. What are the rules?"

A sense of relief washes over me and a wide grin spreads across my face. Maybe I can make her night a little better. "Easy. Each time I ask a question and you answer, you get to ask me one."

She sits up a bit straighter and one side of her lips start to show the slightest hint of that smile I want to see.

"I can ask you," she points a finger at me, "any question I want and you'll answer?"

I smirk and flick my eyebrows at her. I know what she's implying. I'm notoriously private, especially since I retired from Teal Tigers and all but left the music scene. I don't do interviews, I don't do appearances, I don't do questions.

"Yes. Any question, but you have to answer mine first."

"That doesn't sound like much of a game. What if I don't answer?" she asks, knowing it can't be that easy.

I tilt my head toward the bar. "If you don't answer, you take a shot of tequila."

"What about you?"

"I'll answer anything you want to know. No shot needed. But if it makes you feel better, fine. Same rules for me."

Her lips curl into a wide smile, exposing the slightest dimple, as she claps her hands in front, rubbing them together. "Alright, fire away."

I tilt my head back across the bar toward her grandparents.

"You looked like you were in the middle of a root canal with that conversation. Figured you could use some rescuing."

She juts her chin out at me with a questioning hum. "You know that's not a question, right?"

I nod, taking another sip of my beer. "I know. So why did you look like you would rather be anywhere else? It's your brother's wedding and I know you're happy for them. So why don't you want to be here, all together, in Jackson?"

Her surprise is quickly replaced with irritation. She pulls her hands into her lap and huffs, looking up at the ceiling for a second. I watch while she tilts her head side to side like she's debating quitting my game already.

Finally, she lets out a long sigh, reaches across the table, and plucks my beer right from my hand.

"You know what, screw it." She takes a long pull from my beer and I chuckle. Before I realize it, she stands up, drags her chair next to mine, and sits so close our thighs are touching.

There's the woman I remember from before. It only took one long weekend with her and the rest of the Chapman gang to realize she gives no shits about personal space and seems to be comfortable around everyone.

The problem for me is that this level of closeness is clearly clouding my judgement, because I don't move at all. In fact, for some stupid reason, I lean in closer and she doesn't budge an inch.

She sets my beer back on the table and looks right at me. "My life's kind of a mess." The tone of her voice raises at the end, almost like a question.

I arch an eyebrow at her, beckoning her to continue. She takes another sip of my beer and goes on. "I got laid off last week, I don't have a new job yet, and for once, I don't really have a plan. So yeah, a mess is a pretty accurate description right now." She raises her hand in a fist and makes a train conductor gesture. "All aboard the Hot Mess Express."

She takes another sip from my bottle. "Oh, and I'm too afraid or proud — I don't know — to tell my family because if I do, I know they'll smother me and treat me like 'fragile, little Gracie' again."

What the hell? A million thoughts run through my head, but mostly I just feel a burning sense of rage I try to bury down. I remember her gushing about how she had her dream job working at a non-profit. Her eyes sparkled whenever she mentioned the place and anyone with a pulse could feel the passion she had for it. So the idea that anyone would take that away from her makes my blood boil because I never want her to feel hurt.

"What happened? Why would they do that? They can't—" My hands curl into fists when the questions all flood out of me in a rush.

This is not what I expected. Well, I don't know what I expected exactly. Maybe something more trivial, but definitely not something as life-altering as that.

"Nope. You already asked your question and I don't want the pity party." She holds a finger up to my lips in a shushing gesture. "My family doesn't know and I'd like to keep it that way. I'm going to make the most of it, enjoy ski season bumming around in my van."

I nod, seeing the determined look in her eyes. Her immediate response takes my rage down a notch. She must see it, because her playful smile returns.

My mind can only register her smile for a second before my brain spirals down a new path. Living in her van like a nomad, as a single woman in the middle of winter? I know I shouldn't be one to judge. I did it too, in those early years before our first record deal. I get it. Those were some of the most exciting days of my life, but I'm also six-two and can handle myself. Something about her being alone like that doesn't sit right with me. I pack those thoughts away though when I see just how confident she is in her choice.

"So." She swirls my beer around, mimicking my gesture from earlier, to see how much is left. "It's my turn now."

Her smile is playful, if not a bit mischievous. I'm just glad she's looking more like herself.

She lets out a long hum, tracing a finger over her lips, a shade of pink that matches some of the strands in her hair. Everything about her is so beautiful and bright.

She tilts her head to one side, which lets the strap of her denim overalls fall just off her shoulder and over her flannel button down shirt. I figured she wasn't big on formal wear and dresses, but there's something so refreshing that she wanted to get into her comfort clothes the second she could following the ceremony. I can relate to that. Jeans and t-shirt, or maybe a flannel, is always what I feel most comfortable in.

I turn my palms up in surrender. I never want to hide anything from her and I want to make sure she knows that. I don't even think I could hide something from her if I wanted to. "Whatever you want."

There are so many things in my past, even in my present, that

I would rather keep to myself. There's a reason I'm a private person and only let in people I trust.

Shit. She could ask me if I'm into her and I'd tell her the truth.

I scan her face, watching her eyes beam as she considers what to ask. "So I can really ask you anything I want? Aren't you worried I'll ask about something scandalous and go to the tabloids with the sordid details?"

Shrugging, I reach over, grabbing my beer back from her. My fingers graze the backs of hers, sending sparks up my arm like I just hit the perfect note on a guitar solo. I take the last pull of my beer. "I won't count that as your question," I say, giving her a wink. "There'd have to be something scandalous in my past, but sure. I told you the rules. Ask whatever you want. I'll answer."

Her forest green eyes narrow on me like she doesn't believe it's that simple.

I tip my beer at her. "Besides, I trust you. That's not the kind of person you are. Now ask. I know you've got something you've wanted to ask about."

She holds her chin between her thumb and forefinger in thought, her lips part just before asking. "What Teal Tigers' song was your favorite?"

"Really? That's the best you got? I'll give you a do-over if you ask me something you can't Google."

She throws her head back and groans. "Fine."

I watch as her gaze lowers to my hand holding the beer, exactly where I figured she would start.

"What does *that* mean?" She points down at my hand, or more specifically, the tattoo wrapped around my ring finger.

I stare at my finger, looking at the small music notes tattooed in a ring around it. I still remember the day I got it. Not my first tattoo, but the one I was so damn excited about getting. I got it right after we landed our first record deal. Now, it's just a reminder of something that's gone, something that left me. Well, two things that are gone and left me.

"You know the rules, sir." Grace tips her empty champagne flute, highlighting the lack of contents. "Answer or you're getting a drink."

I roll my neck, exhaling as I hold out the empty beer in front of me, tilting my hand back and forth, inspecting the small notes. "Music was my first love. In my teens and early twenties, it was everything to me. It consumed me. Every thought, every idea, every action - I loved it and lived for it."

When I look up, her eyes have softened. She's wearing a kind, compassionate expression, hanging on each word. My words.

"Is that a good enough answer?" I deadpan.

"Yes, it was." Her expression shifts into a devious smirk. "And you just wasted your question."

"Oh, come on."

"Nope. They're your rules. My turn again." She hums thoughtfully, playfully grinning back at me. Instantly, I don't care that she snuck that one by me. Seeing a genuine smile on her face sends warmth all the way through to my bones.

I mock glare at her as she takes her time picking her next question. I raise my hand and look down at my bracelets like they're a watch, gesturing for her to hurry up. Her eyes lock on my hand again.

"Was that your only love? Music?"

Yeah, maybe a cheap shot of tequila is a better trade than answering this question.

"I'm sure you know my dating history, or lack thereof. It's all out there on the internet."

She looks unamused at my answer. "I know I could look up your dating history, but that wasn't my question. I asked if music is your only love."

My hand clenches the bottle and my answer comes out as a

reflex. "*Was*, not is." Shit. That came out harsher than I meant for it to. I can see it by how her eyes widen and her lips part like a deer caught in headlights, not knowing how to react to that. "And yes, it *was* my only love." There was a time when I might of answered that differently, but it's been the truth to me for years.

"I'm sorry. I thought you said I could ask anything."

I reach out and grab her hand. To my surprise, she doesn't pull back. I wrap my fingers around hers, rubbing small circles across the back of her hand.

"I did say that, you're right. It's just an old wound that feels like it never closes."

She leaves her hand in mine while her eyes stay fixed on me. She swallows hard and nods. "I get that."

Fuck. I'm a jackass. As soon as she says that, I remember if anyone would know about old wounds, it's the Chapman siblings.

I need to dig myself out of this hole. The entire reason I even came over here was to try and distract her and cheer her up, not be a downer. So I blurt out the first thing that comes to mind to fix what was bothering her in the first place.

"Work for me?"

That's my next question? Why did I ask that? Why can't I think straight around her?

I watch as her face scrunches. The look she gives me is part shock, part disbelief, and a whole lot of what-the-hell.

"Did you really just ask me to work for you?"

This could go bad quickly. I raise a shoulder in a half shrug, doing my best to play it off casually. I could hire her, maybe she could work with Jake for me.

"Yeah, work for me. I could use someone to help with my charitable giving."

I do give a small fortune to non-profits each year, albeit anonymously for a list of reasons. Jake always picked the causes he thinks I'd like and handles all the paperwork and finances. Maybe I could unload some of that to her?

She's still looking at me like I have two heads and I don't like the feeling.

"Is this some kind of a messed up joke or are you being serious?"

Shaking my head, I stretch my arm around the back of her chair and lean in closer. I already opened this can of worms, so I might as well go all the way. It's hardly the worst idea I've had and she's the kind of person I like to have in my circle, personally and professionally.

"No joke. I'm serious." Her shoulders relax when she sighs. She looks down, tracing a finger over the rim of her empty glass. Maybe this will work? She's actually thinking about it, until I fill the silence. "Come on, what do you have to lose?"

Her head whips up, her green eyes filled determined fire again.

"No pun intended, but I'm not some charity case, TJ. Thanks though." I can see the resolve in her expression.

I want to push back, but I'm caught off guard by an excited shriek from the back door of the bar. Clay strides out of the back hallway with Lizzy clung to him like a koala bear, draping her arms over his shoulders. Lizzy catches the attention of Veronica and Grace, pointing at the sizable ring on her finger.

Oh, damn. Clay did it. He proposed.

Grace jumps from her seat so fast, leaving me at the table alone. I know they're my friends, but this is a huge moment for them. I decide to cut my losses, lick my wounds, and call it an early night.

They should get to celebrate this together as a family.

CHAPTER 5

GRACE
TWENTY-FOUR HOUR

I DON'T KNOW what karmic good graces I've finally conjured up, but the twenty-four hour gym in Jackson has turned into my safe haven. One thing I learned from all my van trips over the years is that the two S's — sleep and showers — can't be overvalued. Jackson has limited campgrounds, especially in the winter, and they are so dang expensive.

Even after I bought my van while I was in college, I still had savings left over from my settlement after the accident. I've done a good job of keeping that nest egg for emergencies and I don't want to burn it on campgrounds. I want that money to be there for when I really need it.

Normally, when I'm in town, I just stay with my grandparents. If I want my own space, I'll park my van behind Tanner's barn. It's the ideal spot, close to his cabin, where I can get a shower, and have access to electric to recharge the van batteries.

Of course, doing that now would mean having to explain why I've still been in town for the last week, and not back in Utah. Clay and Lizzy have been so busy with their own post-engagement celebrating they haven't noticed yet. Tanner's gone with Veronica on their ski road trip honeymoon. He loved my van enough that he eventually built his own, so he could take trips and bring his dog, Rex. Which means V's brother, Collin, is housesitting for them and would know I'm around.

Enter my new home away from home: the twenty-four hour gym.

On days like this, where I know I can get a hot shower after my run on the treadmill, I'm glad that Josie shared that little life hack. Even in a pinch, I can sometimes get away with parking overnight and sleeping in their lot. If anyone asks why I'm here in the middle of the night, I just say I was here for a workout. Obviously, it helps me stay in shape too.

Taking care of my body was something that became a priority after spending weeks in a hospital bed, and then months in physical therapy. It was so easy to take my health for granted before, but I will always prioritize it now. It's not for looks, it's not for vanity, it's because I never want to feel like a prisoner to my own body again. I love being able to go on a long hike or backcountry ski just because. My mind will always be that free and I owe it to myself to make sure my body will keep pace.

I reach down to increase the speed on the treadmill, but stop when the music cuts out. Looking at my phone, I feel a smile spread across my face when I see the name. Speak of the devil herself.

I swipe to answer the call. "What's up, girl?"

"Just making dinner after skiing." I hear the sound of pots and pans banging in the background. "Figured we should chat about meeting up in Jackson. I am so excited to see your face."

I met Josie in college. She dropped out after our freshman year, when she rented a van that summer to visit national parks. She's been living full time in her custom van ever since. While I love van life for short stints, I don't know how she does it full time. It takes a whole different level of determination and independence to not have a place to come back to, when you just need a breather from being on the road.

"You're already bored of Taos, aren't you?" I tease.

She scoffs, her normal reaction to getting called out on her constant on-the-go ways. I can just picture the dismissive hand wave she's making right now.

"No. It's a cool mountain. I just miss you." I'm starting to feel like I've been a bad friend because I miss her too. Blocking the guilt, I reach down to slow the speed on my treadmill, winding down my run. "You're my backcountry buddy. There's no way I'm skiing out of bounds if you're not with me."

Skiing in the wilderness, outside of the confines of a ski resort, chasing down untracked stashes of snow has been a passion of mine ever since my mom first took me out with my brothers. "What day are you getting to town? Maybe we can get a backcountry day in?"

"I'm going to head up to Utah first, ski around the Cotton-wood Canyons before I head to you. Need me to grab anything from your place while I'm nearby?"

This is why Josie is my best friend. Outside of Kayleigh, and now I guess TJ, she's the only one that knows I got laid off and that I'm taking some time for myself. She would totally go an hour out of her way to my apartment without a second thought.

"If you end up nearby, I have one request."

I hear Josie's manic laughter on the other end. "Oh my god, did you forget your vibrator? Do you need me to go through your nightstand and pick one out for you? I would be honored."

"Josie! No. Do not, I repeat, do not go through my night-stand." Fortunately, I did remember to pack that. Living in a van for a few weeks requires a bit of minimalism, but I always remember the essentials and I'm not planning on finding a man on this trip. I'm used to having to take care of myself.

She pouts. "You're no fun."

I snort a laugh. "Anyway, I was going to ask you to grab my extra ski bibs. It's been wetter than normal, and I want my other pair as a backup."

"You got it. So where are we parking when I get there? Campground or?" she draws out the last word.

I know what she's getting at. Tanner will be back by next weekend, so maybe I could finally tell him about Wasatch Wishes, and we could park by his barn. I just don't want my family making a big deal about this. "I'm still working on that, but I'll figure out a good spot. I don't think a campground is in the budget though."

"You know, if you're still looking for a side gig in the mean—"

I cut her off, laughing. "For the last time, I'm not doing the cam girl thing."

I hop off the treadmill and head over to the water fountain to refill my bottle. Being a faceless cam girl is how Josie finances her nomad lifestyle. More power to her, but that's not for me.

"I know you'd love not having a boss," she teases.

I let out another laugh. I'll give her credit, she's persistent. "Hey, I need to get going. Going to hit the shower and make myself some dinner too. Let me know if you have any issues getting into my place or finding my bibs. Thanks, Bun."

"Of course. Can't wait to see you soon!"

IN THE BASICALLY EMPTY LOT, the only sound is my van's diesel heater.

Winter nights in Jackson are downright cold, even compared to Park City. Fortunately it's not windy, otherwise my post-workout sweats that double as pajamas wouldn't cut it. I don't remember nights feeling this cold as a kid growing up here, but maybe I'm just becoming a bit more sensitive as I approach thirty.

If the kids at Wasatch Wishes taught me anything, it's that they're resilient. Playing in the cold all day, falling and getting right back up without getting hurt, it never seems to bother them.

The bone-chilling, crisp night air is just starting to get to me when I reach the back corner of the lot, where I parked. My black van with tinted windows and no logos or accessories on the outside does a good job of not attracting unwanted attention. I open the sliding door, once again thankful for my height when I make the step up into the lifted van easily.

While it might look like a simple cargo van on the outside, inside it's my home on wheels. Insulated for winter, a few storage cabinets, a small kitchenette, and my cozy queen sized bed all make it feel more like home than my apartment sometimes. I even have a composting toilet, but I prefer to only use that for emergencies if I can't find a public restroom. Either way, it's the perfect size for my solo travel shenanigans.

To some, it might look like I'm living out of my car. To me though, there's always been something so freeing about being able to grab a few things, hop in, and head off on an adventure.

After stowing my gym bag in one of the cabinets and putting in my privacy window covers, I snuggle into bed and scroll on my phone. Most of my feed is skiing clips or van life influencers, but after taking a few book recommendations from Lizzy, there's now a smattering of romance book content.

I'll give it to Lizzy. Romance novels renewed my love for reading. I love the characters, but I'm always envious of their connections. I've never felt loved, at least in a romantic sense, by another person before.

It's not a surprise that my options in Utah for local, but non-LDS men, were less than ideal. Even when I was in college, most of the guys were looking for someone to settle down right away and start a family. They wanted the traditional wife, which let's be real was not, and is not, ever going to be me.

The more interesting guys I met in Park City always ended up being emotionally immature ski bros that were only worried about which après bar had the cheapest drinks that night. While that's a handy trait on a night out with friends, it's not what I want in a life partner.

Then there were the transplants, the obnoxious rich boys that moved to the fancy ski town and were constantly on their phone checking their investment portfolios.

And don't even get me started on how many guys, I won't even dignify them by calling them men, were put off by me being as tall as them. That's on top of them having no clue what to do in bed. I hate to even think about the number of times I'd get home from a date, only to have *another* date with myself.

I crave physical stimulation and I'm not shy about taking care of my own needs. Chalk that up as another unintended consequence of spending months recovering from nerve damage, savoring every little regained sensation. I want to feel that physical connection to the world around me however I can.

Still, I have never found an unapologetically authentic person. Someone confident, but kind. Someone bold enough to take chances and not settle for taking the easy paths. I dream of someone that's decisive, ready to go off on an adventure with me at the drop of a hat.

I just don't think those men exist in real life. Maybe in Lizzy's books, but I haven't found one in the real world. It would be great to have a teammate though, someone I could share my adventures with.

That wonderful idea is interrupted by a sound I'm all too familiar with in the winter. I hear the telltale whoosh of my van's diesel heater and the burner kicking on. That's a normal sound. The whining of the fan that circulates the hot air around, that isn't so normal. It's been getting louder and louder each night I've stayed in the van, and I know I'm going to need to deal with it sooner or later.

I throw my head back into my pillow and groan. As much as I might not want to think about the next phase of my career, I'm going to need to do something if I don't want to blow through my savings. I don't necessarily need my next long-term job, but even something part time to help cover some day-to-day expenses or van repairs.

I could probably talk to Kelsey at Cowgirl Coffee or Sutton at Gloria's about picking up shifts. I worked in the service industry during college and those places are always looking for help during ski season. But working at either of those places does increase the chances of running into my grandparents or someone else that would spill the beans. This is one problem with being from a small town.

I love Jackson. It's my home. It's my favorite place in the world. But here, everyone knows me as Grace Chapman, little sister of local big mountain skiing legend, Tanner Chapman.

Back in Park City, I'm the little sister of Clay Chapman, former skiing prodigy whose Olympic career was cut short by injuries.

Or worse, I hear the hushed whispers in both places, I'm the girl that survived the tragic car accident that claimed my mom's life.

I don't want to be known as any of those things, and now I'm the girl that lost my job.

While it hurt, I don't need rescuing. I don't know why, but that makes me think of TJ's offer at my brother's wedding reception. At the time it felt like he was trying to rescue me, but I also remember on our trip to Bend, he was so genuine when he asked me about Wasatch Wishes.

He never stopped asking about me or what I did for fun, what

I did for work, why I took up cold plunges on a whim. For being an aloof rockstar, he was awfully chatty to me.

Maybe I could text him. I still have his phone number from the group chat when we stayed at his place.

I don't know what the hell he meant by work for him, but I haven't been able to forget the look in his eyes when he asked. We never talked much about his professional life.

Even though V might be a huge Teal Tigers fangirl, all we know is that he quietly left the music industry about a decade ago, and he does some kind of real estate investing now. So why on earth would he have wanted me to work for him?

CHAPTER 6
TJ
SLADE

STANDING in the corner of the empty first floor storefront, the view looking west over the Belltown neighborhood in downtown Seattle is great.

Why do I ever doubt Slade? He seems to have a sixth sense for finding the perfect spots to open restaurants.

Generally speaking, that means they're also good places to rehab into apartments, condos, or office space.

The sun is starting to set over the horizon and I can just picture sitting in a booth, looking out at the busy street, on a night like this. I imagine the sounds of the restaurant and people walking by the trendy new concept that Slade wants to open.

Groaning, I admit to myself that Slade is right yet again. This building is a gem. While he's only been to Seattle a handful of times, I spent my life here, before I hit the road with Teal Tigers. I know this city, even if I don't live here full time anymore.

Fucking Slade nailed it. The location, the architectural style, all of it.

This is why I trusted him, sight unseen, to work with Jake and make the offer two weeks ago while I was in Jackson. I knew he wouldn't waste my time or let me down.

Looking through the dirty window, I take in the surrounding businesses. It's been over twenty years since the first time I performed in the seedy bars and venues that once littered almost every corner of the area. There are still plenty of bars, but none are the type that would have given us a gig.

No. This place has definitely gotten trendy.

We were some unknown punks back then and getting slots to play was a grind. The places here now are the ones that would have taken one look at a twenty year old me, and said absolutely not. My shaggy hair was a shade or two lighter and a few inches longer back then — a tribute to Washington's original blond grunge icon, my idol. My white tank tops, or cut off flannels, showed off the cheesy barbed wire tattoo I thought was so edgy on my bicep. My pierced eyebrow only added to the fact that I looked like trouble, even if I was far from it.

Hell. I wonder if these places even do live music anymore. I'm sure they have a curated streaming playlist, ironically with some of my old songs. I guess the joke is on those places that turned us away when we first got started. They aren't here anymore, and I own yet another building in this neighborhood where I enjoy fixing up these properties.

The sound of footsteps, plodding along the worn, old hardwood floors, has me turning to spot Jake and Slade walking over to me.

Slade is wearing his ever-present, confident scowl. His dark hair is parted to the side in a way that reminds me how controlling he is about everything in his life, from the way he plates his dishes to how he runs his kitchens right down to how he folds the cuff of his over-priced selvedge jeans.

"You love it, don't you?" he says smugly, holding a finger up and circling it around the room.

I put on my best concerned look. "Well it doesn't really matter since I already let you two make the offer."

I hold his gaze but he doesn't flinch. He's always so damn serious. Finally I give in and roll my eyes. "Yes, you were right. I fucking love it." I point over my shoulder with my thumb back toward the street. "I forgot just how nice this area is now."

Jake slaps me on the shoulder and I immediately remember that my younger brother makes me feel small with his linebacker build. "You know, if you made it out and hit up a bar more than once a year, you'd have realized how much it's changed."

"Did I come here to get ribbed all night by you two, or for you to show me the rest of the plan for this place?" I scoff playfully.

Slade cocks his head to the side, still with a smug smile before reaching out and plucking a piece of dust off my shoulder. "Nope. I just wanted to hear you say I was right. I need to get going."

"Do you always have to be so dramatic and cocky?" I mutter, prompting Jake to snicker.

Slade just shrugs. "Does it even matter? Anyway, I'll see you when you're back for the party."

I shift to the side to let him head toward the door. Jake watches Slade walk away before turning back to face me, tipping his chin. "You got a sec?"

I lean against the exposed brick wall, folding my arms across my chest.

"Yeah, what's up?"

"You coming to dinner at Mom and Dad's tonight?" He gives me his normal shit-eating grin, damn well knowing the answer.

"Yeah, you know I wouldn't miss it. I need to be back in Jackson tomorrow though. I'm supposed to meet Sutton for lunch."

He shakes his head. "I swear you're going to become an honorary Sterling brother."

I lift a shoulder. "You're not getting rid of me that easy." Jake smiles back softly and we share a knowing look.

Somehow, fate brought us together. The foster parents that took me in my freshman year of high school took him in only a year later. Although I aged out of the system, they ended up adopting Jake before he graduated. We bonded almost instantly the day we met and have considered ourselves brothers ever since.

"So what did you *really* want to talk about?"

"Oh, just your favorite thing. Taxes and finances."

"Fuck me," I groan, running my hand through my hair, pushing it back. "Do we have to do this now?"

Jake knows I hate talking about this stuff. He's three years younger than me, and for the life of me, I will never understand why he wanted to get a business degree. But by the time he was looking at law schools, the band's second album had taken off and I had more than enough to put him through school.

"I know you don't like talking about money and business around Mom and Dad," he says, pulling out a folder from his messenger bag.

"Fine."

Our last family, they were the first people that ever chose to have me in their life, the first ones that made me feel wanted. I owe them so much, and Jake feels the same way, calling them 'Mom and Dad'.

But he's right, it's not that I don't want them to hear because they'd ask for money or something like that. I've offered to buy them a new house, cars, whatever, dozens of times and they always turn me down. If they ever did ask me for anything, they'd get it. No questions asked.

I just don't want anyone to know that much detail about my business. Outside of Jake, no one knows what I actually have.

Thanks to his brains and very pricey Stanford law degree — which might be the greatest investment I've ever made — we've built layers and layers of trusts, corporations, and other entities.

All of it was done to help maintain my anonymity in the business world.

He spreads the contents of the folder across the makeshift, sawhorse work table. He looks up, then back at the papers.

I squint and raise an eyebrow at him. "You know I'm not going to read this shit, right?"

He shrugs. "I know, but don't say I didn't offer."

I step forward and stand beside him, looking at the mess of statements, tax forms, reports, and god knows what else. "We're two days into January. Isn't it a bit early to start this?"

"Wow. It's only taken you a decade to catch on," he teases.

I glare back at him, but he's right. I've been successful, not because I'm great at numbers or tax law, but because I've surrounded myself with good people. People that I trust, mainly Jake, but also people like the Sterlings and the Chapmans. The rest has been a combination of good timing and having a feel for my hometown, but also a whole lot of luck.

"So what'd you want to show me?"

"Well, we're still waiting on a few things to come in, but it's no surprise, yet again, that you had another record year."

"*We* had another record year," I correct him. He's just as much a part of this as me, even if he likes to deny it.

"Right." He nods and smiles softly at me before tilting his head toward a paper with a few colorful charts on the table. "That summary would show you that, if you want to look, for once."

"Can we cut to the chase?" A smile crosses my face when I look back up at him. "You know she's making him wait to eat until we get there."

His shoulders rise and fall with a laugh. "That's pretty much it. I did increase your charitable donations for last year. Partly because your ass can afford it and I know you like giving. Partly to offset more of your gains. We should do even more this year though."

"Great. Sounds good to me. Did you just give more to the same places?" Part of staying anonymous is also being hands off. This is where I let Jake have a lot of free rein. I trust him to pick the right causes to give to, but even he's limited in how involved he can be with how much time the real estate and other investments take. Maybe I was on to something trying to hire Grace to help with this. It would be great to have someone more focused on just this aspect.

"Mostly. Picked a few new ones, cut back on some of the older ones. We can always pick some new places to give to this year. Figured we share the wealth a bit. Well, I guess *your* wealth." He tosses me a smart-ass wink.

"Cool. Well if that's it, let's get going. I'm starving." I pat him on the back and turn toward the door.

I've got a long twenty-four hours ahead of me, and as much as I love seeing Jake and my former foster family, I can't wait to get back to Jackson. Normally, I don't care which one of my places I'm staying at — whether it's here in my hometown, out on the river in Bend, or down in Jackson — I feel comfortable in all of them.

But lately, Jackson's felt more and more like home. Maybe it's because I'm finally putting down roots there. I'll admit that making friends with Tanner and Sutton has been nice. Or maybe it's because a certain tall, energetic woman is there.

Even though I haven't seen *her* the last two weeks, I've seen her van around, and I just can't shake her from my mind. Everywhere I go in town, I find myself hoping I'll bump into her or even just get a glimpse of her.

CHAPTER 7
GRACE
FRISKY FOX

WHILE THE CHAIRLIFT might be my family's favorite local bar in town, Frisky Fox is a legend. Located right at the base of the ski resort, it's the perfect après ski bar. Old wood paneled interior, random knickknacks and trinkets line the walls, and a giant stuffed moose hanging from the ceiling. All of it is just the right mix of cheesy tourist photo op and original 1960s ski resort vibes. I wasn't surprised this was the first place Josie wanted to visit when she got to town earlier today.

"Oh my god." She throws her head back and practically moans. "I've been craving a Frisky Fox spicy marg so bad."

I shake my head and laugh. "When was the last time you were here?"

Ever since we met, she's been my partner in crime. We always seem to get up to something, and judging by the look in her eyes, I have a feeling she's thinking the same thing.

"Probably last April when we came up for Jackson's closing day," she says, twirling a short lock of hair in her fingers. "Glad to see Agnes is still here."

Agnes is the moose that's always spotted around the ski resort village, snacking on shrubs with one of her calves. Tonight she was in her usual spot when we came into the bar.

In some ways, Josie reminds me of my brother's fiancée, Lizzy. I think that's why I immediately connected with her, even though she was Veronica's friend. Their short stature somehow only intensifies their fiery and spunky attitudes into some kind of superpower. Both of them are outspoken, shameless flirts, and don't take shit from anyone.

On top of that, Josie always wants to be moving and going, constantly doing something. In hindsight, it shouldn't have been a surprise that she fell in love with van life instantly. While I'm satisfied with spontaneous, short trips, her wanderlust is insatiable.

She looks down at her now empty drink and nods confidently. "Yep. It was definitely last April. Right before I headed South to Telluride, then to Cali for the music festival." She points a finger at me across the table. "You know, you still need to make it out there with me one year."

"I will try this year. Who knows, if I haven't found a full time gig by then, maybe I can join you for a change."

Her eyes scan my face and she reaches across the table, grabbing my hand in hers. "Girl, you know you're going to find a new, even better job." She smirks at me. "Now seriously, stop sweating it and let's have some fun."

I feel the corner of my mouth lift into a smile. "Well, not *too* much fun. We still have to drive back to the gym to park tonight."

Groaning, she rolls her eyes at me. "Are you seriously still worried about running into someone you know? You need to relax. They're going to find out eventually."

I drop my head and sigh, taking a long drink of my margarita, the salted rim making my lips pucker. "I know, you're right. I just don't want everyone to make a big deal about it, which I know they will."

It's been over ten years since the accident, but even now, if my family sensed something was wrong in my life, they'd drop everything to focus on me. I love them for that, but it's the last thing I want.

The accident was just that; an accident, a fluke. That's not who I am and I don't enjoy feeling like it's going to define the rest of my life.

Her hand tightens around mine. "It's going to be fine, Grace."

I let out a long breath and take a second to clear my head. I might not be ready to tell all of them just yet, but she's right. I will get there.

I look down at my empty drink in my other hand, seeing Josie's glass is empty too. I push back and stand up from our table. "I'll go get another round."

She starts to say something, but her eyes drift up over my shoulder and I see her tongue dart out over her lips. That's her telltale sign that she's found something, or more likely someone, she's interested in.

I turn and bump into what feels like a brick wall.

"Oh, I'm sor—" My words get stuck in my throat when I look up to see Collin Perry, Tanner's best friend and now brother-in-law. Fuck. Me.

He looks down at me with that gentle, kind smile that reminds me of his twin sister. "Hey, Little Chapman. I thought that was you. Even from behind, this hair is a giveaway." He ruffles my hair. "Didn't realize you were back in town."

That's because I didn't want anyone to know and I was doing just great at keeping it that way, until now. Leave it to Josie to get me out on the town and blow my cover.

Maybe I can tell a little bit of the truth. I've practically known Collin since I was born, and he's always been cool. He even caught me sneaking out to see a boy, the summer before we moved to Park City, and I know he didn't say a word to Tanner or he would have freaked out. Tanner's nine years older than me and definitely protective.

"Hi, Collin." I shuffle awkwardly on my feet, a nervous hum working its way up my throat. Here goes nothing. "To be *back* in town, that would have to mean I actually left."

"Oh dang, I wish I knew you were in town. We could have hung out." He shrugs and I notice he's holding two drinks.

Awesome, maybe he won't push this any further if he's here with someone. But then again, leave it to Collin to double fist drinks.

He squints, eyeing me for a second. "Wait a minute. Why am I just now hearing about this? I know you're not staying at Tanner's or your grandparents' place or I'd have seen your van."

I fidget with the two empty glasses that I wish were full right now.

"That's because I'm not staying at either of their places."

This time his brow raises in surprise, but I see the moment it clicks.

"They don't know you're in town, do they?"

"Um, rude," Josie interrupts, eyeing Collin like a piece of meat. "Are you not going to introduce me to your friend?" I can't blame her, Collin is a hottie. Six foot-something, part time personal trainer, part time property manager with Tanner.

I'm about to introduce Collin when another voice cuts me off.

"This would be my boyfriend, Collin." I watch as the tall, handsome cowboy I've only met once, at my brother's wedding, walks up. He extends his hand to Josie, taking hers and placing a kiss on the back of it. "And I'm Walker. Pleasure to meet you."

Damn, Walker is smooth. I turn and my jaw drops. Josie is grinning and I swear, she actually blushes.

❄

AFTER A COUPLE ROUNDS of Frisky Fox spicy margaritas, I finally spill the beans to Collin and Walker. I'm glad I did, it feels like a weight has been lifted. They understood why I don't want my family knowing yet. I should have known Collin would get it. He might be Tanner's best friend and even though he's almost ten years older, we were still pretty close. I remember he came out after high school years ago, so if anyone would understand keeping things from your friends and family, it would be him. My worries feel almost trivial in hindsight now, even if I still don't plan to tell anyone else yet.

"I know, I know. I'm probably being overdramatic. Even TJ offered me a job," I say, taking a sip of my drink. The salted rim stings my lips, chapped from a day of skiing.

The table goes quiet for a second and Josie turns to me. "Excuse me? TJ, as in *The* Tommy Jacob? As in Teal Tigers' Tommy Jacob?"

I nod, licking more of the salt off the rim of my glass.

Collin chimes in. "As in TJ, the notoriously private retired rockstar whose house you stayed at with your brothers earlier this year? And side note, still bummed I missed that trip."

I shake my head, jutting my chin out at them. "Yeah, and? He probably just felt bad for me or is bored since he can't fish right now."

They both hum curiously and look at each other. Simultaneously, Collin and Josie both look back at me, pointing at each other when their mouths open.

"I like her."

"I like him."

"What?" I groan, wishing they'd clue me in on their inside joke. I remember Collin could make friends with anyone and clearly that hasn't changed.

Walker leans forward, letting out a low laugh. "I think these two here believe that good ol' TJ has a thing for you."

Between what they're saying and Walker's way too cool drawl, I can feel my cheeks heating. "No way. He's just pity offering me a job. Tanner's pathetic little sister. Besides, I barely know him and he didn't even say what the job is."

Josie shrugs. "I can't believe you kept this detail from me. Who cares what he needs you to do? He's Tommy-freaking-Jacob. You should absolutely take that job."

I want to object, but she's not wrong. I didn't take him seriously in the moment and then there was all the commotion and celebration after Clay proposed to Lizzy. But would it really be the worst thing?

I was considering picking up shifts at the coffee shop or somewhere else around town. I'm sure whatever TJ's offering would be better than that — and probably pay better too.

Would it be weird to text him? I told him I'm not a charity case. What if it was just a joke or he's changed his mind?

Collin looks at Josie and gives her a few enthusiastic nods. "Hell yeah, she should. Plus, TJ's a total daddy."

I nearly choke on my drink and Josie cackles. Walker is quirking his brow at Collin but gives an approving shrug.

"Screw all of you, seriously." I manage to get the words out after I stop coughing on my drink.

They continue on with their conversation, but I can't help but think they're right. Not the hot part, even though yeah, TJ is definitely hot. It would be worth reaching out to him, even if it's just to have another friend in town. If only I could just work up the nerve to do it.

CHAPTER 8

TJ
THE WORST

"YOU KNOW, this might be the worst pasta you've ever made." I lean across the chef's tasting counter at Gloria's, while Sutton cleans a set of knives in the open kitchen.

"Well, damn. That hurts," he says while focusing on putting the fancy Damascus steel knife on the magnetic holder along the back wall. The neat row of knives, all made by Chapman, is orderly, but not quite up the standards that his neat freak brother, Slade, would keep. Slade still runs their first restaurant in Denver as well as their other one in Park City, Utah. They opened Gloria's here after both restaurants' success. I started getting lunch or dinner here at least once a week if I was in town, and befriended Sutton. Ever since then, it seems like one of the Sterling brothers is always close by, which is fine by me.

Sutton puts the last knife away before turning back to me, still sporting his ever-present, shit-eating grin. "You do know that you still have to pay for it though, right?"

I finish the last bite, exposing my lie. His food is always exceptional. I'm still tired from the flight earlier this morning and I barely have enough energy to deal with his constant teasing and playful personality today. But Saturday lunches with him have become routine for me when I'm in town. I practically have a name plate on this seat, where I get to try the new dishes he's been working on before they go on the menu.

"What happened to 'the customer is always right'?" I grumble, still not quite myself because of the flight. Or at least that's what I've been telling myself.

He laughs and shakes his head. "I swear, you're the cheapest multi-millionaire I know. And now the grouchiest. What happened to chill, laid-back TJ?" He leans across the counter, taking in my empty plate and smirking back at me. "This wouldn't have something to do with the very off limits woman you're obsessed with shooting you down?"

I groan, dropping my fork into the empty dish with a clang. He's not entirely wrong. I haven't seen her since the reception, but that doesn't mean I wasn't doing a double take every time I saw a black Sprinter van around Jackson, hoping it was her.

He grabs a rag, laughing to himself as he polishes a wine glass. "I still can't believe you offered her a job. Way to be subtle there, big guy."

"What happened to this being a safe space to talk? I didn't order a side of judgement with my lunch." The look I'm giving him is probably conveying that I wish there wasn't a counter between us so I could tell him how I really feel about this conversation. "And I didn't offer her a job because of whatever crush you think I have on her. I did it because I wanted to help her."

But Sutton is always going to be Sutton, enjoying himself at my expense. I swear he always has a playful joke or witty comeback queued up. "Yeah. Keep telling yourself that. And for the last time, I'm a chef, not a bartender. I don't know how many times I have to explain that even if I bring you a drink and you sit on a stool at this counter, I'm not a bartender. So you don't just get to dump your drama and baggage on me like I am one."

"I take it back. This *is* the worst pasta you've ever made." I stand, putting on my jacket. I take a look around the restaurant, seeing the lunch crowd has cleared out. "Now come on, let's go get a coffee."

"HOW'S IT GOING, KELSEY?" I say before looking up to the menu board at Cowgirl Coffee. I don't know why I even bother though. After Veronica wouldn't stop talking about iced Honey Badgers, I've been addicted to them. It's one of their speciality drinks with espresso, cayenne, honey, cinnamon, and milk. She was right. They're too good and now I get them every time I'm here.

"Same old, same old," she says, seemingly unamused by us and unfazed by the busy coffee shop around her.

She might be a Jackson local, but she's got the grumpy, edgy feel that would be right at home in a Seattle coffee shop. I almost feel honored that I even get a smile from her most of the time.

"Having your usual?"

I nod. "Plus whatever Sunshine back here is having."

I step aside and when she sees Sutton, any sense of that soft smile from earlier vanishes. She rolls her eyes, enters something into the point of sale, and flips the tablet for me to pay before turning away to make our drinks.

I look over at Sutton with a questioning glance. He frowns, something I rarely see him do and mumbles. "She already knows my order."

I look back to Kelsey, who's facing away from us and making our drinks before looking back to him. "Do I want to know what that's about?"

"Maybe, but I'm not telling you," he says, his tone regaining its normal playful luster.

"Right. Whatever. I'm go—" A bright laugh from the back of

the coffee shop catches my attention and I instantly forget what I was just thinking. I step to peer around the corner, but I already know who I'm going to see.

I freeze like a statue when I see Grace, facing away from me, her brother and Veronica on the other side of the table.

A hand rests on my shoulder and I feel Sutton peek around me. "Oh shit. Dude, she's here. Go talk to her."

I step back closer to the counter to wait for our drinks, hoping they didn't see me. All the while though, I can still hear parts of their conversation.

I look at Sutton. "Didn't you say I should avoid her because she's very off limits and her brothers will kill me?"

He snorts a laugh. "Well yeah, then you spent all lunch telling me how bad my pasta was. And while I know that's a lie, right now I kind of want to see you get your ass kicked."

"One large iced Honey Badger and one black coffee with three sugars." Kelsey hands me my drink with the same soft smile from earlier before glaring at Sutton and setting his down on the counter.

He carefully reaches for it like it might be poisoned and something about this entire interaction between them is instantly fascinating. I'm definitely going to give him shit about this later.

"Thanks," he mumbles under his breath before looking at me. "Seriously, go talk to her."

I sigh. I guess Chap and V are there too and we're all friends. It would be weird if I kept hiding from them.

"Fine. I will." I look to Kelsey. "Please keep being mean to him until I'm back."

Her soft smile turns into a mischievous grin. "With pleasure."

I step around the corner and start to walk to their table. My eyes are fixed on her though.

Her long, colorful hair is hanging out from underneath her black baseball cap with her sunglasses resting on the brim. I learned in Bend that was her normal après ski look, much like her oldest brother.

But that's not what gets my attention. Even from behind, I can tell her posture is off. Her shoulders are sagging and she's fidgeting with her hands in her lap, just like she was at the bar when her grandparents were peppering her with questions. And that's when I hear her brother ask why she's still in town.

Shit.

CHAPTER 9
GRACE
FLUSTERED

AFTER GRABBING MY TEA, I find a seat at Cowgirl Coffee in front of the fireplace in the backroom. While getting drinks at The Chairlift or Frisky Fox after a day on the slopes is fun, sometimes I just want to relax a little and this is exactly what I needed today. I called it a day at lunch, but Josie wanted to keep going. We'll still meet up later.

I figured I would come into town, treat myself to a tea here by the fire and do something I've been putting off for the last three weeks. I set my Nalgene bottle down next to my tea, set my laptop up on the coffee table, and pull up job listings.

I've enjoyed these last few weeks. Kayleigh was right, it was good to take some time for me. I know I should at least start to see what else is out there for me, even if I'm not ready just yet.

"Oh my god, I missed these!" An all too familiar voice catches my attention.

No. No. No.

"I know, Ronni," my brother's deep, unmistakable voice rumbles out his nickname for Veronica, "which is why we're stopping here first before we even go back home."

They weren't supposed to be home for another week from their honeymoon ski road trip.

This would be my luck. As always, karma gives and karma takes. Noted.

I do my best impersonation of the shrinking woman and sink down into my seat. My brain quickly ticks through all the excuses I could give them about why I'm here. Maybe they won't even notice I'm here.

"Grace?!" Veronica's voice calls from behind me. I guess it was optimistic to think she wouldn't notice my brightly colored hair, even under my beat-up, old baseball hat.

I turn and put on a shaky smile. "Hey! You guys are back early."

I start to stand to give them a hug, but before I'm even out of my chair, Tanner leans over, places a kiss on top of my head, and they plop down on the loveseat across from me.

I keep my smile on and take a deep, cleansing breath.

I can do this.

I know deep down, I'm glad to see them. I just wish I had a little more warning.

"What brings you guys back early? Got tired of skiing already?"

Tanner chuckles, his chest rising and falling. "Fat chance of that. You know it's impossible to keep her off the mountain." He looks to his wife and it's impossible to miss just how smitten they really are with each other.

"Hey, I've got to make up for lost time. We're just passing through. Wanted to get our favorite coffee and grab a few things from the cabin." She rests her free hand on Tanner's thigh, taking a sip of her iced coffee with the other before continuing. "We were up North in Big Sky this morning and heading down to Salt Lake this afternoon. Planning on skiing around there for the next few days before we make our way to Taos."

I hum to myself and nod. "That's a solid plan. You should make it there for dinner if you don't stick around here too long."

Tanner nods, but I see a look I'm all too familiar with creep in. It's that questioning, big brother look — a much more intimidating version of the one Collin gave me last night.

Last night it was my pseudo brother, and today Tanner is laying it on even thicker. I can feel his gaze burrow into me.

"Yeah. On that note," he starts, setting his coffee down and leaning his elbows on his knees, "we were planning to call you once we left here and see if you were free for dinner."

I shrug, flare my palms up at my sides, and put on my best, innocent little sister smile. "Well, look at that. We could have dinner here, in Jackson."

He raises an eyebrow and I see him fight off a laugh. "I meant dinner in Utah, which is where you live."

Well, shit. I guess he's not going to drop it. Maybe I should get this over with and tell them. It felt good to tell Collin and Walker last night.

Here goes nothing. "So—"

I'm about to lay it all out when a hand rests firmly on my shoulder. Across from me, V's eyes go wide and her lips part in a big, uncontrolled smile. From behind me I hear yet another voice that's becoming all too familiar, even if I've known it for years from the radio. "There you are, Rainbow. I've been looking for you."

Fucking TJ.

I guess that explains her reaction. Even after spending a week in Bend at his house, she still can't help but fangirl a little whenever he's around.

I should be irritated with him. This is the second time he's surprised me like this in the middle of a conversation. But I'm not, because it's also the second time he's shifted the attention away from me, like he knew I needed a lifeline.

Any bit of anxiety I had about making up an excuse for my brother and his wife is instantly gone. I look over to see Tanner tip his chin to TJ in greeting

"Hey, man," Tanner looks from TJ to me with a curious expression on his face. "Have you two been hanging out?"

TJ rubs a few small circles over my shoulder through my t-shirt, just to the side of my overalls strap. The sensation sends a shiver down my spine and prickles my skin. My body reacts to the touch and I start to lean into his hand, just before he removes it. This is the kind of stimulation and feeling I crave and I find myself wanting him to put it back.

OK. That's a new one for my traitorous body.

Then to my pleasant surprise, or dismay, I'm not sure yet based on the mixed signals my body and mind are still sorting out, TJ pulls up a bistro chair from a nearby table. He spins it around and faces the three of us. Everything about the way he moves and carries himself always looks so calm and comfortable. It's like being around people, in any setting, doesn't faze him.

TJ looks to me, winks, and looks back to Tanner and V with a wry smirk. "I guess you could call it that. She's my newest employee. Isn't that right, Rainbow?"

I'll give it to him, TJ is shameless. The look he's giving me is everything all at once, playful and knowing, challenging and pleading.

I match his wink with a roll of my eyes before turning back.

"Surprise!" I raise my hands up beside my head and wiggle my fingers for some convincingly enthusiastic jazz hands.

V practically jumps off the loveseat with a squeal. "No way. Are you serious? Does that mean you're going to be in Jackson more?"

TJ looks back to me with a pleased grin, his dimple popping in a way that is far too attractive to be fair. He brushes his shaggy hair behind his ear and turns back to V.

"It's up to her. I give a lot to charity each year and thought it would be a good idea to have someone who knows what they're doing advise me on it for a change, especially when it comes to picking causes. I think she'll be great at it for as long as she wants to do it." He looks at me, his expression still cool but confident. There's no sign that he's just putting on an act and every sign that he means what he says. Something about that vote of confidence in me makes my stomach flutter.

Tanner nods before bringing his attention back to me. "What about Wasatch Wishes?"

Alright, if TJ wants to play whatever game this is, I can play along. I cross my legs in a very ladylike posture, one that instantly feels foreign to me, and turn to face my new *boss*. "Well, as Mr. Jacob so eloquently put it, this is a very open-ended opportunity."

I use my best professional, secretarial voice and smile, displaying what I hope is way too much gratitude and enthusiasm. "Wasatch Wishes said I could come back if something changes. But this was just too good to pass up."

It's not a total lie. They did say that 'if something changes', I'm always welcome back. At the very least, whatever this is with TJ buys me some time.

"That's so cool! You'll have to tell us all about it when we're back in town again," V bursts out, hardly containing her excitement. Turning to my brother, I see that his questioning expression has shifted to one of quiet indifference. "TJ's not that demanding of a boss. I'm sure he'll be great to work under."

Thanks, Tanner. Those words immediately take my subconscious, which is apparently agreeing with my traitorous body now, to a very unprofessional train of thought.

After finishing his drink, I notice Tanner checking his phone.

"Well, we better hit the road before it gets too late." He stands and tips his chin to me. "Maybe we'll try and see if Dad and Clay are free for dinner in Utah, but when we're back in town here, we need to get dinner too."

I nod. "I'd like that."

I get up and hug each of them before they make their way out of the shop.

When I hear the bells ring against the door closing behind them, I turn all my attention to TJ.

"You really need to stop sneaking up behind me, *Boss*," I say, flaring an eyebrow at him and folding my arms across my chest.

"Don't call me that. And consider it payback for sneaking up behind me on the river every morning," he says with a nonchalant, one sided shrug.

"What's that saying? Fool me once, shame on you. Fool me twice, shame on me?" I scoff, reaching for my tea which is thankfully still warm.

I feel him watch me as I lift the mug and take a long sip of my Earl Grey tea.

When I look up, sure enough, those baby blues are locked right on me.

"What?" I wipe a stray drop of tea from my chin. "Oh god, did I have something on my face that entire time they were here?"

He smirks and takes a sip of his iced coffee. "Work for me, Grace."

Jeez. I guess he is very serious about this, but I feel like maybe making him sweat a little first would be fun.

"We're just going to dive right into this? No courting or wooing me like the prized asset I am?" I lean forward in my chair, propping my elbow on my knee and my chin on my fist. "You know a girl likes a little foreplay. Ease into the main event, you know?"

He nearly chokes on his coffee and suddenly, without my brother or sister-in-law here, he looks a lot less at ease. Almost nervous. I swear I even see a hint of red creep up from his stubble over his cheeks.

"Do I make you nervous, Mr. Jacob?" I tease, my voice laced with amusement and maybe a touch of flirtatiousness. OK, more than a touch.

He glares back at me, but I still see a hint of that nervousness as he squirms in his seat. I savor this moment before he replies. "Something like that. You have a knack for seeing through me, Rainbow."

Something like that.

Seeing through me.

I don't know what to make of that, but I don't have time to think about it. TJ grabs the arm of my chair, and slides me closer to him, turning it so we're eye to eye. With his jacket in his lap, the motion draws my eyes to his defined biceps and chorded forearms, barely straining to move me and my armchair. He literally just turned the tables on me, or I guess chair.

I'm starting to get it. My Grandma, Veronica, Josie, even Collin and Walker. I can see TJ's appeal. He is hot. I'm just going to tuck that away though because I might actually be crazy enough to work for him.

He crosses his arms over the back of the chair. "I mean it this time. I'm serious. I want you to manage my charitable giving. You'd be working with my brother, Jake, who also happens to be my accountant, financial advisor, and lawyer."

There's no playfulness, no doubt, no nervousness, in his voice now. That has completely vanished. This doesn't feel like the spur of the moment question he blurted out at the bar the first time he asked me. His blue eyes are so intense, unflinching in holding my gaze, leaving no doubt that he means it.

This time, he's all business, all confidence, all conviction. I'm used to cocky ski bros or arrogant finance guys and their irritating swagger. But this look — this matter-of-factness in his tone — is something different. It's almost a presence more than an attitude.

I swallow, sitting taller in my chair. "OK."

His eyes soften and his grip on the back of the chair relaxes. "Wait, what? That easy?" He looks both shocked and relieved, which is exactly what I'm feeling right now. Collin and Josie warmed me up to the idea last night and now, seeing TJ in person again, it feels like the universe is back on my side, giving me a sign.

"Yep. So is this a full time job?" I hold my fingers together like I'm holding a pencil in one hand, scribbling notes on an imaginary note pad in the other. "What will my responsibilities be, Mr. Jacob?"

His eyes flick upward in annoyance. "Can you stop calling me *that* too? TJ is more than fine." He grabs a napkin off the coffee table and scribbles something on it with a pencil that was tucked behind his ear.

Wait, was that there the whole time? Hidden by that shaggy blond hair? Maybe it's some kind of musician quirk, always ready to jot down a lyric when the moment strikes.

He quickly folds the napkin and hands it to me.

Our fingers graze as I pull my hand away with the napkin note. I feel the brief warmth of his touch and the tension in him that spreads into me. His hand recoils, almost like a reflex and he drops to his side. I notice how his hand curls into a fist before flexing his fingers back out and resting them on his thigh.

I sigh and tilt my head. "Really? Handwritten notes on napkins? And who carries a pencil? You know you could just text me it if you don't want someone else to overhear. God, you really are old." I meant it as a playful jab, but he seems both unamused and unaffected.

"Look. If I gave you that much to manage," he points to the

number on the napkin, "to pick causes for, when and how to donate, would that be a full time job?"

I pull the note to my chest like I'm hiding my poker hand, wearing a sheepish grin. He watches me, the corner of his mouth curling into a smile as he leans forward over the back of the chair.

I fold the note open and look down. My mouth hangs open and I'm not sure when I stopped blinking.

That's a big number.

"TJ," my voice comes out as a breathy whisper. I find myself almost speechless for a change. "That's like seven figures. Is this a joke?"

"Oh, shit," his brows furrows and forms a line in between them, drawing my eyes to that little piercing. He reaches over and snatches the napkin. He scribbles something on it and hands it back. "Sorry. I missed a zero."

I open the note again, and wow... OK, now there are eight figures.

I have so many questions.

I knew TJ had money. I mean he's a rockstar, or retired rockstar, or whatever he's calling himself. I know he has the amazing houses all over the place, but an eight figure charitable donation is so rare. I never got to work with donors, individuals or corporations, anywhere remotely close to being that large. Our biggest donor at Wasatch Wishes was a one time donor for a million dollars and they were handled by our founders.

"I don't see how it's a full time job to manage this for you. We'd spend a few months picking the charities and disbursing the funds, but then what work would be left?"

"Sorry, I wasn't clear." His voice is steady and he still has that calm, matter-of-fact presence. "I give roughly that much, *every year*. So let's consider this a trial run. Jake had to handle the end of year donations, but I could use his focus on some other projects this year. So you could work on making a plan for this year and see how we could be doing better."

Reality sets in that he's very serious about this and it might actually be a real job, not a pity offer. It also might be something I enjoy, and I'm good at. I spent so much time working on finding donors and keeping them. We were an established cause too. Everything we did was tied to getting kids exposure to the outdoors. For once, I'd be looking for other causes that would interest me... well I guess TJ technically. It's his money after all.

"A trial run? What? Are you afraid I won't do a good enough job?" I finally answer.

What is wrong with me? Why did I just antagonize him when he's offering me what really is a fantastic opportunity? I should know better than to piss off the universe when it's dropping job offers from retired rock gods into my lap.

A muscle ticks in his jaw and he folds his arms across his chest, showcasing those damn forearms again. "No. I'm afraid you won't like working with me and Jake."

"So tell me more about this *Jake*. Is that like your alter ego? Dr. Tommy and Mr. Jacob?" I ask, holding my hand to my chin looking as inquisitive as possible. Also, does he really think I'd reject a serious offer from him? The time at The Chairlift was one thing, but this time I can tell he's serious.

He rolls his eyes and looks back at me. "Jake is my brother from foster care. I told you he works for me."

"Oh, I didn't realize you had any siblings," I say, slightly shocked. He's opening up to me, something he's not known for and I don't take that lightly. I sit up a little taller in my seat at that realization. "Wow. Talk about unfortunate names, Jake Jacob. But still this all sounds great. I just have one last question. Why me? I told you, I'm not a charity case." Maybe part of me is being self-indulgent, hunting for a compliment or some kind of validation from him. But I do genuinely want to know why on earth he wants to hire *me*.

His eyes narrow and his lips shift into a frown. "First, it's not charity. It just seems like good karmic timing. You needed a job and Jake wants me to donate even more in the future. Second, Jacob isn't his last name but that's beside the point."

Karmic timing. I think he already has me sold with that. Maybe we have more in common than I thought.

He must sense my optimism because his frown disappears when he unfolds his arms and grabs his iced coffee. "You have more experience with non-profits than Jake and me combined. Sure, we give a lot of money. But I've never been able to be as involved as I want and stay anonymous at the same time."

He takes a sip before a smug grin spreads across his face. "And in case you haven't noticed, I try to surround myself with good people. I've hired both of your brothers over the years, the Sterlings — Sutton and Slade. I like people I can trust." He tilts his drink toward me, emphasizing the last two words. "Like you."

Something about those two words from him feels like such a compliment. I might have been playfully looking for words of validation from him, but to hear that from someone I know values his privacy so much feels different. It feels more validating than anything else he's said this entire conversation. It feels intimate and personal.

"I'll do it," I say without hesitation, feeling sure of myself and him.

I can practically see his body relax at my words, a wide, unrestrained smile spreading across his face. I can't help but notice that it's not the same smile that he showed around my brother and V or my grandparents the other night. This one is almost sheepish with a hint of boyish charm. Both of his dimples flare in a way that's both endearing but also impossible to look away from.

His soulful eyes peer into mine and I can feel my skin heat under his gaze. He's been hanging on my every word for this entire chance run-in today, just like he did at the reception, but this feels different. Between his presence and the look in his eyes, I cross my legs, trying to ignore my body's reaction.

I feel like we're lost in this stalemate for way too long before a deep, playful voice cuts the silence. "You're an ass. I can't believe you unleashed Kelsey on me like that."

We both look up to see Sutton Sterling, Gloria's chef who catered the wedding, rounding the corner from the front room and glaring right at TJ. "Did I miss anything good?"

TJ looks both irritated with his friend and almost giddy at the same time. "Just that I hired Grace over here finally."

Sutton grins back at him before turning to me, holding out his drink for a mid-air toast. "Hell yeah, welcome to Team TJ."

What did I just get myself into?

CHAPTER 10
GRACE
FRESH TRACKS

IT DOESN'T MATTER what is going on in my life, this feeling never gets old. Waking up early to get to the mountain and get in the lift line before eight, when they don't even open for another hour, probably sounds horrible to most people that don't ski. Throw in the fact that today, it's below freezing with gusty winds. But on a powder day like this, when it dumped almost ten inches of fresh snow overnight, there's no place I'd rather be.

I love chasing storms to catch a powder day. It's part of why I got my van in the first place. Utah gets great snow. Sometimes though, you have to go on a little adventure if you want to find the best untracked, fresh snow.

It might sound silly to anyone that didn't grow up loving the sport but for me, there's nothing like the rush of laying down fresh tracks on the mountain. Those elusive first runs in pristine untouched, knee deep powder. Floating through the snow down a steep slope is pure bliss. The satisfaction of skiing down a run and looking back up the mountain to see my tracks like brush strokes on an untouched canvas. It never gets old.

Fortunately, Josie feels the same way. She has skied with me

— run for run, turn for turn — all morning. It's Sunday and some might be at church, but this is our place of worship.

"You ready for a break?" Josie says between labored breaths at the bottom of the run, near the chairlift. She props her goggles on the brim of her helmet and skis over to me. "I could eat and maybe a bio break."

I pull my neck warmer down under my chin and prop my goggles up like hers, savoring the feeling of the crisp, cool air against my skin. "Yeah, I packed lunch but I wouldn't mind going inside for a bit."

I turn for the lift line and gesture for her to follow along.

We shuffle toward the chair before we're scooped up and on our way to the mid-mountain lodge.

Josie bites down on the hose of her hydration backpack. A moment of silence passes and I can feel her eyes on me while she takes a long drink. "So when do I get to meet Hot Boss? Oh. Or is he more of a Hot *Daddy* Boss?"

I turn and level a glare at her. "Don't call him that. I'm trying to take this seriously. It's really a good opportunity."

"Don't call him which one?" She smirks before shrugging and shamelessly taking another loud slurp from the hose. "You can take it seriously *and* still call him Hot Boss. They aren't mutually exclusive."

"Look at you, busting out the big words," I tease.

"Hey!" She slaps my thigh with her gloved hand. "Believe it or not, I did pay attention in school and I'm an entrepreneur. I know things."

I smirk at her, knowing that as fun and crazy as she might be, she's hyper -intelligent. On top of being a faceless cam girl by night, she knows how to hustle, market, and manage herself to make it into a successful way to fund her life.

"OK. How about you don't call him Hot Boss or Hot Daddy

Boss?" Bleh. It feels cringy just saying either of those out loud. But she's not wrong, my new boss is pretty fine.

Alright, he's hot. TJ is rockstar hot. That's just a fact.

And he's going to be my boss starting tomorrow, which is another fact. But the two aren't related, at all.

Worst case: I help him find some charities he likes, then we part ways and I have a cool new bullet point on my resume all while keeping my family off my back for a little bit.

Best case: maybe this could be something amazing. If he's serious, I'd have a chance to make such a big impact on even more people. I think about what donations like his could have done for Wasatch Wishes.

I lock eyes with Josie. "I mean it. I'm actually excited about this. I really think something good will come out of this," I say with far more conviction now.

She gives me a look of understanding that feels reassuring. Then, I watch the corner of her mouth pull up into a smirk. "Yeah, you'll be coming if Hot Daddy Boss crosses his arms and looks at you like *that* again."

I glare at her, but that doesn't change the fact that I can feel my cheeks heat against the cold air. I only told her about that an hour ago and I already regret it. But there was just something about his presence, his calmness, that stuck with me.

"Josie! Don't go there," I warn.

To be fair, she wouldn't know the first thing about having a boss. Yes, she has to have boundaries with her subscribers, but she doesn't have to see them in person and be in the same room as them.

"Fine, I'll stop. But if you get the chance to introduce us, I want to meet him. I've never met anyone famous before."

I shake my head at her — trying to show my irritation — but I can feel the wide smile that crosses my face despite my protest. I missed seeing my best friend more than I realized.

"We'll see. I'll be sure to mention it to him first thing tomorrow."

"Wow," she says, raising her eyebrows. "Diving right into it Monday morning after you just told him 'yes' yesterday? I guess he's not big on foreplay."

I throw my head back and cackle. "I guess I was channelling my inner-Josie, because I told him the same thing."

Our laughter is drowned out by the chairlift cables whirring overhead, pulling my attention to the lodge coming into view.

As our ride comes to an end, she leans closer to me, wrapping her arm around me, resting her helmet on my shoulder. "You know you've got this, Grace. All of it. Working for TJ, telling your family, just life. I know you'll be fine."

The sense of warmth and relief I get from hearing that from my best friend is everything.

I have to admit, a morning like this with Josie is exactly what I needed. Honestly, I needed every minute of these last couple weeks, taking some time for myself back in my hometown. Somehow, talking with her always helps put things back in perspective. Throw in the powder day — skiing run after run in fresh snow — as the cherry on top, and now I feel like a weight's been lifted off my shoulders.

I can take some time for me *and* still make a difference the way I want to.

Things have a funny way of working out sometimes. Maybe leaving my old job behind will open up a new, untouched run for me. I'll finally have a blank canvas to leave my own fresh tracks on.

CHAPTER 11
TJ
YOU SURE ABOUT THAT?

WALKING from my kitchen down the hall to my office, I do one last survey of the post-wedding cleanup. I normally keep my places clean, a product of growing up in foster homes and moving a lot. In the weeks since the wedding, I've been spending more time in Seattle with Slade and Jake. So to say my house wasn't looking the best when I got home from Cowgirl Coffee yesterday is a bit of an understatement even with my housekeeper.

Stepping into my office at the end of the hall, next to my studio, I look around the second least used room in my house. The only person that occasionally uses it is Jake, and even then I can't remember the last time. Most of the work I do now is scoping out buildings in person or approving plans and signing paperwork, which Jake forces me to do digitally. I would much rather him overnight me papers to physically sign, but he likes to remind me that wastes time and paper.

Walking around the desk and stepping up to the console table in front of the large floor to ceiling windows, I admire the view of the mountains from this spot.

At this time of night, the sun has set and the lights from the groomers going up and down the ski slopes are visible in the distance. My house might be closer to the slopes, but the view is similar from all over Jackson. I wonder if Grace is looking at the twinkling lights on the slopes now too, like her very own stars.

Hell, I wonder where her van is parked. It's freezing out. I know she said she winter camps all the time, but I still wish I knew she was alright.

The feeling of my phone buzzing in my jeans pulls me from that thought. I look down to see an incoming call from Jake.

"It's about time you called," I say, reaching down to clear off the corner of the console table and make some room.

He groans. "I called as soon as I was free. Mom and Dad wouldn't let me leave until I had dessert. And to be fair, your voicemail just said 'call me when you can, no rush'. So, here I am, calling. Also, just send a text message like a normal person."

"Yeah, sure, next time. Anyway, I need you to get our new—" My voice trails off and I hum to myself in thought.

What do I even call her? Consultant? I already hate the idea that I'm her boss. I like to work *with* people. I hate the power dynamic of a business hierarchy. I hated having to deal with my agent, our manager, and our label. At least when it came to making music, we could ignore them and just do the part we enjoyed. That was the part of being in a band I loved — when we got to work together, collaborate, and not have a real boss.

"I need you to get our new consultant up to speed tomorrow. Figure out what to pay her, get her whatever documents she needs, just make sure she's taken care of. I'll give her your contact info in the morning."

"Woah. Pump the brakes for a second." I hear keys clank against glass through the phone, meaning he must of just gotten home. "What consultant? And are we talking your definition of morning or mine?"

"I hired a consultant to help with our non-profit work and create a better plan for what we're doing. She's going to look at the charities we give to, stuff like that. It could be long-term, who knows. But for now, we're calling it a trial run."

"OK?" his voice trails up and I can picture the questioning look that's probably on his face. "When did you hire her?"

"This afternoon. Why?"

I hear a long, frustrated sigh through the phone. "I know you like to go with your gut all the time, so this checks out but who is she? Where did you find this *consultant?*" he asks, his tone still skeptical.

He's got a point. That probably would have been helpful to lead with. "Grace Chapman, Tanner and Clay's little sister. You remember them, right?" Clay designed my house in Bend and Tanner is the property manager that takes care of my place here in Jackson, so Jake's worked closely with them over the years.

"Yeah, the two giant mountain men that look like they could kill a bear with their bare hands. Hard to forget them."

"Good, because, dude, she's awesome. You're going to love working with her. She's so smart. And funny too. She's worked for a non-profit for years and has so much experience from volunteering with ski school to working with donors. Her passion is just contagious."

I feel like I'm talking a million miles an hour.

I actually hired Grace.

It's Sunday night and she'll be here tomorrow to get started and squared away with whatever she needs for this project. So I need Jake to be on board quickly.

"Why do you sound like you're out of breath?" he says, laughing to himself.

I pause for a moment and realize that I'm now at the door to the hallway instead of by the window. Shit.

"I've been pacing around cleaning the house." It's fine. I just want to make a good impression on someone that I hired, right? That's a totally normal thing to do.

"Oh shit," he says with another loud laugh. "You're worried what she thinks about you, aren't you?"

I guess Jake answered my question for me. I swear he can read my mind.

Outside of him and my small inner circle, I've never cared about other people's opinions of me. People can think what they want. It's never stopped me from doing my own thing. With her though, he's right. I clearly do care what she thinks and my own brother can see right through me enough to know it.

"Fuck off, Jake," I chide, stepping back over to the desk and straightening it up. "I hired her because I think she can help us. Sure, did she need a job? Yes, and I wanted to help. But that's it."

That's a lie and I know it.

Would I do anything to make her smile? Probably.

I know I'll take every excuse I can to be around her because I like her, way too much. I can keep it professional though. Or at least I hope so.

"You sure about that?" he says, knowingly.

"If you were here, I'd punch you," I grumble, not answering his question. "Now can you make yourself free tomorrow morning so you two can video chat?"

He snorts a laugh. "Yeah, that's fine. You said she worked for a non-profit and has experience?"

"She worked for a non-profit back in Utah. They did stuff like getting kids into outdoor activities." My mind goes back to when we first met in Bend with her brothers. She was so thrilled to talk about her job and what she did. Her excitement practically radiated off her.

"Oh, perfect," he says, sounding pleasantly surprised. "We've given to some places like that before."

"Great. Well, you two can chat all about that tomorrow morning. Now I need to finish cleaning."

I'm tired and, yeah, I guess I'm stressed too. Telling Jake

suddenly makes this entire arrangement very real. She's going to be in my house, working with me, learning details about my business and finances that very few people know.

"Whatever, old man. I'll talk to you in the morning."

"Three years, Jake. I'm only three years older than you. You know that, right?" I shake my head. "Anyway, goodnight, little brother."

"Night, TJ," he says, and I can hear his voice soften before he hangs up.

Tucking my phone back in my pocket, I look around the office. She's welcome to use it, but maybe she'll want to hang out in her van instead or work from Cowgirl Coffee. I realize we have discussed no real details about what this arrangement will look like.

My heart warms though when I remember how sure she was when she said yes. She's definitely free spirited, but also so confident and sure of herself.

If she's so sure about this, then maybe I am doing the right thing.

CHAPTER 12
GRACE
HOT DADDY BOSS

AS FAR AS first days on the job go, today has been interesting. Not that I really have much to compare it to.

When I met TJ at his house first thing this morning, I was glad to see that he's a morning person like me. I sort of already knew that from when we were all in Bend and he was up at the crack of dawn to fish, but it's winter now and I wasn't sure if that was a year-round thing. He also reminded me of that last night when he texted me what time to come over today.

As soon as I arrived, he insisted that I'm welcome to use his home office, despite me offering to stay out of his hair and take the video call from my van. He welcomed me in and said to let him know if there's anything I need.

The point was made before he disappeared somewhere into the depths of the house and I haven't seen him since, leaving me to spend the rest of the morning on a video call with his brother, Jake. He was less than thrilled about the early morning video chat because he's an hour behind us in Seattle, but he was still nice about it.

The call was productive, not just because I spent it learning about the business and getting access to the files and shared drives I'll need, but I feel like Jake gave me a peek into TJ's life.

I already knew he was generous, but there are so many lasting scars and traumas that come from growing up the way he did in foster care. I've seen it firsthand with the kids in the programs at Wasatch Wishes.

Now I find myself trying to picture a twenty-something year old TJ dealing with his newfound fame and fortune, and still having the wherewithal to put his brother through college. That's a bond and level of dedication not even some biological siblings have.

So, after spending the better part of the day going through the intimate financial details of this part of his life, I've realized two things. First, he's given to so many different charities over the years. I started as far back as their records went. I figured what better way to learn where he'd like to make an impact than by seeing where he started giving first and how that's changed over time.

Right now, I'm a few years back into his history and I can't really pick out a pattern except that he really likes the outdoors. He's given to charities supporting parks and forest preservation as well as places that get kids outdoors. There's also programs that run summer camps for those in foster care. All of that makes sense given what I know about him. Those are all things I can relate to, and I already have so many ideas on how he can make a huge impact for those types of causes.

One thing that's notably absent though is music.

Outside of the first few years, he hasn't given to anything related to music. I did a little internet snooping and sure enough, that's about when they stopped touring. I found headline after headline about them breaking up, which makes the timing hardly seem like a coincidence to me.

Note to self: maybe don't ask about that though. Based on

how he answered my question after the wedding — 'was, not is' —
I get the feeling it's a thorny topic. Something about it still feels
sad though.

The second, far more pressing thing I've realized this
morning is that I still don't quite know exactly what TJ does these
days. I mean I know he got into Seattle real estate decades ago.
Which — another note to self — maybe ask him more about that
because he seems to be doing *very well*. Between this house, his
one in Bend, and how much money he plans on donating every
year, I'm starting to realize he might be wealthier than people
think... and it's from more than just his Teal Tigers' fame.

But still, I don't know what he actually *does* on a day-to-day
basis. Like what's a day in the life of the infamous Tommy Jacob
look like?

It's nearly lunchtime and I still haven't seen him again since
he set me up in his office. Hunger finally gets the better of me and
I decide to take the risk of getting lost in this place to see if he's
around. Maybe he wants lunch with his newest coworker. Or
maybe he's at Gloria's like he is most days getting lunch with
Sutton. Who knows, maybe he's even a horrible gossip that loves
water-cooler talk.

OK, I guess this isn't a normal first day at a new job. I'm
wandering around a gazillionaire, rock band frontman's house to
see if he wants to get lunch. That might take a while to get
used to.

I grew up here in Jackson, my parents only moved right
before I started high school. There has always been wealth here,
but all of the new mansions like this will always be a bit jarring.
We grew up just down the road from here, but even just a decade
ago, there definitely weren't as many places like this.

Still, TJ has taste. The modern architecture somehow blends
right into the wooded lot at the base of the ski resort. The large
windows everywhere are placed just right to look out onto the

granite mountain peaks surrounding Jackson. I could get used to the views in an office like this.

Making my way down the hall, I pass TJ's studio and the bathroom which I've made a point to commit to memory, when an open door right before the kitchen catches my eye. I step closer and see that the lights inside the room are on.

I don't know what in the universe possesses me, but I quietly step toward the door and peek in. It's clearly a home gym, a nice one.

"Hello? Anybody home?" I call into the room, but don't hear anything. My curiosity continues to get the better of me and I walk in.

The back of the room is a wall of windows with the same stunning views, no surprise there. When I turn toward the other corner though, I freeze, dead in my tracks, taking in a different stunning view.

There's a squat rack in front of the floor to ceiling mirror, but it's the shirtless man busting out pull-ups with ease that I can't look away from. I guess I know why those forearms and biceps are so damn enticing now.

I stand there for a second, shamelessly admiring the view, my head following TJ up and down with each repetition.

I'll admit it. I'm a Goldilocks when it comes to what I find attractive in men's builds. Too scrawny? No thanks. Too big, bulky, and defined like some vain fitfluencer? Nice, but also not my type. I grew up with two big brothers that are huge mountain men and my dad. I don't need more of that in my life.

What I'm watching now though? This is perfection.

He's more muscular than I thought, his lats and biceps flexing with each pull up. He's got that just right build of sneaky muscles that I can tell are from years, decades even, of staying active and working out to stay healthy. Fit and functional. A masculine body.

OK, Josie. Hot Boss might be right.

I can literally feel my mouth go dry. That's fine, right? Just a normal biological response to looking at this objectively attractive man.

I make the mistake of trying to look around his body into the mirror to sneak a peak of his chest and abs, but his eyes meet mine.

Shit.

I try to lift my jaw off the floor before I start drooling, just another normal biological response, right? But TJ has already seen me and I've been caught like a kid with their hand in the cookie jar. I might as well own it, so I grin back at him.

He lets go of the bar and turns to face me, smirking, but still not saying anything. He reaches up to tuck a loose strand of hair away from his ear, revealing the earbuds he has in. Now I know why he didn't hear me when I walked in.

"Hi," I say, drawing out the syllable, knowing full well that my cheeks are probably fire engine red right now. I know he said to make myself at home and come find him if I needed anything, but I don't think this was what he had in mind.

Now would be a good time to remind myself that yes, he's hot, but he's my boss. I'm also more than mature enough to keep those two things separated.

"Everything OK?" He gives me a confused look, his blue eyes flashing concern when he takes out one of his earbuds.

"Oh, yeah. I was just getting hungry and was wondering what you were doing for lunch."

He takes out his other earbud and slips the case into the pocket of his gray joggers. The motion pulls my eyes — my stupid, slutty eyes — down to where his sweats hang perfectly off his hips.

Alright, I'm definitely drooling over him now.

The subtle dips and valleys of his abs are toned just right. He has a faint dusting of chest hair running down to his waistband which is infuriatingly hot.

Snap out of it, Grace. Stop eye-fucking shirtless Hot Boss. Damnit, Josie! I'm going to get her back for planting that nickname in my head.

I bring my eyes back to his, realizing he just caught me ogling him. I note the corner of his mouth lifting into a subtle grin. Yep. He knows exactly what I was looking at.

"I could eat," he says with a shrug. "Just let me put a shirt on." That subtle grin grows wider when he reaches down to pick up his shirt from the gym bench. He holds my gaze while he stretches those long, toned arms over his head, slowly pulling on the shirt. My eyes clearly have a mind of their own because they drop to the defined V diving into his waistband, where I see the top of a small tattoo that I can't make out and will no doubt obsess over now. He finishes pulling down the shirt, catching me yet again and he winks at me.

He fucking winks at me!

I just smirk and shrug because the jokes on him. Just because I'm a strong, independent woman doesn't mean I can't look. He's a hot, shirtless rockstar that just so happens to be my new boss. My brain can keep those things separate.

AS I SETTLE BACK in his office after getting lunch with TJ at Cowgirl Coffee, I make sure to let Josie know about the hole she helped me dig.

> Me: Thanks a lot.

> Josie: You're welcome, babe! What exactly are you thanking me for?

Me: That was sarcasm.

Josie: Rude! What did I even do?

Me: Hot. Daddy. Boss.

Me: I just saw him shirtless.
SHIRTLESS!

Me: I'm blaming you for practically
banging him with my eyes.

After firing off that message, I get back to reviewing more files. So far, day one is off to a great start, even if TJ caught me eyefucking him before we even had lunch.

I'm opening a new folder when a knock pulls my attention to the hallway. I look over to see a fully clothed and freshly showered TJ leaning in the doorway. He looks so damn confident and relaxed like that, his ankles crossed and his arms folded over his chest.

"Still going OK?" his smooth, deep voice floats across the room.

I lean back in the leather swivel chair, surprisingly enjoying the feeling of authority it gives off, even if I'm the one working for him. I shrug, push off the desk with one foot, and spin the chair, making the room blur around me.

"Yep, hasn't changed much since lunch." On my first spin around, I catch him huff a laugh. As I spin around again, I see him striding toward the desk. And as the chair slows down, he's now beside me, behind the desk.

"Was that fun?" he says, reaching out and grabbing the armrest, stopping the chair with his flexed hand.

I nod, a huge smile spreading across my face. "Absolutely. You should try it sometime. Way more fun than fishing."

His lazy smile widens, popping his dimples. Suddenly, I feel a little lightheaded and I don't think it's from spinning around in the chair.

I reach out, grabbing his wrist and lifting his hand off the chair so I can turn back toward the desk. I can't help but notice the warmth of his skin and the tattooed music note on his ring finger again.

Prying my eyes away, I look back at my laptop screen and reach for my Nalgene to take a sip of water for my now very dry mouth.

"Jake was really helpful." Smooth Grace, real smooth.

He just nods, casual as can be. "Good."

He's really pulling off the laid-back rockstar vibe. I'm starting to envy how relaxed he is right now because I'm trying hard as hell not to think about those abs under his fitted black t-shirt. "So do you workout every morning? Your gym's nice."

He leans back against the desk, bracing himself with his knuckles wrapped over the edge. "Oh, I get morning workouts in four or five days a week. Sometimes I go to the gym downtown to swim laps though. I only have the hot tub here."

I look up at him, raising one eyebrow. "Wow, really slumming it with *only* a hot tub to go with your state-of-the-art home gym."

"You're welcome to use either if you want. That's what I actually came to talk to you about."

"You came to tell me I could use your gym and hot tub? Is that part of my benefits package?"

An amused smile crosses his face. "Yeah, sure. What I actually came to say was that you can use this office as long as you want, whether I'm here or not. Like I said, make yourself at home. Come by whenever you want, work whatever hours you want. It's fine with me. And if you get tired of this place, you're welcome to work remote too, if you prefer. You don't have to always come here. I know you like to travel. I really don't care what schedule you keep or where you work from as long as the work gets done."

"Oh," my voice rises up in surprise. He clearly has thought more about this than I have. I've barely had time to start this job and he's already thinking about where I'll want to work from in the future. It's endearing that he's already so trusting of me. "I appreciate that. You sure you don't mind if I'm popping in and out? I'm normally a morning person, but I can be a night owl every now and then. I don't want to intrude."

He shakes his head. "Nope, not a problem at all. Shoot."

I roll my neck, taking an exaggerated glance around the room before looking back at him. "Well if you really don't mind, I think I'll plan on working here. I like the views."

Oh no. Did I really just say that? A pleased grin crosses his face and a muffled laugh rumbles in his chest.

I quickly tilt my head to the window. "The views of the mountains, I mean. It reminds me of growing up down the road."

He nods. "Yeah. I can't get enough of the views around here." I notice that his eyes stay fixed on me though and don't even hint at looking out the windows. A moment passes before he curls one hand into a fist and rasps his knuckles on the desk. "Still, I get it. I lived in a van once and loved the freedom. So if you change your mind, it's totally fine."

I turn my chair to face him head on now. "You lived in a van?"

The look on his face is a mix of pride and nostalgia. "Back in the early days of Teal Tigers. We were driving all over the Pacific Northwest from gig to gig. It was a blast being that free."

I hum thoughtfully and he watches me, his eyes brightening. "You're full of surprises, *Mr. Jacob*. I love van life, even with its drawbacks."

"Drawbacks?"

I nod. "Yep. Seems like there's always something to fix."

"What's wrong with your van?" His tone is short and he tenses.

"Oh, it's not that bad. The diesel heater's fan has been struggling lately. I've dealt with worse. It'd help if I could charge my batteries and run my backup electric heater though." He still gives me the same, intense look, like he doesn't believe me.

"Seriously, it's not a big deal." This time, I hold his gaze until he blinks and I can see his posture relax. He nods once, but I can see the hint of concern there when the corners of his eyes crease. Still, I see the understanding in his eyes and there's something refreshing about it. My brothers and Dad wouldn't back off, no matter how many times I tell them I can take care of myself. I love them for caring so much, but I'm strong and I don't need to be treated like a broken, frail little girl.

I'm about to ask him what their band's van was like, but a notification crosses the top of my laptop screen, pulling my attention away. My eyes widen in horror when I see the message from Josie sitting there on full display.

> Josie: Is Hot Daddy Boss there? Please tell me he's still shirtless. Send a pic. Your girl is lonely and needs spank bank material.

My whole body goes rigid and I want to crawl under the desk. Definitely regretting telling her about seeing him in the gym now while I frantically try to clear the notification. I feel like I'm going to crush my mouse, clicking it over and over hoping that it will actually make the message go away faster, but he had to have seen that.

He shifts on the desk next to me, catching my attention. I look up and to his credit, he looks cool as a cucumber. Maybe he didn't actually see it?

He hops off the desk, brushing the tops of his quads with his hands. "Anyway, I'm glad you're here. Let me know if you need anything."

He strides toward the door and I look back at my laptop, trying to focus on work instead of my boss's body and that smile.

"Oh, and Rainbow," he calls from across the room. I look up just in time to see him smirk. "Next time, I'll keep a shirt on in the gym."

I wish he wouldn't is the first thought that goes through my mind, almost drowning out whatever embarrassment I should be feeling.

CHAPTER 13

TJ

GYM LIFE

I TAKE one last long stroke before letting out a long breath. The water runs over my bare skin when I reach out to grab the side of the pool and finish my lap.

Two sets down, one to go.

Taking a drink from my favorite dented aluminum water bottle, I look around the empty indoor pool. It's eerily quiet, almost like a scene out of horror movie. I guess I shouldn't be surprised that it's empty on a Friday night. Everyone's probably out at the après ski bars, so I have the place to myself which is fine by me.

Maybe Jake and Sutton are right. I need to get out more often. I see Sutton at Gloria's all the time and I've gotten to know Kelsey and Monica at the coffee shop, but otherwise I don't really get out much. Building a social life can wait for another night though. The last time I really even went out with anyone was that night in Bend with the Chapmans for karaoke.

Swimming, fishing, kayaking — anything near the water is always how I like to clear my mind and relax. Maybe I could have more of a social life, but I'm still always going to find time for myself like this. Something about being around water always lets me zone out and block out the noise from the rest of my life. It used to be my way to drown out the lyrics and riffs constantly running through my mind and give myself a moment of calm. Whether it was school field trips, summer camps on the lake as a foster kid, or relaxing by the hotel pool when I was touring with Teal Tigers. Maybe I was a diva back then asking them to shut down the pool so I could have it to myself, but I needed that quiet time for me. Even today, I always keep getting drawn back to water.

After catching my breath, I turn to start my last laps for the night. I push off the side of the pool, starting a backstroke. Looking up, I watch ceiling tile after ceiling tile go by, hearing the water rush past my ears with each stroke.

I see the skylight above me creep into view, meaning I'm near the far end of the pool. I start to reach out to push off the side when I hear a whoosh underwater and I feel a spray of water across my face.

What the hell?

Did someone just jump in the damn pool?

I turn toward the source of the sound, irritated that I'm not the only one here anymore and that someone would jump that close in a giant pool like this.

"Hey! What the—" I yell out, but my voice gets stuck in my throat when I see Grace, treading water in the corner, grinning at me mischievously. Any trace of irritation I was feeling is instantly gone.

My eyes soak her in and I can feel my pulse hammering, not just from my workout. Her long, color streaked hair clings to her shoulders, covering some of her tattoos but I can still see the straps of her floral bikini top. Her perky, full breasts are just above the waterline, with water beading down between them. Her hard nipples push against the wet triangles of fabric and I can see the outlines of her piercings.

My mind goes back to that morning on the Deschutes and the memory of just how perfect her tits look with nothing covering them. That image and the way she smiled at me has haunted my dreams for months.

I feel the blood rush to my cock and I'm instantly glad I'm in chest deep water. Perfect tits aside, it's her damn smile I can't look away from.

Her smile always steals my breath away. The way her nose scrunches and the apples of her round, freckled cheeks lift, radiates her unbridled passion for life. Her wet bangs stick to her forehead, finally bringing my attention to her emerald eyes.

It feels like far too much time passes by silently as the waves from her jumping in finally ebb to a stop.

"You really need to stop sneaking up on me," I finally say, taking a few strokes to swim closer to her from my lane.

She smirks and cocks a tattooed shoulder, bringing my eyes back to her top, where one of the straps is dangerously close to slipping off. "Karmic retribution."

I shake my head. "Fair point."

Her lips part like she's about to say something else when I see her eyes flick to something behind me. I raise an eyebrow at her in question, but it's too late. A flurry of limbs and hair comes flying from the side of the pool and in an instant, Grace and I are both covered in water from the splash.

I scrub my hand over my face, brushing my hair out of my eyes to find Grace cackling with a strawberry blonde woman that I don't recognize. She shakes her head, sending beads of water flying from her short hair before looking at me.

"Hey, Hot Boss. I'm Josie." She grins and looks back at Grace. "You weren't kidding, he's even hotter IRL."

I'm not sure if I should be flattered, knowing Grace has noticed me enough to tell her friend, but something about it strokes my apparently still existent male ego. Maybe I should be more worried though because I can only describe Grace's expression as pure mortification.

I decide to spare her any more embarrassment and ignore the nickname that I'm not entirely mad about. As much as I want to savor the notion that a world might exist where I have a shot with her, I probably shouldn't pile on.

"Nice to meet you, Josie. You can just call me TJ."

Josie turns back to me, her eyes shamelessly track down my chest and back up.

"Seriously, like really hot," she says to Grace, as if I'm not even here.

"Hi," I say, waving a hand. "Still right here."

Grace finally makes eye contact with me, her eyes pleading a silent apology, before she turns to glare at her friend.

"This is why I can't take you anywhere." She raises one arm out of the water, cupping her hand, and splashing Josie.

I snort a laugh. "You two enjoy your Friday night."

And with that, I swim back to the lap lane to finish my workout.

AFTER HITTING the sauna to wind down for the night, I make my way out of the gym. From the lobby, I can see a few inches of snow coating the ground and more coming down by the minute. I'm sure the roads aren't great at this point, but the sports car I keep here has all-wheel drive and snow tires. That's just life in the mountains.

On a Friday night, I'm used to the gym parking lot being empty. As I make my way outside, I see two camper vans parked toward the back of the lot. Standing next to them, I spot Grace and Josie. Curiosity gets the better of me, and I start to walk through the snowy parking lot. Even in my grippy boots, I mind my steps so I don't slip or fall and look like an idiot in front of them.

Nope. Too late.

My feet come out from under me on an icy patch only a few steps away from them. Between my post-workout soreness, the cold weather, and the hard pavement, everything in my body protests the sudden impact. I rock side to side on the ground groaning, but glad it seems like I'm intact, except for my pride.

"Hey! You OK there, Hot Boss?" Josie looks down at me with a smirk.

"Josie! Shut up!" Grace whisper shouts with a mortified expression.

I'm starting to see that Grace's friend is a handful. I'm also starting to understand why Grace and Lizzy get along so well now that I think about it.

Josie ignores Grace, still smirking at me. "Can you get up or did you break your hip?"

An exasperated Grace tosses her head back before giving her friend a playful shove and gesturing at me. "You're the worst. Help him up."

I raise a hand, signaling for her to stay where she is. "I'll manage, but thank you." I prop myself up on my elbows before carefully standing, dusting the snow off my sweats and jacket.

I look at Grace who's leaning back against her van and that's when I notice what she's wearing. She's in a gray robe, chunky socks, and slippers. I notice Josie's dressed just as casually in plaid pajama pants and an oversized hoodie. I guess they're not going out anywhere tonight and heading straight back to their campsite. Something about knowing she's just having a low-key Friday night with her friend instead of hitting the bars takes the edge off my nerves.

"The roads are going to be pretty rough tonight. Let me

follow you back to your campground. Make sure you get there safe."

"Oh, Hot Boss is protective too," Josie says, flicking her eyebrows at Grace, who glares back unamused. "Are escorted rides on snowy roads part of her benefits package?" She pops her lips, emphasizing the last word.

"Oh my god, Josie. Stop," Grace says under her breath.

I chuckle to myself, waiting for Grace to look back at me. "If you want that as part of your benefits package, sure." I smirk at her playfully, earning me a cute little eye roll. "But really, I just want to make sure you two get back alright."

They exchange a knowing look before Grace sighs. "We're actually already at our spot for the night."

I look back and forth between them trying to understand. Grace must sense my confusion because she gestures between the very empty parking lot and their vans.

The realization finally hits me.

No, they've got to be kidding.

There's no way they've been parking and sleeping in their vans in the gym parking lot. I thought they'd be somewhere safe, like a campground or in one of her relatives' driveways or something.

I guess that explains the slippers though.

My face must give me away because Grace rolls her eyes and glowers at me. "Oh relax, TJ. You said it yourself, you lived in a van while touring with a band."

"I know, but—," I start before Josie chimes in.

"But what? You think us girls can't handle it?" She gives me a look that says she knows I just dug myself a hole. Shit.

I run my hand through my hair and sigh. "No, that's not what I meant. I would just feel better if you were somewhere safe. And what would your brother or grandparents think if they knew you were working for me and staying overnight in the gym's parking lot? They'd think I'm the shittiest boss."

Grace's eyes flick to mine, worry flashing across her face.

I raise my hand between us. "Not that I would tell them," I reassure her, remembering she was very adamant she wanted her family to find out she was in town on her terms. "Seriously, do I not pay you enough?" Jake was supposed to make sure she was paid more than fairly.

She shakes her head adamantly. "No. You're paying me more than enough. Honestly, too much probably," she says softly before smiling and tilting her head to her friend. "We'll be fine. This isn't our first rodeo."

Something about this still doesn't sit right with me. "Why don't you follow me back to my place? I have a guesthouse."

"Oh, that sounds fun," Josie says grinning, but Grace's expression hardens.

"No, TJ. We're not taking your guesthouse. I said we'll be fine." Her expression doesn't waiver and I find myself admiring her even more for being so determined to not rely on other people.

But I can be just as determined.

"OK then. At least park your vans in my driveway so I'm not worried about you getting hassled by a security guard or the sheriff." I know law enforcement in town has started cracking down on places not designated for camping, especially when they need to plow after a big storm like this. The last thing I want is for them to get in trouble when I could do something about it.

Her stance softens and I can tell she's considering it, so maybe I can sweeten the pot and seal the deal. "You're welcome to use the hot tub too, if you want. I won't bug you."

"I wouldn't complain if you joined, Hot Boss," Josie says, prompting both of us to look back at her. She shrugs and raises her palms. "What? He's *your* boss, not *mine*. You know I prefer to work solo anyway. Don't rain on my parade by complaining about your job perks."

Grace shakes her head and smiles. "Are you sure?"

"Yes, absolutely," I say emphatically and relieved. "And you said it yourself, your heater's been acting up. So please, give me some peace of mind. You can plug your van in, charge your batteries, whatever you need. Hell, use my gym if you feel like it. Come and go as you please."

Josie claps her hands together. "You drive a hard bargain, but looks like we have a deal. Lead the way, Hot Boss." She heads toward the driver side door of her van, opening it and hopping in.

Once she shuts the door, Grace turns to me. "Like she said, lead the way," she says with a soft smile, her eyes expressing the gratitude she doesn't want to voice.

"Is she ever going to not call me 'Hot Boss'?" I ask, tipping my chin at Josie's van.

She lets out an amused laugh. "Nope, you'll forever be known as Hot Boss to her. I'm sure the notorious Teal Tigers' frontman Tommy Jacob has been called worse."

"Yeah. You'd be correct on that one."

She looks back at me and those green eyes that haunt my dreams soften. "Are you really sure it's OK if we are hanging around your place?"

"Yes. I already have Sutton coming and going all the time like he owns the place." I shake my head and snort a laugh. "I still travel a decent bit too and I'm not around all the time. So yeah, it's totally fine."

"Thank you," she says softly and I can see by her smile that she might finally feel OK about the idea.

"Anytime." I nod and start carefully walking to my car, taking one last look over my shoulder. "See you at my place, Rainbow."

CHAPTER 14

GRACE
BENEFITS PACKAGE

TJ MIGHT BE the best boss I've ever had. Not that there's a long list, but it feels like he'd always be on top, no matter who I work for next.

Thankfully, I've been spared Josie's constant teasing and calling TJ 'Hot Boss' the last couple of days. I know we give each other shit all the time, but she's also the only person that gets my love for being impulsive and sporadic. The weekends we've spent camping somewhere new on a whim and hiking or skiing have been some of the most memorable moments in my life.

Right now, she's off in Big Sky with her van for a few days and should get back later this week. I swear though, I tell her one time in confidence that I think my new boss is hot — he is a famous rockstar after all — and she embarrasses me every chance she gets. I love her to death, but she's not shy about giving anybody, including her friends, shit. I would never want to be on her bad side.

It doesn't matter that he's effortlessly good looking and charming, that's not why he's a great boss, even though I'm starting to consider it an added perk. It's everything else.

I've been working for him for about two weeks and already

I've seen how he treats the people around him. He's on the phone all day with Jake or Slade, giving them the go-ahead on real estate deals or the Seattle restaurant project. Or when Sutton or Tanner stop by. It doesn't matter who it is, he's kind and respectful and listens to whatever their concerns are.

I was lucky at Wasatch Wishes. People there were great, we had an amazing mission. But I know plenty of people that have worked less than great corporate jobs or had terrible bosses.

But TJ is just different.

He listens. He actually listens instead of waiting for his turn to talk, and then makes his decision. If he doesn't agree with something Sutton or Slade or even my brother says, he will drop what he's doing to painstakingly explain it and then hear their side. Slade even convinced him to change his mind. I've seen more than my fair share of egotistical men with unswayable opinions and it's refreshing to see the opposite.

Then there are the gestures.

Today, his cleaning lady came by for her weekly stop. He made sure her favorite breakfast pastries from Cowgirl Coffee were out in the kitchen with a fresh coffee. It reminded me of my first day with the electric kettle and box of teas set up in the office. And I don't even know what to make of him inviting me to stay in his driveway for as long as I need. He walked the fine line of wanting to make sure I was safe while not overstepping. He's given me every bit of space I want.

I just keep asking myself if there actually are people out there this nice? Everything in my gut tells me TJ really is this genuine. Even in Bend, the way he was so generous letting all of us stay there like it wasn't an inconvenience. It was one thing when he was supposed to be out of town, but then his plans changed. I don't know why, but a voice in the back of my mind keeps saying it might have been fate, like we were supposed to cross paths that weekend.

I finally manage to focus on the screen in front of me, on the dozens of folder icons with all of the records of charities TJ's worked with. Each one of those folders represents a different organization, a different cause helped over the years. Everything here tells me the same thing that my gut does, that TJ is different.

It also tells me that he's not the most organized person, even with Jake's help. I'm still catching up to the last few years, but I already feel like a kid in a candy shop, with so many options to choose from and resources to use.

He's made big donations and small ones. He's set up some endowments that will go on for decades. I know some of it has to do with what was the most advantageous for his taxes that year. I've been working with non-profits and donors long enough to not be that naïve, but I still see bits of him shining through all of it. In the early years, I saw how much he supported organizations involved in the outdoors and parks. That hasn't changed in the more recent years, but I have seen more and more giving to groups supporting kids in foster care.

On one hand, all of this is great. Actually no, it's amazing. It's flat out amazing what he's done.

Part of me thinks he doesn't even realize the impact he's made. I know he gives anonymously because of unwanted attention. But I don't think he realizes what he could do if he was actually involved and publicly backed some of these organizations. One donor his size could practically make or break an organization like Wasatch Wishes.

When I finally have a free moment, I rummage through the desk and find a pair of scissors in one of the desk drawers. Taking them out, I start the mindless habit of trimming my bangs. I hold them between my fingers in front of me, confident enough to not use a mirror because I've done this hundreds of times. I'm about to take that first snip when a firm knock in the doorway has me looking up to find TJ there. He is looking delicious as ever in his gray sweats and black t-shirt.

"You want to grab some lunch? Figured since your sidekick is gone, it'd be safe to ask."

"Hi." I awkwardly hold my bangs in one hand and scissors in the other when I look up at him from the desk. "You were more than welcome to join us for lunch while she was here."

He stays put in the doorway, but I can hear his low laugh from here. "She's a bit scary. Figured I would let you two have your girl time. Also it seemed like you don't get to spend a lot of time together. So I'd rather stay off her bad side."

I tilt my head to the side and smile at him curiously. "Trying to stay in her good graces?"

"I just—" He drops his eyes and shifts awkwardly on his feet. I didn't miss the hint of doubt in his expression before his eyes find mine again. "Look, do you want to go out for lunch or not? It's on me."

"Sure." I nod, as I slip my laptop into my bag. He turns to the side, gesturing with his hand to come with him. I pull my messenger bag onto my shoulder and make my way to the door. I catch the way he smiles when I walk past, showing off his dimples, making my heart flutter.

Lunch might be on him, but I can't help but find myself thinking I'd like to be on him too.

Damnit.

Stupid. Slutty. Eyes.

I TAKE another bite of my salad, crunching it loud enough that I suddenly feel TJ's eyes on me from across the table in the downtown café.

"What? Do I have something on my face?" I have always

been a messy eater and suddenly knowing that he's watching me makes me self-conscious in a way I'm not used to. "I know I'm not very lady-like." I drop my fork to make an air quotes gesture.

He chuckles and shakes his head. "That's not it at all. You just remind me of Jake and me."

"Wow. I remind you of a man?" I add, raising an eyebrow hiding my tinge of disappointment. I've always been sort of a tomboy and lumped in as one of the guys.

"Shit. That came out wrong. That's not what I mean," he says, setting down his sandwich, looking off to the side in thought. "It's a foster kid thing. We always ate so fast. Food wasn't always consistent, so we were probably a little too eager to eat when it was meal time."

I raise an eyebrow at him. "So you're saying I eat like a child?"

He palms his face and sighs. "Damnit. I'm digging myself a hole here." His eyes find mind again and soften. "Even after I ended up with that last family and Jake, we still ate that way for a long time. I was self-conscious and hated eating around other people. I was never comfortable and always thought someone was judging me."

He tilts his head at me. "But you? I love that you're comfortable around me and don't put on some act. Seriously, don't ever change."

That admission instantly makes me feel way less self-conscious about how he's watching me. Leave it to TJ to always say the right thing and put people at ease.

A long, silent moment passes before I change the subject. "So this lunch is actually good timing."

He raises his scarred, pierced brow, eyeing me curiously. "Already bored working with me?"

He smiles, but I still catch the slightest bit of worry in his eyes. As if I could ever not enjoy working with him and his brother. Add that as yet another reason he's a terrific boss I guess. He practically refuses to say I work *for* him. He always says working together, collaborating, or consulting, and then he actually backs it up with his actions.

"Definitely not," I say, setting down my fork and grabbing my laptop out of my bag. "Far from it actually. I wanted to show you some charities I picked for this year, but if it's ok with you, I also want to work on a plan for the future to make the biggest impact."

Any hint of that worry disappears as he sits back in his chair and watches attentively as I pull up a presentation and spin my laptop around.

"So some of these are ones you've given to in the past, but haven't in recent years. I thought they seemed like something you'd still be interested in supporting. Any reason you stopped?"

He points at the screen and gestures for me to go back through the first few slides, studying them. I take the moment to admire his features from this close. The way his lips pull to the side as he thinks, popping one of his dimples. The way his square jaw tightens under his salt and pepper stubble and the way that muscle in his neck ticks as he focuses. Or the way his shaggy, dark blond hair with that perfect dusting of gray mixed in hangs over his ear just enough for him to keep tucking it out of the way.

He looks delicious. So delicious that I completely didn't notice that he's still staring at the screen, which is great because I'm practically salivating over him.

"Did you forget your reading glasses?" I tease.

He doesn't move his head, but his eyes flick to me in a playful glare. "How old do you think I am, Rainbow?"

Not old enough to turn me off. That's for sure.

Every time he calls me Rainbow my heart flutters and my skin tingles. In Bend, I thought he was picking on me — being the little sister, that's usually the case — but I'm starting to think that's not it now.

"I know how old you are. You're just too easy to tease."

He shrugs in acknowledgement. "Just easy for you and Sutton."

His mouth lifts into a boyish grin, popping that damn dimple again before he winks at me. Is he flirting with me? No.

"Seriously, he never stops." My mind practically tunes that out, still fixated on the flirting situation.

There's no way that Mr. Way-Too-Hot-Famous-Rockstar, and the bad boy frontman of Teal Tigers would ever flirt with me. Then again, this guy apparently gives eight-figures a year to charity and cares enough about it to hire a consultant to do an even better job at being an impossibly good human.

Yeah, maybe I'm just in my head. He's just being friendly. Unfortunately, that doesn't change the fact that the image of him doing shirtless pull-ups has been living rent free in my head for weeks. I shake my head, burying that memory away, and focus back on my laptop.

"So why'd you and Jake stop working with that one?"

He looks at the screen then back at me before picking his sandwich back up. "It's not that we didn't like them. We'd give to them again. We just always had this 'share the wealth' mindset and wanted to change it up every now and then. We thought we would be making a bigger impact that way instead of always giving to the same places."

I get his sentiment. It's truly not the worst idea, but it is one that could really hurt some of these organizations. With the size of his donations, if he gave to a charity for years then suddenly stopped, it could wreak havoc on their operating budgets.

"Fair enough," I add, flipping to the next slide. "So here are some of the new ones I wanted to add to your list for this year."

He must see the look on my face when I read back over the list. He follows my eyes, humming thoughtfully to himself before reaching toward the screen and tapping Wasatch Wishes.

"That's the one you worked for, right? I think I already give to them."

I swallow my feelings, choosing to remember the good times. It's not their fault I wasn't in the budget anymore. "I did work there. And no, you don't anymore. I looked at your donations for last year."

I know I really need to finish going through the last few years, but I know who he gave to last year. And it may be too late to save my job, but at least if he gives to Wasatch Wishes, it'll help the kids that I loved working with and I would do anything to make sure they're taken care of.

He nods, but his eyes stay focused on the bottom of the list.

"I figured give to the ones you're already working with plus add a couple new ones." I turn my laptop back around. "I can send you this list and you can go over it. Jake said you're not really on a time crunch, so there's no rush."

"Nope, I'm good. I like your plan. Make it happen." He smiles softly at me before nodding and taking a bite of his sandwich.

I'm too caught up in that damned smile to realize what he just said.

"Wait, TJ. That's it? Just 'make it happen'?" I blurt out, holding a bite of my salad on my fork mid-air in stunned confusion.

He couldn't have said that. Working with donors was always fun, but it could still be a headache because getting them to commit can be like pulling teeth.

But this? This is the kind of decisiveness I like. That's the kind of thing I would do. No hemming and hawing, just action. *Make it happen.*

He looks back at me, every feature of his face etched with conviction. "When I feel it, when I know it, I don't waste time and fuck around. I just do it. You of all people should understand that."

I look back at him in a mix of amazement but also understanding. He's right. I am spontaneous. I love it, but this is different. He's talking about choosing to give away millions of dollars just because he vibes with my idea and it feels right. My decisions to go on a weekend road trip or get a new tattoo or piercing on a whim seem so trivial now.

He clearly senses my trepidation because he sets his sandwich back down and leans back in his chair.

"Look, I'm serious. This is how I do things," he says, laughing to himself. "You want to know how I started in real estate? By making decisions with this." He taps his chest, right over his heart.

He sighs and his eyes drift up, like he's lost in a memory. "I bought my first investment property in Seattle when I was twenty-three, not too long after our first record deal. I didn't see it as a business though. A friend I met in foster care called me because his landlord was a shitbag. He was just venting, but I went over to try and help him out. I fell in love with that old, Art Deco building the second I walked in. I ended up getting ahold of his landlord and that night I made an offer on the building. All because it felt right."

Add another reason to the list of why he's possibly the perfect boss, or maybe even the perfect man. The combination of spontaneity and helping others is something that strikes a chord down to my core.

"Alright," I say, still thinking that wasn't the answer I was expecting, but again, a sentiment that I can appreciate so much. "I'll make it happen, Boss."

He rolls his eyes. "Good." Those beautiful blue eyes linger on me just long enough to make my lips part before he winks at me again with a smug grin. "Now finish your lunch so we can get back to my place. Seems like you're about to be very busy with work."

CHAPTER 15

TJ

MAKE ME FEEL OLD

MY PHONE BUZZES in my pocket and I want to ignore it. The only reason I'm even up this late is because I'm too restless to sleep and came to my studio to just clear my head. When I pull my phone out and see my brother's name, a smile crosses my face. We might give each other shit all the time, but we're still always there for each other.

"Hey, what's up?" I answer.

"Well, nothing's really changed since the last time we talked. So same old shit I guess."

I huff a laugh. "Fair enough, so why are you calling?"

"You're still coming up in a couple weeks for the closing, right?" he asks.

OK. I guess it is business.

"Yeah, I'll be there," I say, grabbing a chair and spinning it around toward the window of my studio.

"Good, because Slade won't shut up about this place. He wants to have a party to celebrate closing on the building and starting construction. He keeps saying you have to be there." Jake drags out the word *have* as if there will be dire consequence if I don't show my face. Judging by his mildly irritated tone, I can just picture how Slade has been hounding him in his typical persistent, methodical way. Better him than me. I guess that's what I pay my little brother for though.

"You said before construction? He knows it's just going to be a vacant shell of a building, right?"

He snorts a laugh. "Yeah. Apparently, he's got a whole plan for that. Something about an industrial warehouse vibe before the renovations. I think his exact words were 'Seattle Grunge meets New American Cuisine'. So you're good if I invite the typical crowd?"

The *typical crowd* is his code for the marketing and PR team that will be there, along with my old bandmates and crew. I don't mind seeing the ones I'm on good terms with like Vince, but the others I prefer to avoid unless there's a compelling reason to see them. I guess this is one of those times. Jake has known them almost as long as I have, but he wasn't around them every day like I was, especially while he was in college and I was touring. That's probably why he's on better terms with most of them than me. Still, I appreciate that he asks, given how much I've removed myself from those circles. But those guys are good for business if we're trying to build hype around a new restaurant I'm investing in.

"Yeah, that's fine," I reply.

"Cool. Well, that's all I needed." He pauses for a second. "So how's it going with Grace?"

I hear the teasing tone of his voice, but I'm not going to give in.

"Oh," I reply with mock surprise, dragging out the word. "So, that wasn't the real reason you called? Let me guess. You wanted to check and make sure I haven't scared her off yet?"

"I mean it's been almost two weeks since you hired her. So..." His voice trials off in question.

I groan. "To answer your question, she's great. She'll probably be reaching out to you tomorrow actually. She finished the list for this year."

I think about the list that Grace showed me at lunch today. I liked her plan. She's thorough and does good work and I'm not surprised the least bit. It was clear she did her homework on me based on the organizations she picked. But I can also tell she puts her heart into it. I wasn't lying when I said I liked her plan and I wanted to make it happen. But something is still nagging at me in the back of my mind.

"Hey, on that note, can you send me the list of charities we gave to for the last few years?"

"I already sent them to Grace. Wait, are you actually going to read something I send you for a change?" he says with mock incredulity.

I deserved that one. He knows I never read anything, but that's only because I trust him with all of this. "Very funny. Just send them."

"Alright. Anything else?" he says.

I'm about to hang up, already somewhat dreading the upcoming party for the restaurant when an idea crosses my mind.

"Actually, yeah. There is one other thing. Put Grace on the guest list for Slade's party."

Jake's laugh comes through loud and clear. "Are you bringing her as a date?"

Again, I walked right into that one. "No, I'm her boss. And do I need to remind you that I'm your boss too?" I wish I was bringing her as a date is what goes through my mind, so again, I settle for a half truth trying to fool my brother and myself. "I just want her to get to see this side of my business a bit, maybe meet you in person too."

That's assuming she says yes. But I think she'd like Seattle. She told me she's never been before and I know how much she likes to travel. Seeing her in Cowgirl Coffee, it was so easy to picture her at home in one of the neighborhood coffee shops back in Seattle I used to spend so much time in, sipping on her hot tea. That's why I made sure she had tea here in my office. I want her to feel at home around me. I want her to be comfortable with me and feel like she can come and go as she pleases.

"Sure thing there, Boss," he says with a tone making it clear I'm not fooling him either. "Keep telling yourself that."

"Whatever, ass. I'll talk to you tomorrow." If Jake and Sutton can both pick up on how I really feel about her, I'm clearly not as good at hiding my feelings as I thought. I can't help it though and I don't know if I want to anymore.

"Love you too," he replies with a chuckle before hanging up.

With that interruption over, I turn my attention back to what brought me into my studio in the first place.

For the first time in years, I find myself looking down at the notepad in front of me. I remember how the blank pages staring back at me were once a reminder of how I fell out of love with music. It felt like a day came where I felt nothing for it anymore. There was a time when it was my emotional outlet, a way to turn the big, complicated feelings from my childhood and early adult life into something that made sense to me. Somehow, I could turn a jumble of notes about what I was feeling or going through into lyrics to help me process my feelings. The truth is though, I haven't had feelings like that in ages, ones that felt so intense and worthy of being sorted out and explored. Lately though, I've started to feel that itch again.

I reach out to the old acoustic guitar in front of me, the one Sutton was goofing off with on the day of the wedding, when I was hiding out in here. I run my finger over one of the frets. My hands might not be worn as much as when I played every day on tour or in the studio, but those calluses are still there. Even now, the sensation of those strings running over my fingertips is a feeling that is so familiar but so foreign all at once.

Out of the corner of my eye, I see a flicker of light. I look out the window of my studio toward the guesthouse and see the glow from the TV. It's nearly midnight and suddenly I'm glad I couldn't sleep tonight. I pull my phone out, grinning to myself as I type out a message.

> Me: Are you sleeping in the guesthouse? I know I'm a pretty great boss, but I seem to remember you declining that part of your generous "benefits package".

As much as I enjoy teasing her, I'm glad she's making herself comfortable here. She's welcome to use the guesthouse however she wants. That's why I built it in the first place, even if I don't have many guests. But I know that she appreciates her independence and she's confident enough to tell me to fuck off if I push her too much.

Three dots appear on the screen and my knee bounces in anxious anticipation.

OK. I think I can admit to myself where at least some of the feelings that brought me into my studio tonight are coming from.

> Rainbow: If I'm texting you, I'm not asleep. 😏

I start to type something out, but three dots appear again, freezing me in my tracks.

> Rainbow: I've got wine. Do you want to come hang out?

Fuck me. This is dangerous.

IT TOOK me all of two seconds to realize that when it comes to Grace Chapman, I have no resolve. I was practically sprinting out of my studio as I texted back to say I was on my way over to the guesthouse.

Way to play it cool and look like a desperate weirdo, Tommy. But I was drawn to her and that light in my guesthouse like a moth to a flame.

When I get to the door of the guesthouse, I pause for a second, trying to catch my breath and not be so obvious that I was just running through my own house and across the patio to get here.

Seriously, I work out. I shouldn't be out of breath, even at high altitude like this.

I knock before walking in the door to find Grace pouring herself a glass of wine at the kitchen island.

"Hey." She smiles and gives me a little wave.

"Do you want a drink, Boss?" she asks, holding the bottle of white wine out to me in offer.

"Is that my wine or yours?" I ask playfully. "And really, stop calling me boss."

I know she's teasing me, but I still feel a knot in my stomach when she calls me 'boss'.

She rolls her eyes and smirks to herself. "Fine, TJ. I assumed my benefits package didn't include wine. This is just left over from the wedding. Veronica left some of her bridal party stash out here. I'm just using your glasses."

"Pour a glass for me then. Your brother might only drink yellow jackets, but Veronica has great taste in wine."

Grace pours a second glass and steps out from behind the island.

Dangerous was an understatement.

I saw the cropped, spaghetti strapped cami she was wearing when I walked in. With her tall build, it shows an overly generous amount of her mid-drift, highlighting the dip of her waist and the thin, baby blue fabric does nothing to hide her nipple piercings. But now I can see the short flannel sleep shorts she's in, barely covering her ass and showing all of her long, toned legs.

I look up just in time to see her already watching me. Judging by the little smirk she gives me and hint of pink on her cheeks, I'm pretty sure she just caught me staring. Seems fair after the way she was staring at me in my home gym.

"Come on, this way," she says, leading me toward the living room carrying both glasses of wine.

"I know where the TV is. My guesthouse, remember?" I raise my pierced eyebrow, but follow behind her.

Saying those shorts barely cover her ass is generous. I'm struggling to think of a view I've seen that I enjoy more than this one, which is saying something. I've paid millions for properties just because of the view and none of them are better than this.

She looks back catching me staring again, but grins to herself this time. "Seems like you're a little distracted. Wanted to make sure you don't get lost."

God damnit. Is she flirting with me? I know I'm not exactly thinking straight because seeing all of her curves from her full tits, her waist, and down to the curve of her ass has all my blood leaving my brain and going south. Still, there's no way she'd be flirting with me. She's just that kind and friendly to everyone. She makes everyone around her feel special and cared for. That's just how infectious her personality is. This doesn't have anything to do with me.

"Very funny." I reach out and take the glass of wine from her, before sitting on the far end of the sectional couch. I stretch out along the chaise, kicking my shoes off and propping my feet up.

To my surprise, she sits down next to me. "Scooch over."

Before I can even move, she's pressed herself right against my side, stretching out next to me. My brain short circuits and my body goes rigid at the sudden, overwhelming amount of contact with her.

Her long, smooth bare legs touch mine. She rests her hand on her leg, but her fingertips graze my thigh. I know it's unintentional, but my swelling cock doesn't know that. The only thing going through my mind now is a desperate hope she doesn't look at my lap because my thin lounge shorts are doing nothing to hide what she's doing to me.

She must sense my reaction because she laughs, clinking her glass against mine. "Relax. I know it's your house, but you're not hogging the chaise all to yourself. I've been dying to get out of my van and stretch out for a change."

I let out a long, shaky breath. OK. I know Grace clearly gives no shits about personal space and boundaries. I get it, I'm not great about it either. I'm a touchy, feely person — always shaking hands and bringing people in for hugs.

I can do this though. This is just sitting together on the couch, late at night, with a friend. A friend that you're obsessed with. A friend who is barely wearing any clothes. Yeah, I can do this.

"So what are we watching?" I look up just in time to catch her eyes widening.

"Oh shit," she says, her cheeks reddening as she reaches for the remote.

That's when I see it. Right on the screen is a video from an old Teal Tigers concert, paused mid-frame on a close up of me.

I can't contain the grin spreading across my face. Oh, this is good.

"Nope." I lean forward, grabbing her wrist right before she can click the remote. "You're going to tell me why you're watching *this* in the middle of the night."

Her shoulders sag and she groans in exasperation. "Fine. I was doing research."

I quirk an eyebrow at her. "Researching what? How I used to be way cooler and had fewer gray hairs?"

I can see her relax at my joke. That's when our eyes go to my hand, still holding her wrist, my thumb rubbing the back of her hand. I loosen my grip, but she doesn't immediately pull her hand away.

She takes a sip of her wine. "It's going to sound silly."

She sinks back into the couch and I note the subtle shade of red that's still spread across her cheeks. I can't look away. Those freckled cheeks, the way her bangs and hair frame her square face, and those stunning emerald green eyes that always seem to sparkle.

"Try me," I say, slumping back into the couch matching her posture and taking a swig of my own wine.

Her eyes stay focused on my frozen image on screen, her lips curling into a warm smile. "I like to know what makes people tick. Especially when I'm working with them. Figuring out the kids I'd volunteer with, or learning what a donor is passionate about. You though? You're different."

"You mean because I'm a famous, washed-up rockstar?"

Her eyes flick back to me with a playful glare and she shoves me in my shoulder, melting my heart. "No, silly. You're just harder to read." She closes her eyes and shakes her head. "It sounds so dumb, but I thought watching some of these old videos would help me figure you out a bit more."

That little glimmer of hope that she might want to know more about me, for reasons outside of work, is crushed.

"Rainbow," I say, my eyes locking onto hers. "If you ever want to know anything about me, just ask. That said," I tilt my head toward the TV. "That was a good show. You can hit play, even if you're going to make me feel old as shit watching this. Were you even born yet?"

We both settle into the couch, as the video resumes. She takes a drink from her glass and my eyes can't look away from the way her lips part.

"For the record, you're way cooler now, even if you don't have the whole bad boy thing going on anymore. So knock it off with that self-deprecating shit, TJ."

A deep laugh rumbles up from my chest, prompting her to look back at me like I have two heads.

"What's so funny?" she asks, almost defensively.

"I was never a *bad boy*. Apparently you fell for my act, just like everyone else. It was great for selling magazines and albums. What do you kids call that now? Clickbait?

She grins at me before looking at the TV, pausing it at the opportune moment when I jumped across the stage and decided to kick an amplifier over. "Not a bad boy, huh?"

I wince and tuck a strand of hair behind my ear, noting her eyes lingering on me. "OK. That looks bad, but still just an act."

"You're telling me the cut off flannels, pierced eyebrow, messy hair, and barbwire tattoo was all an act? You still dress like that and that tattoo is still very real. You're telling me it was already just an act for you at that point? You had to be what, maybe twenty-five at that concert?"

I take a gulp from my glass and set it down on the coffee table to gesture at the screen. "You're right. I could get pretty riled up on stage, performing. I'll tell you what I remember about that concert though. Or after, I guess, if we're being technical about it."

She sits up, turning to face me and crossing her legs, her knees pressing into my thigh. Her sudden focus on me makes my mouth go dry. I remember what it felt like when she stared into my eyes all those months ago singing karaoke. Or what it felt like having her listen to me on the river. Knowing that she's choosing to give me the time of day does things to me.

"We were back at our hotel. Vince and the other guys were

up way too late partying. That's why we always got adjoining but separate rooms. After a show, I always just wanted to go to bed. That rush of adrenaline would wipe me out. Sometimes if I was really still feeling it, I'd stay up and try to write."

"Vince was your drummer, right? And who was the guy that played bass?" she asks, looking eager for me to continue.

"Yeah, Vince," I nod before continuing, "and that would be Stan on bass. So that night, I'm laying in bed. I have a throbbing headache and my ears are still ringing. I can't fall asleep, then I hear shouting next door. I get up and go into their room to find them all standing on the balcony looking down at the pool. Fucking idiot, Vince, was convinced he could throw the hotel TV off the balcony and reach the pool. It wouldn't have been a huge deal if there weren't people still down there. He's lucky no one got hurt."

Shock flashes across her face. "I remember hearing that story. You got banned from that hotel chain for that stunt. But everyone always blamed you."

I grab my wine, smiling back at her, not saying a word.

Her lips part and I see the moment of realization. "You were just letting everyone think you were the troublemaker? Tommy Jacob, the bad boy frontman was all just an act?"

I clink my glass to hers. "You got it."

The surprised smile she gives me is nearly blinding. "But why? Even as a kid, I knew your reputation from Veronica gushing over Teal Tigers to Tanner and Collin."

"That's exactly why I did it. The other guys, they had real problems. Drinking, drugs, rocky relationships. Vince always meant well, but he was just so impressionable. And Stan, well, he always thought the next girl was 'the one', getting distracted and missing sound checks. It was hard enough keeping those things under wraps and the band together through it all. I just wanted to keep everything together because I loved the music and performing so much. I lived for writing songs and pouring my heart out on stage."

She still looks back at me with a mix of stunned disbelief, slapping me on my thigh. The impact quickly reminds me of my aching balls from what she does to me. "Who would have guessed the infamous Tommy Jacob was such a softy?"

"I never said I was soft." I'm definitely anything but *soft* right now. I try not to focus on that thought as I grab the remote, pressing play and relaxing back into the couch. She doesn't look back at the TV though, just fixed on me.

"You really covered for your friends like that for years?"

I shrug. "I was the kid that grew up in foster care, bouncing from home to home for years. The guys were all from nice neighborhoods and had money growing up. No one batted an eye that I was the bad boy in Teal Tigers."

She leans forward to top off our wine before readjusting back next to me, still pressed against my side. This close, I can smell her shampoo — a mix of lavender and lemon that I know I'll never forget.

"Where did the name Teal Tigers come from?" she asks, keeping her eyes on the TV, but resting her head on my shoulder. "I've heard rumors, but are any of them true?"

Jesus. I know she's not one for physical boundaries and I'm probably reading too much into it, but sitting with her like this feels intimate and I like it.

Snorting a laugh, I think back to those early days when we were just riffing in garages. "That's another Vince story. He was drunk one night and kept saying he wanted to see a 'real tiger'. He was slurring so bad, it just sounded like he kept saying 'teal'. Teal Tiger. I guess his parents never took him to a zoo or something. Anyway, we never let him live that down. Clearly."

She laughs to herself and I can feel the vibration in my own chest, craving everything about her being this close. "He sounds like quite the character."

I think back on some of the better memories from those days, reminding myself they weren't all bad. "Yeah, he was. Still is. You'll actually get to meet him soon."

She doesn't lift her head, but her eyes flick up to mine. "Is he coming here?"

"Nope. We're going to a party for the new restaurant that Slade is opening in Seattle. You'll get to meet Jake in person too." I point back to the screen. "On that note, I should probably give you the run down on the rest of the guys that worked with the band that might be there."

I grab the remote and start typing out the letters, searching for a different video I want her to see. If she wants to get to know that time in my life, I know just what to show her.

"You know, you could just look up the video on your phone, then stream it to the TV. So much faster that way." She smirks up at me and adds, "Boomer."

"Very funny, Rainbow." I tap her on the head with the remote, rolling my eyes at her. "Again, I'm not that ancient. Technically, I'm a millennial, just a geriatric one."

She rests her head down on my shoulder, pulling a blanket over herself while the video I was looking for buffers. My attention stays solely on her as the video starts to play. This close, I take in the winding tattoo of vines and flowers, starting at her elbow, working its way up and over her shoulder and down her back, below her cami. It's a beautiful mix of brightly colored flowers and greenery, but that's not what catches my eye. It's the barely noticeable, but slightly dulled patches of her skin under the tattoo, maybe the scars from the car accident she was in as a teen. I find myself desperately fighting the urge to reach out and run my fingers over that skin, wishing I could soothe away whatever pain she once felt.

Touching her like that — caressing her skin — feels like a line I shouldn't cross though, as much as I want to.

On screen, the band walks out on stage and I remember it like it was yesterday. Miles is standing just off stage, and I get a sinking feeling in my chest. I let out a deep breath, trying not to dwell on the upcoming party for the restaurant, seeing my former band, and everything that comes with it.

Grace turns to me and my face must be giving away my feelings, because she narrows her eyes on me. "You don't look thrilled about watching this."

I sigh and take another drink of my wine. "I know Miles will be there and I still haven't given him an answer about this reunion tour."

She raises her brows and her lips part in surprise. "You're still hung up on *that* seven months later?"

CHAPTER 16
TJ
AVERT MY EYES

Seven Months Earlier

I PRACTICALLY JUMP out of the water, turning toward the sound of the splash.

What the hell was that?

I look around and see the water rippling out from the swimming hole just underneath the giant boulder along the river bank. I stare at the spot, but there's no sign of what caused it.

I start to turn back, to focus on casting my line into the river, when I hear another splash. I watch as wet streaks of hair emerge from the spot about twenty feet away. Even though she's facing away from me, I immediately recognize Grace, Tanner and Clay's little sister, in the neck deep water.

"Are you OK?" I call out, prompting her to spin around.

She lets out a long, whoosh of air, shaking her head sending beads of water in every direction around her. "Wow. It's cold."

I chuckle and shake my head. "Yeah, the river's fed from melting snow. What are you doing out here?"

She rolls her neck and shrugs. "I wanted to take up cold plunges after my workouts to help with inflammation. They're supposed to release dopamine and endorphins. I thought this would be the perfect spot to start. It's beautiful here."

"It's one of my favorite spots." I nod, looking around us as my heart settles down from the sudden surprise of her arrival. I'm glad she appreciates the beauty of this treelined spot on the river.

She smiles back. "How about you? What are you doing out here?"

I quirk a brow at her and raise my fishing pole at my side. "I thought it was pretty obvious."

She paddles in the water, laughing in amusement. "No one fishes because they want to catch fish. You're out here for something else."

Her green eyes match the evergreen trees along the river and I feel like they can see right through me. All my barriers crumble under her gaze and I blurt out what I've been thinking about all morning.

"I got a call from my old manager. He wants me back for a reunion tour."

She tilts her head expectantly, silently telling me she's waiting for more, so I continue. "I thought I'd come down here and think about it."

She still doesn't say anything, but swims over from the deeper part to where I'm standing in the waist deep water. I'd almost find it unnerving, but it just feels so natural to open up to her about something I haven't told anyone else yet.

She stays neck deep, kneeling in the shallow water. She looks up at me, studying me, the only sound is the water rippling around us and a gentle breeze through the treetops.

"Say less and just say yes," she says before grinning. "Or say no and tell them to fuck off. Either way, don't get hung up on it the way you are now."

A laugh bursts from my chest, prompting her to giggle and I can't look away from her smile and how her cheeks are perfectly covered in freckles. "I like that. *Say less and say yes*. But 'fuck off' sounds pretty good too."

She smiles and crooks her neck, running her fingers through her hair to wring out the cold water as she starts to stand. My eyes track the movement. My heart stops in my chest when I see her emerge from the water and I see her perfect, full breasts.

Fucking hell. She's out here topless.

"Oh, shit. Sorry." I avert my eyes, but not before I see her nipples pierced with little black barbells, hard from the icy cold water.

"Relax. They're just tits, TJ."

Present Day

"THANKS again for getting out on short notice," I tell the electrician, shaking his hand.

"Anything for Tommy Jacob. Pleasure doing business with you, sir."

Sir. I know he's being polite, but that makes me feel old.

I can't complain though. I called their twenty-four hour line first thing this morning. It took every ounce of self control to not call last night when Grace said she wished that she could find a high power outlet she could use to charge her van's back up batteries. She could use a normal one, but I want her to have the best and a normal one charges so much slower anyway.

That was right before she fell asleep in my arms last night on the couch. Nothing happened. We stayed up late and had another glass of wine and kept watching videos, but when I woke up with her snuggled up against me this morning with her leg thrown over mine, the reality of what I want sunk in.

I'm head over heels for the Chapmans' little sister, who's

fifteen years younger than me. And as much as I don't want to acknowledge it, I'm her boss too.

So I snuck out of there as fast as I could this morning, even if every fiber of my being wanted to hold her tighter and watch her wake up.

That's how I ended up here, sneaking in an electrician while she's out skiing with Josie this morning. She barely took me up on parking in my driveway so that I would know she was safe. I'm actually glad Josie was there because she helped sell it. That's why I know there's no way she would have let me do this if I had told her ahead of time.

Still, the electrician was happy to show up right after Grace left to ski for the day, especially after he realized who I was when I gave him the address and my contact info. I guess there are still some perks worth having from being famous.

Normally, I'd call Tanner and have him find an electrician for me. He might be out of town on his honeymoon, but he would have one on speed dial and here in minutes because he's a fantastic, reliable property manager. He does a great job of handling repairs and maintenance around the house, even if he's busier now with his blacksmithing business making knives. But he's also Grace's brother and I know he would have been wondering why I was installing a camper van power outlet right outside my guesthouse. He might know that she's back in town and now working for me, but I don't think he knows she was camping in the gym's parking lot. And I sure as shit don't want to get on his bad side if he finds out she's staying in my driveway now. As far as he knows, she's been staying at one of the local campgrounds but I know she wasn't going to overpay for that.

I know I'd do it again though.

And that heater? Damnit. If she didn't take her van to the mountain this morning, I'd have found an RV repair man to make a house call and fix it, no matter how much she objected.

I know myself. I know I wasn't going to be able to sleep thinking about her being in her van like that at night. Who am I kidding? Every thought of her seems to keep me from getting to sleep recently. Even if she's been staying in my driveway for almost a week now, I still want to make sure she's as safe as can be.

CHAPTER 17

GRACE
LESSONS

"SO YOU'RE GOING to Seattle with him?" Josie asks, sitting next to me on the chairlift.

"Yep. It's supposed to be some kind of hip, warehouse vibey party to celebrate Slade's new restaurant before they start construction. He said he also wants me to meet his business manager, who also happens to be his foster brother, Jake."

Josie hums to herself, tapping her finger to her lip. I already know what's on her mind. Since she got back in town this morning, she's had a one-track mind, demanding to know everything about her new favorite topic: *Hot Boss*.

I can't really blame her though. I know I'm lucky to have a gig like this. I'm sure there are far more qualified people that would kill to 'collaborate' with someone like TJ, especially with the budget he's given me. That doesn't change the fact that Josie wants to know everything about being up close with the mysterious and conveniently very easy to look at retired rockstar. Still, I was happy to get a few laps in with her this morning since I need to work later today.

"So is anyone else famous going to be at this thing? You're going to have to give me all the juicy gossip. You know that, right?" She turns toward me and her head drops the slightest bit. Even with her goggles on, I know she's raising her eyebrows at me expectedly.

"Yeah, some of the other Teal Tigers guys are supposed to be there to hype the new restaurant. He gave me the run down on them while we watched their old music videos and live performances last night before we fell asleep," I say before taking a drink from my hydration backpack.

I turn to see Josie's mouth open, but saying nothing.

"What?" I ask, jutting my head out toward her.

She slowly lifts her goggles and looks at me, her eyes wide.

"You said *we* fell asleep." She keeps staring at me and it clicks.

"It was nothing. It was late, he saw the lights on in the guesthouse, and I asked if he wanted to hang out," I say calmly, not giving in to her hopes for *juicy gossip*. "We had some wine, talked, watched those videos, and it was late so we just fell asleep on the couch together. Seriously, it's not a big deal."

The corners of her mouth lift into a smirk. "First, he drinks wine. Big yes. Second, you two fell asleep on the couch together?"

"Seriously, Josie. Nothing happened. The guesthouse only has the one couch. We were sitting there all night and just hanging out."

"Really?" She raises her eyebrows again in question. "*Nothing* happened? Then why are your cheeks so red, girl?"

Damnit. Thanks again, traitorous body.

My mind goes back to last night, remembering how it felt to be so close to him. But still, it was just a casual night hanging out with a friend, right? Yeah, I did fall asleep on him. And yes, he smelled so, so good. Something about that bergamot and pine scent put me at ease. Waking up with him gone, I breathed in the lingering traces of it and wished he was there.

Still though, he knows I'm just an outgoing goof with no personal space boundaries. I'm sure it didn't mean anything to him.

"Nothing, except I might have fallen asleep *on* him. Just his shoulder," I admit, trying to convince myself it was nothing and shrug it off.

"There it is," she says, her smirk widening. "I knew there was more. And, where was his arm?"

"Around me," I say, the realization that she might be onto something slowly settling in. I keep thinking about how his arm was slung over the back of the couch. Or was he wrapping it around me?

She laughs to herself, shaking her head. "Only you would find yourself cuddled up with a rockstar and think nothing of it."

I keep that thought to myself to sort out later. With the Seattle trip coming up and being in Jackson longer than I was originally planning, I need to go back to my place in Park City to grab some things I didn't even think to ask Josie to bring. Suddenly now I'm finding myself with a surprisingly crammed schedule.

"Anyway, let's talk about the Tahoe trip. We need to pick some dates soon if you still want to squeeze that trip in," I say.

She throws her head back and groans and I get it. Neither of us are huge on pinning down dates and prefer to live in the moment and be free and spontaneous. "You know my calendar is clear. Just say when and I'll show up. I'll even make sure we can get that one campground we like, right on the state line."

I love that campground in South Lake Tahoe. It's been one of my favorite places to stay since it's right on the water. Being on the state line between California and Nevada, we can walk to all the bars and casinos, and there's even a shuttle to the ski resort village.

"If we go after President's Day, we'll avoid the holiday

crowds. A week next month would be perfect," I say, knowing that's well after the Seattle trip. It will also give me enough time to go back to Park City to grab some more things from my apartment.

I TURN into TJ's driveway, pulling all the way down toward the guesthouse. After a morning of skiing, I'm secretly glad I'm staying here. The shower at the gym is nice, but the one here in the guesthouse with full body spa sprayers is flat out heavenly. I can't even imagine what TJ must have in his bathroom.

Hopping out of my van, I start down the path to the guesthouse, but something stops me right in my tracks.

There's a new wooden post where the edge of the driveway meets the walking path. It matches the fence posts around the property, but this one is only waist high and standing by itself. On the front of it are two small, metal flip-up lids. I flip one open, but I already know what's under the lid. Sure enough, it's a high powdered outlet, just like the one at campgrounds to charge RVs and vans like mine.

Freaking. TJ.

Maybe that's why he left the guesthouse so early this morning because he damn well knows that if he would have asked me, I would have said no. Part of the fun of van life is the adventure of not always having it easy and part of me is irritated that he just did it on his own. The rest of me though, that's another story. Something about this gesture feels so personal, so heartfelt. And again, there's that decisiveness about him that I can't resist.

I flip open the second lid and find there's a note taped under it.

It's too late to say no, Rainbow. Now

please, don't make a geriatric millennial worry all night and keep your van warm.

I keep trying to tell myself these little gestures don't mean anything, but that feels like more and more of a lie.

EVEN AFTER BEING AROUND HERE ALMOST every day for the last couple of weeks, I still feel like I could get lost in TJ's house. He should put up street signs or something so I don't end up in the wrong room again.

When I came here, I planned to give him shit for putting an RV pedestal in his driveway. I thought I'd even tell him that I'm going to have Jake take it out of my pay since he's already paying me way too much. I'm sure he'd just figure out someway around that though and pay me even more. Wait. When did I start complaining about getting paid well? It's not that I'm not grateful, it just seems like overkill and he's being far too generous.

After not finding him in the living room, kitchen, office, or his gym, I'm starting to lose my resolve and find myself less irritated with him. Maybe I should accept that he's just a giver — move on, and let him do his thing. I'm about to do just that when a sound at the end of the hall grabs my attention. That's when I see that the door to his studio is ajar and the lights are on.

As I step toward it, I realize that I haven't heard him playing music or seen him in his studio the entire time I've been working here. I lean against the doorway, listening to the notes drifting through the cracked door. The soft notes from the acoustic guitar feel tentative, like he's searching for something.

I quietly walk into the room to find TJ sitting on a stool in the corner of the room, facing the window toward the guesthouse, his back to me. Even from this angle, in his black t-shirt, it's hard not to see how gorgeous he is. Holding the guitar, those perfectly toned back muscles rippling under his well fitting shirt while his triceps flex, strumming the notes. I stand there quietly, admiring the view when something else dawns on me.

Watching his body language, the way he hesitates and replays notes, I don't think he knows this song. I think he's feeling it out and writing it.

Suddenly, I feel like I'm intruding on something I shouldn't be. From everything I've ever heard of him, he all but gave up on music after the band broke up. I'm sure there's more to the story, but I still can't imagine giving up something I loved like that. I'm about to sneak back out of the room, but something deep inside me says stay. That's when my indecisive, clumsy legs betray me. I trip over my own feet, falling to my knees, and swinging the door wide open and loudly into the wall.

Shit, shit, shit.

To my surprise, he hardly moves, crooking his neck just enough to look over his shoulder and see me on the floor.

"I'm so sorry, I didn't mean to interrupt you," I say, standing up and wiping the knees of my overalls.

"You weren't interrupting. I knew you were there," he says, the corner of those full lips lifting into a smirk.

He must see the surprise on my face because he tilts his head toward the window he was facing. "Saw your reflection."

Oh. Yeah. I didn't think about that.

"And I heard you."

"You heard me?" I ask, trying to think of what he could have heard over the guitar.

He turns to face me, shrugging, and huffing a laugh. "Musician's ear. You'd think I'd have lost more hearing, but I still have a knack for picking up sounds."

He places the guitar on the stand next to the stool and I

notice a notepad at his feet. "Did you need something? I assume you're sneaking around my house for a reason," he says with a smug grin.

I fold my arms over my chest, trying unsuccessfully to regain my normal confidence. "I was not sneaking. I clearly announced my presence."

"Yeah. Not very gracefully though. So seriously, what's up?" he says, raises a brow, bringing my eyes to the scarred piercing.

"Oh, yeah," I say, looking around the room suddenly at a loss for words. "Thank you."

Damnit. Thank you? That's all I can come up with after he just installed an electric hookup for my van because of my wonky heater. I'm supposed to tell him that it's too much and he's being too generous. There goes my strong, independent woman streak I guess. What the hell is wrong with me when I'm around him?

And this always smooth and smug man must know that, because he just smirks back at me knowingly and shrugs. "For?"

My eyes dart to his popped dimple, which is infuriatingly distracting at the moment.

"I don't even want to know what it costs to get an electrician here on a few hours' notice and run power for those RV outlets you put in." I glare back at him, but it quickly fades when my eyes find that damned pierced eyebrow again.

"Good, because I wouldn't tell you even if you asked. And no, I won't take it out of your pay, even if you tell Jake to." Yep, there goes that idea I guess.

Leaning forward on his stool, he props his elbows up on his knees. "Consider it a gift. So what are you getting into tonight? No plans to watch old music videos of me again?"

I groan, rolling my eyes, but I still find myself grinning and looking back at him. "Nope, I'll let you get back to playing. Don't let me keep you up. Well, anymore than I already have. Thanks again, TJ."

I start to turn toward the door when he calls from behind me. "Tommy." I look back to see him, his eyes fixed on me.

"Tommy?" I ask, not sure what he's saying.

He stands up next to the stool and nods, but I catch the slightest bit of pleading in his eyes. "Call me Tommy."

"OK." I'm certainly not going to argue with him. "Night, Tommy."

That heart melting, boyish grin returns to his face, making my stomach do a weird, flippy thing.

He waves a hand down at the stool. "Don't leave. Come over here."

I don't even have time to think about saying no before my body follows his command, stepping to the stool, and sitting in front of him.

"You came in at the perfect time," he says, kneeling down in front of me. "I was stuck and about to call it for the night."

I look down at him, finding it once again hard not to admire all of the details of him when he's kneeling between my legs, smiling up at me. He's breathtakingly masculine, but in that subtle way I crave. Suddenly my mouth feels dry and I'm at a loss for words.

"Have you ever played?"

Before I can process or much less answer that question, he's reaching his arms around me, hanging the strap of his acoustic guitar around my neck. He rests the guitar in my lap before appraising me, his blue eyes looking over every inch of me. Like everything else about him, they're so stunning. The blue is so deep and vibrant, contrasting the whites of his eyes. It's like looking into a crystal clear lake, surrounded by snow. I follow those eyes and when he looks at my shoulder, a line creases his brows.

My eyes follow his, but he's already reaching for where the guitar strap meets the straps of my overalls. He straightens it out, but I can feel the warm, callused tips of his fingers graze my pounding pulse point. My lips part at the contact on that oh so sensitive patch of skin just below my ear. Just like that though, he pulls them away, but that doesn't stop my body from following him, craving more contact.

"There. That's better," he says, looking pleased with himself.

Suddenly, even breathing around him feels like a monumental task with the charged air between us. But he doesn't even seem affected. He just keeps looking up at me with that pleased expression.

"Better how? And no, I've never played before," I say, finally collecting myself enough to be a functional human.

I watch his nostrils flare when he snorts a laugh. "Well you look like a natural. Overalls and a flannel? You look like you would have fit right in with us in Seattle twenty years ago."

I drop my chin, lowering my eyes on him. "I can't tell if that's an insult or a compliment because I would have been seven years old."

"Woof. There you go making me feel ancient again." My eyes meet his and he winks at me. "But it's the best compliment. Now give me your hands. Time for some lessons."

I reach out to him, turning my palms up. He grabs me by the wrists, placing my hands on the guitar in the proper spots. I look at his hand, wrapped around mine over the neck of the guitar. I can see so many spots where the finish of the neck, the frets and everything else are worn. "Tommy, this looks old."

He shakes his head, keeping his eyes fixed on our hands where his fingers are bending mine into the right position. "That's because it is old. It's the one I learned on, my first guitar."

My eyes fly to his at the sudden realization of what I'm holding. "There's no way you can let me play this. I'll break it or something. You saw how clumsy I am literally minutes ago."

He grips my hand tighter, looking back at me with nothing

but that pure conviction of his that makes me swallow hard. He leans forward, leaving just inches between us. "There's no one else that I would rather have play with this old thing than you, Rainbow," he says, voice dropping deeper with a gravelly rasp that hits me low in my stomach.

Those piercing, sparkling blue eyes stay fixed on mine. His delicious scent fills each of my breaths. His fingers stay woven between mine. I savor the warmth of his body kneeling so close between my thighs. All of it so, so overwhelming, fulfilling that craving to stimulate all of my senses.

Yes, I told myself I can separate my lust for him from the rest of our intertwined lives. But I don't know if I want to anymore. Maybe this is a problem for future me. Maybe this is one I should take head-on — right now — and solve the way I usually do.

So I give into that spontaneous voice in the back of my head, doing what I always love to do. I live for moments like this that feel so right in every part of my body. I lean forward, closing the distance between us, planting one soft, slow kiss on those full lips.

In an instant, all of those overwhelming sensations take over in an electric blur. I let go of the guitar and let it hang on my neck so I can bring my hands to his face. I feel the tension in his body when I hold my lips to his, savoring the feeling of his stubble under my palms with our foreheads pressed together.

A second of charged silence passes, but it feels like an eternity.

Shit. Did I read this entirely wrong?

Another second passes before I feel his chest heave between us. Then his lips part and he lets out the hottest moan I've ever heard.

That sound wakes up every nerve in my body and makes my nipples peak. My piercings drag against my ribbed tank top under the straps of my overalls. With no bra on, it makes me crave even more contact.

"Rainbow," he practically growls in a low, husky plea, making my thighs clench and hold him tighter between my knees.

He lets out another long, shaky breath before kissing me back. His tongue explores every bit of my waiting mouth. Everything about this kiss feels needy and desperate, like the curtain on whatever he's been hiding has finally dropped.

And I love it.

He drops his hands to my waist, holding me tightly. I nip at his bottom lip, prompting another moan to rumble in his chest before his tongue glides along mine, claiming my mouth. My hands run down his neck, over his toned shoulders, and along his back. Suddenly his tight, well fitting t-shirt is far too much clothing between us, not to mention this damn guitar. I can feel the tension in his muscular body, at odds with the passionate kiss. His hands cautiously explore the dip of my waist, his thumbs tracing the bottom of my ribs under my shirt, making me suck in a breath, breaking the seal of our lips.

I bring my lips to his ear, breathing in every bit of him while my heart races.

"Tommy," I whisper against his ear.

He pulls back and for just a moment, I see the intense, blazing hunger in his eyes, matching my own craving for him. It quickly fades though. Alarm flashes in his eyes and he drops his hands to his side.

"Shit, Grace. I'm-" he starts, before I cut him off, missing the name Rainbow on his lips.

I take my hand off his back, pressing one finger to his lips. "No. Don't apologize. I kissed you, remember?" I smirk at him, but the alarm in his eyes remains while his chest heaves with labored breaths.

"It doesn't matter. We can't do this. I'm your boss. I'm your brother's friend. I'm fifteen years older than you." He runs his hand through his hair, palming his face, but I don't miss the pained expression. "Fuck. I'm pathetic."

"I told you, stop with the self-deprecating bullshit." I stare him down and this time I'm the one not wavering in my convictions. "And who cares? I'm a big girl, Tommy. I can handle myself. I know my limits and I know what I want. I thought you wanted the same thing."

I reach for his hand, grabbing him by the wrist. He quickly pulls it back and flexes it at his side again like my mere touch pains him.

"I know what I want," he says, shaking his head before bringing his eyes back to mine. I can see the lingering temptation, but he still looks so torn, like his mind and body are fighting a war with his heart caught in the middle. He stands, trying to create distance between us, but I stand with him. "It's just not that simple."

I quirk an eyebrow at him, crossing my arms over my chest, pressing against my still very hard nipples, reminding me just how wound up my body still is. "What happened to all that 'I don't hold back when I know what I want' shit? I'm pretty sure you want me."

"You're pretty sure I want you? What makes you so certain?" he teases, flicking his brows in question.

Damnit. Am I in over my head here? I don't want to throw a wrench into our friendship and work dynamic, but I also know I'm right. He just told me as much, except he left that *it's just not that simple* hanging out there with no explanation.

CHAPTER 18
TJ
THAT KISS

THE LOOK that Grace is leveling on me tells me that even I might have been underestimating her. She's confident. She's outgoing, and I know she doesn't hold back. But she just made a move on me and she's not backing down. Instead she's flipping the script on me. Now I'm the one on the spot, having to explain why I'm saying no to her.

Only in my wildest dreams did I ever let myself think she'd be interested in me. And now she's the one looking at me like I'm some indecisive, immature fuck.

Clearly, I'm a dumbass.

"Yeah, I heard that little moan. And I can see it." Her eyes drop to my waist. I suddenly realize my sweats are not doing me any favors right now hiding my throbbing dick. "So maybe if you get your brain, heart, and *that* on the same page, you'll be a little more sure about what you want."

Shit. That was harsh, but she's not wrong. I've been internally denying this since we first met. I'm more than interested in her. I just don't know how to sort this out. I meant it when I said it's not that simple.

The idea of possibly loving anything ever again terrifies me.

She said I go with my feelings — my heart— and that's the problem. I've never been called to something like I am to her, except
music. She already feels like something that will consume me.
Hell. She already does. I can't do anything without thinking
about her.

What if I get burned out like I did with music and I wake up
one day and that magic is just gone?

Or what if I'm wrong like I was with my ex?

My fears swirl in my head like a storm, making me feel a level
of self doubt that I haven't felt in ages.

I let out a long, labored breath, and look her in the eyes.
Those gorgeous, deep green eyes pin me with a look of determination and frustration that no one ever shows me.

"I'm sorry, Grace. I don't know what to say."

Her nostrils flare in a long exhale. "You don't have to say
anything. We can just go back to being friends and collaborating.
Pretend it never happened."

I instantly hate those words 'go back.' I want this, but I'm too
in my own head to think clearly. There's also no way I will ever
forget that kiss.

So I nod and turn to leave, but she grabs my wrist, forcing me
to turn back to her.

"No, I'll go. It's your studio. Keep playing. And if you finally
figure out what you want, you know where to find me." She
shrugs and I see the faintest hint of a smirk. "Who knows? Maybe
I'll still feel the same way."

She loops the guitar strap over her head and hands it back to
me. I reach out to grab it from her, our fingers grazing on the neck
of the guitar. I feel that electric charge sizzle across my skin at the
contact. Her eyes meet mine one last time and I don't miss how
her teeth dig into her full, bottom lip. Then she turns and walks
out of my studio, closing the door behind her.

Just like that, in a matter of minutes, I went from having

exactly what I wanted in my hands to finding myself alone with one thing, or more accurately, one person on my mind.

Damnit. I fucked this up.

"WHY ARE YOU HERE?" Sutton looks at me from across the counter at Gloria's while I try to enjoy my lunch. He points over his shoulder to the calendar hanging in the hall to the backroom. "You know it's Friday, right? Our usual lunches are Saturday."

I feel my shoulders slump. "Got it. Still not a safe space anymore."

"Not when you're in here moping like this for almost every meal." His smug grin grows. "Do tell me, what ails the retired rockstar that has everything, so much so that he's spent the last week and a half hiding at my tasting counter?"

I lower my eyes at him, which is hard because Sutton is taller than me. "You know, your cooking just keeps getting worse. I'm going to start worrying about the menu for the new restaurant if Slade lets you anywhere near it."

"OK. Again, you, me, and your empty plate all know that's a lie. So are you going to tell me why you're still here after you finished eating half an hour ago?" he asks, looking as if he already knows the answer. "You know, instead of at your house? That giant place you own, where you live? This wouldn't have something to do with a certain tall woman living in her van in your driveway, would it?"

I roll my eyes and groan, already knowing that he's enjoying this way too much. "I think you alre—" I start, but my voice trails off when his eyes start tracking something over my shoulder.

I turn to see Kelsey from Cowgirl Coffee come in, carrying a large box of bagged coffee beans that she can hardly see over.

Sutton practically leaps from behind the counter to go over to her.

"Here, let me get that," he says, reaching toward her.

I assume she's glaring back at him based on her tone when she replies. "No, thanks. I already got this far, scrawny arms."

She breezes right past him, walking over to the counter and dropping the boxes in front of the espresso machine with a thud. "Here's your weekly order, Chef," she says, emphasizing the last syllable with a hiss.

Kelsey turns and finally notices me, a sweet smile gracing her face. "Oh, hey, TJ. Nice to see you."

I nod, taking a sip of my water. "You too."

Her smile fades as she walks right past Sutton, bumping her shoulder into his, leaving just as fast as she came in. I definitely notice the puppy dog look on his face as the door swings shut behind her.

He finally looks back at me, shaking his head.

I point at the door. "Alright. I'll tell you my shit if you explain what the hell that was all about," I get out through a grin.

He drops his chin, looking back and forth between his arms. "She called me scrawny," he says, disbelief plastered on his face. "I spend more time in the gym than you."

"Maybe it's that stupid chef's coat. You should try having it tailored." It feels good to be giving him shit for once.

"Stop looking so pleased with yourself," he says, glaring back at me. "And if you're going to keep hiding here, let's at least talk shop. You're coming to Seattle for the party next week, right?"

Shit. I had blocked that out of my mind for a few days, but it's coming up fast.

"Yeah, I'll be there." I look down at my empty plate, rearranging the remaining garnishes with my fork. "Grace is coming too."

I look up to find him watching me with an amused grin.

"What?"

He shakes his head, pointing back at me. "I knew it! You're hiding from her." His shit-eating grin only widens.

I let out a long sigh. He's right. I am, not that I'd admit it to him. I know she said it's not a big deal that we kissed, but I've felt like an ass since then. Everything she said was right. I'm into her. We're both adults. It feels like something I shouldn't say no to. It feels like something I should at least take a chance on, but I still can't get out of my own head.

I finally look back at Sutton. "Oh, so now you want to play bartender therapist? At least get me a beer or something."

He throws his head back with his far too loud, booming laugh before turning to grab a beer from the under-counter fridge.

He pops the top and hands it to me. "Oh, this is too good," he says, palming his face with a muffled laugh. "I've known you for years and I've never heard you even talk about a girl. Now she's got you afraid to be at your own house. What happened?"

I take a sip of my beer, staring daggers at him.

"Less talking, got it." He leans against the counter across from me, still looking far too please with himself. "Well, figure your shit out before Seattle. I'm not going to be your awkward third wheel buffer on the jet there. But if you ask me—"

"I'm not asking you," I say dryly, cutting him off.

He just shrugs and continues anyway. "But if you did ask me, I'd say go for it, man. If you're this torn over her, you owe it to yourself to give it a shot." He smirks back at me before grabbing a bar towel and wiping down the counter. "Either way, stop hiding here. Your moping ass is starting to scare off customers."

Someone calls from the stock room and Sutton finally leaves me to my beer. Despite his razzing, I love him like a brother. He's right though. I need to figure my shit out.

I've spent nearly every minute of the last two days replaying that kiss in my mind. I still can't believe she leaned down and kissed me.

It was perfect.

I don't know why I'm surprised by that. Everything about her makes my heart race. Her smile, that laugh, the sparkle in her eyes when she's about to do something impulsive. I haven't been able to get it out of my head and it's nearly driven me mad. Thinking of the sounds she made makes my dick inconveniently hard way too often.

If I could go back in time, I'd have told her to stay and talk through this with her.

Sutton isn't the only one who's right. She was too. She said I don't hold back and, ninety-nine times out of a hundred, she'd be right.

If I want any real shot with her, I need to be myself. The real version of me. The one that apparently Grace Chapman is into.

CHAPTER 19
GRACE
CRACKED

I'M STARTING to think TJ, no Tommy — shit, what do I call him now? Boss? Mr. Jacob? Definitely not Hot Daddy Boss. Whatever I'm calling him now, I'm pretty sure he is hiding from me.

I've barely seen him since last Wednesday night. I've just gone straight from my van to his office when I've come into the house. Even when he has been around, he quickly found a reason to leave and head to Sutton's restaurant, or there was this awkward tension between us. It's not like I've had much free time anyway.

Ever since he was so quick to agree with my recommendations for charities, I've had this other idea I couldn't get out of my head. I know he wants to make a difference and he certainly has the budget to do it. While I know he wants to stay anonymous with his giving, I think there's a way for him to make so much more of an impact. I've spent the last week and a half working on this proposal.

I'm probably crazy for obsessing over this on a Friday night. I know Josie is out with Collin and Walker tonight and I can only imagine the trouble those three have been getting into.

I'm just so inspired by this idea, I feel like I need to tell him.

He was very clear that I could work whatever hours I want, so I'm going to do just that. I still can't get the other night out of my head. And here I am walking through his house looking for him once again.

Obviously there was that kiss though. The sound of him moaning and rasping my name has been echoing around in my head so much that I've had to keep my earbuds in, constantly listening to music loud enough that I'm pretty sure I've sustained hearing loss.

Ugh, men who moan. Forget rent free, that moan has its own Presidential Suite in my brain.

Not helpful, Grace.

I need to remind myself that tonight, I'm here for business. Or that's what I tell myself as I walk down the hall to his studio, the room I've avoided since our kiss. I haven't found him anywhere else in the house but I spot the door cracked with a sliver of light creeping into the hall. The image takes me back to the night of that kiss again.

I still don't know why I left so quickly instead of staying to talk with him. Maybe pride, maybe stubbornness, or maybe that's just what I do — go with what feels 'right' in the moment. And in that moment, I didn't want to stick around to hear an explanation about why I wasn't thinking straight or not actually feeling what I thought I was feeling or some other bullshit. I wasn't going to let him mansplain my own mind to me, not that I think he would, but I'm just used to men doing that.

That's not the only thing that stuck with me though. I might have walked out of his studio confidently and quickly, but I didn't make it that far. I stopped just outside, in the hallway, exactly where I'm standing now. I stayed and argued with myself about going back in to talk to him.

I was there long enough that I heard him start playing the guitar again, the same notes that he played earlier.

This time, there was a depth and vibrancy to them. They were more powerful and forceful, but there was something else that wasn't there before, an unmistakable, harsh, frustrated edge. I could practically feel the emotion in the cords.

Clearing my head, I take a deep breath and push open the door. To my surprise, the light is on but he's not here. My curiosity takes over and I walk around the open studio, looking at all the little things I was too distracted to notice last time.

There's black soundproofing foam on most of the walls, but there are open sections covered in memorabilia and photos of the band. There also has to be at least a dozen electric guitars around the room and a few stacks of amplifiers and speakers. It's the two acoustic guitars in the corner, by the window, that I'm drawn to.

Standing in front of the floor to ceiling windows, I can just make out the lights from the groomers on the mountain, cleaning up the ski runs for tomorrow, in the distance. Maybe that's how I'll spend tomorrow morning.

From here, I also have a view of the backyard and looking across the patio, I see the hot tub and guesthouse. I can even make out the front of my van in the driveway. I wonder if this is where TJ was the other night when he noticed the light on in the guesthouse.

Finally, I look down at the guitar on the stand next to me, the real reason I came to this corner of the room. I sit on the same stool as the other night in front of the guitar, running my finger-tips down the well-worn neck, along the strings, feeling the tension in them, just like that tension I was so sure was between us. Actually, I'm pretty sure it's still there if he really is hiding from me.

I pick up the guitar, holding it in my lap. My eyes drift shut and my hands run across the curves of the smooth wood. Folding my fingers across the neck, I can practically feel TJ's hand wrapped around mine, placing my fingers on the right strings.

I open my eyes, looking at the instrument when I spot something on the floor at the base of the guitar stand. I reach down to grab the notebook, wondering if it's the same one he was writing in the other night. There are music notes, but no lyrics or words besides a few scribbled words in the margins.

"Really regret picking dance classes over music right now," I mutter to myself, flipping through the notebook on my lap, resting the guitar against my side.

Going through the pages, I recognize the handwriting as TJ's, matching it to the note he left me after installing the electric post. I notice the handwriting on the last half written page toward the back is the boldest, least faded bit. It must be recent, if not even new.

Did I really interrupt him in the middle of writing a new song?

I look back down at the page, running my finger over the little drawing of a rainbow in the bottom corner.

No. There's no way.

I immediately shut the notebook, tossing it back on the floor where I found it. I know he's been abundantly clear that I can make myself comfortable here and make use of his home, but this feels different. Reading that feels like a boundary that might be too far, even for me, to cross.

I settle for something that feels safer, picking the guitar back up and holding it in my lap. I look at it and feel my body heat, remembering his gravelly voice saying my name, his hot breath against my neck. Just thinking about it sends sparks of heat across my skin, making me restless.

"Looks good in your hands, Rainbow," TJ's deep voice rumbles from across the room.

I practically leap out of my skin, turning to see him here in person, not in my mind. My hands fly to my chest in a startled reaction. He smirks before his eyes fly to the same place mine go.

Shit. No, no, no.

I watch in horror as the guitar I was holding falls toward the ground, feeling like it's unfolding in slow motion. I reach out trying to grab it, but I only make it worse, pushing it further away.

I wince when it hits the hardwood floor, making a mangled mess of sounds before it skids across the floor and stops. I fall to my knees and grab it, hoping that I didn't just damage his guitar. This thing has to be almost priceless, in so many ways.

I feel him kneel beside me. "Shit. I'm so sorry. I didn't mean to scare you. We really need to get better about not sneaking up on each other so much."

"Sure," I say, hardly able to pay attention with my heart anxiously racing. "I'll get right on that, Boss."

I flip the guitar over in my hands and my heart sinks when I see the long, wide crack down the back, splitting the beautiful wood.

I groan. "Oh, TJ. I'm sorry, " I say, running my finger along the crack, feeling the splintered edges. "I shouldn't have been messing with it. I'm such an idiot."

He leans closer to me and I feel the warmth of his body as he reaches around me, pulling the guitar from my grip. Something about his presence sends alarm bells off in my body again. As tall as I am, I'm not used to feeling small around another person but it's hard for me to miss his imposing presence.

I look up to see him holding the guitar, a soft smile spreading across his face as his eyes follow the crack in the instrument. He says nothing when he runs his finger along it, just the way I did. He presses his palm against the dark, gorgeous walnut, like he's soaking up the memories contained in it.

"I'm so sorry. I'll get it fixed," I say, looking for any reaction. I'd expect most men to get angry, if not even fly into rage. With him, there's nothing. Just calmness. "Take it out of my pay. You already give me too much."

The corners of his mouth continue to lift when he lets out a single, lighthearted laugh. Did he seriously just laugh?

Another one rumbles up his chest, leaving no doubt that he did in fact just laugh. Is he laughing at me?

Finally, he outright bursts into a fit of laughter, his shoulders rising and falling. Slowly, I start to nervously laugh with him.

At the sound of my laughter, he looks up from the guitar to me. Something about my expression must show my nerves because his smile fades. He sets the guitar down and reaches out toward me. He rests his thumb on my chin, tilting it up so I have to look him right in those endlessly deep blue eyes.

"It's just a thing, Rainbow. It doesn't matter. I can replace *things*. It's the memories that count," he says, his eyes never leaving mine while his thumb traces the bottom of my lip. "And believe me, this guitar has given me more than its fair share of memories."

My lips part when I suck in a breath at the contact and those words. Is he just as stuck as me on the memory of that kiss?

His eyes fall to my lips and I see his nostrils flare and I know that he is.

"Did you get yourself all on the same page yet?" I ask, my voice almost a whisper. I feel the tension between us, the air humming with electricity.

"Rainbow," he says, his voice radiating conflict and I already have my answer. "I—"

"I'll take that as a 'no' then," I say, his eyes flaring up to mine and I can see the anguish in them. He looks like he's about to say something until for some stupid reason, I bite down on his thumb. Both of our eyes drop down and then find each other's again.

He quirks that pierced eyebrow at me and hums in confusion, looking at his thumb and back at me. I let go, realizing just how unhinged I probably seem right now.

I stand up to start walking out of this room, wondering what I'm reading wrong about this again.

"Goodnight, TJ," I say, reaching the doorway and looking back to see him still kneeling by the guitar stand.

He runs his hand through his hair and lets out a long, frustrated sigh. I still see the mix of emotions swirling, but more than that, I see a look of compassion.

He finally shakes his head and smirks back at me. "Night, Rainbow. And I mean it, don't beat yourself up. It's not a big deal."

I CANNOT SLEEP. When I left TJ's house, I went straight to my van, which now thanks to him, is more than warm running on the electric heater with ample power. It was yet another reminder of how infuriating he is.

So now, I'm wandering around in the dark in his guesthouse, on my way to get a hot shower to try and relax.

Somehow, he's always doing the right thing. Being a great boss, being overly generous with his time and energy, not treating me like I'm some fragile doll that needs to be constantly watched and cared for. The man gave me free roam of his house and guesthouse, but doesn't push when I want to spend every night in my van like the feral little heathen that I am. Then there's the whole part about him smelling and looking like a damn snack that I literally just nibbled on. He definitely has to think I'm unhinged after that.

But he's been so compassionate too. I still can't believe he didn't even bat an eye when I broke his first guitar. How did he not care? I know guys who would lose their shit over way less than that. He just shrugged, smiled at me, and moved on. His compassion doesn't end with me either. The amount that man has given to charity over the years is astounding.

Then there's the decisiveness, which is the most maddening of them all. He's been decisive with every suggestion I've made to him at work. He was the same way with running power for my van.

But when it comes to whatever is going on between us, he's been the opposite, palpably conflicted about it.

I see that same, magnetic pull to spontaneity in him that fuels me to my core. That same lust for living life to the fullest. I just want him to let go and give in to it like I know he wants to.

I know there's something here. Maybe he just needs a little more of a push than I thought.

CHAPTER 20
TJ
INDECISIVE LOSER

SOMEHOW, I find myself sitting alone in my studio again, holding my old guitar. For the last half hour, I've been staring at this old piece of wood, turning it over in my hands, thinking about all the memories we've shared.

I remember learning to play on this guitar. I remember the feeling of having something of my own that went from foster home to foster home with me. I remember the way she smiled when I tried to teach her a couple chords.

But most of all, I remember the feeling of her lips on mine, the smell of her lavender shampoo, and the way she looked at me through her bangs with unfettered longing in her beautiful emerald eyes.

Shit. Those perfect, heart stopping eyes that feel like they cut right through me and strip away every façade I could ever try to put up around her.

For the first time tonight, I saw worry — no — terror in them when she broke my guitar. I can't believe she thought I'd be mad about it. That's not me. I couldn't care less about things like that.

What I do care about is her. Maybe it's time I start thinking about what I should do next. Maybe I should give her more credit. Hell, she clearly wants me and isn't shy about it. And god knows I want her.

Part of the reason I'm drawn to her is because she seems like such an old soul, not bothered by things that most people seem to obsess over.

Yeah, I need to talk to her.

I get off my stool, setting the cracked guitar back on its stand by the window. Stepping up to the glass, I see the lights in the guesthouse are on.

Damnit. I hope she's not inside because there's a problem with the power for her van heater. Grabbing my phone, I shoot her a text.

Me: Are you still up?

I watch as three dots appear, disappear and reappear for what feels like an eternity. Maybe she's pissed at me for being an indecisive loser. Or maybe she didn't buy it that I'm truly not mad about the guitar. I'm about to start spiraling when my phone buzzes and her name flashes across the screen, prompting me to fumble my phone and nearly toss it right into the window. I secure it and bring it to my ear.

"Oh, hey. I guess you are still up." Real cool, Tommy. Real fucking cool.

She hums to herself and I can just picture her fluffing her bangs with a puff of air. I instantly find myself thinking about how she just had the tip of my thumb between her lips and what it would feel like to have my aching cock between them.

"Yep. I guess you are too." Her voice is almost breathy.

"Is everything OK with your van? You can use the guesthouse if you need somewhere to sleep and I can get the electrician or a repairman out in the morning."

I stand in front of the window, anxiously watching for motion in the guesthouse. I don't want to be a creep and just constantly look for her, but I need to know she's safe. Finally, an amused laugh comes across the line. "The van's fine. I just want to get a long, hot shower. I really need to unwind."

Shit. Maybe she is still worried. "I told you. Don't beat yourself up about the guitar. It's just bits and pieces."

She scoffs. "I know, I believe you. That's not why I need to unwind." A second passes before she speaks again. "I see you're still in the studio, Tommy."

What the hell does she mean? And she called me Tommy? My eyes search the guesthouse windows when I see her tall, dark silhouette step toward the window.

I wave. I wave like a dumbass. Who waves to someone that just had your thumb in their mouth?

"Taking advantage of your benefits package I see."

"Something like that." Her tone shifting from amused to almost playful. "This job does have lots of perks."

I'm about to come up with some witty retort when I see her step all the way up to the window, completely in the light now, giving me one, subtle wave back.

At least I feel a little less dumb for waving now, but that's the least of my problems.

My heart stops at the sight of her, wearing nothing but that pair of tiny plaid sleep shorts and little cami again. I remember how perfect it felt to have her fall asleep, dressed in that, in my arms. I remember how much I wanted to just stay there the next morning and watch her wake up.

I pry myself out of that memory, clearing my head and hopelessly trying to not picture her wearing even less. "I told you, make yourself at home. Use that shower as much as you want. Move into the guesthouse if you want. I don't mind."

"More perks of the job?" she asks playfully. "I do really like that shower. Is yours bigger?"

Jesus. Christ. She is fucking with me like a cat playing with its prey.

"You're welcome to come use it and see," I say, trying to not sound too desperate, but more like my usual, confident self. If I'm going to have any shot with her, I need to get out of my own head.

She lets out a dismissive hum. "No, it's late. I'm sure you're tired. I think I'll stay here and get in the shower."

Before I realize what's happening, I watch as she holds her phone in the crook of her neck, stretching her arms out to lift her cami up and over her head. She never looks away from the studio window, telling me she knows full well that I'm watching.

My eyes rake over her, taking in the sight. Even from this far away, I can see the clear dip of her waist, how full her tits are, and those beautiful tattoos running down her body.

I already know this image will be burned into my psyche, just like that time at the river, for as long as I live.

Unlike that time though, this feels different. That time, I hardly knew her. She caught me completely by surprise. She was just being her goofy, shameless self, clearly indifferent to my presence on the river with her.

This time, she damn well knows what she's doing to me.

"Rainbow." My voice drops low and I can hear my own desperation in it. I want to say more, but the pathways between my brain and mouth stop functioning, probably having something to do with the amount of blood rushing to my cock.

Suddenly, my normally comfortable joggers feel far too restrictive. Actually, everything feels too restrictive. The one very clear thought that runs through my mind is that I wish there weren't two panes of glass and fifty feet of patio between us. But my legs freeze and I stand there, just admiring her, not knowing what I should do.

I hear a long sigh come through the phone that borders on a moan.

"It's too bad you can't get your shit together, Tommy," she sounds breathy and flirty and lingers on my name, the one I don't let anyone call me except her, "because I know what I want and I don't mind giving it to myself."

I'm not sure what she means until I watch helplessly, with what might as well be an ocean between us, when she slides a hand down into her sleep shorts. "Tell me. Do you think you'll figure out what you want soon?"

"Fuck. Rainbow," I say, pressing a palm against the window, grinding my pulsing erection against the glass through my joggers, desperately needing any friction. "I'm trying. I told you, it's not that simple."

Well, that's a half-truth. For my painfully throbbing cock, it's extremely simple right now.

"I wish you could make it simple," she says between labored breaths.

The sound of her breathing sends chills through me, heightening every little feeling in my body. I run my hand over the front of my pants, grinding my palm against my dick, only making my need for her even worse. Shit, I'd settle for making out and dry humping on the couch right now if she'd let me. I'd probably come just from that judging by the precum I can already feel through my joggers.

"I want you. I mean it. Yes. I fucking want you." Finally, my brain starts to function and get on the same page as my heart and the rest of my body.

She hums again before I hear her whimper. "Good, that's what I wanted to hear to help me unwind."

"Do you want me to come over?" I ask, suddenly regaining enough of my brain power to form a sentence, still pressing myself against the window, reveling in her stunning, unrestrained lust and confidence.

"No, I don't think you can come fast enough," she says, her

breaths getting louder and shorter. I strain to get a closer look at her in the window and I see the quickening, movements of her wrist at the waistband of her shorts.

Holy. Fucking. Shit.

"Are you fingering yourself, in my guesthouse, for me to watch?" I ask, but I already know the answer.

Even from here in my studio, from fifty feet away, I can see the wide grin on her face, matching the laugh that comes through the phone. "I already told you. I knew what I wanted and I'm going to give it to myself."

She has made her point. She's perfectly fine without me if I can't make up my own damn mind.

"Now say it again."

This time, I don't hesitate.

"I want you. I'm tired of trying to dance around it. We can talk about it, we can figure out what this looks like, but all I know is I need you." The confession pours out of me and for the first time in weeks, I feel a weight lifted off my shoulders. That doesn't stop the tension in my body, the need for release growing to an impossibly frustrating, urgent level. I squeeze my thighs together, craving that pressure on my tight balls — I'm going to take care of as soon as I can get to my own shower.

I stop and watch as she drops the phone from her ear and her eyes shut. I can see her body shutter as she finds her release, collapsing against the window and throwing her head back.

"Tommy." My name is one long, breathy moan.

My cock is so fucking hard it's painful and I grind myself against the glass, desperately wishing she was breathing my name against me. Her words, that friction, the sight of her making herself come from hearing that I need her, it's all too much. I need more. I need—

No. No fucking way.

I feel my body uncoil, coming so hard in my joggers I drop the phone, bracing myself against the window.

"Fuck!" I can't control myself around her. I can't think straight. I can't keep my cock from getting hard. I can't even keep myself from coming like a horny teenage boy. As much as I want things to be simple with her from now on, I'm back to wondering if that's possible.

I quickly collect myself and grab my phone, hoping she didn't hear me or worse, see that I just blew in my damn pants. Hopefully she was too busy coming down from her own release to notice that.

Putting the phone back to my ear, I look across the patio and spot her in the window. She's sitting on the floor, her back to me. Her long, color streaked hair hangs over her shoulders, blending into the colors of the floral tattoo running down her side and over her shoulder. "Thanks for that. I needed it." Her voice is content and relaxed. "I think I'm going to go get that shower and clean up now."

"Have fun," I say, trying not to sound out of breath, enjoying the view of her with her back to me. "And I meant it, we'll talk about whatever this is."

Somehow, admitting that there's a *this* between us feels like another important weight off my shoulders.

She lets out a cute little giggle and I can see her shoulders rise and fall. I can't make myself look away from her, admiring every little beautiful detail. "We'll see. I already had plenty of fun, but talking sounds good."

This time, I'm the one huffing out a low, gruff laugh. "Night, Rainbow. See you tomorrow."

"See you later, Boss," she teases, before standing and walking away from the window. I shamelessly enjoy the view of the curves of her ass hanging out of those skimpy shorts and how her long hair hangs just above the small of her back.

This fucking woman. She owns me.

She owns me and she doesn't even realize just how much she does.

SOMEHOW, I can't make a decision again. It seems to be a recurring theme for me lately. I spent the morning at the gym downtown trying to burn off some pent up energy and work on my clearly lacking stamina. Now, I'm sitting in the locker room staring at my phone.

Should I call her? Should I text her? I said we can talk and she said that'd be good, but is that coming on too strong? I tried to find her this morning, but her van was gone before the sun came up. If I had to guess, she's probably out skiing. Either way, I have no fucking clue how to talk to a woman now, much less a wild one like Grace.

With one hand, I run my fingers through my damp hair, and in my other, my thumb hovers over her contact info when my phone buzzes.

My pulse quickens, hoping it's her and she made my decision for me, but that hope quickly fades when I see my brother's name scroll across the screen.

I click answer and bring it to my ear. "Yes?"

A single laugh comes through the phone. "Is that how you greet your favorite brother?"

I shake my head, a grin spreading across my face. "My only brother, so my favorite and least favorite. What's up?"

"Not too much. I was taking care of sending out the last of the donations to the organizations Grace recommended," he says matter of factly.

A moment passes, but he doesn't say anything else so I guess

I'm doing the conversational lifting on this call that he started. "So why are you calling me?"

"Did you know we used to give to Wasatch Wishes?" he asks bluntly.

It takes a second for my brain to register that name as the organization Grace used to work for.

"No, I didn't. And what do you mean used to?" I emphasize those last two words, my tone taking on a serious note. "When did we stop? Why did we stop?" My mind races, wondering why he's asking this and if we screwed something up.

"Woah. Slow down there, bud. I don't think it's a huge deal, but if you want to look into it, Grace has everything you'll need."

"No," I cut him off. "Just send everything to me. Is that it?"

"Yeah, that's it. I'll send it right over. You alright? You sound a little out of it."

I sigh and palm my face before grabbing my shirt from my gym bag. "I'm fine. Just finishing up at the gym and didn't get much sleep last night. I'll be fine when I see you at the party this week though. Don't worry."

"Good," he says, his tone more upbeat, "I just wanted to make sure you hadn't changed your mind and planned to bail at the last minute."

"Great. I need to get back to the house. See you soon."

I hear him laughing on the other end when I hang up and put my phone away. Maybe some time back in Seattle will be good for me. Jake always seems to ground me and that's just what I need right now. I do need to talk to Grace, possibly about more than just whatever is going on between us. But that can wait until she gets back to the house.

CHAPTER 21
GRACE
BACKCOUNTRY BUNNI

"ARE YOU OK BACK THERE?" Josie calls over her shoulder, hiking up the steep trail toward Cody Peak — just outside the ski resort in Jackson.

"Yeah," I bark out from behind her, always surprised at the pace she keeps with her short legs while hiking with a full ski pack on her back. Going uphill on skis, even with climbing skins covering the bottoms, is always exhausting. "Just a little tired. Didn't get much sleep. Stop at that outcropping ahead. That's the end of our trail."

I should be much more rested and I'm glad this hike is almost over. I got a nice relaxing shower and slept in my warm bed, all after hearing TJ finally confess that he wants me. His confession was enough to make myself come so hard I needed to catch my breath on the cool tile floor of the guesthouse. Something about hearing him panting into the phone, already knowing how his breath feels like on my skin, completely undid me.

So even after all of that, I still woke up restless and needing to blow off steam. This hike with Josie is exactly what I needed, even if my body is saying otherwise. I've made this hike countless times over the years, starting as a teen with my family. Our parents, but especially Mom, always loved teaching us the finer points of backcountry skiing. It was her way of teaching us to connect to nature and know how much joy it can bring, but also how insignificant we are in comparison to these timeless mountains and Mother Nature. She made sure we were always prepared: having our hike up mapped out, our ski path planned to get down the mountain safely, knowing the snow conditions and avalanche risk and making sure we had our safety gear. We learned to always have a buddy in case anything bad happened, close but not too close though. Staying spread apart in case of an avalanche meant there might be someone there to help dig you out to save your life.

Even though they taught all of us, it was still my special thing to do with Mom. Tanner was always into extreme skiing on big cliffs and crazy runs. Clay was qualifying for the Olympics, training with Dad and then the Jensen family. Mom and I though, we spent so many mornings hiking up at dawn, catching our breath at the summit, then skiing completely fresh lines down the mountains, untracked by anyone else. *Earn your turns* as she would say. Sure we could ski in the resort and take a chairlift up, but this is just different. Even after we moved to Utah, we kept doing it in the Wasatch Mountains, bonding over exploring a place new to both of us.

Yes, backcountry skiing has always been therapeutic. And today, I want to make sure my head is clear before I talk to TJ after last night. Not that Josie is going to be any help with that. She's keeping a pace up that has my heart pounding in my chest so hard I can feel it against the straps of my avalanche beacon under my jacket.

Finally reaching the crest of the trail, I take the moment to shed my pack, sit down in the snow and take a long gulp from my hydration pack. From here, I can see the entire Jackson Hole valley below us. The town, the ski village, I can even make out my brother's cabin — every place I've known for years. Somehow, I find myself looking down into the woods on the outskirts of the ski resort village, looking for a certain rockstar's house, wondering what he's doing right now.

"You're dragging ass today." Josie's voice breaks the nice, quiet moment. "Normally you're the one kicking my butt on the trail. You alright?"

I take another long gulp of water and smack my lips. "Totally fine," I say way too enthusiastically, hiding my very unfamiliar nerves about talking to TJ tonight. Am I going to get confident, decisive TJ finally? Or was last night just a fluke, never to happen again, and he's going to go back to being too scared to explore whatever chemistry is clearly there between us?

I look over to catch Josie eyeing me skeptically. "So how's Hot Boss?"

"He's good," I say and I hear the pitch of my voice go up. "Or at least he seems like it."

"He's good?" Clearly, Josie heard my voice go up too, judging from her knowing grin. "How *good* is he?"

I roll my eyes at her, but can't fight the matching grin growing on my face.

Her eyes widen at my reaction. "Spill!"

"I don't know." I look up at the sky and squint. "We kissed a few days ago." I don't know if I should tell Josie about last night because she'll be like a dog with a bone, but I need to get this off my chest and maybe she can help me make sense of it.

Yep. Screw it. "But then we sort of had phone sex last night? My knee buckling orgasm was definitely real though."

A shiver runs through my body just thinking about it again and every thought in my brain is replaced by one driving need. I want to see him, preferably sooner than later.

Josie laughs, bringing my attention back to her. "Girl, again, only you could find yourself in that situation with someone like him. So are you two, like, just hooking up or?"

"I don't know. It's not that simple," I say, borrowing TJ's words and shrugging. "We have this weird chemistry and I want to give into it and see where it goes. Let the universe take the wheel." A nervous laugh escapes me. "I was hoping to talk more with him tonight. That's where we left things. So yeah, I think that's it for now?"

Josie nods and hums to herself. "Well, I will make myself scarce tonight. I'll see what Collin and Walker are up to."

I smile back at my best friend, knowing she's always looking out for me. Not that she'd really be in the way if she came and parked and camped next to my van in TJ's driveway tonight like she has been, but I appreciate her wanting me to get TJ alone. "You're the best. That would be perfect."

She turns away, looking back over the scenic valley.

"This would be a great spot to film some content. Talk about a view."

I burst out laughing, feeling much less anxious. "Are you serious right now?"

She looks back at me, shrugs, and winks. "Don't act surprised. Backcountry Bunni never sleeps." She waggles her brows suggestively. "That's why I'm a top content creator."

She has a point. I can't argue with her success.

"Seems a bit chilly though, even for you," I say, watching my breath float through the freezing air, as snow flurries around us. I might love the cold, fresh air on my skin, heightening all my senses, making my skin tingle, but I know that's not for everyone.

She just laughs, reaching down to put her ski pack back on. I know that's her cue that she's ready to go back down to the trail-head. "Come on, let's get going. If we leave now, we'll have time to hike back up and get another run in." She looks over her shoulder at me smirking. "Don't worry, I'll make sure you're back to TJ soon enough."

PULLING UP TO THE GUESTHOUSE, I throw my van in park and hop out of the driver's side. When my feet hit the snowy driveway, my legs wobble and my muscles ache. When Josie suggested we get a second run in, I was all for it until halfway through the hike back up the mountain. My eyes were definitely bigger than my stomach, or I guess legs. Whatever. Either way, I'm beat.

I throw my tote bag with a change of clothes over my shoulder, ready to head inside the guesthouse for a luxurious shower that I have to admit I'm getting very used to. As comfy as my sweats and hoodie I threw on after skiing are, I'm dying to change out of them and relax.

I stop at the charging pedestal to plug my van in for the night. When I flip open the outlet cover, a familiar little bit of paper falls out and flutters down into the snow. I grab it and read the handwriting I'd now know anywhere.

> I'll be in the hot tub if you want to hang and talk.

That sounds just as good as a shower, even better if he's there.

I make my way down the evergreen shrub lined path, past the guesthouse, to the patio separating it from the main house. Sure enough, TJ is there, sitting chest deep in the bubbling hot tub that's sunken down into the stone patio. He has his back to me, looking out toward the sun setting behind the mountains.

His arms are stretched over the sides of the hot tub along the patio, the water dripping off of them highlighting each dip and ridge of muscle. I find myself ignoring the beautiful sunset in favor of this.

I reach out to the shrub beside me, grabbing a fistful of snow, and balling it up. If he doesn't know I'm here yet, he's about to.

I rear back and send the ball of snow at him, satisfied with the direct hit into his broad back that sends a puff of snow into the air.

"You know you didn't sneak up on me, right? I heard you walking down the path. You're losing your touch," he groans, running his fingers through his hair and looking over his shoulder. "Take it you found my note."

I step toward him and set my bag down on a nearby patio chair. Standing over him, I look down to see him smiling back up at me, his piercing, deep blue eyes meeting mine.

Now that's a view I like.

"Hi." My voice comes out as a high pitched, mousy squeak. Really, Grace? Now's when you lose your confidence? You've been thinking about seeing this man all day and 'hi' is all you come up with?

He snorts a laugh and I know I would blush now if my cheeks weren't already red from the frosty air. "Hop in. The water's great," he says, tipping his beer to me.

"That's why I came over here, dumb dumb. My legs are spent after skiing with Josie. I've thought about this all day." I've thought about him all day too, but that's not exactly new.

I brace myself with one hand on the back of the patio chair, kicking off my shoes and shuffling out of my socks.

He gives me a quizzical look. "Oh. Did you change in your van already? I didn't see you go in the guesthouse."

I reach down, pulling my hoodie up and over my head, revealing my sports bra.

His eyes flare while he watches me undress. "No, wait," he

says, raising his hand to object, "that's not what I meant." I loop my fingers into the waistband of my sweats and drop them to the ground, leaving me in just my tight boy shorts.

I step right over him, plucking his beer out of his hand, and lowering myself into the steaming water, sitting right next to him. We're shoulder to shoulder and our thighs press against each other under the water.

"I hope you have more of these," I say, taking a pull from his beer.

He rolls his eyes and his low laugh makes his shoulders shake. "I don't know why I'm ever surprised by you. You know you could have thrown a swimsuit on first? It's not like I was going to leave before you came back."

"What? Are you complaining about what I'm wearing?" I relax into the water, desperate to soothe my aching muscles and joints. I arch my back and roll my shoulders, trying to stretch out. The motion pops my breasts out of the water and I notice the way his eyes drift down. "I can still go in and change. Or maybe I could just take this off."

I run a finger under the strap of my bra, inching it down my shoulder. His eyes track the movement and I see his pupils darken. "It's not like you haven't seen me topless before."

I watch as he looks up with lust in his eyes as a crimson flush creeps across his cheeks. He shakes his head slowly.

"I couldn't care less what you're wearing. I just want you around me, all the time," he says, blunt and matter of factly. The way his eyes comb over me only heats my body more, even in the hot water. He turns, reaching toward a small metal bucket on the edge of the hot tub. The motion shows off the toned muscles of his back, his wet hair clinging to the nape of his neck. Somehow he looks even better like this than in the gym, satisfying my goldilocks needs: not too muscular, not too lean, just right. He pulls another beer from the ice bucket and twists off the top, tipping it at me. "And we have plenty of beer."

He takes a long swig from the bottle before setting it on the edge of the patio and hot tub. I look around us, noticing the snowflakes melting as soon as they hit the steaming stones. "Heated concrete? Nice touch."

He shrugs. "It's not a long walk from the house to here, but it's nice not having to clear it all the time. Paying your brother to plow my driveway is one thing, but I don't want him out here with a snowblower or shovel all the time. So, how was your day skiing?"

I raise a brow, clasping my beer in both hands in front of me just above the bubbling water lapping at my chest. "I know you said we could talk, but you really want to know how my day was?"

He leans toward me and I see that look of conviction in his eyes. His gaze makes my pulse quicken and my hands fidget with the peeling label of the beer bottle.

"I want to learn every little thing about you." His voice is low and commanding, leaving no doubt that he intends to do just that.

I take a sip of my beer, drumming my fingertips along the neck of the bottle. "Well, you know I have no problem over-sharing."

I stretch out more, pressing my thigh against his. He sucks in a breath through his teeth and looks down into the water where our legs are touching. I reach out, running my fingertips over his shoulder to play with the strands of hair hanging over his ear and I can feel his pulse pounding in his neck.

His eyes flick back to mine. "Grace, I need to know you want this. I need to know—"

I lower my hand, pressing it to his chest. "Stop. I already told you, I can handle myself. I know what I want and I know my limits. Don't give me those weak *'I'm your boss'* or *'I'm friends with your brothers'* or *'you're too young'* excuses."

He swallows and nods slowly. "If you're sure—"

I cut him off again. "I'm not the one you need to be worried about. It's you I'm worried about. I need to know you're *sure* because I'm not going to waste time on a boy who can't make up his mind. I am interested in a man that knows what he wants."

His nostrils flare and he grins at me. "So I guess there's no one back home in Park City then, is there?"

"Nope, hopelessly single," I say, watching his grin grow wider. "What about you? No girlfriend at any of your houses all over the country?"

He shakes his head. "I've been holding out for someone that caught my eye months ago. So yes, I'm sure."

That admission sends a spark down my spine to my achingly needy core. I can practically feel the tension between us about to snap.

"Good," I say breathily, running my other hand through his hair, "now do what you've been dying to."

He gives me a confused look.

I groan and roll my eyes. "Do I have to spell it out for you again?"

I reach down with both hands, peeling my wet sports bra off and over my head, flinging it behind me. I turn and throw my leg over him so I'm straddling his lap. He looks up at me in stunned disbelief. His eyes dart between my bare chest and my lips, before locking back on my eyes. I wrap my arms around his neck, smirking down at him, watching his chest heave with each breath.

"You are never short on surprises," he says, his eyes still locked on mine.

"Maybe you need to stop being surprised that I'm into you." I lean forward, bringing my lips to his ear, breathing in that bergamot scent. "Now just kiss me already, Tommy."

This time, he doesn't hesitate.

He palms my waist with one hand and my skin tingles at the touch of his strong, calloused hand on my side. His other hand cups the nape of my neck, bringing our mouths together in a hot, longing kiss. This one is even more electric than the first, his tongue already deep in my mouth, gliding over mine. His hand slides up over my ribs, his fingertips leaving a trail of goosebumps along the way.

I lace my fingers into his shaggy hair and I pull our bodies closer, feeling my nipples drag over his hard chest, sending another jolt of electricity through me.

I break the kiss, both of us panting to catch our breath. Our eyes meet and I can see the hunger consuming him, completely laid bare.

I lean back, pressing myself into his hard erection under me. The friction against my throbbing clit through my shorts isn't enough and just has me needing more. He groans and his eyes drop to my chest and a little laugh escapes my lips.

"Play with them. I know you want to," I say, smirking at him.

He looks back up at me with a feral grin. "You have no fucking idea."

His lips find mine again while he cups one of my breasts in his hand. I whimper into his mouth when he rolls the tight bud between his thumb and fingertips, putting pressure on my piercing. His tongue plunges into my mouth, our tongues stroking and flicking each others. His other hand firmly grasps the curve of my ass, his fingers dancing along the hem of my underwear. I feel the snow falling down around us hitting my exposed back, bringing my nerves to a fever pitch. Every single thing is stimulating me right now.

And I still need more.

I spread my legs open, grinding myself down against his hard length, back and forth, building that tension even higher.

He presses his forehead to mine, letting out a moan. "Fuck, Rainbow. You're going to make me come in my pants again."

"Again?" I ask, my eyes whipping up to meet his. Did he just say that? He must see the question in my eyes.

"Last night, on the phone. I meant it. I want you," he says, pushing his cock against me, giving both of us another jolt of pleasure. His eyes roll back into his head and he lets out a ragged breath.

I reach down between us, dipping my fingers into the waistband of his shorts. "I think your dick and I are on the same page."

He lets out a huff of laughter, but grabs my wrist, stopping me from going further. I look up at him, alarm flashing across my face. He shakes his head, but smirks at me.

"Believe me, I want nothing more than to be buried in you right now." I graze the tip of his hard cock with my nails, prompting him to close his eyes and shudder. He takes a deep breath, pulling his gaze from my hand between us and meets my eyes again. "But the first time I fuck you isn't going to be in a hot tub."

My shoulders sag and I let out a long, desperate sigh, my head dropping into the crook of his neck. I nuzzle into him, whispering into his ear. "Fine, but I need more than this right now."

He chuckles to himself and I pull back to see him wearing that same feral grin. "Don't worry. I'm going to take care of you."

To my surprise, he grips my ass in his big, strong hands, and turns me around in his lap so I'm facing away from him. "Now take these off for me."

I look back over my shoulder, enjoying the way his eyes are fixed on me. "Sure thing, Boss."

Slowly, I slide my shorts down and set them on the side of the hot tub. His eyes stay transfixed on me, tracing the long floral tattoo running down from my shoulder, over my ribs, and to my waist.

"Fuck, you're beautiful," he pants, his voice low and raspy.

His words and the way his eyes take me in only stokes the fire in my core. I reward him, sitting back down in his lap with my back to him, swiveling my hips, pressing my throbbing clit and pussy against his erection. Leaning back into his chest, he reaches around me, cupping my breasts, his fingertips toying with my piercings. He kisses my shoulder, then my neck, and finally that perfect spot just below my ear. I feel his warm exhale when his lips part.

"Now you said something about a long day and being sore. I think we need to fix that."

I feel him shift under me and I watch over my shoulder as he grabs a fluffy towel and unfolds it on the edge of the tile behind him.

I give him a quizzical look and he tilts his head toward the towel with a hungry grin. "Now get your pretty ass up there."

I stand up in the waist deep water, turning to face him. His long, lean arms are outstretched. He looks like a damn king leaning back, comfortable but in charge. I extend a finger toward the towel, giving him a coy look. "You want me on that towel?"

He nods, his eyes darkening. "Lay back, relax, and let me eat that pussy. I want to look in your eyes when you come this time."

My heart jumps and my pussy clenches. This is the decisive commanding man I wanted to see and now that he's focused that energy on me — it's exhilarating. I step toward him, and he cups my ass and looks up at me, nodding. "Please."

"I like where your head's at, but my legs aren't that sore," I say.

He looks at the towel over his shoulder and back at me, raising that pierced eyebrow that I find so hot. "Then what do you have in mind?"

I step toward him, pushing him further back against the side of hot tub until he's leaning back and resting his head on the towel behind him. He looks up at me and this time, I nod at him.

"I want to show you what I was thinking about last night." I step up and out of the hot tub, lifting myself over him. He licks his lips while his eyes track every little movement with lustful anticipation. The crisp, cool night air instantly makes my skin chill like one of my cold plunges after a workout and I savor the feeling.

I place a knee on either side of his head on the towel. Kneeling over his face, I look down at him and lower myself onto his mouth like he's my own personal saddle. "Now let me ride your face."

He grabs my hips, stopping me before I sit all the way down.

"Rainbow." His voice is low and raspy. I look down at him between my thighs to find his blue eyes smoldering.

I smirk at him, raising my eyebrows. "See something you like?"

"You could say that. Fuck," he says, planting a kiss on my sensitive inner thigh. "Always full of surprises."

"Didn't know about that one, did you?" I tease.

"Nope." He laughs against my wet heat, slowly tracing my hip bones with his thumbs. "Now, sit. None of that hovering shit."

His fingers curl around my waist and he pulls me down against his mouth. He wastes no time finding my swollen clit, gliding his tongue up and down before flicking over my hood piercing. That little touch lights the fire in me that he's been building. I moan, squeezing my legs together, feeling the stubble of his cheeks against my inner thighs.

He hums in amusement and the sound vibrates against my clit piercing. I look down to see his face between my legs, him looking up at me in awe. His tongue stops for a second, leaving me aching for more when he plants another kiss on my inner thigh. "That's right, baby. Give those gorgeous, long legs a rest and sit that ass down. I want you riding my fucking face until you come. Fuck my face with your drenched pussy as hard as you need. I'm never going to stop thinking about how your wet cunt tastes."

I reach down, running my fingers through his hair, tightly grabbing the shaggy, wet locks, grinning back at him. This is what I was hoping was hiding behind that laid-back exterior. "Then you better get back to work, Tommy," I say, blowing him an air kiss.

And that's what he does. His lips curl into a wicked smile and his dimple pops before his tongue laps at my clit, teasing my sensitive bud. Each stroke flicks my piercing, already pushing me dangerously close to coming undone. I watch his eyes drift to my breasts, the cold air chilling my piercings and hardening my nipples into tight peaks. Reaching down, I lift one of his hands and place it over my breast. His fingers find the metal barbell and he moans against me, taking me that much closer to the avalanche of pleasure I know is coming.

I hold onto his hair, my nails grazing his scalp, rocking my hips with the rhythm of his tongue. He opens his mouth wider, humming his approval against my pussy when his tongue spears me. I gasp at the welcome intrusion and clench my thighs around his head. His tongue pulls back and his deep voice rumbles against my heated skin. "So fucking beautiful. Keep chasing it. We're going to get you there."

I smile back, nodding breathlessly. His tongue finds my clit again, this time with more pressure, flicking faster. With just a few strokes, I'm barreling toward the orgasm of my life.

This is definitely a man, not a boy.

He runs his other hand from my hip to my back, his worn calluses igniting every nerve ending on my exposed skin. I arch into his touch, feeling his hand on the small of my back and the warm steam rising from the hot tub behind me. The contrast with the cool air against my pebbled nipples is glorious. The snow still falls around us, melting on my heated skin, adding to the stimulation.

And then there's him, the man between my legs worshipping my body. His eyes, the intensity, the calm confidence in them, peering back up at me.

It's all perfect.

I finally combust, giving into the overwhelming flurry of sensations, coming apart on his face. I close my eyes, throwing my head back, crying out into the cold night air.

I LOOK up at the hottest, sexiest sight in my life. Watching Grace come, pulling my hair, nearly made me blow my load in my swim trunks without even touching my cock. Apparently she just has that effect on me. I've had crowds of thousands of people scream my name before, but the sound of her calling my name out into the night is something that's going to play on repeat in my mind for the rest of my days.

She takes her time coming down from her high, still sitting on top of me but loosening her grip on my hair and resting her palms on her thighs. Her chest still rises and falls heavily with each breath, a pink flush spread across her tits. Her dazzling emerald eyes finally drop to mine, lazy and drunk from her orgasm. I would give anything to make her look that sated over and over. She grins at me and ruffles my hair. "That was fun."

A laugh erupts from my chest, shaking her on top of me. "You were right."

She cocks her head and smirks down at me. "I'm normally right, but humor me. What was it this time?"

I swipe the tip of my tongue back across her still swollen clit and that fucking piercing, making her thighs squeeze my head again. I didn't know it was there and I'm already fucking obsessed with it. I want to taste it on my tongue every day now. "Having you ride my face was more fun."

She grins, and then climbs off me, sitting on the edge of the hot tub. I watch as she grabs her boy shorts, slowly sliding them up her long legs and shimmying them back on. Reaching over, I wrap my arm around her waist, my fingers again finding the hemline of those shorts, ghosting her thighs. "Get back in here. I seem to remember we wanted to talk?"

She laughs before lowering herself down into the water, sitting right against me. I drape my arm over her shoulders, pulling her tighter against me. An impossibly cute whimper escapes her lips when she rests her head on my shoulder. "Talking is good, but this is nice too."

I plant a kiss on top of her damp head, twirling a strand of purple and orange streaked hair in my fingers. I have met lots of people in my life, but no one has ever captivated me like the woman in my arms, endlessly full of life and freewill. I know one thing, that I never want to let go.

She plants a kiss to my neck, sending chills down my spine again. "I like you."

I chuckle, looking down at her — still topless and sexy as hell — tucked into me. She's radiating confidence, but somehow equally peaceful. "I like you too. I'm just," I hesitate, searching for the right words, something I've never had a problem with before her, "I don't know if I'm good at dating or whatever it is you want."

She lifts her chin, resting it on my shoulder looking at me curiously. "You don't know if you're good at relationships? Well, if it helps, you're clearly good at the intimacy part because the way you made me come—" she trails off, giving me a knowing, flirty look.

"Well, that's an ego boost, but that's not what I meant," I say, snorting a laugh. I reach out with my other hand, tilting her chin up so we're eye to eye. "I mean I don't know because I've never been in a real relationship, Grace. Or at least one worth thinking about. I put my career ahead of everything else for years, decades even. I don't want to let you down because you're special. I just want to give you what you want, whether that's just more orgasms or being with me or both."

I lean in, kissing her soft lips, feeling them part at my touch. Pressing my forehead to hers, I feel her breath on my cheek and I inhale her lavender scent I've become addicted to.

"Preferably both though," I rasp.

She laughs and pulls back, eyeing me for a moment. I watch her gaze shamelessly roaming over my body.

"Let's keep this simple," she says, her lips curling into a wide, amused smile. I take her in, loving how her eyes sparkle in the evening light, reflecting the steamy water, and how her freckled cheeks are still flushed from coming on my face. She is always so wild, practically glowing. "You kept saying it's not that simple before. I told you, I don't care about all of those excuses you could list about why this is a bad idea and I meant it. None of that matters to me. What does matter is that you and I clearly enjoy whatever this is between us. Because at the end of the day, that's what this is about — you and me. So I'll make it easy for you. Just be the decisive man I think you are, because I'm not looking for a boy."

"You think I'm decisive? Because I've been anything but that when it comes to you," I reply, still amazed at her confidence and outlook on life.

She leans into me, resting her head on my shoulder again and placing one of her hands on my chest, over my pounding heart. Her fingers curl into my chest hair, making my pulse quicken again.

"Some people might think you're impulsive, but I think you know what you want. We both seem to have a knack for going with the flow and doing what feels good. So I say let's stick with that. Stop ignoring that we both want this, whatever *this* ends up looking like, and just see what happens. Let the universe and our hearts guide us."

I nod, watching her twirl some of my chest hair in her fingers. "So what, is this a situationship?"

She laughs softly. "I don't care what we call it. I'm not seeing anyone else and don't plan on it, only you."

I hum to myself, rubbing the back of her shoulder, my fingers tracing the scar underneath her bright tattoos.

"Wait," she looks up at me, "you know what a situationship is? Aren't you too old to get that reference?"

I roll my eyes and playfully glare at her. "I'm forty-two and have social media. I know what a situationship is. Seriously, you're going to have to come up with some better old man jokes. And also, that's fine with me."

"What's fine with you?" she says, still looking up at me.

"Just seeing where this goes, and not seeing anyone else." I feel the corners of my mouth lift, and I give in, letting the smile take over. I can think of nothing I want more than getting to be in her orbit and knowing she wants me there.

She lifts her chin off my shoulder, planting a quick kiss on my lips. "Good." To my pleasant surprise, she climbs into my lap, facing away from me to enjoy the view of the night sky over the mountains. She settles back against me and I wrap my arms around her waist, holding her exactly where I want her.

We sit there for a moment in perfect, peaceful silence, the only sounds coming from the rippling water and the gentle breeze rustling the treetops.

"Do I really make you nervous?"

I lean down and press a kiss to her neck. "Why do you think I'm nervous?"

"I can feel your heart pounding in your chest against my back."

"Yes." I wrap my arms tighter around her waist, holding her closer to me. "You make me feel a lot of things, Rainbow. A lot of things I haven't felt in a long time and some things I've never felt before."

She lets out a long, contented sigh and relaxes against my chest, resting her arms on top of mine. I watch the snowflakes falling onto her hair and all I can think is that I could spend a thousand nights like this and still need a thousand more.

She shifts in my lap and looks over her shoulder at me. "Hey, are you expecting company?"

"No, why?"

Her head turns toward the driveway and I see the light coming from in front of my house, shining toward the guesthouse, and getting closer.

She looks back at me again and I can see the alarm in her eyes. "So you have no idea who that could be?"

"There are only three other people besides you and me who have the gate code. Josie, Sutton, and Tanner."

"Well it's not Josie. She's hanging out with Collin and Walker tonight and staying at their place."

I nod, my pulse quickening again. "And it's not Sutton. He'll still be at Gloria's. They're always slammed on Saturday nights."

"It can't be Tanner," she says. "They're still on their—" she stops mid-sentence.

"Grace?" She turns back to me and I see the panic in her eyes.

"What day did you say it is?" she asks with a nervous smile.

"Saturday. Why?"

"They were supposed to get back from their honeymoon today. And it's snowing. A lot."

Realization of what she's saying finally sets in. Tanner, her brother and my property manager, is driving his snow plow down my driveway right now, probably to salt it to get ahead of the snow coming overnight.

And I have his baby sister in my lap in my hot tub with no top on.

Fuck.

I lift her out of my lap and jump up to look around us, searching the water and the sides of the hot tub frantically.

"What are you looking for?" she asks, watching me do circles around the waist deep water.

"Where's your top?"

"Oh. Yeah. That. We might have a small problem there."

I turn to see her grinning, trying to contain a laugh. "Define small."

She snorts, covering her mouth and then pointing over my shoulder. I turn and look, spotting her sports bra hanging from the branch of a small pine tree behind the patio chairs.

I groan and scrub my hand over my face. That's not ideal. "You flung it that far?"

Looking back at her, she snorts again and shrugs. "I was really excited and didn't think anyone would be coming."

For a second, that actually makes me feel better that she was that excited to take her top off for me. But the sound of a door shutting and footsteps on the walking path grabs both of our attention and quickly erases that sentiment.

Pulling at my hair, I finally spot my t-shirt sitting by her bag. I grab it and toss it to her. "Just wear this."

She catches it, pulling it over her head and sitting back down in the water on the other side of the hot tub, just before Tanner turns the corner and spots us.

I tip my chin to him but before I can speak, Grace chimes in from across the hot tub.

"Did you really ditch your new wife the second you got home to go work?" She kicks one of her feet up, splashing water toward her brother.

He shakes his head, walking around the hot tub toward the patio table. He stops and leans against the back of one of the chairs.

"No. Your friend is a bad influence on Collin. He drank too much and couldn't get out and plow tonight. Believe me, I'd rather be home with Ronni instead of out here in the cold," he says, tossing his head back groaning. "Not all of us are crazy like you with your cold plunges."

He turns his attention to me. "Didn't expect you to be around, TJ. Figured you'd be hounding Sutton for dinner or something. Anyway, I just wanted to make sure your driveway was good for tomorrow. The salt should give me a solid head start when I'm back to plow in the morning and keep it from getting too icy overnight."

I nod, feeling my heartbeat slow down to an almost normal rate. That is until he takes a step to the side and I see the bra hanging from the branch just a few feet behind his head.

"Perfect. Thanks as always."

He nods. "No problem. Well, I should probably get back to Ronni. You were my last stop on my way back to the cabin."

"Yeah, don't let us keep you," I say with a laugh.

He takes a few steps back toward the walking path to the driveway and his truck, not noticing his sister's bra in the tree.

"Hey, what are you doing out anyway?" he says, stopping and turning to face Grace. "I saw your van and the patio lights on and that's why I came back in the first place."

To her credit, she just shrugs nonchalantly. "I was out hiking and skiing all day with Josie. TJ said I could always use his hot tub if I wanted. I stopped by for a dip and he was already out here, so just hanging and talking about work."

He looks at me for a second before looking back at his sister, seeming to accept her answer which is mostly true.

"Well, be nice to him," he says, pointing a finger at her. "He's been more than generous to all of us."

She rolls her eyes at him. "Yeah, I know. Now get out of here. Tell V 'hi' from me too."

He nods and I see his expression harden. "Speaking of V, we were thinking you could come stay at the cabin. You could take our guest room or park your van out by the barn like you used to if you want."

I turn to see Grace's eyes narrow and I see a flicker of irritation in them. "Thanks. I'll keep that in mind. Now seriously, get home to your new wife." She makes a shooing gesture toward him.

He laughs and starts to head down the path back to his truck before calling back over his shoulder. "See you later, guys."

Once I hear the door to his truck shut and the engine start, I look at Grace who looks like she's about to burst with laughter.

"I'm glad you found that so amusing." I cup my hand and splash her with a fistful of water, but she doesn't flinch and just keeps laughing. I could listen to that sound on repeat all day.

"Seriously. He might look big and scary, but he's a big softy. You don't have anything to worry about." Her eyes soften and she lifts a hand, curling a finger at me.

"Maybe, but I'd rather not take any chances." I wade over to her and sit down next to her. "Also what was with that look you gave him? You looked irritated."

She groans and shakes her head. "Just him being overly protective as usual. Nothing new."

I sense the irritation in her voice and decide to not push that topic. "On that note, do you want to tell him about us or just keep it between us for now? To be clear, I'm perfectly fine if you want to tell anyone. I just don't want to make anything messy for you. There are strings attached to being with someone like me."

The last thing I want to do is drag her into the spotlight that still haunts me every now and then. If she doesn't want that, I will do whatever it takes to keep it away from her. As far as I'm concerned though, the entire world could know I'm into her and it wouldn't bother me for one second.

She hums and wobbles her head. "We said let's keep it simple. So maybe let's give it a beat before we tell anyone else?"

I wrap my arm around her, pulling her tight against my side. "If that's what you want, then I'm good with that. But maybe be a little more careful where you throw your bras next time? That was dangerously close."

She leans over, pressing a kiss to my cheek. "You and I both know that's not going to happen. What about me says careful?"

I can't argue with her there because she's right. Both of us go with our guts. Nothing about what we're doing seems careful. But even with that little scare just now, being here with her tonight just feels right.

"Do you want to come in and watch more of my lame old videos again?" I hook my thumb over my shoulder toward my house. "Or we could watch something made in the last decade."

She looks that way and then back at me, her teeth digging into her lower lip. "That sounds tempting," she says and I can hear the hesitation in her voice, "but I'm supposed to leave for Grand Targhee first thing in the morning. We're going to ski there tomorrow to switch it up a bit. So I should probably get to bed soon."

"You know the offer still stands. You can stay in the guesthouse if you want. Or my house. I know you love your van, but if you want a real bed for a night, you don't have to ask," I say, hoping I'm not pushing her too far. I want her to keep choosing to be with me.

"Suuure. That's it. Purely altruistic," she says, smirking at me before resting her head on my shoulder and I love the way she rubs her cheek against me. "And I know, but I don't want to bother you in the morning. I'll probably be up even before you."

"Alright. Fair enough," I say, still wishing to spend more time with her but knowing damn well she's going to do what she wants. Besides if she needs sleep, coming to bed with me right now is the last thing she should do, because there would be no sleep happening.

"But I'll see you Tuesday morning." She stands in the water, leaning down to kiss me, before climbing out of the hot tub. I hook my fingers into the waistband of her shorts, not wanting to let go of her just yet. She looks down and lets out a short laugh. "We can pick up where we left off then."

"Tuesday? You're lucky that you have such a flexible boss who lets you work remote," I say, running my hands up the backs of her thighs.

She shakes her head grinning. "I'm lucky for a lot of reasons."

Me too.

"Alright, I'll be here when you get back," I add, trying not to sound too desperate.

"Good, because I have something I want to show you."

I raise an eyebrow, my eyes roaming her body. I'm going to memorize every inch, every tattoo, and every piercing on her. My mouth waters just thinking about tasting those little pieces of jewelry again. She picks up on the gesture, snorting a laugh.

"Something for work, not for play," she teases, leaning down and grabbing my towel. "Now, I'm going to go get a shower in the guesthouse before going back to my van."

She turns away from me, bending over, running the towel up

and down those long legs. She looks back over her shoulder, grinning when she sees me shamelessly watching her.

"Night, Tommy. Don't have too much fun out here." She tosses me a playful wink, my towel wrapped over her shoulders and my t-shirt clung to her body, showing the silhouette of her curves. "And I'm keeping these."

With that, she turns and walks into the guesthouse and this time, I don't feel bad admiring every detail of her body. I slip my hand into my shorts and stroke my throbbing cock, still tasting her sweet pussy on my lips.

"REMIND me why I got up at the crack of dawn to do this again?" Sutton glares at me from across the small gondola. He takes his glove off and rubs his temple with his thumb and forefinger, letting out a long groan.

I reach my ski pole out, tapping the top of his helmet. He bats it out of the way and flips me off.

"You know for someone so young and spry," I say, making air quotes with my hands, "you look awfully hungover there, big guy. Party a little too hard with the staff after closing?"

He playfully kicks my shin with the toe of his ski boot, which would hurt like hell if I wasn't also wearing ski boots.

I hear my phone ping in my chest pocket. I race to take off my gloves and quickly rip it out, hoping it's her. I'm trying not to be too clingy, but I asked Grace to text me when she and Josie were out on the mountain. Grand Targhee is only a couple hours away, but I hate being this far away after being around her so much the last few weeks.

Looking down at my phone, I'm quickly disappointed when I see the message.

Miles: You're still coming this week, right? The guys will all be there. Can't wait to talk.

I put my phone away and look up to find Sutton watching me with his knowing grin.

I throw my head back against the gondola window behind me. "What?"

"Wasn't her? You're in deep, man."

"I have no idea what you're talking about."

"You mean *who* I'm talking about?" he asks, raising his voice in a flirty tone.

I pull my phone back out, showing him the message. "It was Miles. See? He won't back off."

He hums thoughtfully. "Alright, but I know you weren't racing to get your phone out of your pocket to check a message from him. And you're going to have to give him an answer about that tour sooner or later. Just pull off the bandaid one way or another."

"I know," I say, sighing in frustration and put my phone away again. I level a glare back at him. "You know, you still haven't told me why Kelsey hates you. So we're not talking about this either."

He cocks his head to the side and gives me a smug grin. "Fair enough."

A few minutes later, we finally reach the top and get out of the gondola, seeing the crowded area just outside the mid-mountain lodge. He takes one look at the crowd before turning back to me.

"Seriously, TJ. I know you like her, but why are we out here today? She's not even skiing here. I can't remember the last time you asked me to go out and ski, especially on a powder day with fresh snow and crowded lift lines. And for someone who used to be in front of huge crowds all the time, you really always hate them now."

I shrug. "I don't know. Seemed like it'd be fun."

He lifts an eyebrow, narrowing his gaze on me and I can tell he doesn't believe me, which is fair because I don't believe myself either.

Sutton's right. I like skiing, but I never go on busy days at the resort. I just know that when I woke up this morning and looked out in my driveway to see her van gone, I wanted to be close to her some way, somehow.

Being out on the mountain that she loves just called to me.

CHAPTER 23
GRACE
EVERYTHING ALL AT ONCE

THIS IS NOT how I wanted my Tuesday morning to go. Instead of being back at Tommy's house, Josie and I are still on the other side of the mountain pass at Grand Targhee, sitting in my van waiting for the resort to open.

I click call and hear the phone ring through my van's speakers.

"Morning, Rainbow." Tommy's deep, smooth voice comes through my speakers after picking up on the first ring. "You almost here? Can't wait to see you. I still can't stop thinking about how good you—"

I cut him off. "Morning! You're on speakerphone."

"Hi, Hot Boss," Josie says, snickering to herself and quietly mouthing his pet name for me. Still, every time I hear him say it, the butterflies in my stomach get kicked into a frenzy.

I hear him clear his throat. "Morning, Josie."

"So, good news and bad news. Which do you want first?" I blurt out, sounding way too excited from trying to hide my disappointment because I hate to deliver bad news.

"Is everything OK?" he asks, his voice instantly taking on that commanding tone I've become so familiar with. I can just picture the imposing look on his face right now.

"Yeah, we're totally fine. We're just not going to be back until tomorrow at the earliest."

"What happened? Are you guys having van trouble? That snowstorm that came through the last two days has been brutal here," he says and I can hear concern in his voice.

"So good news first. Nope, the vans are totally fine and toasty warm. The storm has also brought tons of fresh snow and the skiing has been epic."

"Seriously, it's been crazy," Josie chimes in between bites of her breakfast burrito.

Tommy's bright laugh comes through the speakers. "Yeah, I know. I went out skiing on Sunday. I even dragged Sutton with me. So what's the bad news?"

"Well, there might be too much snow. Teton Pass and the backup route are both closed because of avalanche hazards until tonight. We might just stay here and get some more skiing in. I'm still going to work remote a bit since we have good cell service though. This presentation is coming together. I can't wait to show it to you."

Normally, it might only be a two hour drive, but with the weather like this, the detour is nearly six hours and an absolute headache.

"Totally fine. We're not leaving for Seattle until Thursday. So just stay safe and have fun." There's a hint of disappointment and concern in his tone, but it's subtle. It's nothing like the over-bearing way my Dad and brothers can be. They would have probably already been in the car, taking the six hour detour around both passes to get here. While that might make some girls swoon, I appreciate the trust and the space he's giving me to take care of myself.

"Oh, we'll have fun. Don't worry," Josie says, leaning back into the passenger seat.

He chuckles. "Well, don't let me keep you two any longer. Have fun getting first chair. See you soon, Rainbow."

"Bye, Tommy," I say, trying not to sound too much like a girl freaking out over how much I'm into him.

I swipe to end the call and look over to find Josie, grinning ear to ear. She leans forward, propping her elbows on her knees, pressing her hands together under her chin.

"What was he going to say before you cut him off?"

"Nothing." My voice betrays me and comes out as a high pitched squeak.

"Oh, come on. Kiss and tell, Rainbow," she says, dragging out that name and enjoying this way too much.

"Nope," I say, smirking at her before standing up and walking toward the back of my van to get ready for the day on the slopes.

I turn to find her still watching me. I raise my hands to my side, turning my palms out. "What?"

"Hot Boss likes you," she says, raising her eyebrows at me.

"Tell me something I don't know, Josie." My face heats, remembering the other night and the feeling of his stubble on my thighs.

She shakes her head and laughs. "You like him too, clearly."

I'm starting to realize that might be more of an understatement than she knows.

I HAVE ALWAYS loved sunrise in Jackson. The sight of the low valley of the Snake River concealed in fog, bracketed by the low rolling hills painted in iridescent sunlight to the east and the tall, imposing granite peaks of the Teton Mountains to the west, still cloaked in darkness, is something I will never get tired of. It's a view I will always cherish after growing up here... a feeling of home.

Today though, when I pull into Tommy's driveway and head to his backdoor at the crack of dawn, nothing can compare to the thrill I get when I see the lights in his studio on from the patio, telling me he's already awake.

I rush in the house, quickly making my way straight to the studio. It only took a few weeks, but I'm much more familiar with how to get around in his house now without ending up in the wrong room.

I get to the studio door, finding it cracked open with a familiar sliver of light trickling out into the hallway. I stop and collect myself before slowly pushing the door open. That's when the familiar notes of the song I heard him playing the other day float through the air. I stand there and lean against the doorframe, listening to the notes while he plays looking out the window.

I watch the muscles of his back ripple under his shirt as he reaches the point where the song stopped before, but now he keeps going. The song continues, the notes building tension as they go until he stops abruptly, dragging out one note that vibrates through the room. It's both beautiful and harsh, grungy and lively, all at once.

He scribbles something down on his notebook in his lap before carefully setting the guitar on the stand by his side. He reaches up, brushing his unkept hair away from his ear and plucking out his ear bud. I take that as my cue to come in.

"For someone who's allegedly retired from music and says they don't play anymore, you're in here an awful lot."

He looks over his shoulder, his eyes immediately finding mine. The bright smile he points my way with his dimples popped, makes my thighs clench. I take a second to admire that shade of blue that reminds me of the sky on a perfect bluebird day on the slopes.

"Missed you, Rainbow." His deep, smooth voice comes out as a caress.

I step toward him, standing between his thighs, looping my arms around his neck. He wraps his hands around my waist, pulling me closer to him by the waistband of my sweatpants, looking up at me and I can see the longing in his eyes, making my heart flutter. I lean down, pressing my lips to his for a short, breathy kiss. When I pull back, he tugs on my lower lip, letting out a low growl.

I let out a short laugh, playfully pushing him in the chest. "I missed you too."

My eyes roam over him, starting at his ruffled hair, down to his stubble that he clearly hasn't shaved since I've been gone with that just right dusting of gray. He smirks at me, making the corners of his eyes crinkle, as my eyes drift down, admiring how his black v-neck hugs his chest and shoulders. I reach out, playing with his leather necklace, my fingertips lazily grazing his chest hair. I look down between us, spotting that familiar, dusty old notebook in his lap.

"I know you get asked this all the time, but why did you guys stop playing together?"

He follows my eyes to the notebook and nods before tossing it down by the guitar. He pulls me into his lap, pressing a kiss to my neck, prompting me to hum contentedly. His hands run under my hoodie and find the hem of the thin bralette I slept in. He may not be much taller than me, but something about the way he confidently handles my body in his hands is enough to make my core thrum with need.

He reaches up, brushing my bangs out of my eyes. His callused fingertips drift over my neck, over my pulse point, before he cups my nape. "I'm never tired of talking with you. I will always be an open book for you." His eyes drift to the notebook on the ground and I feel him sigh, his other hand resting on my hip.

"The other guys just cared more and more about money and fame. When we started, they were both good guys. Sure, Vince was a dumbass and would get into trouble all the time, but he was always well-meaning. Then Stan was a blast to hang out with and was creative as hell, but he was always chasing the next girl. You add money and fame to the mix though, it just brought out the worst in them. All I ever cared about was how music made me feel. The longer it went on, the more it killed it for me. And one day, I just woke up and that feeling was gone. It's like it didn't love me back anymore, no matter how much I wanted it to. And then finally, I didn't love it anymore either." I watch his eyes close and his throat bob when he swallows. He chuckles to himself and shakes his head, looking back at me. "There's something ironic about it all now."

I've heard the rumors from years ago that there was drama in the band and creative disagreements, but hearing this is different. It's such an intimate confession and I can feel the tension and pain in him, even after so many years. I nod and raise my eyebrows in question, hoping he continues.

He takes another deep breath, holding me tighter. "I never cared about all of the crap that comes with succeeding in that business. Somehow though, I'm the one that ended up being successful outside of music when I only did it for the love of music."

I press a kiss to his cheek, rubbing circles on his back. "I can't exactly relate to all of that, but I'm glad it brought you here."

He tilts my chin up, peering into my heart with those perfect baby blues. "Me too."

The look in his eyes is everything all at once. The unashamed longing focused on me, making my skin tingle. The confidence and the openness to share what he just did, which is so wildly different than the boys I'm used to.

I'm realizing this thing between us is more than just hormone-driven lust. It's a kind of deeper connection I feel in my soul that I've always craved, but never thought I'd find.

I COULD DIE RIGHT NOW and be more than happy with the life I've lived. Never in my life have I felt this connected to someone. Sitting in my lap, her arms draped over me, hanging on my every word. I don't know the last time someone has looked at me like this, wanting me and not something *from* me.

I just want to sit here like this and take all of her in, from her cheeks with the freckles I'm still determined to count, to her soft lips that I want to feel everywhere on my body, to the column of her neck that I want to feel in my hand when she calls out my name. My eyes are frozen though, fixed on hers, sparkling and young but somehow old and soulful all at once.

"So what's your plan for the day now that you're back?" I ask, begrudgingly breaking the silence. "We're leaving for Seattle tomorrow morning, so if there's anything around town you need to take care of, today's the day. I've got to meet with Sutton tonight to go over some things for this party and the new restaurant."

"That works out well if you're with Sutton. I was planning on working here today and then hanging out with Josie tonight since we'll be gone."

The thought of finally getting some alone time with her the next couple nights in Seattle makes my pulse quicken. I press my head against her chest under her chin, feeling her warmth. I almost don't care anymore that I have to see Miles and my old band if it means getting some alone time with her the rest of the weekend. They aren't going to ruin our time together.

"God, I missed you," I breathe the words against her.

She pulls back, eyeing me cautiously. "Hey, everything OK?"

"Yeah, still just thinking about that reunion tour. I know Miles is going to try and corner me about it."

She gives me a playful smirk. "You know, I might give you shit for being old—"

"Might?" I tease, raising my brows at her.

She wobbles her head. "OK. Fair, but that doesn't change that I was going to say you're still so young. You can get back into music on your terms. It doesn't have to be with them. It doesn't have to be for money. It can just be for you."

I smile back at her lazily, admiring her outlook that seems so far beyond her years. "Thanks," I say, "I'll keep that in mind."

She pecks a kiss on my forehead. "Good. So either say yes or say fuck 'em, but either way I'm here with you. Now can you quit moping? I've got something I want to show you."

She bounces out of my lap, her eyes going wide with excitement, clapping her hands together and bringing them to her mouth.

"Speaking of work, are you free now?" she asks.

She turns and grabs her bag that she set down by the studio door, pulling out her laptop.

I watch her, somehow still amazed by her unbridled enthusiasm for everything she does. "You do realize it's, like, not even eight in the morning, right? You just drove three hours to get here from Targhee. You can take a break. Go get a shower, change, do whatever. I'll still be here."

"Are you saying I need a shower? Because I've been dying to see how nice yours is compared to the guesthouse."

Noted. Shower time with Grace is going to the top of the list of things I want to do in the very near future.

"No, that's not what I meant. I was just saying you don't have to dive into work right now if you have other things to do first."

Before I can say anything else, she's already back in my lap, perched on my thighs with her back pressed against my chest.

"Is this how presentations went at your last job?" I say, grabbing her by her hips and looking at her laptop over her shoulder. "You're lucky I have a soft spot for you."

"I could make this more formal if you'd like, *Mr. Jacob*." Her voice drops low and sultry, doing her best impersonation of a seductive secretary. She shimmies in my lap, making me groan when I feel her ass against my swelling cock. "Also I don't think you and I have the same definition of soft."

I rest my chin on her shoulder, watching her open something on her laptop, breathing in that citrusy lavender scent that's becoming so familiar.

She peeks back over her shoulder at me, turns, and runs her tongue across my stubble and up my cheek before turning back to her laptop.

"Did you just lick me?"

She nods, focused on her laptop. "Asks the man smelling my neck."

I huff a laugh and kiss the spot just under her ear and I feel her suck in a breath. "Sounds like a fair trade to me."

She clicks the trackpad on the laptop and rests her hands on her thighs. "OK. So you already signed off on all the charities and foundations I wanted to give to. Jake already sent the funds to them. So that's all wrapped up." Her eyes flick over her shoulder to meet mine again.

"Yep, I remember all of that."

She nods and looks back at her screen, pulling up a set of presentation slides. I rest my hands in the dip of her waist, my fingertips tracing the outlines of her hip bones.

"So yeah, obviously you know your budget for charitable giving is kind of crazy." She waves her hands in the air, her eyes still focused forward on the laptop. "I mean giving eight figures a year is unheard of unless you're a billionaire or something."

My jaw tenses and my heart skips a beat hearing that word. Obviously people know I'm successful, but I've never liked the idea of people knowing just how successful. My grip on her tightens, but she doesn't seem to notice.

"Alright, so hear me out. Your goal is to do the most good, make the biggest impact, right?" She turns and looks back at me.

"Yes. I mean obviously there are other benefits to giving that much, but that has always been the point."

She smiles and looks down at her laptop. I notice the slide is a collage of places and people. I recognize most of them. National Parks I've been to, places I've lived, even a music school I think we donated to years ago.

"I call this TJ's — well Tommy's — moodboard." She stretches her arms out wide and makes a big, circular gesture. "Think of all the different people and places you've wanted to help over the years. And I'm going to tell you, there are a lot of them."

"That sounds about right," I say with an amused laugh.

"You guys have helped a lot of people, but you have also been so inefficient about how you're going about it. You've been basically taking a scatterbrained, shotgun method just making it rain money to whatever place fits your vibe at the moment." She makes quick, hand gestures out in every direction around her. "Yes, you're getting a lot of money to a lot of people, but you're not getting the most bang for your buck."

She clicks and the next slide pops up, showing what looks like two flow charts next to each other. "So Jake said you never actually read stuff, so I'm trying to keep this as simple as possible. On the left, this really messy looking chart, is what you're doing now. Each place you're giving to, they have their own administration, their own facilities, all of this overhead."

"You mean your old job? I thought it was a good thing to help support them to cover their costs."

Her hand hovers over the keyboard and nods. "Yes. That is true, but someone that has as much of a budget as you can do more."

She points her finger at the simpler chart on the right of the screen. "With your budget, you could establish and build your own foundation. You could hire your own staff and everything. You could pick and choose exactly what projects you want to work on or where your money goes. You could still give to other causes and charities too, but you could also set up scholarship funds and micro-grants to get money straight into the hands of the people that need it."

She looks at me and I can see just how excited she is with her blinding smile and the sparkle in her eyes.

I shift under her, meeting her eyes. "So what do you need from me to make something like this happen, besides a very generous budget?"

She gnaws on her lower lip, her eyes darting between the screen and me.

"I need you. I need *Tommy Jacob.*"

I laugh. "You've already got me."

I reach up and tuck a purple strand of hair behind her ear. She leans into my touch before shaking her head and looking back down at her laptop. "I need you. For this to work, I need your name. I need your face. I need your public involvement."

This time, my heart doesn't just skip a beat, it freezes. I close my eyes, listening to her, already knowing my answer.

"I know you and Jake have given anonymously for years. I get it, so many donors do. But you have the means to make such a huge impact. And if people see your name and your face attached to it, you'll get more volunteers and support. You'll get other organizations wanting to collab with you." I open my eyes to find her looking at me, her eyes pleading.

Everything about her idea is perfect. It's sound. She's right. Pride wells in my chest knowing just how much of a big thinker she is. It's amazing work, for anyone else but me.

"No." The word feels bitter and foreign and I hate it the second it floats off my lips.

I see the look of disappointment in her eyes and it guts me to my core. Being public about my wealth, with my past, is a line I don't know if I'll ever be willing to cross.

To her credit, she nods and gives me a weak smile. I already hate myself for ever telling her no and doing anything to dull her brightness.

"Grace, everything you're saying is right. This is amazing work," I say, shifting her on my thigh so she's facing me now. "I should have been upfront about my boundaries. There are some parts of my life I just don't want to open up, things I don't want people to know about me or what I have."

"OK," she says, nodding again and shutting her laptop. "OK. I'll go back to the drawing board."

I pull her toward me, rubbing my thumb over her cheek and pressing a short kiss to her lips. "I'm sorry. I love where your head's at. I know you'll figure out something amazing."

Her smile brightens and I hate myself just a little bit less now. "You don't have to apologize. This is all new. We're both learning about each other as we go. It's fine."

"So we're good?" I ask, searching her eyes.

She grins and snorts a cute little laugh. "Yes, we're good. I love that you think you're the first person that's told me no."

She stands up and rolls her neck. "Besides, this is workplace TJ and Grace, not romantic Tommy and Rainbow. They're separate."

"Good. So what's next for the day?" It feels like the weight that was sitting on my chest is all but gone, seeing how she's handling that better than I would have.

"Actually, I'm going to do some laundry to get ready for Seattle and take a shower before getting some brainstorming done."

Chuckling, I stand and follow her toward the studio door. "It's all yours. Meet for lunch though?"

She stands up on her toes, bringing her lips to mine. The kiss isn't nearly long enough, but it erases that last little bit of unease in me.

"Sounds perfect." She grabs her bag, tucking her laptop away, and practically bounces out of the room and down the hall.

I was right. She owns me and my heart.

She doesn't even have to try. She owns me and that's what terrifies me.

This is why I'm afraid of falling in love with anything, much less someone so vibrant like her, because what if I lose it again? What if I can't keep her happy like she deserves?

"WE'RE LATE." Grace's voice has a hint of panic in it and I chuckle to myself, keeping my eyes focused on the snowy road. "We're going to miss our flight."

"I told you, it's fine. They won't leave without us," I tell Grace, who's rummaging through her bags in the passenger seat on our way to the private terminal at the Jackson airport. "Seriously, I could ask them to wait all day and they'll still be ready for us to leave on ten minutes notice."

She pulls out some kind of ID card and then a couple hair ties from her bag, tying off her long braids. "You keep saying that, but I don't believe you. I've never flown on a private plane before. Don't they have other rich people to pick up in Seattle or someone that will be mad when they have to wait for their jet to get there? I don't want to get off the plane to have some pretty, perfectly styled blonde waiting on the tarmac with her Louis Vuitton bags, tapping her toes, and glaring at me because she had to wait on her jet."

My eyes flick over to her and I raise a brow. "You mean someone like Lizzy?"

She gives me a surprised look back, her eyebrows raised before she smirks. "I'm telling Lizzy you said that because she'd be flattered, but also yes."

"Well, I guess that could happen, but this one only waits for me."

She squints at me and I can see the wheels turning in her head. Her eyes widen when it finally clicks. "Wait. You're not chartering this flight. This is *your* jet? Like a whole ass private jet?" She holds her flattened hand out in front of her and moves it around like an airplane.

"Yep. You got it," I say, resting my hand on her thigh.

She grabs my hand and places it back on the steering wheel.

"Eyes on the road, please?" A shiver runs through me and I'm instantly focused back on the road again, remembering her history with car accidents and what she's been through.

I see the sign ahead for the private terminal and make the turn, pulling into the small parking area next to the tarmac.

"We're here."

"What about security though? I don't want your crew to be mad at me because we're late."

I laugh. "Not a problem. We can go right from the car to the jet."

She sighs and I can hear the relief in her voice. "Oh, thank god. I'm a mess with metal detectors and body scanners."

I lean across the console, running my hand up her side, cupping her breast, and kissing her waiting lips. She presses my hand against her and I can feel her piercing press into my palm. I'm glad she's not a fan of bras because I'm obsessed with her tits. That's not a surprise though — I'm obsessed with everything about her.

She hums with amusement, pulling back from the kiss, tugging on my bottom lip. "The piercings aren't really the issue. It's more so the plates and screws holding my leg and shoulder together. I'm always afraid I've forgotten my TSA Medical Device card."

"Well you don't have to worry about that today. Now, wait here."

I hop out of the SUV and make my way around to the passenger door, opening it for her.

"Thanks, Boss," she says, tossing me a wink before I grab her hand and help her out.

We head to open the hatch, only to find Stacy waiting for us with our bags already at her side.

"Good morning, Mr. Sorensen. The Captain and Co-Pilot are already on board and we're all set to go on your word." She tips her chin to me and then her eyes drift to Grace. "This must be your girlfriend. Miss Chapman, it's a pleasure to meet you."

I choke on a breath and my grip on Grace's hand tightens. Shit. I forgot that's what I told Stacy the other day when I requested to have the plane ready.

I look over at Grace who wears that ever-present smile and I feel her thumb lightly rub the back of my hand. She reaches out to shake Stacy's hand. "It's nice to meet you. Tommy was just saying he has the friendliest crew." I barely even mentioned the crew to her, but leave it to Grace to make them feel special.

Stacy smiles before taking our bags to the plane. I didn't miss the way she smirked at me though, probably because practically no one ever calls me Tommy in public.

Grace and I walk toward the plane and she whispers into my ear. "Who's Mr. Sorensen? Are we stealing a plane?"

I grin at her smugly, somewhat impressed with myself it's taken this long for her to figure this out. "That's my real name — Thomas Michael Sorensen. Tommy Jacob was my stage name, it's my name and Jake's put together. I still use it for business purposes because it felt fitting, but legally I still have my birth name."

"I like it," she says, stopping when we reach the stairs.

I gesture for Grace to go up them first, but she just stands there, looking at the jet.

"What?" I ask, watching her eye the plane skeptically.

She points at the plane and looks at me. "So this just sits here and as soon as you call, boom the crew comes and gets it ready and has the door open and waiting for you?"

"Well, not literally here. Sometimes it's in a hanger to keep it out of the snow. Otherwise, yep, that's basically it."

She hums to herself, scrunching her nose which brings my eyes to her freckled cheeks. "I just pictured you having a cool key fob or something." She raises her hand and makes a clicking motion. "Meep, meep." She smirks back at me. "Really, kind of takes away from the cool factor if you don't even have a cool keychain for it."

"I'll see if they make Gulfstream keychains. Maybe I can find us matching ones. Also, I'm sorry about the girlfriend thing. It kind of slipped out when Stacy called to confirm who would be in the cabin."

She shrugs and beams back at me. "Don't apologize. I like hearing that word come out of your mouth."

I swallow at the overwhelming warmth crawling out of my

heart and up my neck. "Girlfriend? I'll call you whatever you want, Rainbow."

She nods, smiling back at me. "I like both of those. Have you told anyone else though?"

"Nope."

I can't look away from her. From the way her braids come out from under her black beanie and hang over her shoulders to her rosy freckled cheeks. Everything about her contrasts against the snow white background of the mountains in the distance. Standing here, it dawns on me that she's the first woman I've really let into this part of my private life. Maybe I can do relationships if it means more moments like this with her. Maybe it's worth the risk.

"Hey, kids," a way too cheery voice calls from behind us, interrupting the moment.

We turn to see Sutton with his duffel bag slung over his shoulder, wearing his ever-present grin.

"Oh hey, Sutton! I didn't realize you were coming with us," Grace says.

He laughs, tilting his head toward me. "I'm not surprised your boss left that out."

He steps toward her, leaning near her ear like he's whispering, but clearly speaking loud enough for me to hear. "Here's a little secret. He won't admit it, but he loves me."

She giggles and the sound goes right to my heart. Then she slaps him on the shoulder, smirking at him. "He's pretty terrible about leaving things out. I just found out he had a jet this morning."

He raises his eyebrows, presses his lips together, and nods in approval. "Yeah, that's a pretty sizable omission."

I glare at him. "Are you done yet? Because if you're not, I'm more than happy to make you go to the main terminal and fly coach."

He shrugs and grins back. "Where would the fun in that be?"

I press my thumb and forefinger to my temples, slowly rubbing them. "Why did I agree to this again?"

Sutton laughs to himself and steps past Grace, walking up the stairs and into the plane. She grabs my hand, presses a kiss to my cheek, and whispers in my ear. "You agreed because you care about your friends' success and seeing them happy."

I don't even know how to respond to that because she's so right. She gets me like no one else.

CHAPTER 25
GRACE
BAD PERSON

"HERE YOU ARE, MISS CHAPMAN." I reach out to grab my mimosa from Stacy.

"Oh my gosh. Thank you so much. You're the best. And please, just call me Grace." Stacy smiles and heads over to Sutton in the back of the cabin.

I look to the seat next to me to find Tommy watching me, grinning with amusement.

"Having fun?"

I take a sip and press the button to recline the plush, fancy leather seat back. "I know the carbon footprint is horrible for these planes, but am I a bad person for knowing I can never fly coach again?"

"Oh, you're totally cancelled already," he says, grinning wider and popping his dimples.

"No way. That fast?" I clasp a hand to my heart in mock despair.

"Yep. As soon as you let Stacy take your bag. Cancelled," he says, shrugging and crossing his legs. "Don't worry. I still like you though."

I blow a kiss at him. "Good. Now I want to get some work done. I've got a long list of charities that I want to vet."

He chuckles and rolls his eyes. "Suit yourself, but don't blame it on your boss. I'm pretty sure he told you to enjoy the trip."

I set my mimosa down and grab my laptop out, going through the presentation slides from before. I know TJ said no and it might have stung at first, but like I told him, that's workplace TJ and Grace, not romantic Tommy and Rainbow. I wouldn't be any good at this if I gave up the first time someone told me no.

I look over to find him watching me with those heart melting baby blues. He gives me a soft smile, crinkling the corner of his eyes. I know people say men age like fine wine and right now, I could sip on him all day.

"OK. If I'm going to work, you need to stop that. I can't focus when you do that."

His soft smile morphs into a smug grin. "Do what?"

I raise my eyebrows. "Look at me like that. Get your notebook or watch a movie or something."

He nods before his eyes drift down to my screen, seeing my old slides. I immediately see the worry in his eyes.

"Hey. I'm sorry about saying no. You sure we're good?" his deep voice carries just a hint of concern beneath the surface.

I reach over and hold his hand. "You already apologized and I told you that you didn't even need to do that. Please do not worry about it. Seriously, we're good."

His grip tightens on mine and he lifts my hand, placing a soft kiss on the back.

"So-" I start, but cut myself off when I see his eyes lift to something behind us. I turn to see Sutton coming up from the back of the cabin. Tommy quickly lets my hand fall and sits up in his seat.

Sutton strides past us and stops to sit in the seats facing us. His eyes drift between us with a knowing grin before he turns to Tommy. I know he let it slip to Stacy that we're together, but did he let something slip to Sutton? Or maybe Sutton has just functioning eyeballs and can see that there's a connection between us. Either way, I totally get it if he wants to tell his best friend. I mean Josie basically knows. I just don't want it getting back to Tanner or my family until we really know what this is. I know we're taking it seriously and it's more than just wanting to jump each other's bones, but I could see how someone else would think it's me just trying to sleep with my boss or the hot, famous musician. Deep down, I know it's something that could be serious if we want it to be.

I look over my laptop, watching him and Sutton talk about the restaurant and the plan for the night. The only thought that runs through my mind is that I wish he'd grab my hand again.

WHEN THE ELEVATOR DOOR OPENS, I step right into the kitchen of the penthouse. God only knows how many stories up we are in this building in downtown Seattle, right on the edge of the Puget Sound.

Tommy rests his hand on the small of my back, ushering me into the sprawling space.

I spin around on the toes of my Doc Martens, taking in the open floor plan. Floor to ceiling windows on every side of the apartment showcase views of Mount Rainier, the water, and the Seattle skyline and Space Needle.

"This place is crazy. I can't imagine what something like this costs." I look back at Tommy, still standing just outside the elevator.

He smirks and shrugs, flaring his eyebrows up.

"No, don't tell me. You own this place too?"

He steps into the open kitchen with me, rubbing the back of his neck. "Sort of."

"What do you mean sort of?"

He grimaces. "I mean I technically pay rent, but I pay it to myself. Or I guess I pay it to the holding company I own that owns the building. At least that's how Jake explained it."

"Got it. So total normal people stuff," I say with a laugh before dropping my bags.

Looking into the sprawling apartment, it's hard to choose where to start. The views in every direction are stunning. The floors are gorgeous, colorful terrazzo. In the living area, there's a large, slate fireplace. What finally catches my eye though are the trio of large swings facing the fireplace. I walk over to them, running my hands along the thick hemp ropes holding up the wooden planks. I sit down on the buffalo plaid cushion of the middle one and find Tommy watching me with amusement.

"Why do you have swings in your living room?" I ask, kicking off of the floor, swinging myself up into the air.

"I always wanted a treehouse and a swing set as a kid." He steps toward me and grabs the ropes, stopping the swing in front of him. "A treehouse didn't seem practical as a grown man in the city, but the swings seemed like a cool idea. I'm glad you like them."

"They're cool," I say, leaping out of the swing and finally heading into the dining area with its wall of windows looking out over the Cascade Mountains to the east and south. Even after growing up in the Tetons in Wyoming and the Wasatch Mountains in Utah, the view of Mount Rainier is absolutely breathtaking. I feel like a kid, pressing my face to the window, drawn to the scenery.

When someone says million dollar views, this is what comes to mind.

I can't even imagine what a place like this costs, much less the whole building. Then again, that seems to be a recurring theme with Tommy. The jet, the beautiful houses in Bend and Jackson. I can't imagine what any of that costs. My mind drifts back to the way he tensed at my offhanded comment before. '*Giving eight figures a year is unheard of unless you're a billionaire or something.*'

Holy shit. Maybe this is a billion dollar view. If that's true though, I'm starting to realize why he enjoys his privacy and anonymity so much. Still, that's an incredible thing to keep hidden for so long.

"What are you looking at?" Tommy's low voice grabs my attention. I turn to see him, leaning against the window, looking like an absolute meal.

"Right now," I reach over, running my finger down his arm, over his toned biceps and the veins in his forearms, looping it into one of his leather bracelets, "just you."

He steps closer to me, dropping his hand and cupping my ass. "You can look at me whenever you want." He gives my ass a light slap, making my thighs clench. "Now go on, check the place out. Make yourself at home. You can throw your stuff in the guest suite if you want."

"What if I want to stay in your room?" I flick my eyebrows at him, leaning into his warmth.

He lets out a low, satisfied hum, practically a growl. "You don't even have to ask."

He pulls me in closer and I love the way his strong hands feel on me. I've been craving this contact with him, but both of us have constantly been busy. My body buzzes with excitement and I nuzzle into his neck.

"You can show me now," I breathe the words against his neck.

He lifts me into his arms and I wrap my legs around him, giggling when he starts to walk toward what I assume is his room.

My body molds to his. And for once, I don't feel lanky or awkward or too tall. Instead, I feel like he was built for me.

He nips at my ear, sending a jolt of electricity through me. My hips buck, grinding on his hard length I can feel through my leggings. I run my hands under his shirt, pulling it up to his chest so I can feel the toned lines and warmth of his abs.

"I can't wait to—" he rasps against my neck, stopping in the middle of the living room. I feel his body go rigid, but he grips me even tighter.

"Fuck," he says through gritted teeth.

I laugh, planting a kiss to his stubbled cheek. "Well yeah, I was hoping that's what you wanted."

"Hey, guys," a familiar voice says from behind me. "I see you made it back from the airport."

My head jerks to look over my shoulder to see a tall, imposing man with inky dark hair and a beard standing at the elevator door. It takes me a second, but I realize I know his voice and face from our calls.

"Jake," Tommy says gruffly, slowly lowering me back to my feet. "I thought you weren't coming over until later."

Jake's grin grows wider and he lets out a short laugh. "Missed you too, TJ." He turns to face me and his smile softens. "Nice to finally meet you in person, Grace."

"Hello there!" I wave awkwardly at him, definitely feeling a blush creeping over my cheeks.

Tommy pulls his shirt back down to his waist and steps to his brother. Jake brings him into a hug, patting him on the back.

"Next time, please call or give me a heads up."

They might not be biological brothers, but the bond between them is so obvious. With their hug and the deep sighs of relief coming from both of them, it's impossible not to see how close they are. The other thing that's impossible to ignore is that Jake is freaking huge. Tommy is six-two and my brothers are six-three and six-four. Looking at the way his *little* brother towers over him, it's almost comical when Tommy has to wriggle out of the hug and fix his ruffled hair.

They share a glance and Jake tilts his head to me. "I can give you guys a minute or come back later?"

Tommy shakes his head. "No, it's fine. You two get to know each other. Maybe talk business. I'm going to unpack and grab a shower."

He turns and steps to me, resting his hands on my hips. "You OK hanging with Jake for a bit?"

"Yeah, it's fine. We've got plenty to talk about. I'll see you in a bit."

He leans in and kisses my cheek. "Sounds perfect." I watch as he walks away, taking our bags to his bedroom.

A few seconds later, I find myself alone with Jake. He leans back against the massive kitchen island, watching me with an entertained grin.

"So," I hum awkwardly, grabbing my Nalgene bottle from the island and fidgeting with the lid. I'm not exactly sure what the right words are for '*sorry you just saw me wrapped around your brother like a spider monkey*'. "Sorry about that."

He laughs and shakes his head "Please, don't be sorry. I knew he was full of shit when he tried to tell me he wasn't interested in you. I'm just glad I can give him crap about being right and I don't have to deal with him pretending that he's not obsessed with you."

"Oh." I feel my cheeks heat again hearing that from someone else. Still, part of me is glad that someone else, especially someone so close to Tommy knows about the two of us now.

He looks in the direction that Tommy went and laughs again. "It's still weird seeing him with anyone though."

My lips pull to the side and Jake spots my frown.

"I don't think you get it. That's a compliment. Don't get me wrong, he was right about your work. You're doing great." He stands up and heads to the fridge on the other side of the island, talking over his shoulder. Again, I can't help but notice that he has to be six-five or six-six. "Honestly, I can't remember the last time he went on a date, much less liked someone enough to bring them into his life like he has with you. He seriously can't make it more than a minute without mentioning you when we talk."

"Thanks. That actually means a lot. He's pretty special."

Jake shuts the door to the fridge, after pulling out a bottle of sparkling water, nodding with a pleased smile. "Yeah, he is. Now can I get you a drink or something?"

I hold up my empty Nalgene bottle. "I could use a refill."

He plucks it from my hand and takes it to the sink, filling it from the filtered water tap. When he moves, I spot something familiar on the kitchen counter next to the sink.

I point at a tea kettle and box of tea on the counter behind him. "Is he a big tea drinker? I've never seen him have any but he has that same one in his office in Jackson."

He looks over his shoulder and grins wide when he sees what I'm pointing at. "Nope, not at all. He asked me to put that there after he knew you were coming with him."

I feel my cheeks heat again. Even when he's not here, somehow Tommy finds a way to make me feel special. Jake must see my reaction judging by the smirk on his face. "I told you he's obsessed with you."

"I'm starting to see that," I say, stepping next to him to make myself a cup of tea. The feeling is mutual.

"I LOVE IT." Walking down the sidewalk with Tommy and Jake on either side of me, I look up at the four story corner building. The red brick and carved stone definitely has Pacific Northwest vibes with its old, weathered industrial look. He described it perfectly and I can easily picture people sitting outside at the bistro tables under the awning.

Making my way toward the corner, I feel Tommy's hand on my lower back, gently guiding me back to the center of the sidewalk. I look up just in time to avoid walking into a parking meter.

I stop and turn to find Tommy looking at me with a humorous grin. "I'm glad you like it, but can you watch where you're going? I'm going to have a heart attack if you have another near miss with a pole."

I smile innocently back at him. "Sorry, hard to control my squirrel brain."

Jake laughs behind me. "Not to interrupt, but before we go in," he starts, prompting Tommy and I to both look back at him. He points a finger back and forth between us. "How do I know Grace?"

Tommy's hand finds the small of my back again and Jake must see the look of confusion on my face because he continues. "What I mean is, does anyone know you two are together? I've only told people you're bringing someone that works with us. So if you want to keep it that way, just remember there's some press here tonight and you probably want to keep the PDA to a minimum."

"No one else knows. Well, no one that's here anyway and I'd like to keep it that way, for now at least." Tommy's voice takes on that serious, commanding tone I've gotten used to. The one that makes my heart skip a beat and my palms get sweaty all at once. The voice that makes it clear there's no room for negotiation. "She doesn't need to get hounded by the press or anyone else just because she's with me. If anyone asks, she's here to spend time with you and the Sterling brothers to learn about our businesses. That's why I asked her to come in the first place."

Jake nods and gives a thumbs up. "Got it. Secret relationship. Just my coworker. Say no more."

I give Jake a two fingered salute. "And I will not climb him like a telephone pole."

He barks out a laugh and turns toward the doors, gesturing out with one hand. "Well, shall we?"

Tommy shakes his head. "Give us a minute. We'll see you inside."

Jake tips his chin and heads inside the old wooden entryway doors.

"I appreciate you looking out for me, but you do know I can take of myself, right?" I cross my arms and arch a brow.

His head tilts and the tension in his expression slackens. "Sorry. Some of the crowd here tonight can get under my skin. There's a reason I don't do this a lot anymore."

"You don't have to apologize. I'm just letting you know. I'll be fine." I give him a light slap on the shoulder. "Relax. Have fun!"

He starts to reach for my waist before pulling his hand back as someone walks by the entrance. He drops his head and sighs, looking back at me. "I'm just not used to this."

"Used to what?"

He shuffles his feet and shoves his hands into the pockets of the perfectly faded jeans, drawing my eyes to how they hug his muscular thighs just right.

"Used to doing stuff like this with someone that matters to me."

My mouth lifts into a silly grin and I step toward him. I want nothing more right now than to reach out and hug him and wrap myself around him like earlier today. That will have to wait though. "You matter to me too. Now come on, let's go in, enjoy the night, and then we can finally go back to your place."

The corner of his mouth pulls up into a mischievous grin and I can see the sparkle in his eyes. "I like the sound of that."

CHAPTER 26
TJ
TYPICAL CROWD

I'VE BEEN HERE for ten minutes and I already want to leave. Unfortunately for me, it takes Miles, Vince, and Stan less than that to find and corner me. So I'm forced to watch Grace from a distance.

To my pleasant surprise, she looks more than happy making the rounds to say 'hi' to people and checking out the old building with Jake. Watching her, it makes my heart swell with admiration that she can be so kind to complete strangers with such ease.

Right now, she's with my brother talking to Slade and Sutton. I have to do a double take because I'm pretty sure she just made Slade laugh with her joke. I love the Sterling brothers. They're the best kind of people, but I was also pretty convinced that Slade was incapable of laughing given his generally surly demeanor. Instead, she has him wrapped around her little finger cackling like a schoolboy.

It's also killing me that I'm not owning that we're dating. I know we both said that we don't want everyone to know yet until we have a better grasp on where this is going. I can't help the feeling though that it's my fault we can't be more open about it because of who I am. Even now, the press is far too interested in my life for my liking and I don't want her getting dragged into that with me. That's especially true because I want her to tell her family on her terms.

Deep down, I know where I want this to go. Part of me has known it since the day she plunged into my life, splashing color into the still, stagnant waters I was content existing in. I want her in my life — every day, everywhere, every breath.

Vince pulls me into a one armed hug, patting me on my back, and bringing my attention to the trio I knew I couldn't avoid tonight.

"Look at you. It's like you hardly age. What's your secret, man?" Vince asks, taking a sip from his pint glass. I raise an eyebrow when I see that it's surprisingly filled with water instead of a double Jack and Coke.

"Diet, exercise, and avoiding stress," I say, playing with the pop tab on my Rainier beer.

Stan snorts a dismissive laugh. "Still our goody two-shoes I see."

"Boys!" Miles chimes in with that always too cheery tone that is like nails on a chalkboard for me now. "Look at this. It's so good to see the three of you back together."

He grins at us and I can see that familiar look in his eyes. The one that could easily be mistaken for joy, but really screams dollar signs below the surface. I shift on my feet, taking another sip of my beer.

"Yeah, it really has been a while," I say dryly, forcing a smile.

Stan grabs my shoulder and gives me a light shake. "So are you in for this reunion tour or not, TJ? Miles said he has some great venues lined up if we're all in."

"Wow." I laugh through my nose. "Really going right into this without any foreplay, huh?"

Somehow, the thought of Grace's little quip brings a smile to my face.

Stan rears back in surprise. "Wow, he's got jokes now too."

"Well, some of us do evolve, I guess."

Miles clears his throat, bringing our attention back to him. "Stan's right though. This would be an amazing chance. There's huge interest right now in grunge again."

Vince nods. "Yeah. What do you think, man? We'd really love you back."

There it is. It doesn't take a genius to read between the lines. All three of them need me to come back because there is no reunion without me. And if there's no reunion, there's no payday for them. Unlike them though, I didn't piss away every penny because I knew what it was like to have nothing growing up.

I shrug, hearing Grace's words in the back of my mind again. *Say yes, or say fuck 'em.* Right now, I'm definitely leaning toward fuck 'em even though part of me really wants to give them a chance.

I start to talk until I see Stan's eyes drift to something behind me. He lets out a low whistle and I peek over my shoulder reflexively. Out of the corner of my eye, I see that familiar blur of color streaked hair heading toward me and my blood boils.

Fucking Stan definitely hasn't changed.

I turn to face Grace right as she reaches me.

"Hey, Boss," she says, her voice instantly brightening my mood. I start to reach toward her, desperate for any contact, but bury my hand in the pocket of my jeans instead. I turn back to the guys, noting the curious looks on all of their faces.

"Can you guys give us a minute?"

Thankfully, they all head over to the makeshift bar set up along the exposed brick wall in the back, leaving me with Grace.

"Are you OK? Is everything alright?" I ask, nervous about why she came to find me.

She laughs through her nose. "Me? Totally fine. This kind of stuff is easy. I can do Socialite Grace all day."

I tilt my head and pause. "Easy? I hate this shit."

She gives me a proud grin and takes a drink from her champagne flute, bringing my eyes to her lips. "I think you forget I have been to quite a few fancy fundraisers in my time. There are plenty of rich and famous people back in Park City. It's worth it though if it means helping people."

That reminder of how much she cares about others warms my heart and eases the tension in my shoulders.

She lowers her glass and her eyes find mine and her brows pull together. "How about you though? You look miserable over here. That's why I snuck away."

I shrug half-heartedly. "I don't know. It's going about as I expected. Vince seems like he's doing better though."

She smiles and rests a hand on my shoulder. "Then don't worry about it. You're here for the restaurant. Giving them a chance was just an added bonus. It's their fault if they blew it."

I shake my head and snort a laugh.

She quirks her lips into a smile and pulls back. "What?"

"Sometimes I forget how old you are." Her hand still rests on my shoulder and all I can think about is how much I'd like for her to rub my cheek. Instead, I take advantage of the noise of the crowded room and drop my voice. "You look great tonight by the way."

"OK?" She squints and her eyes drop down, looking at her denim overalls that hug her hips just right, her white ribbed tank top, and a familiar, large flannel shirt. She hums in confusion. "I'm just dressed how I always am."

"Exactly." I tilt my head toward the crowds around the open, former industrial space. "You're the only one here not trying to show off. Also, is that my shirt?"

She smirks. "*Was* your shirt."

I lean forward, tilting my head to the side. We're on the edge of being far too close in public for people that are just supposed to be working together, but I honestly don't give a shit now. Looking at her, it's impossible not to admire how happy and confident she is. She looks like none of this phases her.

It's taking every ounce of my self control to not grab her by the waist and pull her into me. It reminds me what drew me to her in the first place.

7 Months Earlier

CRACKING a molar wasn't on my list of things to do this morning, but my jaw clenched like a vice while I try to keep my eyes focused on the river and not stare at her. She's still standing next to me, humming thoughtfully, looking out on the river to the same place as me.

"So this is where you come to think?" she asks.

I nod. "I like this spot. There's one a lot like it by my house in Jackson too. I don't know. It sounds silly, but my mind is just clearer around the water. Also, aren't you cold?"

"I'm good right now. I brought a robe for when I get out," she says with a light, airy laugh. "It's mountains for me though. The crazy squirrels in my brain seem to calm down when I'm out in the mountains."

I dare to peek out of the corner of my eye, catching a glimpse of her face. Water is still dripping from her hair and bangs, running down over her face. Even with her sun-kissed skin from long days skiing in the winter, her freckles still stand out. Her beautiful green eyes shimmer like the perfect water around us. She smiles, bringing my eyes to her lips before I look to see what caught her eye. In the distance, I spot the silhouette of snow capped Mount Bachelor on the horizon, bringing a smile to my face.

"I do like mountains too." I take a long, deep breath of the cool mountain air, trying to steady myself.

She stays facing forward, but she must have heard me. Her eyes find mine and her smile widens.

"You can't have a river like this without the melting snow from the mountains. You have to have them both."

Present Day

"ARE you going to introduce us to your friend here?" Miles's voice gets my attention from behind. I turn to see him standing there with Vince and Stan, still watching Grace and I with a level of interest I don't like.

"Yeah, who's the mystery girl here?" Stan says, practically salivating and I already want to punch him. That's not exactly new though.

I start to confront him, but Grace bounds to my side, extending a hand to Miles, bright and cheery as always. "Hi. Grace Chapman. I've been working on some projects for Jake and TJ."

Miles grabs her hand, watching her with an amused grin. "Nice to meet you."

She lets go of his hand and turns to Vince. "And you must be Vince. He's told me so much about you." Vince gives me a worried look, probably wondering what I said about him, but shakes her hand.

"And that makes you—"

"Stan." I watch Stan extend his hand to her, tilting his head at me. "So you work for our old friend here?"

She smiles and nods. "Yep, for a few weeks now."

His lips curl into a slimy, predatory grin.

"Good. I was worried you were dating this old stick in the mud. How about you give me your number and I'll take you out for a real night."

"Seriously, do you ever stop?" Vince scolds Stan like a misbehaving child. I guess maybe he has changed a little bit.

I turn to find Grace, smirking and cocking a hip out. "Stick in the mud? What are you? Fifty? I thought TJ was the old man in the band."

Vince snickers to himself and Stan's brows rise in surprise. He quickly regains his composure and nods in approval before turning to me.

"Looks like you hired a feisty one, nice," he says, slapping me on the shoulder. I don't think I've ever seen Stan give up after one failed attempt at flirting.

I'm not sure what to make of these two right now. Maybe Miles is right. They've either changed or they're putting on one hell of a convincing act.

"Yeah. She's really helped me and Jake." I look at her and the smile she sends my way is almost enough to make me cave, wrap my arm around her waist, and kiss her in front of everyone here.

"There you boys are," calls a voice that instantly makes my skin crawl. I look back to see Vince reach out and let the source of the voice loop her elbow into his. Vince looks at me and I can see the unease in his eyes. He looks terrified and he should be.

Bile starts to rise in my throat and it feels like I've been punched in the stomach. There's no way. There's no fucking way that Candace, the last woman I dated almost twenty years ago, is here. The one that broke and then stomped all over my heart.

I'm at a loss for words, stunned by this level of shitbaggery. I would expect someone like Miles or Stan to let her dig her claws into them, but Vince was always my closest friend in the band.

"And who's our new little friend here?" she says, her voice grating my nerves.

To my horror, her eyes are turned on Grace, who has no clue who she is. "Grace. I work for Tommy," she says, reaching out a hand.

Candace quirks an eyebrow and looks at her with a catty grin, catching what Grace just called me.

"Oh," she says, "Tommy must really like you then."

She extends her hand to Grace and I stand there completely frozen.

To her credit, Grace just smiles and nods while shaking her hand. "Yeah, he's been great to work for. I couldn't ask for a better boss."

Some small part of me warms to that compliment because I know she means it, but it's not enough to block out the rage boiling inside me. This is the kind of shit I would expect from them back in the old days, only caring about themselves. It's exactly why I didn't want to give them a second chance, but Miles was adamant Stan and Vince had grown up.

"That's great. Speaking of business, the adults here need to talk." There's no way she's going to talk to my Rainbow like that.

"Can you run and get us some drinks?" Candace makes a shooing gesture at Grace, snapping me out of my silence. There's also no way I'm going to put up with any more of their shit tonight or ever again.

"No." My voice is cold and short when I stand between Grace and Candace, looking right at Vince. "Absolutely fucking not. Let me guess, she came knocking when she heard you might be going back on a tour and money would be coming in? Don't even answer because I already know I'm right."

I would love to punch him, but instead I turn to Miles, jabbing a finger into his sternum. "I'm not going to make a scene here and kick you out, but we're fucking done. You guys are never welcome in any of my properties or my friends' restaurants again.

We're done and I mean forever. Don't ever fucking call me again."

I turn, grabbing Grace by the elbow. "We're leaving. Let's go."

I start to walk for the exit with her following at my side, but I see the alarm in her eyes. "What's going on? What about Jake?"

"He's a big boy. He can handle himself. That's what I pay him for."

I guide us through the crowd to the exit carefully, trying not to raise attention. When we get outside, I start down the sidewalk in the rainy Seattle night. After a block, I get to where my car's parked, trying to stop my heart from pounding, grabbing my chest, just trying to breathe. I lean over, bracing myself against the hood of my car with my other hand.

"Are you going to tell me what the hell that was?" I look up to see Grace looking at me, standing on the sidewalk, her jaw tense but her eyes soft with concern.

"That part of my life is over. It's done. I never want to talk about it again and you don't ever have to worry about seeing them again," I say, still focusing on breathing.

Her head draws back quickly and she blinks. "What are you talking about? Who was that, Tommy?" She throws her arms out to her sides with her palms up.

"I said I don't want to talk about it. Can we please drop it?" I watch her eyes narrow in frustration and she watches me. I slowly catch my breath, hearing the cars driving on the wet street behind me, seeing their headlights flash across the brick building behind her.

She crosses her arms over her chest and looks away, the rain beading through her hair and down the side of her face like tears. I step toward her, brushing her wet hair out of her face, tilting her chin up to me.

I see the frustrated, hurt look in her eyes when she looks into mine. "Just take me back to your place, please."

THE RIDE HOME was quiet and stepping off the elevator into my penthouse, it doesn't seem like the rest of the night will be any different. I'm such an idiot for ever even entertaining working with them again. It would have been one thing if they were just their normal immature, selfish selves.

Bringing Candace back into my life in any way is an entirely different story. If those guys ever cared about me, they would have known that was a hard line that could never be crossed.

I drop my jacket on the counter and walk to the dining area, looking out over the city through the windows.

"I don't get it. What was that?"

I look over my shoulder to find Grace leaning against the window behind me, watching me. The look in her eyes is the second gut punch I've taken in the last half hour.

"I told you. Can we please not talk about that? I never want to talk about them again."

She takes a step closer to me, her face still hardened. "I know you have a complicated past with them, but why did you rush me out of there like that? Why won't you talk to me?" She swallows and I see the worry in her eyes. "Are you embarrassed by me?"

Make that the third gut punch.

I turn to face her, my pulse quickening. "I could never be embarrassed by you. Not in a thousand years. That's not it."

She runs the backs of her fingers over my stubbled cheek. "Then please, talk to me."

"You're just different, Grace. You're special. I don't want people like them getting to dampen your light." I drop my head again, running my hand over my face. "God, I sound like an idiot."

She rubs the back of my neck.

"Dampen my light?" she asks, her voice laced with amusement. "I'm not some shiny beacon on a pedestal that needs to be protected and preserved. None of us are perfect. We all have flaws. Some just compliment the person we're with better than others."

My eyes lift and meet hers. I see the compassion in them while they study me. No one ever looks at me the way she does, like an actual person, not some commodity.

I breathe deep and steady myself. "I'm sorry. You're right. I just don't want that part of my life to drag you down. I don't—"

She squeezes my shoulder and her eyes widen. "You don't need to apologize. But you need to start trusting me when I say I can take care of myself. I've spent my entire adult life having people try to watch out for me. I don't need that. I just need you, Tommy. So please be open with me. What was that about tonight?"

I close my eyes again, pressing my forehead against the window, grounding myself with the cold glass on my heated skin. I've spent years trying to erase this story from my mind, but it still finds a way to haunt me at the worst times. For her though, I'll do it, even if it means ripping open the stitches holding my heart together and reliving all of my worst fears.

"Candace," I start and her name feels like acid on my tongue, "she was my first and really only girlfriend. We met right at the end of high school. We dated for a long time. She traveled with me and the band a lot in the early years."

I open my eyes and see Grace watching me intently. I take another long breath and continue.

"When I told you music was my only love at the bar, I meant it. Early on, I thought I loved her and I thought she loved me. Outside of my last foster family and Jake, she was the first person I ever thought I had a connection with. Love — being wanted — it was so foreign to me and I craved it, trying to fill a void in my life that was there for so many years."

My heart races knowing the worst of the story. She must see the concern in my eyes because she inches closer to me and her warmth dulls some of the ache. "You don't have to keep going if you're not ready."

I shake my head. "It's fine. Better to just rip the bandaid off."

Her lips pull into a halfhearted smile and she nods. "We were practically attached at the hip all the time. When we were finally starting to get going with the band a bit, I thought she was the one for me. So I did what every young, lovestruck dumb musician does and asked her to marry me. She said no. I was heartbroken." Grace starts to talk, but I continue. "That's not why I got upset tonight. It's what happened next. A week later is when we signed our first deal and booked our first big tour. That night, that same fucking night, she shows up on my doorstep saying she thought about it. She said that she was wrong and we should get married. I was this close to believing her until I asked what changed. Vince didn't know that she had told me no and he let the news of the deal slip to his girlfriend and she told Candace."

I feel my fist clench and my molars grind, popping my ear. "She came back for one reason, because she knew we finally had money. I thought she might have actually liked me for me, but it was just the idea of me that she liked. That's why I'm paranoid about my finances. That's why I do all the charity stuff and so many of my businesses under the names of holding companies. It was hard enough for me to trust people after how I grew up. Throw on Candace and dealing with fame so early on, I never trusted anyone. I don't want people knowing that —"

"That you're a billionaire?" My eyes fly to hers and she raises her brows, giving me an amused smirk. "Yeah, I figured that out. You're not as good at hiding that as you think."

My heart sinks until she grabs my wrist and rubs the back of my hand with her thumb.

"You know I couldn't care less about that, right, Tommy? You know me. I'm literally happy to live in my van and take showers at the gym in town. I'd live in a van down by the river with you if it meant I get you. So if you want to give this a real shot to be what it could be, that's what I need: all of you."

"You already have it."

She smiles but shakes her head. "No, I want the good and the bad. I need you to share like this. It doesn't matter to me that you loved or thought you loved and then lost. Are you going to let them win and own the last track of your life?"

I stare at her and reach out, cupping the nape of her neck. "No, not for a second. That doesn't mean I'm not scared though."

She snorts a laugh. "You're scared?"

I nod, immediately loving the feeling of her neck and warm skin under my fingers. "Yeah, I'm fucking terrified. The only thing that's ever felt as right as being around you was music. I'm terrified that I'm fucking this up because I don't know what I'm doing. I'm terrified that I'm going to let you down."

She laughs again, her grin widening and her eyes sparkling, reflecting the shimmering lights of the skyline in the window.

"You think I know what I'm doing? That I'm an expert on relationships? Because, newsflash, I'm definitely not an expert. I've spent most of my life learning on the fly and that will never stop. I just want to keep learning, preferably with you. The only way you're ever going to let me down is if you close yourself off and don't try, OK? I know what I want. I know you said you want me before. Are you still sure?"

The look on her face tells me everything I need to know. Any doubt in my mind that she wants me for me vanishes. I want to give her that same reassurance.

CHAPTER 28
GRACE
A LITTLE WORRIED

TOMMY'S EYES find mine and he gives me that look, that all business, all serious look that lights a spark. His jaw tenses and he nods.

"Say it, Tommy." I inch closer to him, reaching out for him and cupping his square jaw in my hand. My thumb traces over the spot where his dimple would show and I feel his pulse hammering in his neck, just like mine. "I need to hear you say it."

He steps toward me, erasing the last inches between us. I watch his chest heave as he tucks a strand of golden brown hair out of his eyes. He looks down at me and I feel his hands rest on my hips.

"I know exactly what I want. I've known it since the second you jumped off that rock and into my life on the river."

I hear the conviction in his voice, leaning into his grip on my neck, feeling him lace his fingers into my hair. The air between us crackles like the feedback on a speaker before the music starts at a concert. "Say it again. Tell me what you want."

"I want you, Rainbow. I've wanted you every second since I first laid eyes on you." He lets go of my neck and brings his hand to my cheek, running the backs of his knuckles across my heated skin. The corners of my mouth lift into a smile at his touch. "I've thought about this smile every second since you dragged me up on the stage at that shitty dive bar to sing karaoke in Bend."

My lips part as his confession, hearing just how long he's been burying this inside. He brings his mouth to my ear and I feel his breath against my neck, making my body thrum with anticipation. "I haven't stopped thinking about what you taste like when you came on my lips the other night."

I whimper against his cheek and he laughs, pulling back to look at me. His dazzling blue eyes flicker like flames, any signs of his earlier conflict gone. All that's left is that focus, that burning desire, that confident side of him that drives me wild and right now, all of that intensity is focused on me.

"Sounds like you've got a lot pent up inside you," I pant, hooking my fingertips into the waistband of his belt. He steps forward, pressing his thigh between my legs, pushing me against the floor to ceiling window. Leaning forward, he brackets me in with his long arms, splaying his hands on the windows on either side of my head.

With my boots on, I'm nearly eye to eye with him and we meet each others' gaze. I've never felt closer to someone, but those last few inches between our lips feel like a chasm I wish he'd close.

I shift on my feet, grinding my throbbing clit on his thigh and pressing my knee against the bulge in his jeans.

We both react, him hissing through his gritted teeth and me throwing my head against the cool glass, whimpering at the friction that feels so good but isn't nearly enough.

His nostrils flare. "You have no idea what's pent up inside me."

I grin back at him. "Why don't you show me?"

He swallows and I see the question in his eyes. "I'm good. I'm on birth control and my last check up was clean."

He nods. "Same — well, the check up part anyway. And yeah, I've got condoms if—"

I shake my head. I just want him to trust me, but I totally understand someone in his position being cautious. "Only if you want to. I want to feel you, if you're OK with that. I want to feel all of you, but I get it if you still want to use—"

His pupils blow. "Fuck yes. I mean no. I mean—" The charged air between us finally snaps and he crosses that chasm, his lips crashing into mine in a powerful, taking kiss. His hands move to my shoulders, shrugging off my flannel shirt and the straps of my baggy overalls, letting them fall to the ground. I'm left in just my tank top and black boy shorts, my back pressed against the cool glass of the window. He pulls back, his eyes devouring me with seven months of pent up desire.

"Fuck, you're so gorgeous." His voice is low and husky when he leans forward and runs his hands up my thighs to the hem of my shorts, leaving a trail of goosebumps in their wake. I step out of my overalls on the floor and his eyes follow me before he smirks. "The boots stay on."

I flick my eyebrows and grin. "Sure thing, Boss."

I hook my fingers into the belt loops of his jeans, pulling him further into me, pressing my lips back to his. My hands run up and under his shirt, feeling each subtle ridge of his abs before dancing over his ribs and settling on his warm chest. He reaches over his back, ripping his shirt over his head, and tossing it away.

I peek at the skyline, over my shoulder, before turning to him with a mischievous smirk. I drag one of my nails through his light chest hair. "You like being watched?"

His lust drunk grin widens. "I don't give a fuck if someone watches because it means they'll know you're mine."

My heart skips a beat and I drop my hands to his waist, running my palm over the hard ridge of his erection straining the fly of his jeans. He groans at my touch and drops his head to my shoulder.

"I think we should do something about this." I breathe into his ear, tracing my nails over his toned back.

His hand runs up my thigh and he cups my pussy, his thumb circling my already swollen clit over the fabric of my shorts. "Not until I get a taste of this sweet pussy again and feel that little piercing dance on my tongue."

He takes a step back, running his hands up over my hips and waist to my ribs. I watch his eyes dart to my hardened nipples before he cups my breasts, teasing each sensitive bud with his thumbs over the ribbed fabric. "No bra. Fuck, you're perfect."

He takes off my top and brings his mouth to my neck, kissing the sensitive spot just below my ear. I moan against him, running my fingers through his hair, holding him tightly. "I think you said something about taste and your mouth?"

He lets out a huff of laughter against my skin. "Don't worry baby, I'm going to take care of you."

He kisses my neck again before dropping his lips to my collarbone, kissing the flower tattooed over one of my scars. His hands settle on my hips, holding me possessively when his mouth goes lower, ghosting over my breast before finding my hard nipple. He sucks and flicks the piercing with his tongue, sending a jolt of pleasure through me. My nails dig into his back and he groans against my skin, building up more and more tension in me. He kisses my sternum before giving my other breast the same treatment.

His lips let go and I watch as he drops to his knees in front of me. He loops his fingers into my boyshorts and his eyes lock onto the apex of my thighs as he slowly drags them down my legs, his fingertips brushing against my skin the entire way down.

He runs one hand over the back of my calf, stopping behind my knee and grabbing my leg, hooking it over his shoulder, bringing my core to his mouth. I buck at the sensation of his lips on me and his tongue finding my clit piercing.

"You're already so fucking wet for me and we're just getting started." He grabs my other leg and lifts it over his shoulder and now I'm pinned between him and the glass on my back, sitting on his shoulders. His hands find the curves of my ass and hold me exactly where I want to be, at the mercy of his mouth. I drop my hands to his head, ruffling his shaggy hair and pull him against my aching core. "That's it, baby, use my mouth. It's all yours, just like the rest of me."

Hearing those words makes my pussy clench and my legs wrap tighter around him. He groans in approval and I feel it through my whole body.

Out of the corner of my eye, I see the flicker of light from the skyline. Pinned against the glass, I feel like I'm floating, just part of the night sky. I look down at the man taking charge between my legs, reveling in the sight.

"Tommy," I moan, feeling the tension low in my stomach building to a blissfully overwhelming level. His eyes flick up to mine while he keeps stroking my clit and piercing with his tongue, pushing me higher and higher.

His eyes darken and one of his hands lets go of my ass. His fingertips find my entrance, slowly teasing my wet, needy pussy. I whimper and he rewards me, sliding two fingers in.

He lifts his lips from my clit, swirling his thumb over my bundle of nerves and grins up at me. "God, you're so fucking tight. I can't wait to fill you with my cock."

He curls his fingers inside me, working my clit with his thumb. My lips part and breath quickens. I can't take my eyes off his, feeling so connected to him, like he's inside my head, not just my body.

"Come for me, Rainbow," he says, his low, gravelly voice like a command. "I want to see you come knowing that anyone in Seattle could see us. Could see that you're mine."

His stubble rasps over my sensitive inner thighs as he swipes over my clit while his fingers plunge and curl into me. I gasp, feeling my orgasm coming so quick and so hard. The edges of my vision darken and my body gives in. I come completely apart, throwing my head back against the glass, squeezing his head between my legs. I ride out the wave of pleasure, admiring the view of him still lapping at me.

One by one, he lowers my feet back to the ground and stands in front of me. This time, I take my sweet time admiring every inch of his body, from the pleased look on his face with my own arousal glistening in his stubble and down his chest to the belt line of his jeans, where that one vein brackets his abs. All of it satisfies every desire of mine like the universe put him here just for me. His eyes follow mine and he grins, unbuckling his belt and pulling it off in one smooth motion that has no business being that hot.

I reach for his jeans, unbuttoning and unzipping them. My eyes take in the bulge in his boxer briefs, but it's the little tattoo just inside one of his hips that I can't look away from. My finger traces over the small rainbow inked into his taut skin and he shutters at my touch.

"How long have you had this?" I ask, my eyes finding his.

His lips pull into a sheepish smile. "I got it early last summer. Couldn't stop thinking about rainbows."

I lean into him, pressing my lips to his. My fingers toy with the elastic of his boxers before I dip my hand into them, gripping his hard shaft. He's long and thick and he throbs in my hand. I rub my thumb over the velvety head of his cock, feeling a bead of precum.

My grip tightens and he groans against my neck and I let out a short laugh. His hand tilts my chin up and I smirk back at him, seeing the smoldering lust in his eyes. "I think we should do something about this."

His nostrils flare and his chest heaves. "Well, I was planning on fucking your tight pussy if you'd let go."

I let out an amused hum, cocking my head. "Well, if I'm being such a bad girl, do something about it."

He grabs my wrist, pulling my hand off his cock, and pinning it over my head against the window. He kicks off his boots, and shimmies his jeans and boxers off, still holding my gaze.

He takes a deep breath and grabs my ass, splaying his fingers across my heated skin. In one motion, he lifts me up and pins me against the glass. I wrap my legs around his waist, pressing my wet core against the shaft of his cock. The instant pressure of his length against my piercing spikes all of my nerves and starts building that tension again. He closes his eyes and shudders with the friction, pressing his forehead to mine.

He kisses my neck before looking in my eyes.

"Is that what you want me to call you, Rainbow? I could call you my good girl because you're so drenched for me already. Or do you want me to tell you you're my bad girl? Constantly teasing me with that smile and making me cum in my pants, talking dirty to me on the phone, at night, from my own fucking guesthouse." His eyes burn with a focus and intensity that makes my body hum with anticipation. "Because I'll tell you a secret, Rainbow. I don't fucking care if you're a good girl or a bad girl, because the only thing that matters from now on is that you're *my girl*."

My mind melts seeing this side of him.

I thought it was there underneath his calm, confident exterior. But seeing him now with his barriers erased, claiming me as his girl, is more than I even imagined.

He leans forward, pressing his shaft against my aching clit. I gasp against his neck, savoring the pressure before his mouth finds mine in a hungry kiss. He pulls his hips back just enough to notch himself at my entrance. I push my hips forward, wanting to feel the head of his cock in me. He tightens his grip on my ass, keeping himself right at my opening, teasing me, and working me into a needy mess in his hands.

He looks into my eyes and I can see the resolve in his ice cold blue eyes. "Tell me what you want."

I loop my arms behind his neck, running my fingers through his hair. "I want you to fuck me, Tommy. Give me all of you."

He shifts his weight forward, bringing his lips to mine while his cock pushes into me. My lips part and I moan into his mouth, feeling the first few inches of him.

"Don't worry, we'll go slow," he says against my neck. He pulls his hips back before thrusting again, pushing himself just a bit deeper into me than before, filling me and stretching me. My body buzzes with pleasure at the feeling of him, but I still want more.

I look into his eyes and shake my head. "No. I said I want all of you."

His grin turns feral before he kisses me again, thrusting harder. I roll my hips, shifting the angle and he drives to the hilt. My lips part and I gasp, wrapping my legs around him. My core clenches on his length and he hisses through his teeth. I splay one hand across his back, cupping his nape with the other.

"Harder," I breathe into his ear.

He thrusts again, pressing me against the cool glass. The sensation of it against my skin clashes with the warmth of his body on mine. My hips swivel, working my clit against his veiny shaft, building that new knot of tension in me.

"You're so fucking tight," he says, our eyes falling to where we're joined. I watch his shaft piston in and out of me, shining with my arousal. "Look at how good you take my cock. So goddamn perfect."

He drops his mouth to my breast, moaning and nipping. I

hold him against me, loving every second of this but craving even more to push me over the edge. "Harder. You're not going to break me."

He pumps into me and grunts. "I'm not worried about breaking you." His eyes meet mine and he smirks at me. "A little worried about these windows though."

My head sags to his shoulder when something catches my eye across the room. "What about those?"

He follows my eyes and his smile widens, baring his teeth and popping his dimples. He quirks his pierced brow. "Oh, fucking hell yes."

He grabs me, pulling me from the window and holding me against him. He turns and strides across the room, still with me impaled on his cock, my legs wrapped around his waist and my boots against his firm ass. We come to a stop right in front of the swings and fireplace. "Didn't have this in mind when I had these put in."

"Good thing you have me then. Too bad there's no fire though," I say as he slides me off his cock and sets my feet back on the ground, in front of him. My core clenches, instantly protesting the feeling of emptiness and wanting him back inside me.

He smirks and calls over his shoulder. "Alexa, fire on."

The fireplace turns on with a whoosh of warm air at my back.

I roll my eyes. "Show off."

He shrugs and then his hands find my waist. He grips me firmly and spins me around, bringing my ass to his front. "Just for you. Now where were we?"

I feel his hard length press against my ass, answering his own question. I grab the ropes on each side of the swing and kneel on the cushion.

He grabs me by my hips, caressing my sides before one of his hands reaches around me and dips between my legs. He finds my clit and deftly plays with my piercing in his fingertips. His fingers work me like someone that's been strumming a guitar his whole life, making my body sing with pleasure.

His other hand claims me in a possessive way I've never felt, his fingers hooking into my hip bone before he pulls me to him, pushing his deliciously thick cock back inside.

I peek over my shoulder and meet his gaze. "Harder."

"Don't worry, I didn't forget," he says, his voice gravelly and strained. Slowly, he rocks me on the swing, back and forth, bottoming out and pounding me with each relentless thrust. Each push of his cock fills me, making me feel whole and each retreat makes me crave more of him. The satisfaction of him listening to me and not holding back like I'm some fragile thing.

Instead, he's ravaging me exactly how I want him to and it's everything. I want it rough. I want to feel it. I want him.

I drop my head and look down between my legs, watching the muscles in his toned forearm work, his fingertips playing with my clit in perfect rhythm with how he fucks me. Watching him drives me wild and works me to a fever pitch, ready to come undone again.

"Yes, please. Just like that," I cry out.

He leans down, bringing his mouth to my ear, kissing my neck. He runs his hand up from my hip, cupping my breast and tugging on my hard nipple while his relentless pace doesn't stop. I feel his warmth everywhere, from his body pressed against my back to his breath on my skin. Even the fire in front of me reminds me of him. His ragged, frantic breaths ghost over my ear. "That's my girl."

I know one thing in that second, that I want to hear him call me his girl, every day, anytime he wants to. I wanted him to be decisive with me like he normally is in every other part of his life. With each pounding thrust, I know he's made his decision.

My body responds to his words and I shatter on his cock,

moaning his name, and clenching down on him while he's buried in me.

"Fuck, baby. Yes, that's it," he says, pushing into me and pulling me against him in one last driving push, still cupping my breast in his hand. He grunts and holds me there, with him fully seated inside me and I feel every twitch of his throbbing cock when he spills inside me with nothing between us.

He bends over, staying inside me, looping his arms around my front, pressing my back to his chest. We stay there just like that, bonded together in a heated embrace and I feel his heart pound against my sweat slicked skin. He presses kiss after kiss to my neck, my shoulders, my back, to the top of my head, praising me, but all I want to do is praise him for not holding back.

A moment passes before he slowly eases out of me and I feel his cum drip down my inner thigh. He lets out an amused hum when I feel him shift behind me. I look down between my legs and watch as he drags the head of his cock up my thigh and pushes his cum back inside, claiming me and ruining me all at once.

CHAPTER 29

TJ

CEREAL

SEEING my girl's pussy dripping my cum in front of the fire is the stuff of my dreams. Pushing it back in though? That took every bit of control I had not to drive my dick home again and again, even if both of us aren't ready for more yet. Instead, I notch the head of my cock in her tight cunt, holding my cum in her and teasing both of us.

Her lips part with a whimper as I tease her entrance with just the tip. She looks over her shoulder and her eyes find mine. "What was that for?" she asks and I can see the lazy, lust filled haze taking over. She's stunning like this — even more than I let myself picture — completely free, uninhibited and most of all, craving me as much as I crave her.

I run my fingers over her boots, up the soft skin of her long legs, and grip her by the waist. My lips curl into a grin and I swipe a strand of my sweaty, ruffled hair out of my face. "You said you wanted all of me. Just making sure you get it."

A light and airy laugh escapes her lips and I feel the vibration right through the head of my cock. "You think you can put one of these in your house back in Jackson?" She shimmies on the swing, still kneeling in front of me, and wraps her boots around the backs of my knees, pulling me just a bit deeper into her. The feeling of her wet, tight opening grabbing my cock makes me shudder, still sensitive from coming harder than I ever have.

"Fuck," I grit out, grabbing her waist tighter and bracing myself. "Yes, whatever you want."

She laughs again, flicking her eyebrows and I can see the mischief in her emerald green eyes, focused entirely on me. "Good, but you know I just want you, right?" Our eyes lock and I nod, knowing that more than ever now.

Seconds pass like this, but it feels like we have an entire unspoken conversation before I feel the heels of her boots dig into the backs of my knees again. "Now you think we can do that again?"

She pulls herself against me, driving me into her and I know that, right now, I'm a goner for her.

THE SUN PEEKS in through the blinds of my room on a surprisingly sunny and clear Seattle morning. I'm sure if I look out the window, I can see the sun rising up and over Mount Rainier to the east. Propped up on my elbow in bed, the only thing I want to look at today is the beautiful girl of my dreams next to me. Her long, rainbow streaked hair flows over her pillow and face, but I can still see her freckles. I give in, running the backs of my fingers over them, prompting her to yawn and grab my wrist. She kisses the back of my hand and turns to bury her face in her pillow.

"I know we're both morning people, but can I stay in bed a bit longer?" she asks, her voice still sleepy and muffled when she turns enough to look at me with one eye, keeping her face plastered to the pillow.

I plant a kiss on her freckled cheek. "I told you. Whatever you want."

I bring my nose to her hair, breathing her in before sitting up. "Besides, we have no plans today besides dinner with Slade and Sutton and they'll wait for us if I tell them to."

She rolls her one eye and groans into the pillow before mumbling, "You're such a diva."

I laugh and stand up, but not before giving her a light slap on her round ass that was pressed against me in bed all night, making it hard to sleep.

She giggles and I shrug. "Stay in bed as long as you want, Rainbow. I'll go work on some breakfast."

I grab my sweats and pull them on before making my way out of the bedroom, quietly sliding the door shut behind me.

I round the corner into the kitchen, stopping at the fridge to grab yogurt and some fruit. I set a couple bowls on the counter next to the tub of granola before opening the silverware drawer.

"Morning, sunshine," a loud, cheery voice calls from across the room by the fireplace. My head whips up and I groan when I see Sutton, sitting on one of the swings, *that* swing. He rocks back and forth with a bowl in one hand and a spoon in the other, shoveling cereal into his mouth.

I palm my face and shake my head before looking back at him. "I know I give you guys the keys and codes to come over, but you really need to start texting or something before you let yourselves in."

He finishes his spoonful of cereal and I walk across the room, sitting in the swing next to him with my bowl of yogurt. "Seriously, between you and my brother, it feels like a frat house the way you guys come and go. At least give me a warning so I can put a shirt on or something."

He snickers and points his spoon at me. "Yeah, but that makes you the cool older one we all look up to." He eats another spoonful and hums to himself. "What? You got a house guest you're trying to hide?"

I glare back at him. "No."

He looks down at his bowl, but points across the room. "Then who's that?"

I look up to see Grace striding out of the hallway from my bedroom, wearing nothing but my flannel shirt. With her long legs, it barely covers the curve of her ass. In a second, my flight or fuck reaction is triggered by the sight of her almost bare ass and because we're quickly adding to the list of people who know about this.

She turns and spots the two of us and waves, flashing her bright smile. She walks over to us and I study her face. My body relaxes when I don't see any signs of apprehension or misgivings about Sutton seeing her. She strides over to us before sitting in my lap. I wrap my arms around her, instantly relishing in her warmth when she brings her lips to my cheek for a quick kiss. "Morning, boys."

I turn to Sutton who's wearing a pleased smirk. "Morning, Grace. Nice to see you too."

I arch a brow at him. "Really? No witty shit talking?"

"Nope," he says, shaking his head, "but I'm glad you'll finally stop moping around my restaurant now."

He turns back to Grace. "Cereal?" he says with a mouthful, raising his bowl toward Grace.

"Do not say yes," I say, pushing Sutton's bowl back toward him. "I left a bowl of yogurt and fruit on the counter by the granola for you."

He laughs. "I didn't mean my actual bowl. I brought a whole box."

I look over to the counter and, sure enough, I see the red box of sugary children's cereal on the counter that I must have missed walking around half asleep.

I turn back to him, my hands still holding onto Grace's hips in my lap. "For a world class chef, you really make me question your taste."

"Whatever, you still love my food," he scoffs.

Grace stands, taking a few steps toward the kitchen before stopping and looking back at us with a smug grin. "You've got good taste in friends and swings though."

"Swings?" he raises a brow looking at her in confusion.

Grace smirks, "Yeah, you picked our favorite one."

She turns and heads back toward the kitchen and I brazenly watch the way her hips sway with each long stride she takes. Sutton clears his throat, grabbing my attention and I shoot him a glare.

"What did she mean *favorite* swing?"

He gives me a confused look and I choke down a laugh. I look toward the wall of windows on the other side of the room and he follows my eyes to our pile of clothes from last night still on the floor. Then he looks up at the ropes holding the swing and back down to where he's sitting. He shudders and drops his spoon in the empty bowl with a clang and huffs to himself. "Damnit. I guess I'll go eat in the kitchen."

"See, these are things you could avoid if you let me know you were coming over like a normal person." I slap him on the back of his shoulder and get up, cocking my head toward the kitchen. "Come on, I'll join you."

I walk over to the kitchen island and stand next to Grace, grabbing her by the waist and pulling her to my side. Sutton sits at the island across from us, still watching with that same amused grin plastered on his face. He could crack whatever jokes he wanted to right now, but it dawns on me that I wouldn't care at all. I've got the girl that's haunted my dreams for half a year by my side and it feels good that my best friend knows. The only person I'm worried about is Grace, because she wanted her family to find out from her. I want to go at her pace and let her have whatever amount of control she wants.

"Now can we finally eat?" I say, sliding my bowl in front of me.

He huffs a laugh. "You're the one that interrupted my breakfast."

"Your breakfast?" I ask, raising my brows.

He points at the box of cereal on the counter behind me. "Yeah, it's my food. I brought it."

I look at the cereal and back at him. "Why are you even here? I thought you were staying with Slade."

Grace laughs and Sutton and I both turn to look at her.

She smiles wide and rears her head back. "What? You guys are funny. You bicker like my brothers."

Sutton shudders before mumbling. "Remind me never to get on their bad side." Then his eyes widen and he points a finger between me and Grace. "Wait, do they know about this?"

"Sutton," I say, prompting him to look right at me. "They don't know and for now, this stays between the three of us and Jake. She gets to tell them when she wants. Got it?"

He nods and I see the look in his eyes that tells me I can trust him. As unserious as he can be, when it counts, he comes through.

The sound of the elevator door to the penthouse opening grabs our attention and we all turn in that direction. I let out a long sigh when I see Jake come in, still dressed in his gym clothes from his morning workout. I look at him and then Sutton. "Again, changing my locks and codes as soon as I can."

Jake snorts a laugh and raises his coffee cup to Sutton as he sits on the other side of the island. He looks at Sutton but tilts his head to me. "I see he's his normal, charming self."

Sutton takes a sip of his coffee and shakes his head. "Actually, these two were all sweet and cuddly this morning. It's a good look for him."

"Whatever." I mutter under my breath, rubbing my hand down Grace's back, still holding her to my side. I lean down, whispering into her ear. "Are you good? I'm sorry they're all here. You can go change or throw on some of my sweats."

"I'm good. They're just legs, Tommy." She tips her head to Sutton and then Jake. "You think these two haven't seen a pair before? Besides, I grew up with Tanner and Clay. Those two are big presences, literally and figuratively. We didn't exactly have a big place when we were kids so I'm used to crowded houses in the morning."

She might be fine with it, but I want to make sure they know she's fucking mine. Absentmindedly, I kiss her just above her collarbone and she hums contentedly before I pull away to spot Jake looking between Sutton and me.

"Wait, so he knows too?" Jake asks. I roll my eyes and groan. "As of five minutes ago, since he also let himself in. Yeah."

Jake shakes his head. "Wow, you really suck at keeping this under wraps."

I shoot him a playful glare. "You didn't come over here just to tell me that."

Jake's lips pull into a half hearted smile. "No, I came for a couple reasons. I wanted to apologize last night, but you were already gone. I had no idea he was going to bring her. I never thought Vince would bring Can—"

"It's not your fault," I say, my voice colder than I meant. "I never thought he'd be that stupid either."

Jake nods and we don't have to say the rest. "Anyway, as long as it's just us that knows." I start before Grace hums with a mouthful of food, holding up a finger.

"Don't forget about Josie and Stacy," she says.

"Right." I scrub my palm over my face.

I look up to see Jake wincing and my whole body tenses.

"What is it?" I ask.

He takes a deep breath, swiping his thumb across his phone and sliding it across the kitchen island. "Remember I said I had a couple reasons for coming over? Well, the group that knows might not be so small."

I look down to see a picture of me from last night on a local online music blog. I'm standing in the rain, tilting Grace's chin up to me. While I remember the hurt and frustration in her eyes, from the outside in this picture, all I can see is the intimacy of the moment and the longing.

Shit. So much for keeping it simple.

This just got a lot more complicated.

CHAPTER 30

GRACE
LITTLE GESTURE

LOOKING DOWN at Jake's phone, it's jarring to see this scene captured by a stranger. It was only last night and I remember being so frustrated with him. In that picture though, even if he's barely touching me, it's impossible not to see the built up tension pulling us together.

"Grace." Tommy's deep voice snaps me to attention and I turn to see him focusing those blue eyes on me. "I'm so sorry. I should have been more careful. I should have kept my shit together. Are you OK? What do you want to do?"

I see the worry etched across his face. I see the stress and anxiety. I already see that my worries are nothing compared to his. I can see how this has nagged at him for years and years. It makes sense why he likes his privacy back in Jackson or Bend.

I take a deep breath and nod, trying to reassure him. "Yeah, I'm fine. Don't worry about it." My eyes drift back to the phone and I point at it. "How big of a blog is that?"

Jake grabs his phone and tucks it into his pocket. "It's not huge, just a music scene blog really. Lots of Teal Tigers fans though."

I breathe a sigh of relief.

"Good. That's perfect. My family practically lives under a rock and doesn't really use social media."

Alright. Maybe there's a chance no one in my family will find out before I have a chance to talk to them first.

"Do you think you can get them to take that post down?" Tommy's voice is still terse when he looks at Jake and I can see the tension in his jaw.

"I already reached out but haven't heard back yet. I'll stay on them and see what I can do."

"Good." Tommy nods and turns to me, rubbing his thumb over my cheek. "You sure you're—"

I raise my brows and give him a pointed look. "Stop worrying about me."

He sighs and drops his eyes. "You're right." I reach out and rub his arm, tracing my thumb over the faded barbed wire tattoo on his bicep.

"Anything I can do to help?" We turn to see Sutton, sitting there with his hand raised.

I shake my head before Tommy tips his chin to him. "Just get your shit together and be ready to meet us at the airport. I already want to get back to Jackson. We can head back a couple days early. I've already had enough of this shit here."

He looks at his best friend and brother exuding confidence and determination. It's almost enough to convince me that everything is OK, but I see that current of tension beneath the surface, coursing through him, up his spine, and to the spot he's rubbing at the base of his neck. I can only imagine that living in the public eye, under a microscope — the way he did for so many years — must've been incredibly hard. That part of his life seems like a distant, alternate reality, so far removed from the largely quiet, private life he has now.

I told myself it wouldn't bother me and it still doesn't, but now I see that he was right. As much as he doesn't want to have my life impacted by his past, it was still bound to happen at some point.

All I can think of now is that I want what he wants — to be back in Jackson.

I GRAB my mimosa from Stacy and turn to walk back where Tommy and Sutton are sitting across from each other in the middle of the plane's cabin. I stand in front of Tommy, his eyes are fixed on me. "OK. It's official. You've completely ruined me."

He looks up at me with a flirty smirk. "Are you telling me I'm spoiling my girl?"

I cock my head and shrug. "Maybe, but can you promise to stop using this jet like an Uber? I'm having serious struggles about the environmental impact."

He laughs and I give him a slap on the wrist after taking a sip of my drink. "I'm serious. This is so extra!"

"Fine," he says before taking a drink of his coffee. "No promises, but I will try." He lifts my hand and brushes his lips over the back of it with a gentle kiss. Then he pulls me down into his lap and I squeak a surprised laugh, grasping my drink in my other hand trying not to spill it.

He wraps his arms around me, winding his fingers into the hand he's still holding. I curl into him, resting my head on his shoulder, breathing in that comforting, bergamot scent.

I do my best not to worry about what people think or needing validation from others. That doesn't change the fact that I like him being so comfortable with me in front of one of his best friends. It feels reassuring. That little gesture, holding my hand — holding me — in front of his friend, feels bigger now.

"Alright, I'm going to go read." We turn to see Sutton stand up from his seat opposite us. He gives us a wink, grabs his book, and walks to the back of the plane, sprawling out on the couch and opening his book.

Tommy chuckles to himself. "He's such a dork."

"I don't know. I think he's kind of sweet." I look over to see just a hint of worry creep into his eyes. "Oh, don't tell me you're the jealous type?"

He smirks and squeezes my hand. "Not at all. I know you're mine and I'm yours." He reaches into his pocket and grabs his phone and headphones, putting one into his ear. I stop him before he puts the other one in, plucking it from his fingers and putting it in my ear. He gives me a bemused look.

"Wait, your phone's on?" I ask, pointing at his phone.

He nods slowly, looking at me like I'm crazy. "Yeah, we have WiFi on board."

"So what are we listening to?" I already put my phone and headphones away, but I also want to listen to what makes him happy. I want to know everything about him.

He turns his phone away from me, scrolling with his thumb before clicking play. He turns to me with a pleased grin.

I lean against him and he wraps his arm around me as the sound of a distorted electric guitar and rhythmic bass plays in my ear. It's followed by that eery, hoarse voice belting out lyrics with a raw edge. I listened to all kinds of music growing up, especially what my brothers and parents liked, and I would know this grunge song anywhere.

Tommy rests his head on top of mine while my eyes flutter shut. I listen to the song as he starts to talk quietly.

"I grew up listening to Nirvana CDs. There was this one older foster kid in the same house as me and we'd listen to them all night. I was maybe ten or eleven years old, which in hindsight, was hardly age appropriate." His chest rumbles with a low laugh. "But it wasn't like I had the best supervision in that house. I remember the kids at school would talk about waiting for their favorite band's new albums to come out so they could buy the CD."

"CDs? God, you're old. Did you carry around one of those portable players and everything?"

He laughs through his nose and presses a quick kiss to my forehead. "You're something, you know that?"

I shrug. "You're right though. They had a lot of great albums. It's hard to pick a favorite."

I yawn and hold onto his arm wrapped around me.

I feel him nod, dragging his stubble through my hair.

"Yeah. It's probably weird and morbid, but something about their music always grounded me. I think that's also when I really understood death for the first time, realizing I would never get a new album from my favorite band. I don't know, I think maybe that's how I ended up right here though. No drugs, no groupies, just babysitting my bandmates and nursing a few drinks."

I tilt my head enough to look into his eyes and see that nostalgic, contemplative look in them.

I reach up, cupping his cheek with my hand. I look into his crystalline blue eyes, wanting him to know I heard him and love that he just opened up like that.

"I think we all respond to tragedy differently. Sometimes, I feel like I make it too much of a point to live what I think is a full, spontaneous life." I look down in my lap, looking at his hand holding mine. "I try to take advantage of every second I get and sometimes, I forget to slow down and enjoy what I have."

"Sounds like we both still have some lessons to learn."

I nod and lean into him, soaking up his warmth. He presses play and we spend the rest of the flight just like that.

One thought occupies my mind the whole way back to Jackson. Maybe this is why he came into my life when he did. Maybe he's the calm and steady to my fast and free.

✳

I BUCKLE my seatbelt as Tommy puts the car in drive to make the trip from the airport's private terminal back to his house in Jackson. He reaches across the center console and rests his hand on my knee. I love the contact, but I lift his hand and place it back on the wheel.

"Sorry, I still get uneasy in cars when it comes to distracted driving." His eyes briefly flick to mine and they're laced with concern. With my history, it's something that's always bothered me that I've never been able to shake.

"No, you're right. I got it. Hands at ten and two," he says, nodding.

"But you can think about putting that hand much higher when we're back at your house in twenty minutes."

"You don't have to tell me twice." He grins, popping his dimple. "Besides that, anything else you want to do tonight? Thoughts on dinner? We could stop into Gloria's and see Sutton."

"That could be fun." I reach into my bag and pull out my phone, turning it back on. "I should check in with Josie too and see what she's up to. I didn't tell her we were coming back a day early."

As soon as my phone screen lights up, message after message appears. So many notifications pop up that it vibrates nonstop in my hand.

"Baby, if you wait twenty minutes, you won't need your vibrator. I'll take care of you." He waggles his brows and I feel that heat creep up my neck.

"I thought you said you weren't the jealous type? And no, it's my phone. It's blowing up."

I open a string of text messages, all from Veronica.

> V: OMG.
>
> V: What were you and TJ doing last night? Are you and TJ a thing?!
>
> V: Call me! I have so many questions.
>
> V: Also… don't get mad. I might have freaked out and showed Tanner.

The last two text messages came in only about 15 minutes ago.

> V: Jake called Tanner to make sure the driveway was clear. Your brother might be waiting at TJ's house.
>
> V: Wait… OMG! Are you staying there now? I love your brother, but you're seriously living my teenage fantasy right now of dating Tommy Jacob from Teal Tigers.

Shit. I scroll the string of messages to see more of the same. I know Jake said it was just on a music blog, but he did say a lot of the followers were Teal Tigers mega fans. I should have known Veronica probably followed that blog and would see it. I almost love her enthusiasm, but it's the messages about my brother that have my knee bouncing in the passenger seat.

"Everything OK?" Tommy asks.

I hum and nod rapidly. "Yep, totally fine." My voice turns into a nervous squeak.

"Grace." His eyes flick to mine for a second before going back to the road, but long enough for his smile to fade and his lips to press together into a line. "Why don't I believe you?"

CHAPTER 31
TJ
SIBLINGS

GRACE LOOKS at me from the passenger seat wearing a very unconvincing smile.

"So remember how Veronica is one of your biggest fans?"

I nod. "Hardly see how that's relevant right now, but yes."

"And remember how that picture was on a music blog with a bunch of your fans?"

"Yeah. And? What does that—" I cut myself off when it clicks. "No. Please tell me she didn't see it."

"Do you want the truth or do you want me to do what you asked?" I hear a playful tone in her voice. I'm glad she's having fun with this because she's not the one who is probably going to face down her brothers.

"Shit." I strum my fingers over the steering wheel. "You know we already have our bags. We could take an impromptu road trip to literally anywhere — anywhere your brothers aren't?"

"Tommy." I hear the seriousness in her voice, but also the calmness. Then I feel her hand gently squeeze my knee in a comforting gesture, but I keep my eyes on the road. "If we want to keep taking this seriously, we might as well rip this bandaid off. V said Tanner's waiting at your house. So let's get it over with."

I take a deep breath and exhale. "You're right. It's not like we got married without telling them. We're just two adults that are happy together."

She lets out an infectious laugh and a thought I've never even let see the light of day creeps into my mind. What does she want long-term? Would she ever even want to get married? And if I'm thinking about that, is that what I really want deep down? I bury that thought for another day and focus on the task at hand, getting home, and talking to her brother.

"Relax," she says, her calm voice soothing my nerves. "We'll do this together."

SURE ENOUGH, when I pull through the gate into my driveway and past the main house, Tanner's truck is there, parked right next to Grace's van. And leaning against the truck is the six-four, rugged mountain man that I've known for years, who also happens to be the brother of the girl I'm falling for. Correction, I've completely fallen for.

I park behind her van and look at her in the passenger seat. "You think if we sit here long enough he'll leave?"

She gives me a playful shove, but I see her hesitation. "Come on, let's get this over with." She unbuckles her seatbelt, stopping to look back at me. "Besides, if he really does beat your ass, I can nurse your old, frail body back to health."

She tosses me a wink and suddenly, I don't feel nearly as bad about this as I did fifteen minutes ago.

I step out of the car and walk around to the passenger side, opening the door for her. She hops out and hugs me, tapping the door shut behind her with her boot. I hold her against my chest, rubbing her back.

Tanner just stands there menacingly, briefly looking at us

before focusing all his intensity on me. Knowing him, I'm sure his pulse is a goddamn flatline. He's worked for me for years before we became friends and I've never once seen him lose his temper. The look on his face now though is pure, quiet rage and I get it. I'd probably be pissed too if I had a little sister and someone I called a friend was going after her. Much less an infamous rockstar who was fifteen years older than her and has baggage that still follows him around.

I brush her bangs out of the way and press my lips against her forehead before letting go of her and I don't miss the way Tanner grimaces.

I tip my chin to him. "Hey," I start, "I'm sorry you had to find out that way. She wanted to tell you herself when she was ready. This is what she wanted though."

He looks at Grace for a second before stepping toward me, stopping within arm's reach for someone his size. "What the fuck is wrong with you, TJ? You hire my little sister and now you're dragging her into the media for some publicity stunt or whatever it is you're even doing?"

I shake my head. "No, that's not it at all. I hired her because I know she's passionate about what she does. Because she's smart. Because she cares so deeply. Everything else sort of just happened after that."

His nostrils flare and I see the doubt in his expression. "So you're telling me that you never thought about her like this before hiring her?"

I sigh and palm my face. "I'm not going to lie to you. I was interested in her. When we met in Bend, she was just so genuine, so—" I run my hand through my hair and sigh. "So damn energetic and real. But I meant it when I said that's not why I asked her to work for me."

He takes a step toward Grace and holds her shoulder. If he wasn't her brother, I'd have already decked anyone for getting that close and touching her. "Are you alright? I'm so sorry for letting him take advantage of you."

I watch her reaction and the look in her eyes might be more intense than her brother's. She steps into him and shoves him square in the chest, almost knocking him off his feet. Tanner normally dwarfs most people around him, but I can see that she's used to being up in her brother's face with her height. He takes a step back and looks between us.

"Am I alright? Do you realize how messed up it is that you're asking me that?" She takes another step toward him and jabs him in the chest with a pointed finger. "Do you really still think I'm that same fragile girl from high school? You still think I can't take care of myself and make my own decisions?"

He scrubs his hand over his face and shakes his head. "No, of course not. That's not what I meant. But you don't need to date him just because he's our boss."

Her jaw tightens and her eyebrows shoot up. I see the hardened look in her normally sparkling eyes.

Shit. She's mad.

That doesn't change the fact that she is absolutely stunning right now. Her profile is laced with fury and intensity, highlighted by the snowy landscape behind her amplifying her vibrant colors. Those beautiful evergreen pools burn with a fire that I can't look away from, framed by her bangs and freckles in a way that draws me in more.

All of it screams passion, confidence, and determination, the kind I once had. The kind I've started to feel again when I'm with her.

"This is what I'm talking about. Have you, for once, considered that I'm the one who wanted this? That I'm the one who started things with him? No, apparently not. Apparently you think I'm still little Gracie that needs to be protected from herself and everything around her. Do you realize how pissed Mom would be if she knew you treated me like this?"

I wince at that, knowing the history behind her loss, their loss.

She takes a step back and crosses her arms over her chest. She tilts her head toward the truck. "Now, go home. Come back when you get your stupid damn head out of your childish ass. I'm done talking with you."

He opens his mouth to say something, but she shoots him a glare. "Now. I mean it."

I watch in complete dismay as Tanner tucks his tail between his legs and walks back to his truck. He takes one look at the two of us over his shoulder before getting in and closing the door with a solid thud. Grace and I both watch as he backs down the driveway and the gate closes behind him.

I turn to her, seeing her shoulders rise and fall with heavy breaths, her cheeks red. She's still fuming when I reach out and grab her hand.

"Hey. I'm sorry. Are you alright?"

Her brows wrinkle and she looks at me. "Why are you sorry? You didn't do anything wrong."

I step closer to her, resting my hand on her hip over her long, puffy down jacket. "That was brutal and I'm the reason he's pissed at you."

She sighs and shakes her head. Her eyes meet mine and I see some of her normal brightness returning. "We're siblings. We argue sometimes, but that's not your problem. This is between me and him. And honestly, it's mostly on him."

The look on my face must not be convincing because she rolls her eyes and smiles. "Seriously, Tanner and I will be fine. He might look all mean and broody, but he's a teddy bear underneath all of that. You've seen him with Veronica enough to know that."

"More like a grizzly bear if you ask me."

She gives me a playful shove in my chest, unlike the one Tanner was on the receiving end of. "Very funny."

Jake and I have fought, but never like that. Clearly, their sibling bond is strong if she's that confident they'll just get over it. But if I do want this to work, I should take a note from this whole day and trust her and give her the space to sort this out how she wants.

"Just let me know what I can do." I reach up, rubbing the back of my knuckles over her freckles.

"You can start by taking my bags in and letting me see that shower of yours finally." She gives me a wry smile and I give her one swift nod in return.

"Done." Just like me, because I'm done.

I'm not just falling for her, I already have. She has my heart and she has my love.

CHAPTER 32
GRACE
GIVE IT ALL UP

One Week Later

THE LAST WEEK in Jackson has been great. I've been out to ski and I've stopped in to see my grandparents. I've been able to do more work on coming up with a new plan to still make a bigger impact with Tommy's charitable giving while maintaining his privacy.

Then there's the sex.

After Josie left town to meet up with some friends in Oregon, I've finally been able to spend more time alone with Tommy. That night at the hot tub and that night in Seattle were good, but somehow it's been even better now that we're not trying to hide. He can't keep his hands off me and I'm just as bad. I crave how he makes me feel cared for and safe, but alive and desired all at once. He's every bit the man I thought he was and more.

It's almost surreal how easy it has been to fall into a comfortable routine with him back in the town I grew up in. Even stopping into Cowgirl Coffee today takes me back to growing up here. Seeing Kelsey who I'd known for years before we moved to Utah just feels like a normal day.

"This storm system has been nuts," Kelsey says from behind the counter, grabbing a pastry from the case. "I'm so glad I'm off on most Sundays because I'd lose it if I had to miss another powder day tomorrow. The long drive from Victor is bad enough."

I think to myself just how lucky I am to have a flexible work schedule and a very, very forgiving boss.

Drink and snack in hand, I turn to make my way past everyone in line behind me toward the door. When I pass by a group of girls, I notice one lean into the other whispering. I don't hear exactly what she says, but I definitely catch one thing. "Can you believe he's dating her?"

My mind instantly goes to those days back in Utah, worrying that people saw me as something other than my authentic self. Clay's little sister, the girl that survived the crash. I knew being with Tommy would come with baggage, but I haven't given a second thought about this part. Does being with him mean being OK with everyone knowing me as Tommy Jacob's girlfriend? There are certainly worse things I could be known for. I can't think of a better man to be tied to like that. I'd be proud to be tied to him, but that still doesn't mean I don't have reservations about it though.

Distracted by that thought, I turn and nudge open the door with my boot and stop when I bump into someone.

"Oh, sorry about that. I'm kind of a klutz when I have my hands full." My smile falters when I look up and see Veronica, probably on her way in for her second iced Honey Badger of the day.

The corners of her mouth lift into a genuinely warm, but weary smile.

"Hey, girl!" She wraps her arm around my shoulder in a one armed hug, careful to mind my full hands. We're almost eye to eye and I remember that she's nearly as tall as me. "It's good to see you."

I enjoy the short hug because I have wanted to see her, especially since we've both been back in town. She might be my new sister-in-law, but I've known her for practically my entire life since her grandparents were best friends with mine.

"We should get a drink or something soon." I lean into her embrace and look up just in time to see my brother round the corner.

And there he is, the one thing in Jackson that hasn't been great lately. He gives me a quick look and walks past us to get in line to order.

Veronica lets go of me and we both watch him walk by. I can see the sad, frustrated look in her eyes. She sighs. "I've been trying to work on him."

I nudge her in the shoulder. "You're as bad as Tommy. Don't beat yourself up, it's not your fault that he's being an ass. He'll get over it."

She quirks a brow at me. "I mean, I did sort of blab to him about the picture on the blog. So, yeah it's at least a teensy bit my fault." She holds up her thumb and finger with the tiniest space between them.

"Well, I always wanted a sister so I'll let that one slide. At least until Lizzy replaces you," I say, bumping my elbow into hers.

"Thanks." She smiles warmly back at me and this time I don't see any of the weariness from before. "So you're all good then?"

I nod, hardly able to contain my grin that even my moody brother can't completely put a damper on. "Really good."

"Well if we can't get together soon, use the group chat. I know Lizzy and Kayleigh probably have just as many questions as I do. We need details, girl!"

I let out a short laugh. "Yeah. I'll do that."

She starts to say something before the way too obvious sound of my brother clearing his throat interrupts us. She rolls her eyes. "Well, I better get back to working on him."

"Just be you. He loves you and he'll cave if he knows it matters to you."

I KNOW Veronica is working on my brother, but that still doesn't change that I'm annoyed and frustrated. He's being an even more obnoxious, overly protective version of himself than he was when I was younger. I want him to trust me to take care of myself. I need him to understand that, but I also know I need to let go of feeling like I need his approval.

The only thing worse than that is the pain I feel because I am close with my brothers. I love talking to them and now that they know, all I want to do is share how happy I am with them. Clay has at least been texting me back and called me. Clay and I have always been closer since we're only a year apart. We moved to Utah with Mom and Dad, but since Tanner is about eight years older, he stayed here in Wyoming.

I would love to be able to talk with Tanner, especially because he and Veronica are here in the same town. I guess that's the curse of small towns though. There's no hiding from someone in them, good or bad. I know we'll eventually sort things out, but running into him today and having him basically ignore me still hurt. For being my oldest brother, he's the one acting like a baby.

The whole situation has made me restless and I'm dealing with it the best way I know how: using my billionaire boyfriend's very nice home gym. After finishing my tea and pastry, I went right to the walk-in closet in Tommy's room, which I'm convinced is the size of my studio apartment in Utah, and changed into some spandex workout shorts and a sports bra.

Since getting back in town, we've spent every night in his room, and he let me use the extra space in his giant closet. He hasn't been pushy about it. Instead, he's just let things happen naturally and I adore him for it. Whenever he'd spot my laundry, he'd do it for me and put my clothes back away in his closet. Ever since that first night I fell asleep with him on the guesthouse couch watching music videos, I knew there was no place I'd rather be than wrapped in his arms.

When I walk into the gym and find him already there, sitting on the bench and lifting in the squat rack, I can't control the grin that spreads across my face and the warmth that fills my chest. I slowly walk up behind him, admiring the view of him shirtless and his subtle muscles in all their glory — like I did the first time I found him in here. When I get closer, he looks up in the mirror and his eyes find mine. Even in the middle of his lift, his mouth opens into a boyish, toothy grin, showing off his dimples.

I stand behind him, watching him in the mirror while he finishes his set, practically bouncing on my feet between the restless frustration from dealing with my brother earlier and the electric anticipation I get whenever I'm around Tommy. When he finishes, he sets down his weights and cocks his head to each side, swaying his hair in a far too sexy way as he takes out his earbuds one by one.

"Hey, Rainbow." His deep voice is raspier than normal from his workout. "How was Cowgirl Coffee?"

I step forward, wrapping my arms around him while he's still seated on the bench, facing the mirror in front of us. My hands roam over his warm, toned chest and I lean down to press a kiss to the top of his head.

He lets out a deep contented hum and looks back up to me. The view of him looking up at me with those glacial water blue eyes always makes my heart flutter.

"It was fine until I ran into Tanner and V." I splay my hand across his chest and he reaches up, holding onto my wrist when I let out a long sigh. "Tanner's still being an ass, but Veronica is working on him. I just wanted to get a run in and blow off some steam."

He brings each of my hands to his mouth and drags his lips across them. "I'm sorry. I can try talking to him again."

I shake my head. "No, it's fine. And stop apologizing. I told you, it's not your fault."

He huffs a laugh and I see the look of understanding in his eyes. "Well, just tell me if there's something I can do."

I nod and that warmth in my heart threatens to overtake me completely. I know that if I asked him to do anything, he would. I also know that if I tell him to let me figure something out on my own, he will. That's how I know that I've completely fallen for him, because he's the man I thought he was.

WITH EACH MILE I tick off on the treadmill, the last little bits of frustration and irritation with my brother fade away. Instead, I focus on everything I have to look forward to. It's Saturday and Tommy and I will probably go sit at the chef's counter at Gloria's for dinner. I was skeptical at first, but he was right. Badgering Sutton at the restaurant is fun. Tomorrow, we plan on going out to ski and, in a couple weeks, I'll get to go meet up with Josie and some of our other friends in Lake Tahoe for our ski trip.

With each stride, my feet pound against the treadmill and my ponytail bounces against my shoulders. It's what's in the corner of my eye that has my skin heated though. Every time I peek across the room, I'm met with Tommy's eyes on me.

"Hey there," I say between breaths while he takes a break between sets of curls. His eyes fly up just a bit to meet mine and I see red creep across his cheeks, like I just caught him doing something he shouldn't.

I look down at my chest where he was looking and let out a short laugh when I see my hardened nipples and tiny barbells showing through the fabric of my sports bra. I always take the annoying pads out because they just get lost in the wash or bunch up anyway, but the way he's looking at me is more than a perk. It makes me glad I didn't have the patience for those stupid pads.

I slow down the pace of the treadmill and smirk back at him, flicking my eyebrows. "You're really obsessed with these, aren't you?"

He grabs his aluminum water bottle and takes a drink. I watch how his tongue darts over his lips to clean off a stray drop. His gaze sharpens into the intense one that makes my core clench.

"You'll have to be more specific because I'm obsessed with everything about you," he rasps, matter-of-factly.

I press stop on the treadmill and hop off, grabbing my towel before walking over to where he's sitting in the squat rack. I stop right at the edge of the flat workout bench, standing in front of him. In the floor to ceiling mirror, I can see his well-toned back muscles glistening with sweat. I drape my arms around his neck and step into him, my bare knees rubbing against gray sweats that hug his thighs perfectly. He takes his earbuds out and tucks them in his pocket before running his fingertips up the back of my thighs to the hem of my shorts, just under the curve of my ass. If he moved his fingers just a few inches higher, he'd find my spandex shorts already damp.

He turns his face and leans his head against my chest and I feel his breath against my sweat slicked skin, sending goosebumps across my body.

Looking back in the mirror, I can see the closeness of our

embrace. It's impossible to miss the peace in both of our expressions.

"How'd I get so lucky to find you?" I lift a hand to the nape of his neck, ruffling his shaggy hair.

He lifts his head and looks up at me with a confused look. "How'd you get so lucky? I'm the one that has to pinch myself every day to remind myself I'm not dreaming, Rainbow."

I roll my eyes and ruffle his hair again. "Don't be so dramatic."

He leans forward, pressing another kiss to the bare skin between my breast, just above my sports bra, sending another wave of goosebumps across my skin. I whimper at the touch and he looks back up at me.

The look in his eyes nearly stops my breath. Gone is the confusion, replaced by a vulnerable openness I can't put into words.

"If there's one thing I am in life, it's lucky. I'm lucky I ended up with good foster parents and met Jake. I'm lucky I met my bandmates in high school that gave me all of this. I'm lucky I bought places in Seattle when I did." He swallows hard and I feel his grip on my thighs tighten.

"I'm lucky I met your brothers. I'm lucky my trip to Seattle got canceled and I stayed in Bend that week because that's how I met you. Most of all, I'm lucky because you let me be in your life."

That look in his eyes hardens, crystalizing into something I can put into words. One word, to be exact.

Love.

I see it laid bare before me. I don't know if either of us are ready to say it, but I know we both feel it.

He takes a deep breath and continues, "You asked me once if I would do anything different, if I would give it all up. The answer is no, I wouldn't change a thing because all of that brought me — brought us — to right here."

I reach for his cheek, rubbing the backs of my fingers across his stubble, looking into the depths of those blue pools that just stole my heart. "I can think of something else you are." I lean down and slant my lips to his, pulling away just long enough to say one syllable, one word.

"Mine."

His low grunt is the kind of feral, raw response I lust after. His hands move up, molding to my ass and pulling me toward him. I step forward and over his legs, straddling his lap, bringing me almost eye to eye with him.

"I've been yours for months," he says. He runs his hands up my back, his fingertips grazing my spine along the path to the band of my sports bra.

I bring my mouth to his waiting lips and he pulls me into the kiss. Every time our lips meet, it feels hungrier, any trace of his hesitations from weeks ago are gone. All that's left is our undeniable bond, drawing us together constantly.

I give into that bond, melting into him, sinking into his lap. His hard erection presses against my wet core through my shorts and his sweatpants. I swivel my hips, grinding my clit against him, increasing the friction for both of us. He groans into my mouth before breaking the kiss. "Fuck, baby."

His eyes look down to where I'm sitting in his lap and I can see how I've already left a damp spot on his sweats. I grin back at him and slowly, I slide back and forth, my piercing putting more pressure on my clit, building that tension low in my belly.

"You're already so wet for me. You love grinding on my cock, don't you?"

I nod, my lips parting as my breathing quickens. "I fucking love your dick."

He lets out a low, husky laugh and rocks his hips forward,

pressing his length against my core, pushing my need even higher.

My head falls to his neck and I moan. "I want to taste you."

He cups the nape of my neck when he brings his lips to my ear. "Now, hold on."

Before I can think, he stands, and my legs wrap around his waist like a reflex. He turns around and sets me down on the edge of the bench. I look up to find him standing over me, but I can't look away from the bulge in his sweatpants and the spot I left. I reach forward, running my hand over his length and he shudders at my touch. I smirk up at him, seeing the lust and need in his eyes and tighten my grip on his shaft.

CHAPTER 33
TJ
SO PRETTY

GRACE SITTING in front of me grabbing my cock is almost enough to make me come right here, right now. The look in her eyes, the pure needy lust, makes me want to rip those light blue shorts right off and bury my cock in her. Her fucking mouth though. The way her tongue darts out before her teeth dig into her bottom lip has me frozen and I can't look away.

She lets go of my cock and leans forward, hooking her fingers into my pants and shimmying them down. I kick my shoes off and step out of them, but I don't miss the way her pupils flare when my cock springs free.

She rests her hands on my thighs, kissing my stomach, slowly working her way down, torturing me and making my balls tighten.

My dick is painfully throbbing by the time her mouth reaches it and she licks the drop of precum off, making my spine straighten. She grabs the base of my shaft and squeezes, making me buck into her hand and brace myself on her shoulder.

"Fuck," I say through gritted teeth.

She looks up at me with a mischievous grin. "Don't come yet."

I roll my eyes. "I come in my pants one ti—" She lowers her mouth to the head of my cock, swirling her tongue over it and I forget how to speak.

Slowly, she takes me further in her mouth and I watch in awe as she takes me to the back of her throat, humming in amusement. She looks up at me with those big green eyes, water pricking the corners of them.

"So pretty with my cock in your mouth." I reach down and cup one of her breasts over her bra, my fingers finding her hardened bud through the fabric, my thumb tracing the little metallic barbell. She moans with my cock down her throat and it sends a shiver through me, making my balls tighten.

She starts to bob her head up and down, hollowing her cheeks with suction that threatens to make me blow already. We've been fucking all week but I still clearly need to work on my stamina with her. Watching her take my cock in her mouth — shining with her spit, making those cute little whimpers and moans — is intoxicating.

The only thing that can pull my eyes away is her reflection in the mirror. The way she's bent over, I can see the curves of her body and her full ass. Those skin tight light blue shorts do nothing to hide how wet she is and remind me that I want more than just her mouth right now.

I fist her ponytail, somehow finding the masochistic strength to stop her before I come. She looks up at me with questioning eyes, still sitting on the edge of the bench with the head of my cock still resting on her plush lips. I bring my hand up to her lips, tracing the bottom one, wiping off some of her spit. "You said just a taste. Don't get greedy. Now, it's my turn."

I kneel down in front of her and drag my hands up the sides of her long, toned legs, feeling every inch of her smooth, heated skin. My hands find the waistband of her shorts and I peel them down her legs and take off her running shoes.

She spreads her thighs for me and my eyes fall to her already wet pussy and that little black piece of jewelry on her hood. I press a kiss to her soft inner thighs and she squeezes my head between her legs at my touch. I look up at her to find her looking at me with hooded eyes. "Lay back and relax," I say, running a fingertip over her piercing, making her shudder. She's so wet for me already that my finger glides over the smooth metal.

She shakes her head. "No, I want to watch you."

That lights a fire under my skin. "Not yet."

She rolls her eyes and gives me a playful, pouty look. "Fine."

She lays back down on the leather gym bench and I lift her legs, resting them on my shoulders. I slowly ghost my lips over the soft skin of her legs, feeling her writhe with built up tension.

I plant a kiss just above her swollen bundle of nerves and she bucks, pushing herself toward my mouth. I grin, loving how she responds to my touch. My eyes flick up to find her propped up on her elbows, still trying to watch me.

"My girl is so needy," I say, holding her gaze before I lower my mouth and glide the tip of my tongue over her clit. Her eyes close and she lets out a low, contented hum, slumping back down against the bench.

I lap at her clit, tasting her sweet arousal, still lust drunk knowing that I do this to her. When I look past her into the mirror, I see the deep, feral need in my own reflection when I increase the pressure with my tongue. I swirl it around her sensitive bud, feeling the cool metal of her piercing. Her legs tense around me and her heels dig into my back. Reaching up, I dip one, then two fingers into her soaked pussy.

She gasps and she pulls me tighter against her. I laugh to myself before rewarding her, plunging my fingers in and out, curling them against her most sensitive spot while sucking on her clit.

I look up to see her arching her back, pushing her tits up in the air and I see her piercings pressing through that fabric. The first chance I get, that bra is coming off.

I suck harder on her clit, holding it in my mouth while my tongue flicks faster and faster over it. I feel her walls clench around my fingers and I know she's close.

"That's it, baby. Let go. Let go so I can fill this soaked pussy with my cock." She moans and I feel her whole body tense, her pussy grabbing my fingers when she finally gives into the pleasure and comes undone, her orgasm rocking her body.

I give her clit one last swipe of my tongue before I lift my head, watching her chest heave while I still work her with my fingers. She props herself back up on her elbows and looks at me, her sparkling green eyes glassed over. I slide my fingers out of her, prompting her to gasp. I take my fingers to my mouth and lick them clean. "You taste so fucking good."

Her lips part before she bites her lower lip. "Anyone ever told you that you're talented? Like really talented?"

I laugh, extending my hand for her to grab. "Not anyone that's ever mattered to me."

She grabs my hand and I pull her to her feet. She giggles, falling into my arms. I pull her tight, tilting her chin to look up at me. "Now I think I said something about filling your pussy with my cock."

She reaches down, grabbing my shaft and squeezes. "Then get to it."

The playfully wicked glint in her eyes tells me everything I need to know. She wants me as bad as I want her.

CHAPTER 34
GRACE
WORSHIPPED AND WELL-FUCKED

I LOOK into the eyes of the man I know I'm in love with, watching a muscle tick in his jaw when I tighten my grip on his hard length.

"Fuck, baby. I don't know what's tighter, your fist or your perfect cunt."

I lift my brows. "Good thing you're about to find out."

His hands find my waist and he spins me around, giving my ass one deliciously biting slap. "Then go to the end of the bench."

I take a couple of steps forward, stopping at the edge of the weight bench in front of the mirror. He sits down behind me on the bench, bringing his head to my side, running his hands up my thighs and resting them on my hip bones. He kisses the dip of my waist and all I can do is watch him in the mirror, the way he reverently touches me, firm and rough but still lovingly, in a way that makes my body sing.

His grip on my hips tightens and he lowers me down into his lap, pressing my wet core against his erection that's so hard I can feel him throbbing beneath me. His arm wraps around me, pulling my back to his front.

"You have a thing for mirrors and being watched?" I ask, looking at him over my shoulder.

He shakes his head. "You're so fucking beautiful when you're about to come. I want you to see it. Now, take off that bra and eyes on us."

He thrusts his hips up, pressing his hard, veiny shaft against my piercing sending a wave of pleasure through me. I reach for my bra and pull it over my head, tossing it aside. I melt into his lap and he moans against my neck.

He drops his hands to my waist, lifting me off his lap just enough to notch himself at my entrance. I grip his thighs, running my nails along his muscular quads and brace myself. He nudges my cheek with his stubbled jaw, prompting me to look forward into the mirror. My eyes meet his.

"Watch how good you look when you take me."

Slowly, he lowers me. Inch after inch of his long, thick cock stretches me open, and I gasp at the pleasure when he's fully seated in me.

"Fuck, you feel so good," I pant. I rock my hips, needing more friction. I feel my core clench.

I feel him tense beneath me and hear him hiss through his teeth. His reflection shows how his jaw tightens at the sensation. Clearly, this is doing things for both of us.

"You want me to fill you with my cum? Because if you keep that up that's what's going to happen."

I hum my approval, rocking my hips and clenching my pussy again. He drops one hand between my thighs, dragging his knuckles against the sensitive skin until his fingertips reach the apex of my thighs. He starts to rock his hips forward, slow and rhythmically while he fingers my clit.

I lean back into his chest, swiveling my hips in rhythm with him. He cups my breast with his other hand and rolls my nipple between his fingertips, tugging on the little barbells just the right amount to peak my need. I whimper at his touch, throwing my head back when he presses a kiss to my neck.

"See how good we look together," he rasps, his voice low and gravelly. I lower my head back to the sight waiting for me in the mirror.

It's raw. We're sweaty. We're a mess. We're broken in our own ways, but we're one and the same.

He plunges into me over and over and I can see how my arousal is soaking his cock. I watch the chorded muscles of his arm work in beautiful harmony while he strums my clit. I watch the way his fingers play with my breast. Most of all though, I see the look in his eyes gazing back at me.

He's giving me everything I want, placating all of my senses, my never-ending need for stimulation. And most of all, he knows it.

I rock my hips faster, craving that sweet release we both want. He matches my pace, thrusting harder, and increasing the pressure on my clit with his fingers. He kisses my neck again, pushing me closer to the edge.

"Yes! Yes! Please!" I cry out.

He groans against my neck and holds my gaze in the mirror. "That's my girl. So fucking beautiful taking every inch of me."

His warm breath against my neck and his words undo me. I arch my back into him when I come, moaning and digging my nails into his thighs, pressing my core down onto him, bottoming him out in me.

My pussy clenches on his shaft and my thighs tighten around his hand, holding it there while he rings every last ounce of pleasure from my worshipped and well-fucked body.

"Fuck. That's it," he grits out before biting my neck, his grip on my nipple tightening. I feel his cock pulse and twitch as he spills into me, finding his release deep inside me.

We both stay there, molded to each other, riding out our

orgasms. Our chests heave with heavy breaths as we slowly come down from our highs. I whimper as he places a trail of kisses down my neck and along my shoulder.

I relax, opening my thighs and releasing his hand. He brings it across my front, holding me to him.

I can't look away from our reflection. I see the devotion in his expression. The way he holds my spent body, while he's still stretching me, a bead of his cum dripping down my thigh, I didn't know it was possible to be this desired, to be loved this viscerally.

I want to tell him. I know I feel it, but the words are stuck in my throat. "Why me?" I say instead, leaving those other three little words unspoken. My voice is so quiet I almost think I imagined saying anything.

He stops his trail of kisses and wraps his other arm around my front, holding me tightly to him. My fingers trace along his bicep and over his tattoo, when he brings his lips to my ear and whispers. "Because you have the heart of someone who's lived a thousand lives. I wish I knew you in each and every one of them because this one sure as hell isn't enough."

CHAPTER 35
TJ
SHARING MY SNACKS

"YOU'RE TELLING me she ran through the campground topless over a bag of skittles?" I quirk a brow at Grace sitting next to me at the kitchen island for breakfast.

She takes another sip of her tea and nods. "She doesn't mess around when it comes to someone messing with her snacks. My family always thinks I'm the wild one, but Josie puts me to shame. You'll get to see that next weekend when we go to Tahoe."

"I don't know if I want to find out," I say, shaking my head before eating another spoonful of my yogurt and berries.

I've always been a morning person and enjoyed my peace and quiet to start the day. These mornings I've spent with her the last few weeks have me glad that she's an early riser too. Getting up before the sunrise, seeing the fresh snow lit by the moon, and enjoying breakfast with her is how I'd start every day if I could. We've talked about everything from music to the favorite places we've traveled and things in life we still want to do. Each morning has felt like a date almost and I've loved it. She hasn't traveled nearly as much as she's wanted to though and as much as she might object to frivolous use of my jet, I'm going to change that as soon as our schedules allow.

I look at her and she shrugs innocently. "Too bad. You're coming with us next week, whether you like it or not. No changing your mind now." She grabs my thighs, running her hands up my gym shorts, sending blood rushing to my cock. Everything she does seems to make my body respond. "Josie's been blowing my phone up all week asking about Hot Daddy Boss. We can't let her down now."

"She knows I'm *your* boyfriend, right? Not hers?"

She rubs her thumbs over my inner thighs and from the look in her eyes, she knows exactly what she's doing to me. Her gaze drops to my lap before she looks back into my eyes. "I don't like sharing my snacks either."

I lean forward, kissing her soft lips, breathing in her lavender scent that I can't get enough of. I nip at her bottom lip, tugging on it before pulling away. I hear her little gasp before our eyes meet. "Same. Glad we got that out of the way."

"Good." She smiles softly and stands, taking her empty bowl over to the sink. I prop my elbows up on the counter, leaning on my fists while I watch her. She's humming to herself, rocking her head side to side, swaying her hair. Her sleep shorts hang just off her hips giving me a full view of her long legs. I have to remind myself and my hard cock that I can't just drag her back to bed. It's Thursday and she said she actually wants to get some work done this morning. When she's focused, she's a force to be reckoned with and I know there's no stopping her.

I know she says she's happy with what she's doing, but I still can't shake the memory of how she looked when I said no to being more public about my charitable giving. I want to make sure she's happy, that she's thriving, and not giving up anything that she wants, just to be with me. I want her to feel like she's living her best life and I'm not holding her back.

I'm about to ask her about her plans for the rest of the day when lights outside catch my attention. I turn toward the windows and see headlights coming down the driveway toward the gate. I recognize the headlights from the plow truck that Tanner drives. She follows my line of sight and I see her posture sag and her smile fade.

I get up and walk to her side, draping an arm around her waist. "Go out and talk to him. I know you're still mad at him—"

Her eyes flick to mine and she raises a brow.

"And rightfully so," I clarify with a laugh. "Give him a chance. Maybe he'll take the opportunity and apologize."

She takes a deep breath and groans. "Fine."

I swipe away her bangs and press a kiss to her forehead. Then she heads toward the door to the driveway, pulling on her snow boots and a long, puffy jacket.

"Good luck," I call out, as she pulls the door shut.

I head to the other end of the kitchen to make myself an espresso, thinking about what I want to get done today since she's planning to work. I load the grinder when I hear the door open and see Grace coming back inside. Shit. That was quick.

I stop making my coffee and walk over to her. She kicks off her boots and my heart sinks when I see her face. Instead of frustration or irritation, I see hurt and sadness.

"I take it that didn't go well?" I ask, rubbing her shoulders.

She shakes her head and doesn't meet my eyes. I reach up, tilting her chin to look at me. "I'm sorry he's being difficult, but he'll get there."

She sighs. "I know. I just want to be able to share this with everyone. We've always been so close."

I rub the pad of my thumb over her cheek. "Why don't you try talking to the girls? I know they must be excited for you. Share it with them."

That little spark in her eyes that I love returns. She pulls her phone out and starts typing away.

"Wait, I didn't mean this second. It's not even seven in the morning."

She hums dismissively with mischief in her eyes. "Never too early to start shit."

CHAPTER 36
GRACE
SHOW AND TELL

BRUNCH BABES

> Me: Tanner's still being an ass.

Lizzy: What'd he do now? Clay's been such a good boy about this. Come back to Park City soon? I miss my OG Brunch Babe.

> Me: Wait... Lizzy, why are you already up?

> Me: I tried to flag Tanner down while he was plowing the driveway and he ignored me.

V: Ugh. I'm trying to work on him.

Lizzy: Try working on him in a gondola. I heard that goes a long way.

Lizzy: Clay likes to do morning yoga. So here I am. Of course I had to find an accountability buddy that loves waking up early.

Kayleigh: For all the talk about women being dramatic, the moody Chapman boys really make me glad I like women. Also, I second Lizzy's idea. Come down and hang out soon. Miss you, Gracie!

Me: Leave my retired rockstar out of this. He's not being dramatic. Or at least he's less dramatic than my brothers. Maybe I'll come visit this weekend?

V: Yeah. Still not sure how you pulled that off. Still sooooo many questions.

V: Although... tattoos, piercings, cool hair... Rockstar girlfriend fits you babe <3

V: Jealous if you all get together this weekend. I would love to come down, but I have too much going on here with work and I have to go back to Bend for a meeting soon.

I LOOK DOWN at my phone, sitting at the desk in Tommy's office that I've basically claimed as mine at this point.

Rockstar girlfriend.

It reminds me of the girls whispering at the coffee shop. The more I think about it though, the less I care. What matters to me is the man he is and how he makes me feel — how he treats me with respect. I know neither of us have said the words to each other, but I know the love between us is real and growing by the day.

That thought brings a smile to my face and warmth to my heart, thinking of all the possibilities in front of us. Tommy was right, chatting with the girls was a good idea. I need to go down to Park City anyway to grab some things from my place. Going down to spend some time with Lizzy, Clay, and Kayleigh would be nice before Tommy and I leave for Lake Tahoe on Tuesday.

I've spent the morning working on my new idea for him to be more involved with his charitable work, but still stay out of it publicly. It's not as good as my original plan, but still solid. Knowing what I do now about his past, I understand why he wants to keep it this way. That doesn't change the fact that there's a part of me, deep down, that wishes we could do the kind of work I used to do together — volunteering with kids and working fundraising events. I enjoyed it so much and I would love to share that part of my life with him. He could definitely volunteer and attend those events without exposing that he's a giant donor or something like that, but I know the difference he could make if he did.

Walking into the living room, I find him on the couch with his tattered old notebook. He looks up when I come in the room and I see the warmth in his eyes. It makes the butterflies in my stomach do somersaults while also making me instantly feel at home.

"Don't tell me you were actually working for a change?" I ask, pointing at his notebook.

He laughs through his nose. "It looks like you're rubbing off on me."

I walk over, standing in front of him between the couch and the coffee table. He runs his hands up the backs of my legs. Even through the baggy denim of my overalls, his touch still makes my entire body hum with electricity. I ruffle his hair when he looks up at me. "I'm glad. So do you have lunch plans today, *Boss*?" I emphasize the last syllable with a hiss.

His lips pull into a hungry grin. "I was planning on Gloria's for lunch, but I'd rather eat something else."

"You're bad!" I give his shoulder a playful slap. His fingers find the backs of my knees and he pulls me down into his lap so I'm pressed against him. Somehow, I always find myself here with him and I'm more than OK with it.

He cups the nape of my neck, bringing my lips to his for a short kiss before I pull away. The look in his eyes would bring me to my knees if I wasn't already in his lap. Those kind, caring, compassionate eyes overwhelm my senses like everything else about him, almost enough to make me forget what I came in here for in the first place.

"I meant to tell you. I took your advice and chatted with the girls. Thank you for suggesting that"

He nods, his hands resting on my sides. "Good. So V's going to kick your brother's ass?"

I roll my eyes. "No, but Lizzy and Kayleigh said I should come down to Park City this weekend. I was thinking I would go. I needed to grab some things before we go to Tahoe next weekend anyway since I've been up here longer than I planned originally."

I raise my brows at him, because he full well knows he's the reason I've stayed in Jackson. He nods. "Go see your friends and have fun. When are you planning to leave?"

I gnaw at the inside of my cheek. I know he's going to miss me and it's endearing, but I also need him to be OK with me doing my own thing. I'm always going to be impulsive and by my standards, this is nothing. "Probably tonight?"

I see the worry flash in his eyes. "I'll be back Monday night. Then Tuesday, we'll be off to Tahoe together."

He takes a deep breath. "I'll miss you."

I bring my lips to his cheek, kissing the stubble right over his dimple. "I'll miss you too."

"You sure I can't just buy you everything you need from your apartment and keep you here?"

I shake my head and give him a light slap on the shoulder. "No. I like my stuff and I also really just want to see my friends." I lean in close enough to feel his breath on my neck and whisper into his ear. "I also have a nightstand filled with my toy collection. I'd like to bring that back for a little show and tell."

He whimpers into my neck and I feel his erection under me.

Pulling back, I see the hunger in his eyes. "I'll be here waiting then."

CHAPTER 37
TJ
BEING AN IDIOT

I KNOW I'm attached to her. OK. I'm more than attached, but I didn't think it would be this hard to see her leave for a long weekend. Maybe I'm subconsciously worried that I was being too clingy and scared her off. Or maybe I just miss smelling that fucking lavender scent and the feeling of that piercing sliding over the tip of my tongue. Either way, I'm going to miss the fuck out of her and count the seconds until I see her again.

"I will see you on Monday. That's less than four days," she says, dropping her chin and quirking her brows. "Stop being such a big baby. You're almost as dramatic as a Chapman boy."

I hook my thumbs into the pockets of her overalls and pull her against me. Standing next to her van in my driveway, a cool winter breeze wafts over us, blowing her bangs to the side. She might be giving me shit, but I can see that she's going to miss me too.

"Fine," I huff begrudgingly, bringing my lips to hers for a goodbye kiss. "Tell the girls and Clay I said hi."

She nods. "I will."

We stand there for a second and the words I've been wanting to tell her all week linger on the tip of my tongue. I want to tell her I love her, but the words keep getting stuck in my throat because I don't want to spook her. She wanted to keep it simple and I know I can come on a bit strong. I mean, I do have a fucking rainbow tattoo on my hip.

"Be safe. I'll see you soon, Rainbow," are the words I settle on before I place one gentle kiss on her forehead.

"See you soon, Boss," she replies with a wry grin, blowing me a kiss when she hops into her van and shuts the door.

All I can do is stand there and watch as she starts to back out of the parking spot that's become hers. When her van pulls out of my driveway and turns the corner, it feels like a little bit of my heart is going with it.

I TAKE a bite of my pasta, swirling my wine glass with the other hand when Sutton groans. "I thought you were done with the moody, moping act."

I shoot him a glare, but I'm surprised when I find him studying me without his usual shit-eating grin. I set down my glass and shrug, spearing another bite of food.

"Grace is out of town," I reply, unenthusiastically. She only left yesterday and I still can't shake that this is my fault. I know she needed to go anyway and it's good she's seeing her friends. But I still feel like the whole reason this drama started is because she's dating me.

Yes, her brother is being a dickhead after finding out, but that's only because I was famous once and people care way too much about what I do.

Sutton hums thoughtfully, polishing a cocktail glass behind the counter. "Trouble in rockstar paradise?"

I set my fork down and furrow my brows at him. "It's not that simple."

"What part?" he asks. "The part where you're clearly in love with her or something else?"

I drag my hand over my face, sighing in frustration. "When did you become the smart, observant sibling?"

He shrugs. "Always have been. So let's make this simple. What's really wrong?"

"You know cocky looks good on Slade, but I'm not sold on this look for you." I bury my face in my palms and sigh. "Fine. She's back in Utah for the weekend. Partly because Tanner's being an ass about us dating, and doesn't take us seriously or thinks I'm taking advantage of her. Either way, I just feel like I'm fucking shit up for her. Because of who I am. And she's not even getting anything out of this."

That's what's been creeping into my mind lately. What's the point of all the work Jake and I have done to keep my wealth and my life private if it's still going to make my life messy? Not just mine, but hers now too.

He cocks his head in surprise. "Did she tell you that?"

"Well, no."

"Then why would that even cross your mind, man? If you're worried she feels that way, then you need to ask her," he says, again no trace of his normal goofy, unserious self.

He might be right though. I've bottled so much of my own worries up that I haven't even asked her.

He tips the glass he started polishing at me. "I hate to break it to you, but you're always going to be a public figure one way or another. You might as well own it."

I think back to what she said weeks ago. I should just own it and maybe some good will come out of it.

"But if you ask me how you should fix—" he starts before I cut him off when the idea slams into my mind.

I want to make things right. I need to own who I am and I

know just how to start. He's right. I need to stop being an idiot and tell her everything, starting with how much I love her.

"I'm not asking you," I say, standing up from the counter. "Put this on my tab. I need to go."

I know what to do. I start to walk to the door when Kelsey walks in with a box of bagged espresso beans in hand.

I don't stop on my way out, but point at him with my thumb over my shoulder. "Be nice to him. He was actually helpful today."

CHAPTER 38

GRACE
FINCH

"I CAN'T BELIEVE you're already leaving tomorrow," Lizzy pouts, flicking her trademark blonde ponytail over her shoulder. "It feels like you just got here."

She brings her nitro cold brew to her lips, clasping it in both perfectly manicured hands. My eyes flick to her big diamond ring, and I still can't believe she's going to be my sister-in-law.

"You know she's only four hours away. We can literally drive up any day. I'm pretty sure your dad won't mind if we take the time off," Clay says. "So we should absolutely go up."

She bats her eyes at my brother. "If you drive the little sports car, then yes."

"You know that stays under the tarp, in the garage, until winter's over, brat." He sighs. "I'll drive, but we're taking your Bronco."

She taps her pink tipped fingers to her matching pink lips. "If we can listen to that new romance series I've been waiting for you to start with me, then—"

"The werewolf vampire regency one?" Clay asks eagerly.

Lizzy nods, humming in agreement. "That's the one."

I look at Kayleigh and we both snort a laugh. Seeing these

two like this will never get old. Before I left for Jackson, brunch or coffee and pastries was our old routine, stopping into Finch, the coffee shop and book store in downtown Park City. Even on a crowded weekend like this around Presidents' Day, I still love being here with them.

"Deal," Clay says, taking a sip of his drink before turning his attention back to me. "You sure you can't stay longer?"

"I wish I could, but I need to get back to Jackson tomorrow. Tommy and I leave for Lake Tahoe first thing Tuesday morning."

"Interesting. You call him Tommy. Not TJ or Tommy Jacob." Lizzy's lips curl into a feline smile and she leans forward, propping herself up on her elbows. "So how's that going?"

Clay checks his phone before reaching over to grab the empty plates in front of us. "Nope. Happy for the two of you, but I want no part of this conversation."

Lizzy gives him a slap on the ass when he stands. "Go find us a new faerie smut book." She makes a kissy-face at him before looking back at us.

I shake my head and laugh as he walks to the bussing station. He drops off the plates and goes to the rows of shelves in the back of the shop, browsing the romance section.

Turning back to the table, I find Kayleigh and Lizzy curiously eyeing me. "Right, so now's when you two grill me about dating the rich, older man?"

"Basically." Lizzy nods with a wide grin. She gestures with her palms up. "I saw him in Bend and that man's aged well. Is he still a total bad boy or is he a secret softy? He seemed so chill when we were in Bend. Did you make a move on him or did he pursue you? Come on, spill the tea."

I look down at my actual mug of tea, thinking about what to say. I knew they would ask and I want to tell them. It feels good to be able to express all the things I've had swirling in my head for weeks. The truth is though, I don't know where to start. Things have moved fast but they feel so natural and so right.

I've only been away from him for a couple days, but not having him close to me, having his eyes on me or his bergamot scent filling each of my breaths has left an ache in my chest that's overwhelming. That ache, that desire and unquenched need to have him in my life is the manifested confirmation that I do love him.

My calm and steady. My man.

I look up from my mug to find Kayleigh and Lizzy smirking at each other. Kayleigh reaches across the table and grabs my wrist. "Have you told him?"

Her simple question and the soft, kind look in her eyes says everything. I shake my head, breathing in the steam from my Earl Grey tea, the scent reminding me of him. "No, not yet."

Lizzy smirks, shaking her head. "Girl, don't waste time. Just tell him. We know he loves you."

I quirk a brow at her. I've felt it, that pull, that connection between us. But how would she know it? She must see the question on my face because she continues on her own.

"We all saw that picture of you two in Seattle. The only person who's ever looked at me that way is your brother. That's love, babe."

I grin back at her, accepting that she's right. I need to tell him how I feel.

A familiar voice from behind me breaks my focus.

"Grace! Oh my gosh!"

I turn to find Kathy, my old boss, standing with a coffee in hand.

"I thought that was you." She's smiling and pointing at her head. "Always easy to spot that hair."

The last time I saw her was my last day at Wasatch Wishes,

which was a horrible day. I remember the anger, the sadness, the frustration of the days after that.

Seeing her now, it dawns on me that I don't feel that way anymore. I'm actually grateful because it was the universe's own messed up way of putting me exactly where I needed to be.

I gesture for her to come over to our table. "We've got an open chair if you want to catch up."

She comes over but doesn't sit down. "Oh, I need to get back home to the kids. I just wanted to tell you thank you. Your boyfriend, Mr. Jacob." She cuts herself off. "I mean Mr. Sorenson. I just can't believe what he did. He was so sweet and polite when he came to the office today too."

My heart rate picks up and my mind races. He's here? He came by their office? I thought he was back in Jackson with Sutton. Why would they be talking? What would they even be talking about?

"Oh, yeah. He's pretty great." I nervously laugh to mask my uncertainty.

"Anyway, I need to get going. I'll give you a call soon though. Seems like we're going to have plenty to work on." She starts to leave but stops before reaching the exit, smiling widely. "Please, tell him thank you again."

I nod. "Will do."

I wave as she walks out, wondering what just happened.

Clearly I'm not the only one who was bewildered by that. When I turn around, Kayleigh and Lizzy are wearing equally confused expressions.

"What was that about?" Kayleigh asks, tipping her chin toward the door.

"I have no freaking clue," I say, digging into my pocket for my phone, "but I'm about to find out."

Me: What did you do?

> Hot Boss: You're going to have to be more specific than that.

> Me: You know what I'm talking about...

> Hot Boss: 😊 Surprise?

> Hot Boss: Did I do that right? It's supposed to be jazz hands.

> Me: Ugh. We'll talk about this and your millennial cringe use of emojis later.

> Hot Boss: Or we could talk about it now?

> Hot Boss: Maybe over dinner?

My brows raise when I read the text, three dots appearing and disappearing. What does he mean *now*? He's supposed to be in Jackson with Sutton.

"Everything OK?" I glance across the table to see Lizzy eyeing me, snickering with Kayleigh.

"Yeah, I think so but-" I stop when my phone vibrates and Tommy's name scrolls across the screen. I raise a finger to them, standing and facing away from the table toward the back of the café. "Hold on a sec. It's him."

"Hi," I say, my voice a nervous squeak when I hold the phone to my ear.

"Hey, Rainbow," he says, that low, silky smooth voice like a soothing balm to my anxious nerves.

"So do you want to tell me why my old boss was just saying how amazing you are and to thank you for her?"

"Well," he hums thoughtfully. "I do want to, but I was hoping I could talk to you in person about it."

Motion in the corner of my eye catches my attention. I turn to find my brother, Clay, standing right in front of me, new romance book in hand.

"Hey, Gracie," he says, wearing a stupid grin.

"Not now," I shake my head and point at my phone. "It's Tommy. Go show your book to your fiancée." I make a shooing gesture but his grin only grows and he pulls the phone away from my ear. He can be a little shit, but he's not rude and knows better than this. "What the fuck, Clay?"

Instead of saying anything, he simply reaches out, palms my head in his giant, bear paw mitt of a hand, and turns my head.

I see Kayleigh and Lizzy sitting at the table, watching me with matching, shocked smiles. It's not them that have me speechless though. It's the man standing on the sidewalk outside, holding up his phone, waving at me with a scruffy, dimple popping smile that sucks the air right out of me.

It's only been a couple days since I've seen him and still, just knowing he's this close has me ready to go jump his bones right here. I don't care if the bustling holiday crowd on Main Street sees, I just need to be near him.

I slowly regain my breath when his broad smile pulls into a mischievous smirk. He waves at his own phone, reminding me that we're still on a call. My eyes fall to the phone still in my hand and I lift it to my ear.

"So does *now* work?" he says, far too pleased with himself.

I roll my eyes, but can't hide the smile taking over my face when I hang up the phone. I walk past Lizzy and Kayleigh who spin in their chairs, clearly enjoying this spectacle while I walk out of the shop and onto the sidewalk.

The second he sees me leave the door, we both stride to each other, that electric tension between us pulling us together, making the world around us fade into a blur. He pulls me into his arms and even through his thick, wool lined denim jacket I can feel his warmth. My arms instinctively drape around his neck and he slants his mouth to mine. A low growl rumbles in his throat when our lips part and his tongue dives into my mouth and caresses mine. This kiss is passionate, unleashing pent up hunger that neither of us were expecting. More than anything, it's here, on the crowded sidewalk with tourists all around us and he doesn't seem the least bit phased by it. I break the kiss for just a second and his teeth tug on my lower lip, protesting the separation.

I raise my brows and he lets go, giving me just enough space to look into those deep, blue pools. "I missed you."

Another low growl rumbles up his chest. "I missed you too."

I smirk before pinching the back of his neck and tilt my head. "Now are you going to tell me why you're here and why Kathy thinks you're just the sweetest, *Mr. Sorenson?*"

His hand tucks a stray wisp of my hair out of my eyes. His Adam's apple bobs and when I look into his eyes again, I see that calm, but vulnerable openness that makes the butterflies in my stomach do summersaults. "I'm sorry your brother's mad at you. I'm sorry you lost your job."

My jaw tenses and my brow furrows. He must see my irritation when I open my mouth to speak because he shakes his head.

"No, let me finish," he says and I see the pleading look in his eyes.

I nod and he continues. "I know those things aren't my fault, at least not fully. And I know you're more than capable of taking care of yourself and fixing things on your own. That doesn't change that I'm sorry that they happened. I'm sorry we both felt like we had to hide us. I don't ever want that. I want people to take us seriously. And I told you, I'd give you all of me. So that's what I'm doing. If we're going to be together, you're going to get all of me, whether it's just you and me at home or in public."

I cup his jaw, my thumb tracing the hollow of his dimple, up over the crinkles at the corner of his eyes until I feel the cool metal of his eyebrow piercing.

"That's amazing. That's perfect. I just can't believe you're doing it." I press a kiss to his lips. "But that still doesn't explain how it involves Wasatch Wishes."

He sucks in a breath and grabs the back of his neck. "I had Jake move a couple things around and we made a donation to them."

I squint at him. "How big?"

He smiles nervously. "Enough for them to get a new office building, with better facilities, and fund their full time staff for the next five years," his voice trailing up like a question.

"But—" I start, wanting to tell him this is amazing, but then it hits me.

Kathy knows his full name. That means... No. He didn't.

My mouth falls open. He shrugs awkwardly. "They said I can have my name on the building. That it'd really help with their fundraising."

"What did you say?" My voice is a whisper.

"I said I'd only do it if your name was next to mine."

"Tommy, you didn't."

"There's more. Kathy said you could have your job back if you want it."

"What are you saying? Please tell me you're not sick of working with me already?" I shake my head. "No, I want to stay with you. And you can't just go and buy my old job back for me anyway."

He laughs and his warm breath nearly makes me melt into a puddle at his feet. "Good, that makes me feel better about the next part. I spent last night in Seattle. By the way, the swings aren't nearly as fun without you. Anyway, I was there with Jake signing an ungodly amount of paperwork."

I quirk a brow. "Wait, what for? And did you really fly to Seattle yesterday and then here today? Please tell me you didn't use your jet. No amount of drinking from reusable bottles is going to offset that."

"That's beside the point," he says, smirking and rolling his eyes. "Jake and I took your idea and put it in motion. We're going to do it."

"What do you mean my—" The question stalls in my throat when what he's saying registers. For the second time in minutes, he has me feeling like I've forgotten how to breathe.

He nods. "The foundation. Making a bigger impact. All of it, publicly, and I want you by my side doing it."

My heart reels. He hasn't just opened up to me. He hasn't just been vulnerable with me. He's cut open his chest, exposing the deepest wound he has, and handed me his heart on a silver platter.

"I don't know what to say." I fumble for the words, my mind racing, heart swelling with pride.

He pulls me into him by my waist, with the hands I didn't even realize he'd placed there. His nose ruffles my bangs before those warm, soft lips ghost over my forehead in a light kiss.

"I love you, Rainbow." His lips find mine for a slow, lingering kiss. "So fucking much it hurts. I know there's nothing I can do about my past and the attention that brings. So you were right. If we're going to have to deal with that, we can at least make some good out of it, together. I told you, I'm all in. I want your brothers to know that. I want your friends and family to know that. I want the world to know that. But most importantly, I want you to know that."

His gaze meets mine and I feel water prick the corner of my eyes. The pad of his thumb catches a stray tear. Hearing those three words, the ones I've wanted to tell him so many times over the last week, make me feel whole and grounded in a way I never knew I could.

"I love you too." I watch his lips curl into a smile. I palm the sides of his face and bring my mouth to his, kissing him until every last molecule of oxygen has left my lungs.

I don't know who breaks the kiss first, but when we do, I press my forehead to his. I feel his hands run up and down my back in slow gentle caresses over my light sweater, because I didn't even think to grab my jacket when I saw him outside.

A hollow knocking sound grabs our attention and we both look to our side. Lizzy and Kayleigh are standing in the coffee shop window, faces plastered to the glass. They're grinning, like the kids looking into the window displays along Main Street.

He waves and smiles sheepishly at them. Lizzy and Kayleigh both make obnoxious kissing faces and waggle their brows. I give them both middle fingers.

"Do you want to get out of here and talk somewhere a little more private?"

I look into the eyes of the man who just gave me his heart and nod.

CHAPTER 39
TJ
PLANET-KILLING RIDESHARE

MY HEART still pounds against the walls of my chest after hearing her say she loves me.

"But we're still going to talk about the jet and how you use it as your own on-demand, planet-killing rideshare." Even when she tries to scold me, she can't hide her infectious smile.

I shrug. "We'll see." I toss her a wink. "So about getting out of here?" I hitch my thumb over my shoulder toward the half dozen or so people standing around us with their phones out, taking pictures of us. I'm sure this will end up on social media, but now I know that neither of us will care. This isn't a secret anymore and I'm fine with that.

Grace scrunches her nose and turns her palms up. "We could go back to my place? Just let me run in and grab my things." She grabs my hand and pulls me in with her. "Come on, they're your friends too."

"OK SO IT'S NOT MUCH." Grace looks backs over her shoulder at me nervously when her keys jingle in the lock.

"Grace, you could literally live in a shoebox and it would never change how amazing I think you are. You remember that I found you with a barely working van heater in a gym parking lot, right?"

"Alrighty then. Don't say I didn't warn you," she says, swinging open the door to her place.

I step in behind her and she flicks on the light switch. She waves her hand out in front of her. "Welcome to my shoebox."

I take in the studio apartment in front of me. I'm immediately brought back to my first place in Seattle. It wasn't much, but I still remember the feeling of having a place that was mine compared to a bunkbed in a small bedroom at a foster home. Looking around this place, I can see that Grace made this place hers. There's an eclectic mix of Mid Century Modern furniture around a brightly colored southwestern patterned rug in the center of the room. I step past her into the room.

In one corner, there's a cozy bed covered in an assortment of colorful knit blankets and throw pillows. Above the headboard is a slim, wide window letting in a sliver of light, cast all over the room by the little crystals and stained glass trinkets hung in the window. Opposite that is a small kitchenette with plants in macrame hangers in each window, matching the ones hanging behind the bed.

Yes. This is definitely my girl's place. Everything about is so perfectly her.

I set my jacket on the small round table by the kitchenette and walk over to the bed. I hop all the way on it and prop myself up on my elbows. I've spent almost all day on the go and laying back in her bed that smells like her feels beyond good. "I love it. It's one hundred percent you."

She stays over by the door watching me with curious amusement while she unties her boots. She drops her coat by the door and comes over to the bed. She plops down next to me on the bed sitting cross legged. Then she lifts my feet off of it and lays them in her lap before taking off my boots. "Didn't anyone ever teach you manners? Feet off the furniture. Were you raised by wolves?"

I shrug. "Foster families, remember?"

Her eyes widen. "Oh shit, I'm sorry. I—" I smirk at her and quirk a brow. She groans, grabbing a pillow, and throwing it at me. "Ass."

I laugh, reaching over and wrapping my arm around her. She squeals when I yank her down onto the bed beside me, burying ourselves in the pile of pillows along the headboard.

"Oh my god, stop it," she gasps between giggles while I try to tickle her. I wrap my arms around her, pulling her close.

Suddenly, I find myself on top of her, looking down into her sparkling green eyes. Her hair flows over the pillows behind her and the streaks of color flow with the patterns on them.

She flicks her eyebrows and her teeth dig into her bottom lip. "I see you really missed me." She rolls her hips up and presses herself into the bulge in my jeans.

A low groan rumbles through my chest. "You could say that."

I see the mischievous glint in her eyes and she reaches between us, running her hand up and down the seam of my jeans. I rock myself into her hand, desperate for more contact, desperate for her.

Her fingers find the fly of my jeans and deftly open them, relieving some of the pressure on my cock.

"I missed you too," she says, her eyes flicking down between us. She cups my already aching erection.

"Fuck,' I hiss and my shoulders squeeze together when I shudder.

Her hands find the waist of my jeans and boxers and she shimmies them down over my ass, finally freeing my cock.

I sigh in relief, loving the feel of her soft, warm hand when it strokes my shaft.

"I think you're still wearing too much." I thrust myself forward, grinding my shaft against her core, over her leggings. Even through the fabric, I can feel how much she needs me, how wet she already is for me. "You should do something about that so I can feel your tight cunt squeeze my cock when you come."

Her lips part and she whimpers, letting go of my dick. Her hands frantically work to pull her leggings down. In seconds, my throbbing shaft is pressed against her slit and, yes, she's fucking drenched for me. I grab my cock and flick the head back and forth over her swollen clit, watching her eyes roll back at the contact with her piercing.

"Does my girl like that?"

She nods and bites her bottom lip, running her hands up and under my t-shirt. I take my other hand and reach over my head, tossing it on the floor beside the bed. Her eyes track the movement, lingering on something. I follow her gaze and see the nightstand.

"Did you already pack your toy collection?"

"No," she says, shaking her head excitedly. "Take a peek inside. We can play with whatever you want. Your pick."

"You don't have to ask me twice." I lean over the side of the bed, pulling the drawer open.

Fuck. My girl likes to have fun.

I mean I sort of knew that already. I know she needs constant stimulation. Nothing about her is vanilla, but damn was she serious when she said she had a collection. A few different vibrators, a metal and crystal butt plug, some clit sucking toy, and what I think is probably a tentacle dildo? That's just what I can see without rummaging around. I can't make a decision with either head right now, probably due to the lack of blood in one and too much in the other, because I want to explore every option with her. I make a mental note that the rest are getting packed up and brought back with us on the jet.

"I can pick one out for you if—" She starts to tease me while she takes her long sleeve flannel shirt off. One of the toys catches my eye.

"Nope. I got it." I reach in and grab the big, white wand vibrator.

I bring myself back over her, kneeling between her thighs. She's down to just her thin, practically see-through, white bralette. Her pebbled buds and those fucking little barbells I'm obsessed with show right through and I just want to feel them rolling over my tongue. When my eyes drift lower, my mouth waters at the sight of her swollen clit and slick pussy lips.

I hold the handle of the wand, bringing the head of it right in front of my lips. She quirks a brow at me and I tap the head of it with a finger twice like a microphone. I look down at her with hooded eyes and cue up my classic frontman voice. "Is this thing on?"

Her eyes widen and her bottom lip curls over her teeth. "Oh my god, you are such a dork!"

I shrug, grinning at her, unable to hide how much I fucking need her. "Maybe I am, but now it's my turn to make you sing my name, Rainbow."

I flick the switch on the wand and the head rumbles to life. I run my free hand up her inner thigh, grazing her clit piercing just enough to make her whimper before resting my hand on her hip bone. She wraps those long legs around me trying to bring me closer. Looking down, my throbbing cock is only inches from her tight entrance and a pearl of precum is already on the tip.

I drop the head of the vibrator to her, slowly running it up and down her wet slit, spreading her open for me. She rolls her hips, grinding herself against the toy. The head of the vibrator reaches her piercing and it sings, vibrating right against her clit.

"Fuck. Oh my god, that's so good," she says, tossing her head back against a pillow.

I let out a gruff hum of amusement. "Tell me what you need," I say, increasing the pressure on her clit and grabbing my cock, stroking it from the base to the tip. Moments like these are the ones I'm glad I developed the talent to use both hands as a musician. Or maybe it was the other way around. Either way, I'm going to rock my girl's world — that's for fucking sure.

She bucks into the toy, her stomach hollowing out as she arches her back. "You. I want you all in."

I lean down, still holding the toy on her clit, pressing kiss after kiss up her stomach, between her breasts, up to her collarbone. Our bodies are so close I can feel the vibration of the toy on my cock, building that heat at the base of my spine. I nip at her collarbone, looking up to see her eyes already glazing over. "You ready for me?"

"Don't," she says, gasping when I hit the switch on the vibrator, increasing the power level, "Fuck. Don't ask questions you already know the answer to."

I laugh, pressing one more kiss to her neck before I notch myself at her entrance and push the head of my cock in just an inch. Holy shit. She's tight and soaking wet.

At this angle, the vibrator sits right on her clit and the shaft of my cock. I already know neither of us are going to last very long.

Slowly, I thrust in, giving her inch after inch. She grabs my hair, dragging her nails over my scalp. "I said all in."

Before I can think, she rocks her hips up and pulls me deeper with her legs, burying me in her to the hilt.

My teeth clench. "Shit. Shit, your pussy is so damn good. You're going to make me come." My voice is husky and strained.

I pick up my pace, thrusting harder and faster the way I know she craves. I feel her walls tighten as she swivels her hips, grinding the vibrator against my shaft and her clit.

Staring into her eyes, I practically lose it right then and there.

I've spent the better part of my life in the spotlight, but nothing compares to this.

Her pure lust, pure need, pure love, are all focused entirely on me. The way her lips part as she whimpers. The way her hands cup her breasts and she rolls her nipples in her fingertips, bringing herself closer to the edge. The long, colorful strands of her hair blend into her tattoos and the pillows.

She is beautiful in every single way, just like a rainbow. I know I could never find the end of her beauty even if I spent my entire life looking for it.

"Yes, please," she pants. "Just like that." I thrust hard, bottoming out in her pussy right as she clenches and flutters on my cock while the vibrator rocks us both with pleasure.

"Yes. Fucking yes, Tommy," she cries out. I watch the crimson flush creep up over her chest, up her neck, and across her freckled cheeks as she comes with my name on her lips.

Hearing her cry out undoes me and I make it one more thrust before I come undone, draining into her tight wet heat.

I look up at her to see her eyes slowly open, both of us trying to catch our breath. Flipping the toy off, I toss it aside. We stay there, looking into each other's eyes while streaks of iridescent light from the crystals in the window shimmer around us. Our lips meet for one long, languid kiss.

"I told you I'd make you sing my name."

"YOU'RE STILL A DORK."

He shrugs with a lazy, sated smile. "Maybe, but at least I'm *your* dork."

My eyes roll back with a huff of laughter. I run my hands over his ribs, still feeling his heart pound and chest heave, coming down from our post-orgasm high. His smile is something I can't look away from. I reach up and rub his stubble with my thumb.

His eyes feel like they peer into my soul, in an all consuming way that makes my pulse quicken. He's gentle, but still rough with me, the way I need. In a way that reminds me that I'm not broken, that I'm strong.

Somehow, he feels like he was always supposed to be the one for me, the one I was supposed to love.

He might say he's the lucky one, but all I can think about is how lucky I am to be loved by him. Lying here in my room, this place has always felt cozy, but it never felt like a home. With him hovering over me though, any place would feel like home.

I know I never want this feeling to end.

I grab his shaggy hair, pulling him down to me for another kiss, letting my lips say all the words running through my head.

"Now that I have your attention." I wrap my calves around his firm ass, pulling his still impressively hard erection into me, eliciting a low grunt from him. "We're going to talk about how you need to stop using your jet like that."

He chuckles. "Oh. Not fair. You're playing dirty. You could ask me to do anything when I'm buried in you and my cum is still dripping out of you, and I would say yes a thousand times."

"You know you don't need to impress your girlfriend like that." The word girlfriend floats on my tongue and it's never felt more right, while also feeling like it's not nearly enough for our bond.

His smile becomes almost boyishly excited. "Anything you want as long as you keep calling yourself my girlfriend."

I nod. "Good. So next time, keep the planet in mind," I say with a wink. "Still love you though."

"Love you too," he rasps, chuckling to himself.

He rolls over, and my body instantly misses the fullness and warmth of him on top of me. He lays next to me, wrapping his arm around my shoulder and pulling me close. I lay my head on his shoulder and we just lay there like that.

"Grace," he says, his voice trailing up in question.

"Yes?" I trace lazy circles over his chest hair with my fingers.

"Who's been taking care of these house plants?" I look up to see his eyes lingering on the plants hanging over the headboard.

"Oh. Yeah. Kayleigh was taking care of them at first but my dad's been stopping in the last couple of weeks too."

He nods. "Got it. Your dad." I feel his body tense under my head.

Shit. I got so caught up in getting into bed with Tommy that I forgot I already planned to meet my dad tonight.

"Yeah, so about that."

His eyes flick to mine and I scrunch my shoulders innocently.

"I was already supposed to see him for dinner tonight. Would you want to come?"

He looks up and he rocks his head side to side, his tell that he's mulling it over. I forgot that somehow, in the commotion of the wedding and reception, he might not have met my dad that night. I know he's not afraid of a challenge, but I'm sure meeting your girlfriend's dad is never going to be easy.

I splay my fingers over his chest, looking up at him. "It's OK if that's too much too soon. We can do it another time."

He looks back at me, pressing a kiss to the back of my hand. Letting out a deep breath, he nods. "No. It's perfectly fine. I was going to have to meet him eventually."

His warm smile fills me with something that's been missing, a feeling that I do know what's next. One way or another, deep down I know a life with him is next. With the way he said *eventually*, it's like he knows it too.

"DO you guys have a rolodex of dive bars or something?" I ask, holding Grace in my lap at the high-top table with Josie.

"Basically, yeah. If it's a mountain town with skiing, biking or hiking, we've probably found a bar we like. We just add them as starred locations in our map apps." She smirks at Grace. "I think your man, Hot Daddy Boss, is too fancy for us."

"No. Not at all. I've always loved playing in these places, way more than any of the giant venues we played when we got big."

I look out across the room, taking in the vintage, seventies charm. There's two bars, on opposite sides of the room. On the back wall between them is a stage with a small local band playing covers of nineties and early two-thousands rock.

The most unique feature has to be the bright, nearly neon yellow stripe of carpet with a black dashed line running down the center of the room. One side reads 'California' and on the other, 'Nevada'. There are a few places like this in Lake Tahoe, built right on the state line. On the Nevada side there's even a few slot machines, right next to the bar. Just like everything Grace enjoys though, it's cozy and authentic. The crowd is mostly locals and ski bums, having a good time after a day skiing.

"Yeah. I like this place a lot," I say, smiling back at her.

Josie gives me a subtle nod of approval while Grace turns in my lap, wriggling her ass on my groin. I have to focus to not get a hard on in the bar, in front of her friends. She looks into my eyes and my resolve crumbles. I lean in for a hot, breathy kiss. I break it and watch her lashes flutter. "You need another drink?"

Grace slowly nods. "Yeah, I'll take another one of these." She holds up my empty bottle, the second one of mine she's taken tonight, not that I would ever mind. She's already taken my heart and soul, so what's another beer.

"Let me go get a round." We both turn to look at Josie, who's eyeing us with wide, amused eyes. "You two clearly look like you're having fun and it's the least I can do since Daddy here booked us that sweet lakeside Airbnb."

Grace rolls her eyes at me playfully, something she's done every time the Airbnb was brought up. It was my other surprise to her though when we got here. I know they're her mutual van life friends with Josie and I'm sure they'd all be happy just camping. I still wanted her to have a fun, relaxing place to spend the week with her friends. Their vans might all be nice, but they're not exactly a great place to hang out and catch up all night with a group. She insisted it was too much, but after the fun we've all had here the last few days, I'm half tempted to just buy it for her.

I wave off Josie and slide my black credit card across the table. "Just start a tab for everyone on me, Josie."

Grace sighs. "Seriously, you don't have to take care of us all."

"What's the point of being rich if I can't take care of my girl-friend and our friends?" The way she smiles at me when I say 'our friends' wells pride from deep in my chest. It's the truth though. Josie and her other friends have all been beyond welcoming to me. Just like her, none of them put me up on a pedestal or act weird around me and I fucking love that. I don't know why I'm surprised though because they're her friends.

"Yeah, Grace." Josie cocks a hip out. "Daddy here can spoil us, or at least me, all he wants."

She waggles her brows at me before swiping the card off the table and heading to the bar on the Nevada side of the room where there's a bigger selection of drinks.

"Yeah, I see it. She's definitely a younger and feistier version of Lizzy."

Grace laughs, shaking her head. "Yeah, I think that's why I love them both."

"God help the man that tries to lock her down."

She huffs a laugh. "I'm not sure one exists who is brave enough. She's had her fun here and there, but she's been single for as long as I've known her."

Doing the mental math, that's almost a decade because they met in college. I would have been thirty-two then because that's right around when I retired from music.

Holding Grace in my arms, I realize I don't want to waste a single day that I could have with her. She's the one that snapped me out of my funk, reminding me that I could do things just for me. She's the one that made me feel again. Every day with her has brought up feelings and emotions that I haven't felt in ages. It's gotten to the point that I need to sort them out the best way I know how.

CHAPTER 42
GRACE
THOSE EYES

TOMMY'S ARMS wrap around my waist, holding me in his lap. I fiddle with my nearly empty beer and lean back into him, soaking up his warmth.

He lets out a long grunt. His grip on my waist tightens and his lips tease the skin just under my ear, sending a shiver down my spine. "If you're not careful, I'm going to take you into that bathroom and remind you that you're mine."

Peeking back over my shoulder, I see the look in his eyes and I know he's not kidding. "You make it sound like that's a punishment." I take the last sip of my beer, letting my parted lips linger on the bottle.

"Fuck me," he says, pressing a kiss to my neck. "I told you I'm the lucky one."

At the bar, I see Josie struggling to flag down a bartender. I tilt my head toward her. "I'm going to go give her a hand."

He nods. "Grab an extra beer while you're up there. I know you're going to end up stealing mine again."

I shrug innocently and hop out of his lap, pecking a quick kiss to his stubbled cheek. I start to turn to head to the bar, but he grabs my wrist, bringing my eyes back to his.

"Love you, Rainbow." His eyes pierce right through me, making my breath hitch.

"Love you too," I say, struggling to form words under the intensity of his gaze before his eyes soften.

"Just wanted to make sure you knew." He gives my ass a playful slap and tilts his head toward the bar and smirks. "Now, go have fun with your friends. That's why we're here."

I walk over to where Josie's leaning on the bar, with an extra bounce in each step. I try not to overthink how I got here, with someone that pours his love out to me like his life depends on it.

"Good. I need your tall ass to flag down a bartender," Josie huffs when I lean against the bar next to her. The band on stage finishes their song, sending a wave of dancers around us to get drinks. "Maybe someone will see you."

"Josie. Have you looked in a mirror lately? You're hard to miss, babe." She glares at me, ignoring the fact that her very flattering tube top, denim mini skirt, and knee high black leather boots have the attention of practically every man in this bar.

As if on cue though, a bartender comes up to take our order before she can say another word. After he leaves to grab our beers, she raises her brows at me. "See? Came right over when you showed up. People notice you."

I scoff and wave her off. "Whatever."

What I actually mean is that I couldn't care less who is looking at me. Right now, there's only one man's eyes that I care about. Just thinking about Tommy's smoldering gaze roaming over my body has my skin heated and a flush creeping up my neck.

The bartender comes back with a bucket of beers and Josie starts going on about the plan for skiing tomorrow. I lift a beer to my lips, but stop before I take a sip when I hear it.

A distorted, soulful string of notes cuts through the musty air of the old bar, making the hair on the back of my neck stand.

Their beautifully raw sound makes my heart race even though it feels like time stops.

No. It can't be.

> *You plunged into my life*
> *And I never had a chance*

That voice. That deep, smooth caressing voice that lives in my mind, when I close my eyes, fills my ears. And those notes. They might sound different with an electric guitar, but I know them. They're the ones I've heard him writing and playing in his studio.

> *You told me, you told me, you told me*
> *You know what you want*

When I turn around to face the stage, Tommy is front and center with an electric guitar in his hands. The drummer and bass player from the local band are behind him but they might as well not exist in this moment. They're keeping a steady, neutral beat to go with his masterful guitar playing. I barely notice because I can't look away from the man I love. Apparently, no one else can look away from him either.

A small crowd has formed around the stage and a few people have their phones out recording and streaming him. I can't imagine that any of them ever expected to see Tommy Jacob here tonight, not just playing, but performing a new song for the first time in years.

> *You asked me, you asked me, you asked me*
> *Do I want it too?*
> *Baby, I need you*
> *Oh I know that it's true*

Do I want it too? I see the question in his eyes, but he doesn't have to ask me. Neither of us have to ask anymore. Want isn't even a strong enough word. Need isn't strong enough. It feels like somehow we were always part of each other's very being, we just needed to be ready to accept when the universe told us it was time.

Now I know what I am
The man that knows what he wants
So stop with the taunts
It's too late to say no, Rainbow

I suck in a breath, hearing my nickname — my favorite name. That first weekend in Bend, I thought he was being stupid and trying to irritate me. Thinking back now though, I don't know how I never saw it. His need for me has been there, I just had to look deeper into those eyes and I would have seen it. Right now, those eyes make it feel like the room narrowed to a tunnel between us. I watch him strum the borrowed guitar, pouring his mind and body into it. Those tousled locks of hair hang over his eyes, beading sweat down and over his stubbled, flushed cheeks. His forearms strain and tick with each flick of his wrist, reminding me of how they looked between my legs in the gym mirror. His eyes though, they stay fixed on me. Even in this crowded room with people cheering in the audience, this feels intimate and personal.

So baby, baby tell me
Do you need me too?

I still don't know how he thinks he needs to ask me that. What started weeks ago as me being clearly into him, but also curious to explore that connection has turned into so much more.

Right now, that string of tension between us tightens and tugs on my heart and nothing else in the room exists anymore.

Just us. Just that bond we've never been able to ignore even if we tried to pretend we could. Ever since that morning on the river in Bend, it's just inevitable — like it was meant to be.

On stage, he drags out one final distorted note. He finally drops his head, swiping his hair away from his eyes. I see his shoulders rise and fall with labored breaths from exerting himself on stage. He turns back to the members of the band, fist bumping each of them before handing the guitar back to its owner.

I watch in awe, seeing a smile plastered on his face, one so electric and full of energy it makes my stomach flip and butterflies fill my chest. He looks so happy, so at ease, so alive that it's hard to picture him giving this up for so many years. I know it may only be an impromptu one song performance at a tiny bar in a ski town, but it looks like this was the world to him.

He hops off the stage in one smooth leap, striding past the people that had gathered in front of the small stage. His eyes meet mine and he wastes no time in navigating through the tables and crowd until he's right in front of me. His hands find my waist, holding me in that possessive way that makes my body mold to his without a second thought. I hold the beers in both hands against my chest, staring back into his hungry eyes for what feels like forever.

Josie's hand finds my shoulder and she gives it a squeeze, snapping me out of that trance. "I'm going to leave you two alone I think."

She tosses me a playful wink before finding our friends out in the now crowded, boisterous bar.

"Thank you." His voice is low and rough, still strained from singing his heart and soul out to me.

"For what?"

He raises a hand to my neck, his thumb tracing lazy circles

over my hammering pulse point. I lean into the touch and whimper. The corner of his mouth tugs up into a smile, revealing that delicious dimple that I'm half-tempted to lick.

"Reminding me that music can just be for me. That it can be mine." He leans forward, kissing me in a way that's both long and far too short. My eyes shut, savoring every second. When he pulls away, my lips follow his, wishing it would go on forever, like everything with him. "And for making me feel something again. Feel something so strongly that it brought me back to the only other thing I've loved. Writing and playing music."

I set my beer down and drape my arms around his neck. The way he rolls his neck into my arms, craving my touch the way I do his, brings a smile to my lips. He gives me the same focused, lingering gaze he gave me while he spilled his soul — our story — out on stage.

"I do." I nod, playing with the ends of his hair in my fingers. "The answer is yes, Tommy. It'll always be, yes."

He lets out one long, relived sigh. "Good."

He looks back at the center of the room in front of the stage where Josie has found our friends. They seem to be paying no attention to us at this point, as the local band starts to play a new song. "Do you want to get out of here?"

I can hardly contain my smile. "Yes. I know just the place."

CHAPTER 43
TJ
MY HEART WALKS AWAY

One Month Later

"RELAX. I will see you at Gloria's tonight." Grace straddles me in bed, while the sun, just creeping over the horizon to the east, rises behind her. She looks heavenly like this — my perfect fucking angel, sent here just for me.

My hands glide over the smooth skin of her lower back, playing with the hem of her cropped cami, and pulling her tighter to my lap. If it was up to me, I'd already have my boxer briefs and her flannel sleep shorts off. "You could let Kayleigh and Josie go out backcountry skiing on their own today."

She quirks her brow. "Nope. Kayleigh's turned me down forever. I'm not going to miss making her hike up to Cody Peak. She's so spoiled. She needs to earn some turns."

"I could just take back your vacation day. Not let you have the day off and keep you here."

She hums in amusement. "You could, except you're not my boss anymore. We're partners in this now, remember? And what happened to casual work environment?"

My heart wells with pride. For the past month, we've worked

together, hand in hand, to start setting up the foundation she envisioned. It's already been the most rewarding thing I've been involved in and it's barely even gotten started.

"Fair enough." My lips pull into a crooked grin, and I thrust my hips up in a way I know puts pressure on her clit piercing.

She shudders and her eyes roll back, letting me know we both felt that burst of pressure. "Fair? You know that's not playing fair."

I grin up at her. "I never said I played fair. Are you still sure you don't want to stay?"

"You're not the only one with tricks." She gives me a playful smirk, sliding forward on my shaft, eliciting a groan from deep in my chest. "But you could just join us today."

I shake my head. "I think I will pass on the full day of hiking and skiing. Dinner tonight is already going to be exhausting."

Her eyes soften and she runs the back of her fingers over my cheek. I grab her wrist, pressing a kiss to her palm.

"It's going to be fine. Seriously, all of them love you already. Even Tanner is warming back up to you. He liked you before we were together, and I think he's finally realizing you're still the same genuine person."

I take a deep breath before letting out a long exhale. "OK."

She's right. I know how much this means to her.

Her dad is in town from Park City along with Clay, Lizzy, and Kayleigh. Her grandparents, Tanner, and V are all coming to dinner too. It's the first time we'll all have been together with us as a couple, and I want nothing more than for it to be perfect for her.

She gives me a questioning smile and I nod again, grinning up at her. "Yeah, I'm good. Can't wait to see everyone."

Her smile widens and she leans down, kissing me, her teeth tugging on my bottom lip when she pulls away. "Good. So, I'll see you at the restaurant tonight when I come with the girls."

Normally, having someone else's approval of anything I do never matters to me. When it comes to my girl, I know how important her family is and I want their approval for her sake. The surprise dinner with her dad back in Utah went shockingly well.

It's gone well with the rest of her family too, minus Tanner. Even that's been better though. He's stopped being a little bitch and if I can finish patching things up with him, everything will be perfect.

She climbs off my lap and I hold her hand until her fingers slip through mine. I lay there watching while my heart walks away, knowing that nothing has ever felt so right in my life.

CHAPTER 44
GRACE
MANGY MOOSE

"I THOUGHT YOU WERE AN OLYMPIC ATHLETE?" Josie calls back from further up the trail, keeping proper distance ahead of Kayleigh and me. She's far enough away I can just make out the colorful silhouette of her ski gear, but even from here I can still hear her teasing, snarky tone. She didn't earn her nickname, Backcountry Bunni, for no reason. She's just leaving the thicket of trees below Cody Peak.

This high up the mountain, we have a clear view of the jagged granite mountain ridge. The peak juts out into the blue horizon, high above us, to our left. The ridge line extends to the right, curving around us to form a large horseshoe shaped bowl, framed by rocky chutes and cliffs on either side. Great for wide open skiing in the middle.

A smile spreads across my face when I see the pristine mountain without a single track from other skiers. That's why we got up at the crack of dawn and hiked this far, to ski down these beautiful mountains and paint our fresh tracks in the untouched snow. On a mid-March day like this, the temperatures aren't brutally cold like they were a month ago, making the trek a little more comfortable. At this point, I've even shed my outer jacket and stowed it in my pack after working up a sweat.

Kayleigh lets out a long frustrated groan, as she makes deliberate strides on her skis up the path that Josie cleared ahead of us. "I go down mountains, not up them!"

I chuckle and call out between heavy breaths. "We'll take a break soon before we hike up to the top of the ridge line."

She lifts one of her ski poles in the air and I can see that she's giving me a thumbs up. I shake my head, still working my way along, slowly bringing up the rear of our group, on the trail. Kayleigh has made it her life's work to be the best in the world at going down a mountain as fast as humanly possible. I know Josie might be giving her shit, but I'm impressed with Kayleigh and glad she finally made it out with me. We've gone backcountry skiing only a couple times before, but always back in Utah and never here on what still feels like my home turf. She's more than holding her own, hiking up a mountain on skis with a full pack of safety gear, snacks, water, and extra layers.

It's not easy.

We've had to be careful on our way up. With the fresh snow, there are steeper parts of the mountain that are holding plenty of fresh snow that isn't stable after the storm last night.

I take another stride, feeling my legs and muscles protest. No matter how much time I spend hiking or in the gym, this is never easy. I'm starting to think that maybe Tommy was right. The idea of being back in bed with him sounds blissful compared to how sore my legs are. I don't think he realized how close he was to keeping me in bed this morning.

One more sweet kiss. One more thrust of his hips against me and I would have been all his today. That would be if I wasn't already completely and hopelessly his forever.

Peeking back up the wooded trail, I see that Josie and

Kayleigh are waiting at the edge of the trees. A few more strides and I'm there with them.

"Why do you do this all the time?" Kayleigh already has her skis off, leaning them against a tree while she catches her breath.

Josie laughs. "Not all of us get pampered out on the mountain as professional skiers with free lift passes. That shit gets expensive." She gestures her gloved hand around the mountain, just outside of the boundaries of the ski resort. "This is free and there aren't any lines. Just have to earn your turns."

"Yep. Free, a killer workout, and no lines. Hard to beat." I pop my skis off and take a drink from my hydration backpack, smiling back at Josie. "Not that you're hurting for cash."

Kayleigh rolls her eyes at Josie. "Definitely earned my turns today after that hike." Josie laughs before Kayleigh looks around us, taking in the heart stopping views. I see the subtle approval in her eyes. That's the look that makes it all worth it, when someone finally gets it. She takes a drink from her pack, smacking her lips. "So, where to next?"

I gesture toward the more open part of the ridge line, where it's less steep. "We'll go along this tree line, across that snowfield and work our way further up that face of the mountain. Once we're up there, we'll stop for lunch, and then it's all downhill after that."

She lets out a breath and shakes her head, clearly seeing that the hiking portion isn't over yet. "Let's get to it, I guess."

We all take one last drink of water before clicking back into our skis. Josie slings her pack over her shoulders and straps it on, heading out to lead the way again. The snow is heavy and the trip up the mountain is backbreaking today after nearly eight inches fell overnight, but that is what makes it worth it.

I am going to crush some pasta and wine tonight at Gloria's. Refueling with carbs and Cabernet already sounds amazing compared to the granola bars and peanut butter and jelly sandwich I packed for lunch.

After Kayleigh gets far enough ahead of me, I start behind her, still hugging the tree line before going higher up the slope. This area of the mountain is my favorite. The landscape transitions from forested woods on the lower elevations to rocky, barren snow covered terrain on the higher elevations on the way up to the peak above us.

It's breathtakingly beautiful, but also a harsh reminder that Mother Nature can be a coldhearted bitch. Dead trees, taken out from falling boulders or the brutal climate, dot the mountainside.

Following the trail, I see Josie working her way up the far side of the horseshoe shaped bowl, below one of the bands of rocks. Kayleigh's crossing the snowy center of the bowl, we'll eventually ski after we reach the top.

When I work my way out into the open area, past the trees, I have a clear view of the valley below us — down the steep, treacherous part of the mountainside. Like the last time I was out with Josie, my eyes find their way to the cluster of houses near the bottom of the ski resort.

Warmth spreads through me, wondering what Tommy is doing back at home. After spending so many nights with him there, I'm sure he's either in the gym taking care of himself or in the studio, working on another new song.

The sound of a tree branch cracking behind me reminds me that I need to focus on my surroundings and I stop in my tracks.

It's March, it should be too early for a Grizzly bear to be waking up from hibernation. I whip my head around and scan the trees behind me, when I finally spot movement near a large pine tree. I smile when I see the large, lumbering figure emerge from the trees.

Freaking Agnes.

That damned mangy moose made her way up from the village. Probably looking for something to munch on, where there isn't much competition for it, after eating everything good in the village all winter. I'm sure it barely took any effort to get up here with those freakishly long moose legs.

I shake my head, muttering to myself when a shadow behind Agnes draws my gaze back. A small calf comes out from behind her, munching on branches and bark from the same tree as Agnes.

Josie calls from way up ahead, near the rocky outer part of the bowl, with a shrill whistle, snapping my eyes up to her. I can see her waving her hands, gesturing for me to catch up. I point back behind me, toward Agnes, when I hear the sound of hooves beating against the ground. I look over my shoulder to see her and her calf sprinting away from the trees, down the steep part of the mountain below us.

Shit shit shit.

After seeing me, and hearing Josie, they must have been startled. From where she is, she would have had no way of knowing they were there. I watch in horror as they run down and across the steep mountain face below Kayleigh and me. It's covered in heavy, unstable snow. Seconds later, that damned moose and her calf are out of sight, farther down the mountain, and the snow below Kayleigh and me is intact.

I let out a long, relieved breath seeing that the slope is still holding. I collect myself and start to continue on the path when I hear it and see it all at once.

A crackling sound is followed by a long, jagged fracture in the snow that spreads along the path those damn moose took. Seconds later, the top layer of snow begins to slide down the steep terrain. My eyes flash to Josie who's far enough up, along the rocks, she should be safe. Then I look to Kayleigh who's still above the faltering snow like me.

Frantically, I yell and wave at Kayleigh, trying to get her attention. With our climbing covers on our skis to go uphill, we're in no position to ski out of danger quickly. She turns and our eyes meet, just as I hear the roaring sound of the snow base beneath of us give way. I see the moment abject, gut-wrenching terror sets in as she realizes what's happening around us. Just as she begins to open her mouth to yell something, I feel the snow beneath my skis begin to slide.

In an instant, I'm being pulled down the mountain in a brutally strong current of snow. I grab and claw for purchase on anything, but it does no good. I feel myself get pulled under like I'm caught in a riptide. Everything around me goes by in a blur of blinding white, with flashes of blue from the sky, as I'm tossed and turned in the cascading snow. For a split second, those flashes of blue make me think of seeing TJ when I left this morning.

The deep, rumbling sound of the avalanche and cracking branches and tree limbs unite into a chaotic, deafening maelstrom around me, muffling my screams. After what feels like an eternity, everything stops, except for my heart, which feels like it's beating hard enough to jump out of my chest.

I open my eyes to blackness and eerie silence.

Every fiber of my body aches, but I still try to move. I wiggle my feet and hands, and try to shake my head, but I'm met with the resistance of cold, dense snow in every direction.

The always optimistic side of me calls that a small victory that I don't seem to have any broken bones. But that doesn't stop reality from setting in though.

No. No. No. I tell myself no, but I already know the reality deep down.

I'm buried under feet of snow.

Kayleigh probably is too.

My only hope is Josie, or someone else that might be out in

the mountains nearby, saw what happened and can save us before time runs out.

I do my best, trying not to panic, to conserve air and energy. I think of one calming, steadying thing...

This isn't how I go out, because this morning will not be the last time I see him.

CHAPTER 45
TJ
HAS TO BE PERFECT

I TIP my chin to the hostess at Gloria's and walk to my normal seat at the counter. Dinner isn't for half an hour, but I was restless at home, pacing around. Despite what I told Grace earlier, I'm still slightly terrified of seeing her whole family under these circumstances. Admittedly, neither of her hulking, brooding brothers has tried to kill me and if they haven't by now, I'm probably safe. Her dad and grandparents have also been nothing but welcoming. With the childhood I had, it still brings up such a tangled mix of emotions for me.

I'm so happy Grace grew up with a loving family and I'm gracious they're starting to treat me the same way she does, like just another guy. They don't mention my money or act weird about it around me. I knew her family was good people, but it's still refreshing to see. I just want her to be happy and to never feel like she has to choose between me and them. That's why I wanted to have dinner with everyone tonight, to make it clear that I will always be in this with her. I want it to be clear that we're partners. We're always going to be on each other's side.

Looking back into the kitchen, over the counter, my knee bounces as I still struggle to keep my nerves in check. Sutton's normally glued to his perch right behind the counter, in the open kitchen, and I still haven't seen him yet. Finally, the door to the back office opens and he steps out, looking down at the floor as he walks through the kitchen.

"You had me worried there. Thought I was going to have to send a search party for you," I joke, trying to get my nerves in check. He looks up at me and his eyes widen in confusion.

"Why the fuck are you here?" he asks, his tone showing no signs of his normal jovial, always cheery self.

I rear back slightly, furrowing my brow in question. "I have a reservation? The big family dinner I'm nervous as fuck about, remember? The one I said has to be perfect? Please, don't tell me you forgot."

"Josie and I have been trying to call you for half an hour."

Shit. Grace is my only contact that has emergency bypass and I've had my phone on silent all afternoon because I've been worried about tonight.

"Tanner was here earlier," he continues.

"So why isn't he here now?" I interrupt.

Sutton's eyes flick to the ground and his tone softens. "Tommy."

The hair on my neck instantly stands on end. In the years I've known Sutton, he has never once called me Tommy.

He finally looks up at me and I see the pained expression in every striking feature of his face.

"Tanner was at the bar, having a drink with Veronica about half an hour ago. They got a call from Josie."

"What call?" My jaw clenches so tight I can barely get the words out.

He shakes his head, but not before I see the look of sympathy in his eyes. "Grace and Kayleigh are in the hospital."

❄

I RUSH in the doors of Jackson's small hospital, right into the emergency room. My throat and lungs sting from breathing in the frigid winter air after running the five blocks from Gloria's here. It's nothing compared to the gut-wrenching, heart-shattering pain I've felt with every single second that passed since Sutton told me she was here.

The one constant thought that ran through my mind the entire way here was *no.*

There's no fucking way that she comes into my life, adding color, passion, and love to very single minute of what was my boring routine just to be taken away from me. There's no way someone so vibrant gets cut short.

No, this morning wasn't the last time I saw her.

I scan the waiting room, looking for any sign of her or someone I know. My pulse pounds and it's like I can feel each, single, painful beat of my heart as I look for something to grasp onto before I break down into full on panic.

Finally a nurse walks past me and I step in front of her.

"Where is she?" I ask, barely able to think straight and realize I'm not exactly being clear.

My voice cuts through the seemingly calm, quiet ER in the small town hospital.

"Who?"

I barely register her question when I spot all six-foot-four, impossible to miss, Tanner Chapman, over her shoulder. I waste no time brushing past the nurse to head down the hall.

He looks up from his phone as he comes out of the room, shutting the door behind him. Around the corner, I see Lizzy sitting on a bench in the hallway. She gives me a weak smile and quick wave.

"TJ," he says, his voice it's usual deep, gruff tone. "I was just about to call you. I—"

That's the most he's said to me in the last two months, but right now I couldn't give a single, solitary fuck.

"Is she in there? Is she OK?" I don't even wait for an answer, stepping around him. I reach for the door handle, when the doctor swings open the door to her room and steps out. He stops when he looks up from his clipboard and sees me.

Opening my shoulders, I gesture for him to walk past me but he stays standing in the doorway, separating me from her. I'm not normally one for violence, but right now I'm pretty sure I could shove him through the door and across the room with the amount of adrenaline surging through me.

He must sense it because he calmly asks. "It's family only right now. Are you a relative?"

Over the doctor's shoulder in her room, I see Clay sitting on the other side of the room, next to their dad. Clay gives me a look that I think is his attempt to be reassuring, but it's hard to tell with how surly he normally is.

"Sir, are you a relative?" the doctor asks again, a hint of irritation in his voice now.

I seethe, knowing that she's on the other side of the door and he's in my way.

CHAPTER 46
GRACE
JAZZ HANDS

I WAKE up to the quiet sound of mumbling in my bed. I try to sit up, groaning when I feel each and every one of my muscles ache with the motion.

What the hell? Grogginess sets in and I force my eyes shut to keep the light out. I must have gone a little too crazy at dinner with my family because I don't even remember it or leaving.

"I'm going back to bed, Tommy," I murmur, ready to sleep off what already feels like the worst hangover I've ever had. I try to snuggle back into bed, grabbing my pillow and burying my face in it.

The smell of disinfectant and bleach immediately fill my nose with each breath. The scratchy fabric tells me instantly that I'm not in Tommy's bed — *our* bed. My eyes immediately fly open at the unpleasant sensations and I sit straight up, ignoring the pain shooting through my muscles and joints.

There's no doubt in my mind where I am. Before I even look around the room, I already know I'm back in a place I never wanted to be again.

Panic sets in at the thought of those days after the car accident that claimed months of my life as a teenager. Anxiety and adrenaline bring back another rush of memories, reminding me how I got here.

Agnes, the moose. Josie whistling. Watching as Kayleigh got buried. Then silent, hopeless blackness...

My breathing quickens as panic takes over and I fist the sheets at my side. My eyes scan the room, fully aware of where I am now.

Clay is sitting on the far side next to my grandparents. Tanner is standing in the corner, by the door, with Veronica, who is talking to a doctor. All of it reminds me of waking up in that room a decade ago. All the more highlighted by the fact that Dad is at my side, and Mom isn't here, just like that day.

I feel pressure on my wrist and look down to see Dad's hand squeezing me, making my breathing slow down ever so slightly.

"Hey. Hey," he says, making a gentle shushing sound. I see the look in his eyes, beckoning me to stay calm. "You're fine. Everything's going to be OK."

"Where's Tommy?" I ask.

My dad looks to Tanner who simply nods. "I was just going to call him."

Tanner pulls out his phone, and steps out of the room into the hall. I look back to Dad. "How long have I been here? How long was I asleep?"

"Josie said you were buried for about five minutes before she got to you. You were unconscious when she found you, and she called search and rescue. They brought you straight here by heli-copter. That was about two hours ago."

My breathing slows down another notch until a far worse realization dawns on me. "Wait. Where's Kayleigh?"

He winces, causing my anxiety to spike again. The look of horror in Kayleigh's eyes when the avalanche hit us crashes into my psyche, making my entire body tense. She was in the direct path of it compared to me and I was still totally buried.

Clay, Kayleigh's best friend since high school, clears his throat. "Josie's with Kayleigh since she doesn't have any family here with her and they let her in. She's still unconscious." I look over at him to find him wringing his hands and a muscle ticking in his jaw. "They wouldn't let me in, but I caught the search and rescue team that brought her in and Josie has been giving me updates. She broke her leg and they're checking her for other injuries still."

"Clay," I say, trying to get him to look up. My voice is weak and my throat is sore as my adrenaline wears off. This is all my fault. I'm the one who has been begging her to do this with me for years. I should have known it wasn't right to push her to come with me given how important her olympic career and training are.

"Miss Chapman." The unfamiliar voice of the doctor interrupts our silent sibling exchange. I look over to see him eyeing me over his clipboard. "You're both unbelievably lucky Josie was there to dig you out, and call for search and rescue to get there as fast as they did. Your friend, Miss Jensen, is in good hands though. Now please, try to get some rest."

He turns for the door and steps out, leaving it cracked behind him.

I look back to my dad, who's still holding my wrist. "Please, get Tommy here."

He smiles warmly at me and nods.

My mind is overwhelmed by feelings and memories that are coming back to me. But through all of them, one stands out. That feeling of need for him followed by the crushing fear of thinking I would never see him again. That was the last thing that I remember before waking up here and it still hasn't changed.

I need him here, with me — my calm and steady.

Commotion at the door and the sound of raised, agitated voices pulls my attention away from Dad.

"Yeah. I'm related." As if my mere thoughts summoned him, he's here for me.

Even from outside the room, I can feel the urgency in his voice, and the all consuming bond between us. It's ever-present, always pulling us together.

Despite every ache in my body, I want to — no, not want, need — I need to give into it, get up, and walk to him. I shift my body and swing my legs over the side of the bed that I already am committed to getting the hell out of as soon as the doctor isn't within earshot. My dad puts his arm out, trying to stop me.

Then I hear him say it. His voice is a low growl, but still clear enough for my entire family to hear.

"She's my wife."

Every head in the room snaps to the door as Tommy, my husband, pushes his way past the doctor and strides to the side of my bed.

Our eyes meet and it feels like a weight heavier than the crushing snow of the avalanche has been lifted off me. It's like I can finally breathe again.

I see it in his eyes too, his posture visibly softening when he sees me sitting up in the bed. My dad, with a surpassingly calm look on his face, steps aside.

Tommy says nothing, just wrapping me in his arms, pulling me tight into his chest. I melt into his warmth, sinking into his embrace. His familiar scent fills my lungs and I hear the sound of his racing heart, making me feel whole.

"I'm here, Rainbow." His voice is hoarse and ragged. He presses a kiss to the top of my head and rubs soothing circles on my back, bringing my pulse back under control.

"What the fuck?" My brother's deep, gruff voice cuts through the room. Tommy and I both turn to see Tanner standing in the doorway next to the doctor.

The doctor awkwardly shuffles on his feet. "I'm going to give you some time as a family." He steps out of the room and silence sets in.

I feel everyone's eyes on Tommy and me.

"Surprise?" My voice trails up in question. I raise my hands to the sides of my head, waggling my splayed fingers in jazz hands.

Tommy leans down and whispers into my ear. "That was cringier than my use of emojis and you know it."

To my pleasant surprise, Clay and Veronica both cover their mouths to hide their laughter. I'm glad to see they're still on my side.

Tanner shoots Veronica a sidelong glance. "You think it's funny that they got married and didn't tell us? They've known each other for months." He looks back at me. "When did this even happen?"

She smirks, raising her eyebrows at him. "I'm pretty sure you proposed to me after we dated for two months."

He groans and scrubs his hand over his face. "That's different. She's—"

"I'm what?" I cut him off, staring daggers at him. "Too young? Too fragile? Still too broken to make my own choices?"

He winces and stays silent.

Tommy's hand still works on my back rubbing my stiff muscles. It's like he can sense my apprehension about being back in a hospital room, with my entire family, and he's trying to will it away with his touch.

I look back at my family and shrug. "And to answer your question, it was in Tahoe last month. We just knew. It felt right. We wanted this and went to a wedding chapel one night on the Nevada side of the lake."

Tanner looks genuinely stunned and angry. Through his rugged exterior, I don't miss the little bit of hurt in his eyes.

"We were going to tell everyone tonight," Tommy says. I look up to see him still peering down at me with nothing but love and affection.

I smile up at him before turning back to my brother. "So I guess you guys get to find out now instead."

I look over to see Grandma, her eyes flicking back and forth between Tommy and me. She's grinning ear to ear, just like she was at Tanner's wedding when she first met Tommy at the reception. I swear she might burst if she gets any more excitement today. At least this is good news compared to the reason she came to the hospital.

"Dad, are you really OK with this?" Tanner stands there, turning his palms up.

A laugh I haven't heard in ages, practically a boyish giggle comes from beside the bed. Beside Tommy, my dad is smiling and shaking his head. I haven't seen him smile or laugh that way since Mom died.

He ignores my brother and replaces Tommy at my side, who reluctantly takes a step back. "Grace, honey, if your mom would be proud of anything, it would be this. This is the most *her* thing you've ever done."

Tears pricks the corner of my eyes. I only ever wanted my family to accept my decisions. Their approval would never stop me from doing what I want, but hearing him say that, right now, means more than he could ever know. Although from the look in his eyes, I'm pretty sure he might have at least some clue.

"You guys got married on the ranch," Tanner says, still clearly not thrilled.

Another laugh, this time from Grandpa, in the corner of the room. "No they didn't. Your mom and your dad were the most impatient teens we'd ever seen."

Tanner looks to Grandpa and then Dad, whose warm grin only widens.

Grandpa laughs again. "The wedding on the ranch wasn't

their *actual* wedding. We did that because your mom and dad drove to Vegas the day after they graduated high school and got married. We didn't want to upset all of our friends and family in the whole damn town, so we did that wedding. You know how small towns are. We'd have never heard the end of it if there wasn't a wedding for everyone to come to."

A moment passes where everyone in the room looks around in stunned disbelief. Even I didn't know that story, but knowing Mom, it makes so much more sense than the wedding I've seen in the family photo album.

Sensing my oldest brother's lingering apprehension, my dad gestures between Tommy and me. "Look at his face and tell me he doesn't love her as much, or maybe even more, than any of us. I was a bit worried he was going to throw the doc through the damn wall when he got here. As far as I'm concerned, he's part of this family now."

This time, Tanner looks between Tommy and me. I finally, finally see his expression soften. The corner of his lips tug up into a remorseful smile and he gives me one curt nod.

"Welcome to the family, TJ." Everyone in the room looks over to see Dad extending a hand toward Tommy.

A wave of emotion hits me all at once. Never once in my adult life did I think I'd find a man I'd want to call my own. Now my dad, still as tall and rugged as my brothers, is holding his hand out for the man of my dreams — my husband — to shake.

I know how much this means to Tommy too. He might have Jake, but he's never truly had a family to call his own. I don't even think my dad realizes the meaning of what he just said to him. Tommy swallows hard and I can see him trying to hold back his emotions. He extends his hand and gives my dad's one firm pump.

"Thank you, sir."

"Hold on a second." A familiar voice practically squeals. "Did someone say married?"

We all look over to the door to see Lizzy, still in the hallway but poking her head in the cracked door.

Clay groans. "Fuck it. The doctor's gone. Get in here, Princess. Join the party."

She wastes no time making her way to her fiancé and sitting in his lap. It's standing room only in here, fitting given that Tommy finally showed up. She looks at Veronica and then me. "You know you're going to have to spill all the tea later, right?"

I DROP Grace's bag down inside our bedroom door.

She steps into the room after me and I hear her sigh in relief. "Oh, thank god, I'm home. I need a real shower."

Home.

Hearing her call my house *home,* the one I've enjoyed but never felt particularly attached to, makes my chest fill with pride. Even though we've moved so fast, like everything with us, it just feels right, like it was always meant to be.

I think I'd call anywhere with her home. I'd sell all my places and move into her van, without a second thought, if that's what she wanted.

I don't think that's the case though. She brushes past me and beelines for the ensuite bathroom practically skipping. I chuckle and follow behind her. She was only in the hospital for one night as a precaution, but the first thing she asked for this morning was to get home and get a real shower. After checking on Kayleigh, who was out of surgery and awake, and somehow lucky enough to only have a broken leg and dislocated shoulder, we left the hospital.

I walk into the bathroom to already find her stripping down with the water running.

I lean in the doorway, watching her with amusement until her baggy overalls fall to the ground and I see the bruises covering her legs. My body stiffens, but there's no one to be angry at. All I can do is thank every fucking star that she's still here with me now. "You sure you don't want to rest first? The shower will be here when you wake up."

She shrugs her flannel shirt off, leaving her in just her sports bra and revealing more bruises across her toned upper body. Her eyes find mine and she shoots me a playful glare. "Not a chance in hell."

I snort a laugh and walk over to her, standing behind her. I wrap my arms around her waist, pulling her nearly naked body against my front. Even with my jeans on, the feeling of her ass against my crotch sends blood rushing south.

"Arms up," I say.

She looks at me over her shoulder. "I can take my own bra off."

"I know you can, but that doesn't mean I don't want to help." I run my hands up her sides, my fingers tracing over her ribs and the band of her sports bra. She makes a little whimper and leans into me, raising her arms up. I press a kiss below her ear. "That's my girl."

I pull her bra up and over her head, careful to make sure it doesn't snag on her piercings. Pulling her back into me, I look at her in the mirror in front of us. She holds my forearms and nuzzles into my collarbone. The contented smile on her face doesn't give the slightest hint of how sore she must be. The bruises up and down her sides though say otherwise.

"Get in the shower with me," she rasps against my neck. "Please."

I press another kiss to her temple. "As you wish. My girl gets whatever she wants."

I check the water temperature, and steam fills the room, while I strip down with her. I feel her eyes on me every second until I'm fully naked with her.

She laughs to herself and I cock my head at her, raising my pierced eyebrow. "What's so funny?"

"Just thinking about how lucky I am."

"We're not having that argument again."

"You're really going to tell me I'm not lucky? I just survived an avalanche with basically a bunch of bruises and only a light concussion."

I step toward her, pulling her by her hips into me. She looks down at my cock where it presses against her. It's definitely inappropriately hard for the moment, but I don't give a shit. All I want is to be close to her. I spent all night holding her against my body in that tiny hospital bed and that wasn't enough.

"You're right. That's pretty lucky. I'm luckier though because I still have you."

She reaches down, rubbing her thumb over the tip of my cock.

"Fuck," I grit out, bucking into her hand.

She giggles. "You keep selling yourself short. What if I'm the lucky one to have you?"

She tosses her head back, the motion makes her bangs flop across her forehead, before she smirks at me.

"Fine. We're equally lucky." She squeezes me tighter and pulls me toward the glass shower door by my cock. "Now, get in the shower with me."

I step in behind her because I'll follow her wherever she wants to go.

The hot spray from the rainfall shower heads is an instant

relief. I'm not even the one that survived an avalanche, but the stress of the last two days wore on me more than I realized.

She releases her grip on my throbbing dick and turns to face me. The water cascades over her, running through the colors of her hair, making her bangs cling to her forehead. My eyes follow the water beading down over her chest and my mind goes back to that morning on the river.

"Hey, what are you thinking about?"

I look up to see her smirking at me, her eyes flitting down to my erection and back to me.

I step toward her, brushing her wet hair off her shoulder.

"Just you. Always you."

Her lips part and I chuckle.

"Come on. Let me wash your hair. And yes, I know you can do it yourself but I like taking care of you, so don't argue." I reach over her shoulder to grab her bottle of shampoo but she grabs my wrist, stopping me.

I level a questioning glare at her but she just grins.

"I'll take care of that later."

She lowers my hand down over one of her breasts, pressing her hard, pierced nipple into my palm.

Fuck me. That does nothing to help with how hard my dick is right now.

She steps closer, still holding my hand to her chest and kisses me. Her other hand cups the base of my neck and her fingertips curl into my hair. I feel her hunger and need as her tongue explores my mouth. Our bodies press together and she moans when I trace her hip bone with my thumb. I don't know what I ever did to deserve her. I had practically resigned myself to being alone and drifting along. Somehow, the universe put her right where I needed her to be.

I break the kiss, pressing my forehead to hers, the sound of the water falling around us matched by our panting.

"We can wait. I don't want to hurt you. The doctor said to take it easy for a while."

She pulls back, just enough to look into my eyes.

"I'm fine, Tommy. I'm bruised and sore, but I know my body. I'm not broken." She brings her lips to my ear and rasps. "So, please just trust me and fuck me."

I know how much it means to her to be strong. I've seen what her independence and autonomy means to her. Now though, to see her bare it like this, to see how she wants and needs me, makes me feel whole in a way I never thought was possible. Knowing that I'm her person just as much as she is mine breaks my heart and stitches it back together every time I think about it.

This wild and carefree woman chose me. She pushed me. She even helped me find my love of music again, not by trying to force the issue, but just by existing in my world. Her mere presence was enough to break me out of my aimless decade of nothingness and make me feel everything again.

Looking in her eyes, seeing that fire and desire focused solely on me, I make a mental note to never question her convictions again. I should have already known that. When she first kissed me, I doubted her even though she was confident and knew what she wanted. Hell, she knew what I wanted before I was willing to give into it.

Just like getting married that night at a small wedding chapel in Nevada. She knew that every word, every lyric of that song was a question for her. Never once has she doubted herself, or me, and I will spend the rest of my life thanking her for that. That unwavering trust in each other is something I'll never, ever take for granted.

My gaze drops to my hand over her breast, where my fingers rest just above her heart. I feel the pounding rhythm against the pads of my fingers and my eyes drift to the new band of ink woven between the notes tattooed on my ring finger.

"See." She ghosts her lips across my stubbled cheek. "I'm here and I'm fine."

I'm at a loss for words, which is nothing new when it comes to her. Instead of wasting more time, I give her what she wants, what we both want. I tighten my grip on her waist and step to her, pressing her against the shower wall at her back. Her fiery green eyes lock on mine and her lips part into a lusty, playful grin. It's short lived though, because I give my girl — my wife — exactly what she needs.

I bring my lips to hers in a flurry. My tongue finds the back of her throat in seconds, unleashing the pent up lust in both of us after the drama of yesterday. She lets out another surprised gasp before following suit, nipping at my lip. The kiss is sloppy and messy, hot and needy, and so fucking perfect.

I hook my hand under the curve of her ass, pulling her leg up. She wraps it around me, following my lead. The movement puts my cock right against her slick pussy lips. I feel her piercing slide against my shaft, waking up every fucking nerve in my body. She lets out another low whimper as she grinds herself along my length.

I'm not even inside of her and I'm ready to come right now knowing just how needy she is for me. Watching how she works herself on my shaft, driving us both closer to the edge is pure fucking perfection. I shunt my hips forward, increasing the pressure for us both.

She reaches between us. "I need you inside me. Now." Fisting me, she notches the head of my cock at her entrance, and pulls her other leg up, wrapping it around my waist. I grab her ass with both hands now, feeling the pads of my fingers dig into her flesh. She drapes her arms around my neck. I look into her eyes and she smirks at me, relaxing her body into my hands.

Holy fucking hell.

She knows exactly what she's doing because that little movement seats the head of my cock just inside her tight, wet cunt. I shudder, staying focused so I don't come right on the spot.

"Fuck, baby. You're so damn tight and soaked for me."

"I told you I needed my husband's cock deep inside me."

That might go down as the single hottest sentence I will ever hear. Any time I take a shower and hear running water now, my wife's words are going to echo in the depths of my mind.

I rock my hips forward, slowly easing into her so I don't end our fun too quickly.

"My wife gets what she wants."

"Then give it to me. Give me all of you."

Before I can even think, her mouth meets mine in another frantic, clashing of teeth and tongue. She swivels her hips and digs her calves into my lower back, fully seating my cock deep inside her wet heat.

"Fuck," I hiss, breaking the kiss to see her eyes and her teeth dig into her lower lip. Her skin glistens under the water and has taken on a crimson flush from the steamy water and heat of our bodies. "Your pussy was fucking made for me."

She hums her approval, nodding with her eyes still closed. Her lips part and I can't take my eyes off her chest as it rises with each shallow breath. I drop my mouth to one of her breasts, flicking my tongue over her nipple and swirling it over her piercing. Her nails dig into the back of my neck and I thrust forward again, savoring the feeling of her walls tightening around me. My tongue dances over the metal barbell, flicking it again. This time she moans, crying out my name.

"Yes, Tommy. Please, don't fucking stop." She rocks her hips in rhythm with mine, adjusting her position just enough that I feel her piercing sliding along the base of my shaft with each thrust.

I pick up my pace, hammering home and pinning her to the granite shower wall. Her eyes blaze with a fire and passion that bore into my soul and I know that she will always own my heart.

She is my other half and I'm never going to let her out of my life again. I know she thinks she's the one that lives fast and free, trying to seize every precious moment of life she can get. She might call me calm and steady, but right now I'm making a promise to myself to be more like her. I'm going to make the most of every second I have with her.

"Oh. Yes!" she cries out and I feel her pussy start to flutter and clench my cock.

Looking into her glassy eyes, I see the moment she comes undone. Her eyes roll back and that crimson flush on her cheeks nearly hides her freckles from me. I drop my mouth to her neck, kissing that spot just under her ear, making her buck her hips as she wrings out her pleasure.

"Don't come yet," she breathes against my ear, so quietly it's nearly a whisper.

"That's going to be fucking hard," I grit out.

I don't know how, but I find the strength to slow my pace. She's smirking at me with that mischievous little grin I love.

"Sit over there." She tilts her head toward the bench on the back wall of the shower.

"I know you think I'm ancient, but I've got plenty of stamina to stand and fuck my wife."

Her lips part and pull up into a surprised smile.

"I know, but I want to thank my husband. So sit."

She's going to kill me. I ease my cock out of her and begrudgingly sit on the cool bench. She stands over me and my dick aches for her body to be back on me. She's pure stunning radiance, still glowing from her orgasm. She stands right in front of me and I run my fingertips over the backs of her legs until I'm cupping her ass again. I try to tug her forward but she stands firm.

"What do you have to thank me for?"

Her eyes soften and she tucks a wet strand of my hair behind my ear. She gently runs the backs of her fingers over my stubbled jaw.

"For listening to me. You never treat me like I'm fragile. You always see me the way I want to be seen, how I see myself."

She lowers herself down in front of me. The hot water still falls around us, streaking down her hair. I cup the back of her neck, brushing it over her shoulders.

The sight reminds of the morning she found me on the river. Despite her scars, masked with beautiful tattoos, or the bruises from yesterday, everything about her screams passionate optimism and hope. It's enough to block out that little bit of anger in the back of mind that anyone would ever think she's anything but strong. I will never take away her agency like that. I want her to always feel like she's empowered to realize whatever bold dreams she has.

"You never have to thank me for that."

An unimpressed hum escapes her lips as she grabs my cock, squeezing the base. I shudder and feel that need and tension at the base of my spine again. She looks into my eyes with that mischievous glint that I love, just like everything else about her.

"Maybe, but I still want to."

She pushes her breasts forward and slowly drags the head of my cock over her nipples. I rock my hips forward at the sensation of her hard buds and the cool metal, desperate to feel more of her touch.

She lets go of my cock and runs her hands up my thighs, her eyes still locked on mine. As close as I was to coming inside of her when she said to stop, I'm now painfully aware of just how much I need her. She leans forward more, pressing my cock into her chest. I rock my hips up again and she huffs a cute laugh. She scrunches her elbows together, squeezing my dick between her slick, full breasts.

"Fuck my tits. I want to watch you come on them."

We both look down, seeing my cock twitch at her command, a bead of precum already on the tip.

She huffs another laugh. "I won't say stop this time."

She opens her mouth and spits right on the head of my cock. Slowly, she moves her breasts up and down, sliding them along my length. I match her, thrusting into her tits.

"Tell me the truth. You've wanted to do this since that day." That coil of tension at the base of my spine builds to an urgent level as I get closer and closer to coming completely undone.

I nod, not even having to clarify which day she means. "I've never stopped thinking about you."

She hums her approval at my admission. She lifts her hands from my thighs, cupping her breasts and pressing them together even tighter on my dick. She rolls her nipples between her fingertips, whimpering at her own touch. That little sound of pleasure snaps my restraint and I come hard, grabbing the edge of the granite bench. I watch as rope after rope of my cum spurts from my cock onto her wet chest. It slowly runs down her chest and over those little barbells. I'm half fucking tempted to lick it off of her so I can feel those piercings under my tongue again.

"Fuck yes," I groan in relief, knowing that sight will be burned into my mind for the rest of my life. She smiles, licking her lips before lowering her mouth onto the crown of my cock. She hollows her cheeks and sucks, taking as much of me in her mouth as she can. I shudder again, grabbing her shoulder as she takes in every last drop.

"That's my girl. You look so good with my cock in your mouth, baby." I run my hand over her slicked hair and she leans into my touch. Her eyes meet mine and she hums with me still in her mouth. Slowly, she raises her head up and the tip of my cock springs free from her mouth with a pop.

"Come here." I grab her hand, tugging her forward. She

stands up and I pull her down onto one of my thighs. I adjust my still hard and sensitive cock out of the way when she sits sideways, cradled in my arms. I hold her warm body against me and she nuzzles her head under my chin.

I press my lips to the top of her damp hair and she lets out a contemplative sound that I feel against my skin, barely audible over the sound of the water still trickling down around us.

"So, what's next?" She kisses my collarbone, barely moving her head.

I look up at the shower head, humming in mock contemplation. "Well I know you might have the energy to probably try and hike up a mountain or something equally outlandish, but this old dinosaur could use a nap."

She pinches my ribs and giggles. The sound makes my heart, still stressed from the thought of losing her less than twenty-four hours ago, relax another little bit.

"You're not old. And I know this might be contrary to popular belief, but I do actually like to just chill sometimes. A nap with you sounds great right about now. That's not what I meant though."

She rests her chin on my chest and looks up at me with those beautiful evergreen eyes. "I meant what's next for us?" She strums her fingers along my bicep, tracing the faded barbed-wire tattoo.

That question brings an unbridled smile to my face. We've focused so much on what wouldn't work. Our ages, our family and friends. My reluctance to be less private. We took her idea for this foundation and ran with it because we're both actually excited by what we could do together. Outside of that, we've just enjoyed every moment together. I think the truth is that I still might not care that much about what my future looks like. I'll see what rebuilding my relationship with music looks like, but only on my terms. I'll keep working with the Sterling brothers because despite being pains in my ass, I have a soft spot for Slade and Sutton. Beyond that though, I want to take a page from her playbook.

I just know I need to be with her and I want to see where the universe takes us. That should be easy though, because she's my universe.

I rub my hand up and down the back of her neck, feeling her melt into my arms. Her eyes flutter shut and I whisper into her ear.

"Whatever you want to do, Rainbow. I've been the frontman in my life for so long, I just want to get to enjoy the ride with you. This is your show now. I'll follow wherever you want to go."

CHAPTER 48

GRACE
PIZZA

"HOW THE HELL do you look that good?" I watch Tommy walk out of the closet, dressed in a pair of dark blue jeans that hug his legs perfectly. The sleeves on his black and gray flannel are rolled up to show off his toned forearms and the first few buttons at the top are undone, revealing his collection of leather necklaces.

He smirks and shrugs at me, fidgeting with his bracelets before standing in front of me. He palms my hips in his hands, hooking his fingers into the belt loops of my black jeans.

"I could say the same thing about you." He kisses me before letting his gaze roam over my body. We're both in jeans and cozy flannels. Nothing fancy, but that doesn't change the way he looks at me.

I slap him on the shoulder. "Matching outfits? You realize we look ridiculous, right?"

A low laugh rumbles up his chest. The hungry grin on his face when his glacial blue eyes meet mine instantly heats my skin. That damned smile has always gotten to me. If anything, I think it might be getting to me more now. It's been a week since the avalanche, and every single time he smiles at me like that, I count my lucky stars that I still get to see it.

"You know damned well that I've never cared what other people think." With my boots on, I'm practically eye to eye with him and I can't bring myself to look away.

"We look like hipster lumberjacks though," I toss my head back and groan.

His grin grows wider. "Good. At least it will be clear to anyone that sees us that you're mine." He gives me a slap on the ass before smacking his lips at me in a playful air kiss. "Now come on, let's get going. Everyone is going to be waiting."

I giggle when he grabs my hand and leads me out of the bedroom. I know he said he'd follow me anywhere, but I'd do the same with him every day for the rest of my life. The way this man worships me and looks at me, I know he only wants what's best for me.

What makes him so special is that he doesn't feel the need to impose his will on me. He respects and even idolizes my need to make my own choices and decisions. That's what makes him a man — the one I love, the one I married.

WE DRIVE toward the main road to town, heading to meet our family and friends at Gloria's for a second attempt at a big family dinner. Tommy drives, keeping both hands firmly on the wheel, for me, while I look out at the mountains around us. Spring is almost here, but the Tetons are still snow covered after another late season storm.

I hear the turn signal click on and I look over to see Tommy turning onto a side street going the opposite way from downtown Jackson.

"Are you lost? Town's that way." I hitch my thumb over my shoulder pointing the other way. "Oh my god, please don't tell me you're going senile already." I clasp my hands to my face in mock horror.

He shakes his head and rolls his eyes. "I know where I'm going."

I look up again to see The Chairlift coming into view. Sure enough, he pulls right into the bar's parking lot. "Come on. We're here."

I give him a curious look and he grins back at me, looking way too pleased with himself. "Did you plan this or was this a last minute change? Because if it was a last minute change, you know Sutton's not going to be happy when he finds out we're not—"

A knocking sound on the window nearly makes me jump out of my seatbelt. I turn around to see Lizzy, Veronica, and Josie standing outside of the car. All of them are watching me, making googly eyes and kissy-faces at me.

OK. Not a last minute change I'm guessing then.

I hear Tommy laugh and turn back to see him still grinning in the driver seat. "Can we go inside now?"

I nod and hop out of the car. Looking around the parking lot, I see Tanner's truck and Lizzy's Bronco among the other familiar rides.

Josie comes up to me, wrapping me in a tight hug. She's still in town for another night, so I'm glad I get to see her today. I will forever owe her for saving my life that day on the mountain. She was already my best friend, but seriously, how do I repay her for that?

She looks up at me and smiles softly, like she knows where my head is at. "Kayleigh's inside waiting for us. She'd come out, but the wheelchair is less than ideal and she didn't want to get her cast wet."

I follow her, noticing that Lizzy and Veronica are already talking with Tommy. I don't hear everything, but I definitely catch the words *summer* and *music festival*.

I follow Josie into the bar, right on her heels since she's practically dragging me along. When I look around the room, I see that we must have the entire place to ourselves for the night. Everywhere I look, it's our family and friends. I see Sutton and Slade sitting together at the corner of the bar. My grandparents are sitting together at a table against the wall.

I can't look them in the face without blushing now. It was only a couple days ago that Josie told me that doctors did X-Rays while I was unconscious, and that's when my whole family found out about all of my piercings. Josie thinks it's hilarious, but I'm still not sure my grandparents or Dad will ever look at me the same way.

On the other end of the bar, Tanner and Clay sit with Dad, stubby beers in hand. Even Kelsey from Cowgirl Coffee is here since we've been reconnecting now that I'm in Jackson again.

Along the back wall of the bar are a few long folding tables, and sitting on top are box after box of Big Red's pizza. On one end of the table are a bunch of big sodas and reusable aluminum cups, ready to pour. I'm glad he's taking my request to offset his carbon footprint seriously.

I stand there, shocked until Tommy comes up beside me, resting his hand on my lower back. I look up at him, still stunned. "Was this your idea? How did you know I love pizza parties?"

He shrugs. "I do seem to remember you telling me that over breakfast. But no, this wasn't my idea."

"Then who—" I start but don't finish the question. He tips his chin and I follow his eyes to Tanner, who's standing beside us now.

"This was your idea?" I look at my older brother and watch the warm smile spread across his face. Veronica comes up next to him and he pulls her to his side.

She stands up on her toes, kissing him once before turning to me. "Consider it a late wedding gift from both of us. We never really got to celebrate you two properly."

Tanner reaches out with two fresh beers, handing one to each of us. "I'm happy for you two."

We clink our beers together before they head back to the bar. I watch them walk away, feeling like another weight has been lifted off my shoulders seeing Tanner accept us like that.

"I do have one surprise for you though." Tommy's smooth, deep voice snaps my attention back. He points across the room, past the long tables of pizza. Standing in the corner of the room is a pair of microphones and a karaoke machine.

"No. You didn't."

He laughs, rubbing my lower back. "Oh, yes. Yes, I did. Don't think I forgot about that time in Bend. I told you I'd get you back for dragging me up there with you. So later tonight, your whole family gets to watch."

Tommy still grins at me and I know he might think this is funny. Right now though, the idea of my whole family watching us, as mortifying as it should be, actually makes me happy. I know Mom isn't here, but looking around the room, I can't help but feel like her fingerprints are over all of this.

Every choice, every decision, I've always been thinking of her and everything she taught me. All of those little choices and moments — the verses and choruses of life — have led me to being here, right now, with my whole family.

None of us have ever been happier. Tanner has Veronica, and Clay has Lizzy. Even with everything we've all been through, it still feels like it might be the beginning of a new story, a new song for all of us.

"Hey. What are you thinking about?" Tommy's voice brings my eyes up to his. He searches my face. I cup his face in both hands and kiss him.

"I'll get up there with you, but I get to pick the song."

He quirks a brow at me. "Did you have one in mind?"

I nod, holding him tightly and resting my head on his shoulder.

"The one you wrote me. My song."

He rests his head on top of mine, pulling me into him.

"That's not your song, Rainbow. It's ours, and there will be plenty more of them to come."

EPILOGUE
TOMMY

August, Four Months Later

"I PROMISE. You're going to love it." Walking backwards, I pull Grace by the wrist toward the door to the driveway.

She groans, exasperated because the last time I told her that, she said it was 'way too much'.

"Tommy, I swear to god if there's a helicopter or a fancy car in the driveway again, I'm donating it to charity."

The helicopter was my compromise on not using the jet all the time. I thought it was a huge win because it could be used for heli-skiing, but she didn't seem to find the humor in my very serious idea. That doesn't mean I don't still have it stowed away at the Jackson airport until she comes around to the idea.

"I promise it's not a helicopter or a fancy car. And to be fair, that SUV was solely out of love, because it was five star crash rated and the safest on the market."

She sighs and her posture softens. "Fine. Let's go see it."

She told me she didn't need or want a wedding gift from me. With every day that I've spent with her over the last few months, I've felt more and more like myself. I've found that passion again, the one the that drove me to write music, the one that pushed me to help my friends when they need it. I think it was always there, but being around her has brought that joy for life back to the surface and I can never thank her enough for that.

I have a feeling this gift will be perfect though.

When we walk outside, I spot Josie standing in the driveway leaning against a van, arms crossed with a smug look on her face.

Grace rushes to her friend, wrapping her arms around her in a bear hug I now associate with the whole Chapman family. "What are you doing here? I thought you were in Colorado."

"I was. Got a little hiking in. Just had to stop here before heading on to California next week."

I watch Grace with her best friend, glad to see the joy those two bring each other. I will forever be grateful to Josie for being there to help save her that day in the mountains. I will find a way to repay her one day.

"So what's up? Why'd you go out of your way? You know we'll see you next week at the music festival anyway."

Two months ago, Grace, or more accurately, Veronica, Lizzy, and Josie all convinced me to go to the Southern California Music Festival. It's next week, but I spent the last two months working on making sure Grace and I and all of our friends would have the best time possible.

"I know, but I'm not here for you. I needed to come pick up my van and drop this one off."

Grace gives her friend a confused look before looking at the van that's right in front of her. "Wait. Yeah. Where is yours? Did you get a new one?"

"I left it at Collin and Walker's. They're picking me up in it in a few."

"Then whose is this?" Grace asks.

She looks between us for a second and then I see the moment it clicks that it's not Josie's van. Grace walks around the large, blacked out adventure van. She drags her fingertips along every inch of it, checking out the lifted vehicle with off road tires, storage racks on the back for skis, and a roof rack for solar panels.

She finally turns back to me with Josie standing at my side now.

"Go ahead, check it out," I say, tossing the keys to her.

She snatches them out of the air, giving me one more surprised look before opening the sliding door. She climbs up, disappearing inside the van.

I pop my head in the door, watching her explore the custom camper van. I ordered it the day after the pizza party, after she took me out camping for a night in hers.

Watching her, I can feel her giddy excitement. She pops open each little cubby and cabinet, inspects the fridge, and slides open the shower door, combing every inch of the new van.

"I got the high roof one so I don't have to hunch over in yours. I also had them put two heaters in just in case one of them acts up." She looks at me over her shoulder, still clearly shocked. I already feel like this was the perfect gift.

"And no, I didn't get rid of Millie. This one is for the two of us. It's ours."

She finally comes back to the door of the van, standing in front of me. I grab her by the waist and she hops down.

"Thank you. This is amazing. It has everything in it I've ever dreamed of."

I kiss her forehead, smiling back at her. "The only thing I care about is that we're in it together."

We both turn to see Josie standing at the van, watching us.

She smirks. "The guys at the van shop were curious about this little special request." Josie points up at the roof rack, just above the tall rear doors. There's a little bracket with two folding arms.

"Close your eyes. I'll show you both."

Grace and Josie close their eyes and I climb the ladder on the back door and swing out the two arms. After climbing back down, I open the back door, pull out two ropes and a wooden plank.

I quickly assemble everything, pleased with my handiwork and my idea. Josie was right. The guys at the van shop were a bit confused by my idea, but they didn't object after I paid them quite well for the whole custom build. I just said I wanted to be able to a hang a swing or a hammock from the back and enjoy scenic views with my wife. Technically, that was true.

"Alright. Open your eyes now."

They both open their eyes and look at the wooden and rope swing in front of them.

"Hell yeah. You put a swing on the van? That's sweet. You could totally park this thing on the end of a trail and watch the sunset from there."

I look over at Grace and catch the slightest flush spreading over her cheeks. The look she gives me is worth every freaking penny. I know from the way her teeth dig into her bottom lip, she's replaying that night in Seattle, just like I am.

When we got back from Tahoe, the first thing I did was put a set of the same swings in the living room here in Jackson. They're right in front of the fireplace, just like the ones at the penthouse in Seattle. So far, not a single person has given them a second thought except for Josie and Sutton. Everyone thinks they're cool and way more fun than just hanging on a lounge chair in front of the fire. I didn't miss the look on Josie's face. Her grin told me exactly what she was thinking and I'm guessing my wife told her something about that night.

The sound of Josie clearing her throat catches both of our attention.

"Well, you two making googly eyes at each other is my cue to leave." She tilts her head toward the driveway. "Also Collin is here with my van, so I'll see you guys in California."

She hugs us both and we say our goodbyes for now. Then we watch her pull away.

Grace turns to me, shaking her head.

"Please tell me you don't hate it."

She steps to me, putting her hands in the back pockets of my jeans and pulling our bodies together.

"I love it. Thank you, but why?"

I tuck a loose strand of orange and purple hair behind her ear, taking in her smile. I still haven't counted all of her freckles yet, but I'm getting closer.

"It's been nice having our friends over or traveling to see them. I know how much it means to you to see them and spend time with them. I want to do more of that with you."

I cup the nape of her neck and pull her toward me, bringing our lips together for one soft kiss that I wish would last forever.

"I meant it when I said I'll go wherever you want. I'll always want to share that with you and make our own memories together. I figured what better way than to start with something of our own. Something that we can build together, just like our future."

BONUS CHAPTER
SUTTON

My Black Cat - The Pizza Party

Sipping on a beer in the corner of the bar, away from the action, is not my usual MO at a party. Normally, I'd be the one out on the dance floor trying to coax the quiet ones out with me to have a good time. Somehow that always seems like my role as the middle child, but this isn't my party and thankfully that's not my job tonight.

Tonight's an even rarer treat because it's a party that I'm not catering or cooking for. If TJ or Grace would have asked me to cater a party or host an event at Gloria's, I would have done it without hesitation. TJ is my best friend and his new wife, Grace, is quickly becoming a close friend too. I'm so happy for them and that they found each other. That still doesn't mean that when I heard Tanner was throwing them a pizza party at The Chairlift, I was a bit relieved that I could relax tonight and just watch the crowd.

Maybe more accurately, I just want to watch one shadow that's been lurking in my thoughts for what seems like ages now. I look out on the dance floor to watch *her* dancing up near the karaoke machine in the corner that Grace and TJ are setting up. I could watch her all night and never get tired of admiring her. From her black hair with the bangs I want to brush out of her eyes to the low cut tops she wears that show a hint of her sternum tattoo — I want to look at all of her, all the time.

"I thought that was you," a familiar voice draws my eyes away from the only place I want to be directing it. I look to my right and almost can't believe who I'm seeing. If Grace hadn't mentioned that her best friend was hanging around in town lately, I definitely would not believe my eyes right now. Her familiar red hair is now in a pixie cut and she's gots some noticeable tattoos and piercings that she didn't have a decade ago, but my whole family knows that wild personality all too well.

I pull my attention away from the group by the karaoke machine and turn to Josie. "I heard a rumor you were in town, Josie." I tip my beer to her. "It's been what, nine or ten years?"

She nods and takes a sip of her cocktail and doesn't bother to acknowledge my recognition of our shared past. "Yeah. Something like that."

To my surprise, she pulls up a barstool and joins me at my high-top table. I shake my head and look back at her. "Who would have thought that the married couple both happen to have best friends from the same little town in New Mexico? Small world, right?"

"Yep." She pops that syllable and takes another sip of her drink. "Small world. I'm glad to see you and your brothers got out of Sterling Springs too, though."

I shake my head and shoot her a glare. "Not all of us. Just me and Slade."

I let that little bit of info sink in, but she doesn't seem to take the bait again.

"So what has you moping around away from the party

tonight?" her voice trails up in an amused tone. I try not to look over toward the karaoke machine, but my eyes betray me. Josie must pick up on that because her lips curl into a feline grin. "Ooooh. Coffee shop girl. Interesting. I figured you'd be looking for someone bright and cheery to match your always sunny disposition."

I roll my eyes and grin back at her. "I see you have the same sense of humor as always. Glad that hasn't changed."

She hums and flashes that wide smile. "Yep, you know me."

I'm about to say something else when I spot my brother, Slade, walking toward us. Shit. That's just what I needed tonight — more conversation when I just want to relax and enjoy watching the person that I've been obsessed with for a year have a good time with her friends.

Slade reaches the table and starts to say something when he looks at Josie. I see the moment he recognizes her, new haircut and all. "Holy shit. Look what the cat dragged in."

Her eyes roam up and down my older brother and she lets out an amused hum. "Still obsessive about your appearance I see."

He shrugs. "Yeah, whatever." His eyes drift to me and he quirks a brow before looking back at Josie. "What's my little brother's deal tonight? He looks way too mopey for a party."

Josie grins and tips her chin to the girl I've been watching since I got here. Slade follows her gaze and snorts a laugh. "Man, get over her. She doesn't even know you exist and we're going to be opening the Seattle restaurant soon."

"You two are really making tonight so much fun, you know that? I wasn't expecting a Sterling Springs reunion."

"Oh, come on," Josie says, bouncing a little on her feet. "What are the odds of this? Let's have a little fun."

She reaches out over the table with her drink and tips it at me and Slade. "To getting out of small towns?"

Slade reaches in with his beer and looks at me. "Come on, for old times' sake."

I shake my head and groan. "Fuck it. For old times' sake." I clink my drink to theirs, but I don't repeat Josie's toast because I'm in no rush to leave Jackson anytime soon.

ACKNOWLEDGEMENTS AND AUTHOR'S NOTE

To the readers who just finished Fresh Tracks, or maybe even the entire On The Slopes Series, thank you so much for choosing to read my books.

Grace and TJ's story was near and dear to my heart and I hope you enjoyed reading about them as much as I enjoyed writing their journey.

Skiing, especially in Jackson and Utah, is one of my favorite things to do in the entire world. Before this book was even released in October, I had already mapped out my entire winter to visit towns like Jackson and Park City. Sharing that love through a story like Grace and TJ's has been so rewarding. If you know me, I can't stop talking about how each one of these little ski towns and mountains is special and romantic in its own way. Instead of just yapping about it though, I've learned that it's more fun to tell it through the eyes of my characters. Every time a reader tells me that they felt like they were in the town or they want to visit a place I wrote about for themselves now, my heart melts a little bit with joy.

That's why I can't ever thank the people that have supported me along this journey more than enough. Some people in particular I'd love to thank are my beta readers. Jo, Hannah, Abby, Amy, Kelsey, Brandy, and Nessa: you've all been amazing and I loved getting your reading notes and even live feedback. Thank you so much for making Grace and TJ's story the best it could be.

To my loving partner, thanks for always humoring me when I have a wild idea or talking me down from a ledge when I want to delete an entire chapter because I was in a mood. I could never do this without you.

I also couldn't do this without my characters. Each and every one of them has a part of me in them one way or another. Bonding with them over the last year of writing was possibly the most rewarding part of this experience. When I started writing in April 2024, I never expected to fall in love with the Chapman siblings and their friends the way I did. Saying goodbye to them (for now...) has been the hardest part of writing this book.

That said, if you read the bonus chapter, I'm beyond excited about my next project and who knows, maybe readers will be seeing some Chapman cameos again soon.

ABOUT THE AUTHOR

I grew up in and around the city of Cincinnati, Ohio, graduating with a degree in Engineering.

I'm an avid skier and traveler, spending almost all of my free time traveling and enjoying time outside, ideally in the mountains. More often than not, I'm with my partner and our fur babies.

There isn't much that brings me more excitement or joy than getting in a car (or maybe a Sprinter van) and driving across the country and exploring. And besides, twenty-something hour long road trips means we have lots of time to cross plenty of wonderfully smutty romance novels off our TBR list. And who doesn't love that?

instagram.com/dforestwrites

goodreads.com/dakotaforest

threads.com/@dforestwrites

tiktok.com/@dforestwrites

ALSO BY DAKOTA FOREST

Full Send - On the Slopes Book 1

Fall Apart - On the Slopes Book 2

9 7 9 8 9 9 2 7 2 7 1 1 1